In Love with the Enemy

Ignoring the pain in his leg, he found his arms around her. The light scent of roses clung to her, and her body was unexpectedly soft. He told himself to let go, to take a long breath and think things through. Yet the cold, ruthless part of him—honed by years in the navy and with the pirates—wanted to take what had suddenly fallen into his arms, what he'd been desiring . . . a woman who, from the look in her eyes, wanted him, too.

His inner battle raged even as their lips touched, even as they sprawled together on the floor. He pressed his mouth tightly against hers and her hands curled around the back of his neck. He felt her warmth, drank in her sweetness.

A groan reverberated deep in his throat. He was aware of a craving he'd never felt before. Lust was mixed with something deeper, richer, more enticing. And far more dangerous . . .

Star Keeper

Patricia Potter

🐓 BANTAM BOOKS

NEW YORK   TORONTO   LONDON   SYDNEY   AUCKLAND

STAR KEEPER

A Bantam Book / August 1999

ISBN 0-553-57881-2

Published simultaneously in the United States and Canada

Bantam Books are published by Bantam Books, a division of Random
House, Inc. Its trademark, consisting of the words "Bantam Books" and the
portrayal of a rooster, is Registered in U.S. Patent and Trademark Office
and in other countries. Marca Registrada. Bantam Books, 1540 Broadway,
New York, New York 10036.

PRINTED IN THE UNITED STATES OF AMERICA

OPM   10 9 8 7 6 5 4 3 2 1

With affection and thanks to Carolyn McSparren, Phyllis Appleby, and Beverly Williams, who struggle so valiantly to keep my books, and me, on track

Star Keeper

Prologue

The feel of danger prickled along his spine.

John Patrick slid farther down into his seat, his gaze wandering around the noisy, odorous tavern and its disreputable occupants. He had always had an affinity for places like this, much to his older brother's chagrin.

He had never understood it himself. He was a graduate of the College of Philadelphia, which, along with Harvard, represented the best in education in the colonies—and yet he'd always sidled toward the underbelly of Philadelphia. Just as he was doing here, in Glasgow, Scotland.

His brother, Noel, always shook his head in dismay. "If there's a fight within ten miles, John Patrick will find it. If there's a damsel to be rescued, John Patrick will sweep her away. If there's an argument to be had, John Patrick will be at its center."

Noel, on the other hand, would walk ten miles to escape discord—except perhaps in the case of the damsel. Noel, now a staid Philadelphia physician, had inherited his mother's reasoning, compassionate nature. But John Patrick had inherited his father's streak of recklessness, his wont for tilting at windmills and adopting lost causes.

But it wasn't just adventure John Patrick sought, especially on this trip to England and Scotland. As a boy, he'd been passionate about righting wrongs. Now, he had seized upon this trip as an opportunity to right one particular injustice: his father's death sentence.

After the Battle of Culloden, twenty-four years ago, Ian Sutherland had been condemned to hang, along with the other Scottish rebels. Only a twist of fate had saved him from the gallows, and seen him transported to the colonies as a bond servant. Of course, much had changed since then—including Ian's marriage to John Patrick's American mother—but Ian Sutherland still could not return to his homeland without risking execution.

John Patrick had honestly believed he could accomplish his goal. He'd never failed at anything he'd put his heart into. He had stood first in his class and been labeled brilliant by his teachers. He'd studied British law and had prepared a sound case for his father's pardon. Rebuffed over and over again in London, he'd finally hired a British barrister to pursue his action while he took a long-awaited visit to the old Sutherland property in the Highlands.

There, he had fallen in love with the wild, lonely Highlands and become even more determined to reinstate what should be his family's. God, but he detested Fat George, who sat on the English throne and ran roughshod over the rights of both the Scots and the American colonists. . . .

The prickling sensation grew stronger. His eyes darted around the tavern again. *Something* had alerted him. Something or someone.

But no one else seemed perturbed. Every man jack in the room appeared to be roaring drunk; they probably wouldn't feel a sword if it was thrust into their bellies. 'Twas a motley crew, to be sure. Sailors mostly, recounting tales of great adventure, of China and India and pirates. They'd accepted John Patrick as one of them. He had a talent for mimicry and could imitate his father's Scots burr perfectly.

But tonight he chose to listen. The outrageous tales made his life seem staid and stuffy, and his future even more so. He shuddered at the idea of the dull law office that awaited him when he returned.

He held his hand up, and a barmaid flashed him a practiced smile. It was an appreciative glance, full of invitation.

Yet he was too preoccupied for flirtation. He wanted to stay and pursue his father's case, but his funds were nearly gone, and he knew it was time to return to Philadelphia. He would not abandon his fight, though. Somehow he would see it through.

The barmaid brought him another tankard. "I donna' usually see gents like ye in here," she said, leaning against him as she set the container on the table. "Wha' aboot a visit up the stairs?"

Her large bosom brushed his arm, and he received a full whiff of an overperfumed and underwashed body. Suddenly, he wanted to leave. He'd already had too much to drink.

"Drink up, dearie," the barmaid insisted. " 'Tis the best in the house, an' the night is young." He looked at the tankard, wondering whether it was indeed any better than the last one. He had not expected much here, and his expectations had been well met.

"Try it," the woman coaxed.

The prickling sensation hadn't ceased, but now he thought he understood. 'Twas his virtue, such as it was, that was in danger, nothing more. And the devil knew what that was worth.

Well, he would finish this tankard and be on his way to his more respectable lodgings. Sailing was at dawn, only a few hours away. He would not have time to sleep this night, much less sample the dubious charms of the barmaid.

He tipped the tankard and was surprised to find the

brew far better than the last portion. Now anxious to leave, he gulped the remainder. He tried to fathom the distinctive taste and was about to ask its source when the barmaid disappeared. Shrugging, he set the tankard down.

John Patrick threw some coins on the table, then started to rise. He'd apparently had more than he thought, because he found himself clutching the table for balance.

The room started swimming. One man became two, then three. His hand tried to tighten around the edge of the table, but he no longer had any strength. He swayed dangerously.

With a sinking feeling, he knew suddenly that he had been drugged. He reached out, then felt himself falling, and everything went black.

Chapter 1

They came at night.

Annette Carey woke to the sound of hooves and drunken shouts and the flickering glow of torches. She ran to the hall and found her father emerging from his room in a nightshirt.

Betsy, the housemaid, appeared below the stairs, her red hair wild and her buxom body encased in a red nightrobe.

"Dear Almighty," she wailed.

Annette's father hurried down the steps to soothe her. Betsy had been his wife's maid and was as much a member of the family as Annette was. Her cries echoed through the house and summoned Franklin, the man-servant, who came frantically pulling on his coat. His shirttails were only partially stuffed in his trousers.

Someone pounded on the door. No polite knock. No ordinary visitors.

Annette followed her father down the stairs, her slippered feet padding silently and her heart thumping. It was as loud to her as the drums that had accompanied a rebel march down the streets of Philadelphia not a fortnight ago.

The shouts of the men outside filled the house.

"Traitor!"

"Burn 'em out!"

"Come out or we will burn you out!"

Her father started for the door. Annette caught his nightshirt. "Please don't go out there, Papa."

He looked at her sadly. "We can't stay inside forever. I will talk to them. They know me."

"But you cannot reason with a mob." Her words came out low and ragged. She hated the fear she heard in her own voice.

"Child, they will burn the house down if I don't come out," he said gently. "The only chance we have is reasoning with them."

Annette felt her protest crumbling. Weeks earlier, a mob had burned the home of a royalist suspected of selling supplies to General Howe. All the occupants died in the fire.

Numbly she allowed her father to disentangle himself from her. He walked heavily toward the door. Betsy and Franklin, their faces white, had backed against the wall, watching silently.

He'll be able to convince them he means them no harm. Her father was one of the best-liked men in the county. He had sent food to those in need, given substantial sums to the Quakers for the hospital, and often loaned money without interest. But tales of atrocities toward other Tory families were rampant. Still, she'd never thought they would come here, to her home.

Her father opened the door and she steeled herself to stand at his side, to face the hatred, the shadows, the torches. Terror filled her as she saw the masked faces, waiting. She heard a shot, could almost feel it speeding toward her. It was so loud. So were the shouts: "Get 'em!"

Her father tried to yell above the noise, but it was like sighing in the wind. In seconds, he was engulfed by men in hoods and carried away like so much flotsam.

Annette felt her arms being seized. She was aware of Betsy and Franklin being swept along by the mob.

"Burn the house." One voice issued orders, dominating the others. She recognized its owner immediately despite the hood. Jacob Templeton, a man who had tried to buy land from them and been rebuffed.

He had probably gotten these other men drunk, and accused her father of conspiring with the British because he wouldn't sign the loyalty agreement. All for want of a few acres. But her father was innocent. He was guilty only of being true to his beliefs, of being reluctant to abandon the king who had given his family this fine land.

The senselessness of it enraged her.

Her father!

She struggled against the arms that held her, struggled to go to the one constant in her life, the man whose gentleness and wisdom had always guided her.

Dear God, why hadn't she found a musket? Why hadn't they fought back? She would never surrender so easily again. She kicked one of her captors suddenly, surprising him, and jerked away as he sank to the ground in agony. "Papa!" she cried. But two more sets of hands grabbed her, pulling her head back by her long, dark hair.

Pain shot through her neck and scalp, but still she fought them. One man hit her across the face, momentarily stunning her. "Witch," he said.

She spat at him, still trying to twist out of his grasp, and succeeded in freeing her head for a moment. Her gaze went to her father. He'd been stripped of his nightshirt, leaving only the smallclothes.

Her father was pleading. "Jacob," she heard him say. "Don't hurt my daughter."

"We warned you," said a voice muffled by a cloth hood but distinctive enough to be identified. Robert Lewis. "We won't have no Tories here."

Ropes were tied to her father's wrists. The men secured each rope to the trunk of a tree, pulling until he was stretched between them.

Annette smelled the acrid odor of hot tar. Desperate, she struggled even harder against her captors. One of the hoods slipped off in the struggle. Charles Parker. She had given Mr. Parker's son a puppy six months ago, and she had sat with his wife when she was dying. How many others had she shared lives with? Dancing at their weddings, weeping at funerals, and rejoicing at births.

Friends and neighbors.

"No!" she screamed. She heard her father's muffled moan, then his cry of pain as the hot tar was applied. Suddenly the attackers stopped, and she prayed they had come to reason. Her father was slumped against the ropes, but he was looking toward the house. Annette turned, too, and cried out again at this new horror.

Her home was on fire, the hungry flames eclipsing the sky. The roar filled the sudden silence, then embers began to drift from the house to set a series of new fires. One caught the barn just as one of the servants was driving out the animals. The horses, including her mare, Sasha, shrieked with terror. A woman wailed in anguish. A roar went up from the attackers. A cacophony of sound. Of hell. The worst nightmare possible.

Sweat drenched her nightrobe. She wanted to let herself fall, to run far away. But she couldn't leave her father. She had to be strong for him. She wrenched her body out of the hands that held her, surprising the men staring at the inferno they'd created. She ran toward her father, slipping again and again, dodging out of the reach of those who would catch her. And then she was at her father's side.

He straightened, meeting her gaze.

"I love you," she said.

"I know," he answered softly. "Courage, girl."

Then she was seized again, her hands tied behind her back.

Courage.

But she had none. Everything was gone. The room where she had been born, where she'd lived her entire life. The parlor filled with laughter, her father's study where they discussed philosophy, the barn where she'd groomed Sasha and helped birth her foal.

Everything she knew and loved.

Friends and neighbors. Thank God her mother wasn't alive to see this.

She heard laughter and felt herself jerked upright. Feathers were being tossed on the tar that now covered her father. She couldn't even recognize him. His head had dropped, and she didn't know whether he was conscious or not. She heard the bawdy lyrics of a song mocking the king.

The hands imprisoning her fell away then. The men in hoods were dispersing. Betsy and Franklin came running to her. Blood flowed from a cut on Franklin's forehead. Awkwardly, they untied the rope binding her hands, then Betsy put her arms around her, weeping silently.

But Annette had no tears. Not now.

She gently disengaged herself. "We must take care of Father."

Franklin, his face creased with grief, nodded.

She knew now both she and her father should have heeded the mumbling going on in their community. They had heard of other cases of royalists being tarred and feathered. Some had even been hanged. But her father had been known for his fairness and generosity, and while they had not aided the patriot cause, neither had they harmed it by selling foodstuffs to the British.

Friends and neighbors!

She vowed she would never trust anyone again. And

that no one would hurt her family again. Ever. She
would do anything she could to aid the British and bring
about the downfall of the rebels.

Off the Atlantic Coast, October 1777

His beloved *Star Rider* was trapped.

Bloody damned Brits! John Patrick Sutherland cursed
them as lightning streaked through the sky, illuminating
his schooner. He had ceased the firing of cannon, hoping to slip away from the British trap in this cloud-
darkened night. But the sudden squall had given the
better-armed Brits the advantage they needed.

John Patrick, his pilot beside him, took the wheel. It
had been risky, more than risky, this trip downriver, but
he had been told that a merchantman carrying gunpowder to the Brits would make a run this night, and it had
been too tempting a target to pass by. And he *had* destroyed the merchantman. But the resulting explosion
and fireball had summoned help John Patrick had not
expected. His ship, small and deadly against merchantmen, was no match for warships. It depended on speed,
but now there was no place to run.

A cannonball whistled past him, smashing into the
mainmast, toppling it to the deck. Another cannonball
hit the stern of the ship, sending a hail of flaming
splinters raining down on the crew. He heard cries of
pain, then curses as the ship took another blow to its
side.

The *Star Rider* rolled leeward. Its aft decks were
aflame, lighting the river. His ship—and crew—were going down.

"Lower lifeboats," he ordered, then turned to his pilot. "Maneuver the *Rider* as close to shore as you can."

The Delaware River was damnably cold, and he didn't want his remaining men to freeze to death.

He looked toward the enemy ships. They, too, were lowering boats. The Brits would try to capture the American privateers as they escaped. More than the crew, however, they wanted the captain—the man known only by the same name as his ship. John Patrick, the Star Rider, had jealously guarded his true identity all these years, not wanting his family to suffer for his actions.

But now . . .

He had to give his men a chance to get away. The Brits were calling them pirates, and he knew the Crown might well hang the crew of so notorious a privateer as the *Star Rider*, despite the fact that it held a lawful commission from the colony of Maryland.

He had no intention of finishing his life at the end of a British rope, either. And there was no hope of avoiding such a fate once they discovered that the captain of the privateer was really John Patrick Sutherland, a deserter from the British navy. It wouldn't matter to them that he'd been impressed, drugged and taken from a squalid tavern in Glasgow, that he'd been beaten and forced to fight those he had no quarrel with.

He *did* have a quarrel with the king, however. A very big quarrel, and one that wouldn't be settled until every last lobster coat was driven from American shores.

John Patrick supervised the loading of the lifeboats, then ordered the pilot to join them. He and his first mate, Ivy, used the winches to lower them as cannon continued to pummel the ship, one driving a hole just at the water line.

Twenty minutes. They had twenty minutes before the ship sank. No longer.

"Sir," yelled Tower, the second mate. "Drop down into the boat."

He shook his head. "I'll follow you. Make for shore, then inland to Washington's forces."

"We'll wait for you," the mate said.

"No," John Patrick replied. "I can keep them busy until you get to shore. Otherwise, you don't have a chance." He hesitated, hating to say the next words. But he would endanger them all if they waited for him. "You're on your own. Take care of yourself. Take care of each other. You've been a fine crew."

John Patrick moved away from the railing before the man could protest further and joined Ivy, who had gone to the one remaining perrier. The small gun on the quarterdeck was capable of quick fire, but effective only at close range. Desperation gave both Ivy and himself strength. He was only too aware of the limited time they had. Fire was eating its way toward them, even as the ship drifted lower and lower in the water.

John Patrick rammed home powder, and Ivy loaded the balls. The barrel was hot, and they didn't have time to clean it. John Patrick held his breath, aimed at one of the British tenders moving slowly toward his men, and pulled the taut trigger line that tripped the flintlock.

The ball reached the small enemy craft, striking its side.

The *Star Rider* listed even further.

"Time to be going, Cap'n," Ivy said.

"Aye, it is," John Patrick said even as he poured powder back into the perrier, then lifted a ball from the basket under the gun.

"It will be exploding on you," Ivy protested.

"If they're fighting fires, they won't be coming after us," John Patrick said. "Help me move this damn thing."

Ivy shook his head, but came to stand next to his captain, using his huge bulk to aim the perrier back toward the larger of the British ships.

John Patrick prayed as he helped Ivy position the gun. The exhilaration of sinking the British merchantman earlier that night had dissipated in the deadly rain of wood and metal that had wounded his crew. His fabled luck had finally run out.

He pulled the trigger line. The gun boomed and rebounded, forcing them both to jump back. Rifle fire raked the deck, and John Patrick felt his body jerk as a fragment from a cannonball hit him. He fell to the deck as his leg gave way under him. Then his body jerked again as a musket ball hit his shoulder and metal fragments grazed his head. He tried to get to his feet, but his body didn't seem to work anymore.

He felt hands on him, and a rope being tied around his torso.

"Hold on, Cap'n," a voice said. "I have to get you in the water, but you can be depending on Ivy being there with you. I'll see you safe to shore."

John Patrick tried to argue. Musket balls were shredding what was left of the deck. "Save . . . yourself."

There was no answer. He felt himself being lowered, then the shock of freezing water.

He went under, felt himself being tugged back to the surface. The cold seeped into his bones, but he knew with what reasoning power he had remaining that it would, at least, stop the bleeding.

He was aware of being tugged along through the water. He looked toward the ship. It was enveloped in flames and the stern was sinking. In another few minutes, the *Star Rider* would be gone.

John Patrick closed his eyes. He didn't want to see its death.

Still, he fought to remain conscious, to try to help Ivy, whose progress was already slowing.

But instead he felt himself slip away into a dark, warm void.

Chapter 2

*J*ohn Patrick thrashed against the mast, against the bonds that held him there. His body shuddered as the whip came down across his back again and again, and he struggled to keep from screaming. He wouldn't let them win. They wouldn't break him.

"Cap'n?"

A voice, insistent and intrusive, pierced the nightmare.

"Jonny!" The voice was harsher, yet the old, familiar name jerked him back into consciousness. Only his family and Ivy ever called him that, although Ivy hadn't used the name since the two of them had left the nest of pirates who'd both sheltered and imprisoned them.

Slowly, he emerged from the dark terror that had enveloped him.

"Ivy?" he finally managed.

"*Ja*, Cap'n," came the soft reply, and John Patrick opened his eyes. The bulky form above him seemed to sway, become two, then three, until finally the three shapes merged back into one. His head hurt, and his body was racked by alternating bouts of freezing cold and fierce burning heat.

"I have to get you to a surgeon, Cap'n."

The ship! His men! John Patrick struggled to remember. "The crew?"

"I don't know, Cap'n. I couldn't find them. I had to hide you in reeds while the redcoats hunted."

John Patrick shivered in his damp clothes. He looked around and found himself in a shed of some kind. From the looks of the gaps in the roof, it had been abandoned for some time.

"We cannot stay here," Ivy said. "The Brits are searching this whole area. And you need a doctor."

"Maryland . . ."

"You would never make it. Even with that cold water slowing the flow of blood, you've lost too much. And one of those balls is still in you. I have to go for help. We're not far from Philadelphia. Is there anyone . . . ?"

John Patrick hesitated. There *was* someone. A halfbrother who had, at one time, been very close to him. But the unhappy fact was that John Patrick no longer trusted Noel Marsh. His brother had pledged loyalty to the king, and even now was the trusted physician for the British command.

"Cap'n?" Ivy persisted, his broad Swedish face knit in concentration.

John Patrick closed his eyes. "Help me up."

"I don't think . . ."

"Help me up, Ivy." John Patrick was unexpectedly pleased to find steel in his words. He only hoped his body had as much confidence.

Ivy looked doubtful. He was a large man, bulky but without fat. His broad, guileless face belied the sharp intelligence he'd inherited from his schoolteacher father. Like John Patrick, he'd been impressed into the British navy; unlike John Patrick, Ivy had been taken from a Baltimore tavern when the Brits were at war with France. He'd been John Patrick's mentor and protector the first hellish year at sea. But somewhere along the line, the roles were reversed; the protected became the protector, and each had saved the other's life more than once.

"Help me up," he insisted now.

Ivy went down on one knee and put a hamlike arm

around him, guiding him to his feet. John Patrick put one foot in front of the other, then stumbled. Without Ivy's support, he would have fallen.

He felt what little strength he had, hoped he had, imagined he had, drain from him, and consciousness flickered again.

"Philadelphia," Ivy insisted again. "Where can I get you help?"

"Perhaps . . . my . . . brother . . ."

"Your brother?"

John Patrick had never discussed his family, or even mentioned them to his crew. 'Twas safer that way. Safer for them, safer for himself.

And Noel?

He heard Katy's bitter words in his mind. "He's a turncoat, John Patrick. He's against all of us now. General Howe is one of his patients. The general's staff meets in his parlor."

Brother? No. Not any longer. His mother and father had not disowned Noel, but in his heart John Patrick had. The British had inflicted far too much pain on him, on his family, for him to have any understanding for a British sympathizer. He had written Noel a bitter letter, expressing his outrage at Noel's collaboration with the enemy.

And he could not crawl back to him now, even though he knew that the danger of infection from the musket ball that remained in his body was extremely high.

He tried to move and agony shot through him. He couldn't stifle the groan that made its way up his throat.

"His name?" Ivy prodded.

John Patrick tried to concentrate, but the pain was too strong. He wanted to succumb to it.

"Jonny?"

John Patrick blinked. That familar name again. Ivy always preferred "Cap'n" when they were alone together and "sir" in front of the crew. He must really look bad.

"Marsh," he mumbled. "Noel . . . Marsh. But I'm . . . not sure he will not tell the British."

"If he does, I'll kill him," Ivy said in a matter-of-fact tone, and John Patrick knew he would do exactly that.

Philadelphia, 1777

Dr. Noel Marsh listened to the excited conversation with growing anxiety.

The British officers who'd gathered at his home for late-afternoon tea, a misnomer considering that they were there more for his port than his tea, could talk of little except the sinking of the American privateer, the *Star Rider*.

The ship had been a thorn in General Howe's side for months, sinking one British supply ship after another, and the captain's luck—and skill—was legendary. The sinking was an occasion for elation.

"Have they caught the captain and crew?"

A colonel shook his head. "I understand we've captured some of the crew members, but I don't think they've found the demmed captain yet. Bloody pirate. But they will."

"I'll drink to the man's hanging," said a colonel.

Noel turned to pour more port into their glasses, struggling with his own questions. Had they discovered the Star Rider's identity yet? No, or he wouldn't have these visitors this afternoon. He would already be tainted, his loyalty suspect.

"Noel?"

He looked up. The three officers were looking at him strangely.

Major Roger Gambrell leered at him. "Thinking of

Miss Carey? Can't think of a prettier lady to take your mind off war. Lieutenant Sanders tells me he saw you over there this morning. Says he sees you over there often. Too often for his peace of mind."

Noel remembered the man. Lieutenant Ames Sanders had glared at him when Annette Carey broke off her conversation with him to greet Noel. She had wanted to talk to him about one of the British soldiers she was nursing in the private home used as a hospital.

Only the most seriously wounded were placed at the Carey residence. After the battle of Germantown, private hospitals had been needed. The Quaker hospital was full to overflowing, and Noel shuddered every time he entered the military hospital, which he considered more dangerous than no care at all, what with its rampaging infections.

Annette Carey and her aunt—mainly Annette, he knew—had volunteered both their lodgings and their services, and Noel had jumped at their offer. He had, of course, noticed that Annette was a pretty young lady, though he considered her far too serious and solemn for someone her age. But his heart had been given away years ago. He'd cheated one woman by marrying her when he loved someone else. He would never do that again.

The thought brought back the grief and guilt he still felt toward Felicity.

"You can tell the lieutenant he has naught to worry about from me," Noel said abruptly. "I'm still in mourning for my wife."

"I thought she died three years ago," Colonel Swayer said, his voice husky from the port and his ruddy face nearly glowing with the liquid spirits.

"That's right," Noel said, a bit of frost in his voice. "And I have no intention of marrying again."

"Was she that bad or that good?" boomed Major Gambrell.

This time Noel chose to ignore him. He needed these men. He had prospered as surgeon to the British officers.

His Irish wolfhound, Aristotle, however, seemed to take offense. He rose from his favorite place next to the fire, eyed the interlopers with a baleful expression, shook himself, then with extreme dignity retired from the room.

Colonel Swayer looked slyly at the younger officer. "I think he found your remark in poor taste."

"I didn't mean anything by it," Gambrell defended himself. "Where did you find that bloody beast anyway?"

"He belonged to one of your officers," Noel said, not elaborating on the fact that he had found the man beating the dog nearly to death.

Aristotle was not fond of red uniforms, but tolerated them because Noel did.

Noel poured another glass of port and handed around the plate of scones purchased by Malcomb, his cook, butler, valet, and medical assistant.

Swayer took one.

"Where did you say the *Star Rider* went down?" Noel asked, returning to the topic that concerned him most. His tone was somehow casual enough to convince the others that the inquiry was made out of idle interest. Not heart-stopping concern.

"Twenty miles downriver. Bloody cocky bastard," Swayer said. "Came right up the Delaware, sneaked past our gunboats in the fog. Sank the *Sylvia*. But we have him now. There's no way he can escape our patrols."

"Anyone know who he is yet?"

"No. We'll find out, though, when we catch him. And when we question his crew."

Noel took a long swallow of port. He usually drank cautiously. But now he could use more fortification. A great deal more.

He knew the Star Rider was his half-brother, John Patrick Sutherland. The name was a dead giveaway. The Sutherland side of the family had an affinity for constellations. Family legend had it that one of John Patrick's ancestors had been known as the Starcatcher, and more recently his mother had teasingly called his father the Starfinder.

The moment he'd heard the rumors concerning the Star Rider, he'd known his brother was involved.

His brother: British navy deserter, Caribbean pirate, gunrunner, and now privateer.

Katy had told him some of the story. But his contact with her ended a year ago, when he'd refused to sign the pledge of loyalty to the rebel government. Since then his family had been lost to him, as well as the patients he had attended to for years. He'd managed to keep only the custom of those remaining Loyalists, and now the British military. His life and freedom had been threatened. His integrity, which he prized above all, had been questioned, impugned.

Only his stepfather, Ian Sutherland, had looked at him with a steady, appraising gaze as the others burst into recriminations. It was July of 1776, and Katy, his stepfather's sister, had just lost her husband in a battle against the Brits. She'd thrashed him with words more painful than any lash.

Later, his father had walked with him to the Sutherland stables.

"You know what you're doing? You know the cost?"

"Aye," he said as he usually did with Ian. He'd picked up Ian's "ayes" and "nays" as a child and automatically reverted back to them in his presence. He had worshipped Ian then. He loved him now as much as he could any blood father.

"I won't be asking any questions, lad," Ian said quietly. "I know you wouldn't do anything you didna' think was right. If you ever need anything . . ."

"Noel?"

He was brought back to the present by Swayer's voice.

Noel raised an eyebrow in question.

"Mr. Carey? Is there any improvement?"

He shook his head. "Not much." Annette Carey's father was one of his greatest concerns. The man still carried scars from being tarred and feathered by a group of drunken would-be patriots. But the greater injuries were to his mind and soul. He had simply retreated from life, sitting for hours without saying a word, apparently unaware of people or conversation or events swirling around him.

"He still doesn't talk?"

"No," Noel said quietly.

"Uncivilized rabble," the major said.

Noel nodded.

"Don't know why the king wants to keep them," the major continued. "Good riddance, I say. No manners, no breeding. Savages."

Swayer's censorious look silenced him as Noel raised an eyebrow. "But good port," he said wryly.

The major flushed. "Present company excepted, of course," he said swiftly. "Naturally, we don't consider you one of *them*."

"Naturally," Noel said. "I'm honored by the exception, but some of my family in Maryland support the rebels, and I don't consider them savages."

Swayer grinned at the major's uncomfortable wriggling.

"I apologize," the major said. "I meant no offense."

"None taken," Noel said, ignoring the anger crawling in the pit of his stomach. He could take Swayer well enough. He was a professional soldier, and Noel understood that. But he detested Major Gambrell's posturing, his snobbery and his ambition.

Yet Gambrell, as a nephew of one of General Howe's aides, was a man with influence, and even Colonel Swayer trod lightly, though it was clear he, too, did not care for the brash and tactless major.

As Swayer had told Noel, "If you need a favor from Howe, Gambrell can get it done. He's a pompous self-promoter, but he has important ears."

And there were favors Noel needed. Medicines, decent treatment for the residents of Philadelphia, better treatment for the rebel prisoners. And he had to work through the British military to get them.

"Time to be leavin'," a drunken Gambrell said. "Have an engagement with a . . . lady."

"I have to leave, too," Swayer said, rising to his feet. "It has been a pleasure, as usual. Where *do* you get that port?"

"Yes," Gambrell said. "You will have to tell me the source. My uncle would enjoy it."

" 'Tis a very limited supply," Noel said. "But for you . . . I'll see what I can do."

Gambrell took his hat from Malcomb, who had appeared suddenly, as if he had been listening at the door. And he probably had, Noel thought. Colonel Swayer and the other officer followed more slowly.

"Are you planning to attend the general's ball next week?" Swayer asked.

"I was honored at the invitation," Noel said with what he hoped was the proper humility.

Swayer beamed at him then hurried after Gambrell, who was concentrating on keeping on his feet.

As the door closed behind them, Noel looked askance

at Malcomb, whose blank servant look had been replaced by urgency.

"There is someone wantin' to see you in my room," Malcomb said.

"A patient?"

"He wouldna' say."

Noel had learned to sense trouble from miles away, now that he was caught in the middle of a war he abhorred. His instincts prickled.

" 'Lay on, Macduff,' " he quipped, trying to ignore the presentiment of danger.

"It's Malcomb," Malcomb replied indignantly.

"I know your name," Noel said with exasperation. " 'Tis merely a . . . hell, just lead on."

Malcomb gave him a wounded look, then proceeded to his quarters at the back of the house. He knocked once, then opened the door. Noel followed close behind him. He was not surprised when a pistol was stuck in his ribs, leveled by the man standing behind the door.

"You are Noel Marsh?" A slight Scandinavian accent accompanied the words, and Noel slowly turned around to encounter one of the biggest men he'd ever seen. He had blond, almost white hair, and eyes as blue as a mountain lake. And as cold.

"Yes," he answered steadily.

"You will come with me."

"May I ask why?"

"No." The answer was final.

"That is *my* pistol," Malcomb complained behind him.

"*Ja*, and I thank you for it," the big Swede said unapologetically.

"May I ask where we are going?" Noel said.

"No," the Swede said again. He turned to Malcomb. "Bind his hands in front of him."

Noel nodded at the manservant. He had an instinctive

feeling that this had something to do with John Patrick. His heart raced and his pulse pounded as he held out his hands.

The big Swede had already helped himself to the sheets on Malcomb's bed, tearing them into strips. Now he indicated that Noel should be bound with these and Malcomb reluctantly obliged.

The Swede fixed a malevolent stare on Malcomb. "You will saddle the two horses in back. Remember this one's life depends on obedience."

Noel noted that his visitor had evidently scouted out the house, studied its occupants, and located the stables. Despite the fact that his clothes were damp and stained, he was obviously used to command.

Noel nodded again as Malcomb looked toward him for guidance. "Do what he says," he said, "since you so carelessly left your pistol where any . . . thief could find it."

The man frowned at Noel's description. "Go," their visitor said, "and do not take long."

Malcomb gave Noel one last contrite look and disappeared out the door.

"Obviously you are not here to kill me, so I surmise you need a doctor."

The Swede didn't answer.

Noel tried again. "Can you at least tell me how badly the . . . the person is injured? If there *is* an injured person?"

"You are a Tory, a redcoat-lover," the man said, disdainful. "A traitor to your country."

"It depends on the country you refer to," Noel said pompously. It was a role he'd perfected.

The Swede looked at him with contempt. "Are you really brother to John Patrick?"

Despite the fact that he'd suspected this had something to do with his brother, the sure knowledge drove the breath from him as powerfully as any blow. "He is all right?"

"He had better be, or I will kill you."

Noel was a tall man, but the Swede was even taller, and well spoken even with the slight accent. He didn't seem like a sailor. What was he doing with John Patrick? Or was it a trap? The British had bought the services of mercenaries—Scottish, German, Scandinavian. And Noel knew not every Tory trusted him. It was common knowledge that his family in Maryland supported the American cause. "Do we need supplies?" he asked brusquely.

The Swede looked puzzled for a moment, as if he had not considered the matter. At that moment he appeared to be exhausted, as if he was standing only through immense strength of will. Noel had no doubt that, as large as the Swede was, Malcomb could best him—if he weren't armed.

"Instruments? Bandages?" Noel pressed.

His visitor nodded then. "And clothes, water, food."

"I would suggest something else," Noel continued. "If my brother is injured badly, we should take the phaeton, not saddle horses."

His uninvited visitor considered the question, doubt clouding those clear blue eyes. "The captain said not to trust you."

Noel had endured pain for his actions before, but nothing ran as deep as this. Surely, John Patrick knew he would never hurt him. Noel had looked after him as a lad, had taught him to ride and shoot, had fed his curiosity and encouraged him to reach for his dreams.

"Either way, you won't get me through the sentries with my hands tied," he said, knowing any rebuttal would be useless. "And you'll need the phaeton if Jonny can't ride. We'll have to move him. The British army is searching everywhere."

The pistol in the Swede's hand didn't waver. "You should know."

"If he was desperate enough to mention my name, he must be near death," Noel persisted. "I swear I won't turn him in. He *is* my brother."

"You lie, and I will kill you," the Swede said, his emotionless calm more threatening than hot anger.

"You tell Malcomb to ready the phaeton," Noel said, holding out his hands to be released as if taking the Swede's words as assent. "I'll gather what I need." He paused. "What do I call you?"

The man hesitated, perhaps resenting Noel's attempt to assume authority. "Iverssen. My name is Iverssen. The cap'n calls me Ivy." Again, the intruder studied Noel. Finally, as if aware of his growing need for cooperation, he took a knife from his belt and cut the bonds around Noel's wrists.

"Ivy," Noel said, "how did you get into Philadelphia? The roads are guarded."

"The cap'n and I are used to getting where we want to go," Ivy said simply. "We go now. You can hitch the horses while your man gets what you need."

Noel nodded, but now that they would be traveling in the conspicuous phaeton, he needed to convince his suspicious guest of one more alteration to his plan. "You can't go like that. Those are the clothes of a sailor, and God knows they look waterlogged." He went to Malcomb's trunk and pulled out a shirt and breeches. "Put these on."

The Swede seemed to see the logic of Noel's statement, quickly discarding his clothes. Malcomb's were small for him, the cloth stretching across his broad chest, but Noel added a plain wool cloak and a plain hat and was satisfied with the result.

Somehow control had changed hands, and it was obvious that the Swede didn't care for it one bit. Still, Noel thought, the man was loyal enough to John Patrick to see the need, though the pistol was pointed at him even now.

He couldn't waste more time. Noel led the way to the stable. Malcomb was just coming out with two saddled horses. He looked at Noel's unbound hands with curiosity, then at his own clothes on the Swede.

Noel didn't give him a chance to speak. "I'm—*we* are taking the phaeton. Get my medical bag. Food. Water. Brandy. Several blankets. A pair of my trousers, shirt and waistcoat, and—" He looked briefly at Ivy, then back at Malcomb. "And that British uniform we . . . found."

"I'll be going with you."

"No," Noel said. "Stay here to answer any questions. Send a message to Captain Longwaith that I won't be joining him for gaming tonight. A woman in labor."

"Aye." Malcomb hurried off.

Ivy's face went red, then regarded him quizzically. "You trust him?"

"With my life," Noel said. "Apparently as John Patrick trusts you."

"It could well mean your life." The threat was back in the Swede's voice. "Brother to Jonny or not, I'll not hesitate to kill you."

Noel felt a start of surprise at the man's easy use of his brother's nickname. Something more than loyalty between sailor and captain existed here. He chose to ignore it for the moment. Best to concentrate on John Patrick. They hitched the horses to the phaeton and loaded it with supplies. The Swede laid the pistol between them on the seat.

The night was dark, with only a half-moon providing light. His heart pounding at an accelerated rate, Noel guided the horses into the cobbled street and headed

south, toward the sentries. He urged the horses into a
fast walk, heedless of the jarring of the carriage.

He was barely aware of the looming presence next to
him. Noel kept seeing his brother's face in his mind.
He started praying silently.

Chapter 3

John Patrick shivered against the cold. He fought to stay awake.

He had barely escaped the last British patrol, crawling down into the reeds as soldiers searched the banks. It took the last of his strength to climb back out and cover himself with leaves for both warmth and safety.

He was frozen. And God's mercy, but he hurt. As much as when he'd been lashed.

How long had it been since Ivy had left him? Hours? It was nearing dusk. At least twelve hours had passed, and Philadelphia had been what? five, ten miles away?

Would Noel come?

He had not seen his brother since before he'd left Boston for that fateful trip to Scotland. He'd spent nearly a year in England, then three years on a British ship of war as an impressed sailor, and four more as a pirate. When a pirate band had taken the frigate, only he and Ivy had survived the carnage, and then only because they'd been in chains for insubordination, their backs torn by the lash. They had been given an option. Join the pirates or die with the rest of the British crew.

Confronted with that devil's choice, John Patrick and Ivy had joined up, always intending to escape them as they had the British. Yet John Patrick found that his dark side adapted easily to the brotherhood of thieves; since they mostly raided British shipping, John Patrick felt few qualms. The Brits had taken three years of his life, and he didn't mind making them pay dearly for each one of them.

He'd detested the leader's lust for killing, however, and eventually he gained enough support to challenge him for command of the ship. He won after a hand-to-hand battle to the death, but he still was not free. If his crew had thought he might desert them, he knew they would kill him without a thought. As captain, he limited his raiding to British shipping and forbade any unnecessary killing. Within eighteen months he became a very wealthy man and had carefully, very carefully, built a crew loyal to him—not to the brotherhood. . . .

Cold. He was so cold. He tried to think of the Caribbean, of the warm blue-green sea that changed colors in the sun, and the white sands that reflected heat. So different from the icy grayness of the Delaware, or even the Chesapeake where he was raised.

He curled up in a ball. He thought of home, of Noel, whom he'd adored as a boy, of Katy, whom he loved as if she were his true sister. His mother. The laughter on her face as she looked at his father. He'd always wondered whether he would ever find passion like that. Neither Katy nor Noel had.

Noel. Would he come?

He'd avoided Noel since he returned to the colonies nearly three years ago, first running guns to the colonists, then as a commissioned privateer. Because of Noel's Tory leanings and John Patrick's virulent hatred of everything British, he had not sought out his brother despite their childhood closeness. God help him, he hated to do so now.

He tried to move, but pain ran through him, and he felt the seeping of blood again. He fought to stay awake. He had to stay awake until Ivy returned.

Think of warmth. Think of sunrises. He had always loved sunrises, both as a boy and later as a sailor. They always signified hope to him. New beginnings. The sunrises—and Ivy—had been his two lifelines on the British ship.

How long before the next sunrise?

It was Ivy who found John Patrick.

He had been combing the woods with Noel behind him. Noel knew it was risky. He knew he should stay with the phaeton, in case a British patrol came along. But he couldn't.

They'd been lucky so far. They'd passed the British checkpoints easily, describing the Swede as an anxious husband whose wife was in labor. They had been stopped twice more, but Noel was a prominent Tory, a man known to be General Howe's physician. The easy passage was as much an irritant to his companion as a relief. He had not taken his hand off the pistol, though it was now buried under the cloak.

They had driven three hours when the Swede told him to turn off the road and into the woods. He stopped the team at an abandoned cabin while the Swede hopped down, turning to him. "If the buggy is not here when I return, I will hunt you down."

"I'll come with you," Noel assured him.

In the early gray dawn, Noel had seen the Swede's hard gaze, before the man took off in a loping run toward the river. Now, Noel stumbled, blocked by the large body of the Swede as he bent over a still form. Noel urgently nudged him aside, felt the pulse at his brother's throat, then leaned down and placed his ear against John Patrick's heart.

"Jonny?" he said.

There was no movement.

He said his brother's name louder, his hand clutching the bloodstained shirt. He heard a groan.

"Jonny," he said again. It was his family's pet name

for John Patrick when he was a boy, a name that John Patrick himself started. *Jonny wants this. Jonny wants that.*

"Noel?" John Patrick's voice was weak, thready. But he was alive!

Thank God, still alive.

"Aye, little brother. What in the devil have you gotten yourself into this time?"

He felt John Patrick shivering under his touch, heard the chattering of his teeth. He leaned down and started to pick him up, but the big Swede shoved him aside. "I'll take him."

"To the cabin," Noel directed.

The Swede moved quickly. When they reached the dilapidated shelter, Noel retrieved the bundle Malcomb had prepared and followed Ivy inside. The big Swede lowered John Patrick to the dirt floor. "Light a candle," Noel said.

After several attempts, Ivy produced a small flame. Noel quickly inventoried John Patrick's injuries, stripping away the cold, wet clothes and wrapping him in blankets. He wished he could start a fire, but any sign of smoke would likely bring the British. And John Patrick, were he found, would hang.

His brother had three major wounds and a host of minor ones. One ball had apparently gone through his left shoulder, grazing the bone. Another had hit his thigh and seemed to be lodged there. And there was a jagged cut on the side of his head.

It was the ball still lodged inside John Patrick that most worried Noel. The bleeding in the leg had stopped, because of the cold water, he thought, or perhaps the makeshift ligature that had been applied to it by either his brother or the Swede.

The bleeding could start again when he took out the ball, and his brother looked as if he couldn't afford to lose more blood. He was too pale, his pulse weak. He must be in terrible pain already. But it had to come out or he would most certainly die of inflammation.

If only he could get him warm enough. Noel took off his cloak and spread it over his brother. He didn't want to do this here, but it might be even worse if he let the ball go deeper on the jarring ride back to Philadelphia. Thank God he had the opium he'd been able to secure through the good graces of the British. He would need more in the next few days.

He looked up at the big Swede. "Shouldn't you be on watch?" In the flickering candlelight, he saw the doubt in the man's face.

"Go," John Patrick whispered.

Ivy hesitated, then went out the door.

John Patrick seemed to struggle with words. His usually brilliant blue-green eyes were dull with pain and cold.

"You'll be safe with me," Noel said, hating the necessity for the words, wishing that his brother would take him on faith, as he had as a child.

"Home . . ."

"I can't send you home. You would never make it. You need rest and care." He hesitated a moment. "I know a place, but you will have to be careful, very careful. It is the home of a friend, a Tory, who takes in overflow from the military hospital."

"No."

"I have no choice," Noel said. "You can't stay with me. If they learn who the Star Rider is, that's the first place they'll look."

"And you have . . . British officers going in and out. I . . . can't interfere with . . . that." John Patrick's voice was bitter. "I'm . . . surprised you even . . . came."

Noel wanted to explain, but there was no explanation that John Patrick would understand. Not now. Probably not ever. Instead, he took a packet of opium and mixed it with water from a flagon, then leaned over John Patrick, lifting his head. "Swallow this. I have to take out that ball."

"Want . . . to stay awake."

"This is going to be painful," Noel said. "You want to risk crying out and telling the British where to find you and your friend?"

A muscle moved erratically in John Patrick's cheek, but then, obediently, he swallowed the mixture.

"John Patrick, listen to me. A woman named Annette Carey and her aunt are caring for a small number of British wounded in their home. You could not have better care, and no one will be looking for you there. But you must let them believe you are with the British army. You used to mimic our father's burr. Can you still do it?"

"Aye," John Patrick said. "I would not be tainting your . . . credentials as a good Tory." His voice was bitter, strained.

He had stopped shivering, and his eyes were glazing over. The opium was working. A few moments of consciousness, no more. Noel knew he had to make John Patrick understand. Now. "My man, Malcomb, will be with you when you wake. Just remember . . . you are a Scottish mercenary. A burr, brother. A burr. . . ."

"You're not . . . my . . . brother," John Patrick whispered through dry lips. But then his head dropped, whether from the opium or exhaustion, Noel wasn't sure. The last words echoed in his mind. He knew they would for a long time.

He tried to erase them as he bent to his work.

Annette Carey brushed hair from her face. She was exhausted, but there was still so much to do. Betsy couldn't do it all. Recent battles, especially the last at Germantown, had brought a steady stream of severely wounded British officers.

Bed linens had to be changed, bandages washed, letters written. She needed to spend time with her father. But despite the constant, unending demands, she seldom regretted her offer—or her subsequent battle with her aunt and society—to take in wounded.

Even before her father's land had been confiscated, she'd never been able to sit still and knit or embroider or perform other acceptable feminine duties. At her father's side, she'd learned as much about farming as he, and she'd been as good at working with the animals. She'd often assisted at calving and foaling, and never fainted at the sight of blood. Now she would never run a farm, but she could and, by the holy Mother, *would* make herself useful.

She'd fought the gossips and cajoled her aunt, with whom she and her father stayed after the destruction of their own home, until finally they took in one patient, then another, then ten, and finally twenty after the battle of Germantown. Most of them were now well on their way to recovery. And she felt a deep pride as each one left.

If only her father, too, would recover. . . .

But she was afraid he never would. He'd almost died that terrible night, and only tireless efforts by Dr. Marsh had saved him. Yet he'd never spoken again.

Annette leaned against the wall for a moment. Her father's cries still haunted her. At night, she would wake, her body drenched in sweat, her head filled with terrifying pictures. Then she would try to remember how she'd felt riding across the fields on Sasha, her hair blowing in the wind.

She buried her head in her arms. She'd tried so hard to find the mare, but her father was critically ill for weeks, his spirit gone as well as his health. She could only place an advertisement in the paper for a bay mare with three white feet and a white streak down her mane. If found, she'd already resolved to buy her back with the one thing of value she still had, a pearl-and-sapphire brooch that she'd had fashioned into a necklace. It had belonged to her mother and she always wore it, had worn it that night under her nightdress. But Sasha was a living thing, a friend she'd raised from a filly and treated with exquisite care and tenderness. She couldn't bear to think of Sasha being mistreated.

But no one had answered the ad, and she ached for the gentle mare that followed her as a dog might. One day . . .

One day when the British won, she would petition for the return of her father's land. One day, her father would find justice.

Betsy's light footsteps interrupted her folding of washed wrappings.

"Dr. Marsh is at the door with another patient," she said disapprovingly. "You tell him we can't take any more."

Annette studied Betsy a moment. She looked as tired as Annette felt. Her curly red hair had escaped the neat cap she wore, and her normally pristine apron was stained and wrinkled.

"You know the Quaker hospital is filled," Annette said slowly. "And Dr. Marsh wouldn't have brought someone unless he thought it necessary."

She brushed by Betsy and headed toward the door. Dr. Marsh stood just inside. With him was a huge blond man carrying a man in uniform, and Dr. Marsh's man, Malcomb.

"Doctor?"

He had already taken off his hat, and now he made a small bow. "I'm sorry, Annette. I know you have more than you can handle, but this officer is badly wounded.

Malcomb will look after him, if only you have a bed he can use."

Annette looked at the soldier. He was unconscious, thick black lashes covering his eyes. Several days' growth of dark beard covered his face, and the red uniform he wore was stained with blood. He smelled heavily of brandy, and she drew back. Its smell reminded her of that terrible night.

Her reaction must have been evident because the doctor smiled wearily. "I used brandy to clean the wound and spilled some on his clothing."

Of course. She nodded, embarrassed at her reaction. "Who is he?" she asked.

Dr. Marsh shrugged. "He's a lieutenant. That's all I know. He mumbled a name but I didn't hear it. I suppose we'll find out. I found him on the road as I drove back from delivering a child. He'd apparently been ambushed by rebel marksmen. Can you keep him here for a few days? I know Captain Garrett was sent home on the *Marigold*, and I hoped this man could use his room. He needs quiet."

It was Betsy's room, and she'd been none too happy to give it up. She had been planning to move back into it this afternoon.

"Betsy?" she said.

Betsy's bright green gaze rested on the wounded man for a moment, then moved approvingly to the large man carrying him. She nodded, an appreciative gleam sparkling in her eyes.

"Thank you," the doctor said. Annette thought he looked even more concerned than usual. That was one of the things she liked best about him: the way he cared about the patients.

It was after her father's physical recovery that Noel told her how badly overcrowded the Quaker hospital was, and she'd talked to her aunt about taking in some of the wounded. Her aunt, also grateful for Dr. Marsh's efforts but concerned about Annette's reputation, reluctantly agreed.

Annette had found herself looking forward to Dr. Marsh's twice-daily visits, to his quiet wit and thoughtfulness. He never condemned anyone, but his loyalties were well known, as was the fact that they had alienated his family in Maryland. Annette admired him tremendously, but despite Betsy's teasing she'd never felt anything more than friendship toward him.

Now he seemed infinitely weary and sad, the lines at the edges of his eyes etched even deeper than usual. His tawny hair, usually tied back neatly, had come loose and hung untidily around his face.

She looked at the tall bulky man holding the patient, the one who had attracted Betsy's glance.

"This is Ivy," Dr. Marsh said. "He is a friend of Malcomb's and will spell him."

How odd, she thought. Malcomb didn't look as if he considered the large man a friend. He was fairly glowering at him.

"Come with me," she said, leading the way to Betsy's small room in the back. The chamber was plain, but it would afford a privacy that the other patients, crowded on cots in two large rooms, didn't have.

The man called Ivy—such a strange name—carried the wounded man carefully, even tenderly, which surprised Annette. In her experience, most large men were anything but tender. She felt the familiar coldness as she remembered the men who had held her that one night, the night that she relived nearly every day. She'd not realized before then that men could be capable of such brutality. It was those memories as much as any other reason that made her wary of the men who asked to court her. She'd wanted naught to do with them.

Annette led the way, aware that Betsy was swinging

her hips more than usual. The large man didn't seem to care, although Malcomb apparently did. The Scotsman appeared very dour.

When they reached the small room, the large man lowered his burden to the bed. The patient's boots were already gone. She turned as Ivy started to undress the officer.

"If you have a pallet," Noel Marsh said, "Malcomb will sleep in the room. You have plenty to do without caring for this one, too. It's enough that you give us a bed."

"What about that one?" Betsy said, looking up at the big man who now stood uncomfortably against the wall, looking like a giant in a closet.

"He'll stay with me."

"I'll get some water and fresh wrappings," Annette said after a moment. She could have sworn that they were waiting impatiently for the women to leave. But why . . . ?

"Remember," Dr. Marsh said as she turned to go, "I don't want him disturbed until the danger of infection is over."

She understood. Common medical practice dictated giving badly wounded men opium in the belief that the elimination of pain sped recovery and prevented infection. Thank God the British were able to provide the drug. She'd heard that the Americans had little, and though she had disdain for their cause, she couldn't help but shudder at the thought of their pain.

She took one last look at the patient. He was not a particularly handsome man in the accepted definition. He certainly bore no resemblance to Noel Marsh's patrician features. The newcomer's face was striking, with sharp angles and a mouth that, even in unconsciousness, bent upward on one side in a sardonic smile.

An odd flutter moved in her heart. She didn't understand why. She'd helped nurse a number of men, and none of them had produced the slightest fluster. Yet there was something in that face . . . perhaps the expression that seemed to laugh at what must have been excruciating pain.

Imagination, she told herself. Nothing but imagination. She hurried out the door.

Noel breathed a sigh of relief. So far, so good. Getting past the sentries outside Philadelphia had been the difficult part. He had purposely spilled brandy on John Patrick's clothing, claiming they were taking home a drunken British officer.

Now he and Malcomb pulled off John Patrick's uniform. Noel winced as he saw the scars on his brother's back; no one in his family had mentioned them. Perhaps they didn't know. He didn't have to ask how John Patrick had gotten those deeply embedded scars; he'd seen them before on British sailors. Noel's breath caught in his throat as he thought about the pain his sibling had endured, and he understood John Patrick's rage against the British—and against him.

He had to make sure that no one else saw them. They did not fit the cover story of a British officer. He would send over a nightshirt with Ivy later. He checked the more recent wounds. They were bleeding again, but not badly. If only there was no poisoning of the wounds.

But first there was the matter of his brother's mate, or friend, or whatever he was. The man looked to be in a towering rage. He wanted to stay with his captain, and only after Marsh convinced him that Malcomb was equally qualified to tend the wounds and far less apt to produce questions did he grudgingly agree to leave—on the condition he could visit.

Ivy insisted on staying in Philadelphia, despite the danger, and Noel had not been able to sway him. If anything happened to the captain, the Swede had declared on the long ride back from the river, he would personally shoot both Noel and Malcomb. For now, Ivy would become Noel's groom.

"Wait for me outside," Noel instructed the two men when they had finished undressing John Patrick. He moved the chair over to the bed and sat down, alone with his brother. John Patrick had changed much in the years since he'd last seen him. The face was hard, the body lean and strong. He was a man, not the happy-go-lucky adventurous boy Noel had helped raise.

Noel put a hand on his brother's arm, and affection surged through him. It was nearly impossible to think of the boy he remembered as a pirate, but neither was John Patrick's visage the same. It was a map of hardship and survival; lines existed where there should be none. And his back . . .

In these moments he could indulge himself in the compassion and love he could not give the conscious man. John Patrick, he knew, would not accept it. Not from him.

After several minutes, he rose. He left some packets of opium on the table. It was vital that John Patrick be still, that he not utter one word that would betray him.

Noel took one last look at his brother, then left, closing the door silently behind him.

Annette could not stop wondering about the man occupying Betsy's room. She caught glimpses of him when she helped Betsy bring food and water to the room, but whenever she offered more help, Malcomb kindly thanked her and accompanied her out the door.

Dr. Marsh himself stayed for hours at a time, even remaining all night with him one evening. Each time he visited, he emerged from the room with a deep frown.

When she asked about the patient, he would only answer, "As well as can be expected."

"Is he awake?" she'd asked this morning.

"On and off," Dr. Marsh had replied.

"Then he'll need some soup?"

He smiled, his lined face relaxing. "I think that would be well received. Just give it to Malcomb."

She spent the morning making a delectable broth to tempt his appetite. Their other patients were much farther along in their recoveries and clamoring for something more substantial.

When it was ready Annette poured the broth into a bowl and added a cup of milk to the tray. She fully expected to be met at the door by the "dragonkeepers," as she and Betsy had termed Malcomb and the large Swede.

But for once no one was there. She hesitated for a moment outside the door, then knocked. A deep, slightly accented voice summoned her inside.

The patient was sitting up in bed. He looked pale and drawn, although he was clean-shaven. Now that the beard was gone, the face was even more striking than she remembered. His eyes fairly danced with restless energy despite the pallor of the skin around them. She had the impression of recklessness, of a man untamed, although deeply indented lines at the corners of his mouth gave hint of character. A white nightshirt contrasted with his deeply browned wrists.

His brows bunched together when he saw her.

"You must be Mistress Carey," he said with a slight burr. "I owe you thanks."

So he was Scottish. 'Twas not unusual. A number of Scots fought with the king's forces. She smiled, delighted with the progress he'd made in just a few days. She put the milk and soup on the table next to him and busied her hands in her apron. Oddly, she wished she weren't wearing one of her usual rather plain gray dresses. "You are better," she observed, feeling a strange lightness in her heart. "I brought some food."

"I see," he said seriously. For a moment she wondered whether he was laughing at her. He had green eyes, incredible eyes, and despite his grievous wounds she was sure she saw a glint of humor in them.

"Where is Malcomb?"

"I think he went to have tea with a certain lovely woman," he replied.

"Betsy?"

"Redheaded?"

She nodded, feeling suddenly awkward.

Then he moved, and she saw pain ripple across his face, a muscle flexing in reaction as his whole body went still. The roguish light fled from his eyes, and they became intense pools of green.

"Can I help you?" she asked, looking toward the bedside table where Dr. Marsh's packets lay.

She watched the struggle on his face. Finally, with what appeared to be a supreme effort, the corners of his lips turned upward. But it was not quite a smile, only an attempt at one.

"No," he said. "Just a momentary spasm."

"Perhaps some opium . . ."

"Nay, I have had enough, Mistress Carey," he said.

"You are from Scotland?"

"Aye," he said. "But I've been wandering about these past few years."

So that was why his accent was not as pronounced as that of some of the other Scottish soldiers. "That must have been grand," she said wistfully. She'd dreamed about visiting England and Europe. She had, in fact, often wished she had been born a man, with a man's power to roam and right wrongs. Instead, she'd had to fight bitterly just to nurse those she felt were fighting her battles.

"Not always," the patient said, and his eyes seemed to darken.

"Dr. Marsh didn't tell us your name."

" 'Tis John. John Gunn. And your given name?"

She flushed suddenly under his grave scrutiny. She knew she looked plain, even unkempt, with her hair falling from the knot she'd twisted it into at the back of her neck. "Annette," she said.

He looked at her fingers. "*Miss* Annette Carey?"

Annette realized her face was aflame, though she didn't understand why. She'd shared conversations with wounded men before. Of course, she had always been reserved, more comfortable with books and animals than with men. But she felt instinctively she should be particularly wary of *this* man. He radiated a dangerous intensity, even though his lips smiled roguishly. It was partly boyish charm, but she sensed it was more practiced than real.

"It *is* miss, isn't it?" he persisted.

"Yes," she said, somewhat defensively. She was twenty-three, and though many young women were still unwed at this age, most had prospects. She did not, although she'd had callers, including several British officers whom she thought were more lonely than interested in her. She had rebuffed them all, impatient with the art of flirting, and fully aware that she had neither the manner nor the dowry for a good match. Not that she wanted one. She never wanted to be dependent on a man, nor commit herself to someone she did not really love.

She also had her father to consider. She could not leave him, and what prospective husband would want to take on the responsibility of a man struck silent, a penniless Tory whose wits were, according to some, addled?

John Gunn tried to move again, and this time winced.

"You should drink some milk and take the broth," she said. "Please, let me help you."

"Nay," he said. "But I thank you."

His smile was blinding. She felt dazzled by it. His earlier smile had been charming, almost too facile, but this one warmed the room and crawled into her soul. It made her want to smile, too, and it had been a very long time since she'd been so tempted.

"Then I will leave you with it," she said, hoping her words didn't sound as ragged to him as they did to her.

"I thank you, Miss . . . Annette." She thought she saw that glint in his eyes again. She wished she knew exactly what it signified.

She found herself backing up, her fingers behind her, catching at the doorknob and opening it. She stepped out into the hall and leaned back against the door panel for a moment. She took a breath and tried to understand why it was catching in her throat.

What had happened to the responsible, practical, levelheaded woman she thought herself to be?

She looked back at the door.

What was he?

Who was he?

And why did he affect her this way?

Chapter 4

ohn Patrick watched the door close behind the woman. The smile quickly faded from his lips.

Too bad she was a Tory, and he had to watch his tongue. He had been warned about it sufficiently by Malcomb, whom he didn't entirely trust, and Ivy, who worried about everything and everyone, including Dr. Noel Marsh.

But after several days of drifting in and out of consciousness, of fighting waves of pain, he'd welcomed a presence other than the dour, accusing Malcomb or the anxious Ivy. Annette certainly was a bloody sight better looking than either of them, and her brief presence had been like a fleeting ray of sunshine.

She'd entered, in fact, the first time that he'd been left alone for more than a few moments. He smiled at the thought of Malcomb's horror when he discovered that the young lady of the house had visited during his brief absence. John Patrick couldn't help but notice that Malcomb was as protective of Noel as Ivy was of him. It had not made for the best relations between the two men, nor did the fact that both Malcomb and Ivy had eyes for the redheaded maid. John Patrick had been amused at the obvious antagonism between them.

He reached for the bowl of soup with his right hand. His left arm was tied tightly to his chest to protect his wounded shoulder. Every movement cost him dearly. He had not wanted her to see how much. He finally managed to balance the bowl in his lap. His hand shook slightly as he took a spoonful. He hadn't wanted anyone to see that, either.

How long before he could leave this bed, and see to his men? Only this morning, Ivy had told him that nearly half of his crew had been captured. They were being held here in Philadelphia in the Walnut Street Prison, not more than a few blocks from this house. Guilt racked him as he thought of their suffering while he had a soft bed, plenty of food, and more attention than he wanted.

He took another sip of soup and wondered whether the woman had prepared it. But no, in a house this large there would most certainly be a cook. Then why had she brought it? Curiosity? Or was she just one of those good souls like his mother? Gentleness did seem to radiate from Miss Annette Carey, along with a quiet competence.

She was pretty enough, though she did little to enhance her looks. Her gray gown almost, but not completely, hid a graceful figure, and her hair was pushed back in a severe knot. He wondered what it looked like down, framing the strong, oval face and large gray eyes that were by far her best feature. Her lush black lashes had immediately drawn his attention to them. They were the rare color of smoke, tinged with only a hint of blue. He could imagine them smoldering under the right circumstances. And he could imagine what those circumstances would be.

But she was a Tory, in addition to being an unwilling benefactress to the man the British were hunting so frantically. He wondered what her reaction would be if she discovered she was aiding and abetting the Star Rider.

He wasn't any happier about it than she would be. He didn't like lying, or taking advantage of someone trying to help. Yet Noel was right. The best place to hide at the moment was in the midst of the enemy.

He had just finished his soup when another knock came. Malcomb never knocked, nor did Ivy. 'Twas evidently his afternoon for visitors.

John Patrick didn't have time to answer before the door opened and his brother entered, closing the door behind him. John Patrick tried to sit up straighter, but couldn't quite manage it without a groan.

"Stay as you were," Noel said. "Where's Malcomb?"

"He said he was going to get something to eat," John Patrick said stiffly. He still resented the necessity of going to his Tory brother for help. He hated every moment of being in his debt. He wanted to resist the familiarity in his voice, yet another part of him wanted desperately to clasp his brother in both arms. It had been so bloody long. He steeled himself against those feelings.

"More likely romancing Betsy," Noel said with a smile hovering on his lips. "I have noticed that he and your mate are competing for her favor."

"Where is Ivy?"

"Tending my horses. Grudgingly. It keeps him out of sight, except when he sneaks over here at night."

"Horses? He's always been at sea."

"He and the horses *do* regard each other gingerly," Noel said. "But he takes instruction, if not pleasantly."

John Patrick didn't tell him exactly how grudgingly Ivy could take orders. Instead, he studied his brother critically. "You look prosperous." He made it sound like an insult.

Noel shrugged it off. "How do you feel?"

"As well as expected, having been sieved by British musket balls and now resting in a British home. When can I leave?"

"And return to harassing your . . . hosts?"

"Does that bother you?"

Noel ignored the question and started unwrapping the poultices from John Patrick's leg. He studied it for a moment, then wrapped it up again. After examining the shoulder wound, he straightened and looked directly at John Patrick. "I'll ask Annette to make fresh poultices to pull the discharges from the wounds."

"Annette?" John Patrick asked, raising an eyebrow. "That's pretty familiar. Do you have intentions toward her?"

Noel eyed him suspiciously. "No, little brother. She is just a friend, the daughter of a patient I like very much. Why do you ask?"

John Patrick shrugged, ignoring the jab of pain that went with it. "She's pretty enough, especially if she wore more attractive clothes."

Noel's eyes narrowed. "Have you seen much of her?"

"She was just here. She brought some soup." John Patrick had watched his brother's reactions carefully, though he hadn't expected any other answer. He'd always known that Noel married Felicity only after Katy had married someone else. Katy owned his heart. Still . . . a devil inside him had prompted the question, and the answer had pleased him. He didn't quite understand why.

Noel swore softly, and it surprised John Patrick. Noel was usually the most mellow of men, difficult to rattle, even more difficult to anger. John Patrick had spent much of his childhood trying to do both. Usually to no avail. "Does it bother you that she shared a few moments of conversation?"

Noel ignored the taunt in his brother's voice. "I want you to have as little to do with this family as possible," he said curtly. "It's dangerous."

But there was more to it than that. John Patrick sensed it. "Then you *do* care about her? Does Katy know?"

Noel's face shuttered, and his hazel eyes glowered. "Of course I care. She is a friend, no more. But she has been badly misused by the rebels, and her father almost died at their hands. I'm not sure how she survived, getting her father here, after—"

He stopped suddenly as if he thought he was saying too much. After a moment, he continued, "I know about your damnable charm, and I will not have you use her. And leave Katy out of this. She is none of your business."

John Patrick knew that look. He knew it hid deep feelings. He'd last seen it when Noel heard that Katy was going to marry. Although she'd been raised with them, Katy was not related to Noel. She was the much-younger sister of his stepfather, John Patrick's natural father. As confusing as the exact family relationships were, so were their feelings for each other. Katy had married nearly fourteen years ago, long before John Patrick had been impressed. Even as a lad, he'd recognized Noel's internal struggle to accept Katy's marriage, the silent pain he'd tried to suppress.

"Leave Annette Carey alone," Noel continued stiffly. "You are no longer delirious, and I cannot leave Malcomb here without arousing suspicion. So I have to trust you not to do something that will destroy both of us. Or this family."

Noel's comment did not call for an answer, and John Patrick changed the direction of the conversation. "Tell me more about the family."

Noel raised an eyebrow, as if he recognized that John Patrick was pushing him, but he answered, "There's Annette and her maid, Betsy. Maude Carey, Annette's widowed aunt. This is her home. Then there's Hugh Carey, Annette's father, and his manservant, Franklin. You won't see much of him. He spends almost all his time with Hugh. And there's Celia, the cook and housekeeper. She doesn't live in the house, but comes in six days a week. She's a shy woman who takes care of the housekeeping while Betsy helps Annette with the wounded."

"How many Brits are here?"

"Fifteen at the moment. Five left earlier today."

"Good God," John Patrick said. "You mean two females take care of . . ."

"Yes. Franklin helps a little, and I loan them Malcomb when he's needed. But Annette and Betsy are rather special."

"So why has Miss Carey become an angel of mercy to the Crown?" John Patrick couldn't keep the bitterness from his voice. He knew how desperate General Washington was for decent medical care. The British seemed to have a surfeit of it, including his own brother.

"Annette has her reasons," Noel said. "She also has good reason not to like the rebels, so I advise you to be very careful in what you say."

John Patrick was quiet a moment before he changed the subject. "When will I be able to leave?"

Noel frowned. "As soon as I can get you well enough to walk out of here. Infection is still a danger."

"It's been what, three days now?"

Noel shrugged. "Infection usually shows on the third or fourth day. Don't worry, Jonny. I want you out of here at the earliest possible moment."

"Believe me, I don't like being here. I don't like . . ." John Patrick's voice faded.

"You don't like me caring for you." Noel finished the sentence. "I'm not happy about it, either, nor am I happy about placing Annette and her family in jeopardy because of your foolhardiness."

"Because I did damage to the Brits," John Patrick said. He moved his legs, twisting around. Pain surged through him, but he kept moving. He placed his feet on the floor, then held onto a bedpost as he stood. He was so bloody weak. He clung to the post for all he was worth, even as he felt himself slipping.

Noel caught him. John Patrick had forgotten how strong his brother was.

"Does that answer your question?" Noel asked quietly. "You won't be walking on that leg for a week or more, or use that arm for two. Nor should you leave until I make sure there's no gangrene. Those balls drove cloth and splinters into the wounds. The poultices must stay in place."

"I don't want . . ."

"I do not give a damn what you want. At the moment, Jonny, you have damn little choice. And neither do I. Mother and Ian would never forgive me if anything happened to you."

John Patrick felt the guilt digging inside him. Noel had risked a great deal to help him. Yet he couldn't quash the feeling of betrayal. He didn't understand Noel's siding with the enemy. He never would.

"Is that why you're risking your precious friendship with Howe?" John Patrick lashed out. "By the way, what does Katy think of that particular friendship?"

Noel's lips tightened into a narrow line. "I told you to keep Katy out of this."

But John Patrick couldn't drop the subject. He'd visited the farm in Maryland after his return from the Caribbean. Katy had been in mourning, not only for her husband but for Noel's defection. And John Patrick still remembered the almost mystical bond between her and his brother when they were young.

"You're breaking Katy's heart," John Patrick accused.

A muscle worked in Noel's cheek. "A week," he said again, his voice impersonal and curt. "Two weeks at most, and you can leave. Perhaps by then the British will believe you are dead and give up searching for you."

"I can't stay here two weeks. My men . . ."

"I know about your men."

"Can you . . . ?"

"Attend them? A favor, John Patrick?"

"Aye," John Patrick said reluctantly.

"Another doctor is looking after them. I will ask him how they fare."

"Ah," John Patrick mocked. "You would rather treat British wounded?"

Noel turned away. "What did you tell Annette Carey?"

"I just gave her a name, nothing more."

He watched Noel's hands flex. Finally, as if arguing with himself as to how much to say, Noel spoke softly. "Rebels burned her home and tarred and feathered her father. He hasn't spoken since. They lost everything. I shouldn't have brought you here, but I couldn't think of anywhere safer. No one would suspect her of harboring a rebel." He hesitated, then added, "I know your . . . charm with women. But restrain yourself. She's suffered enough without having her heart broken."

"The pot calling the kettle black," John Patrick retorted, wounded by Noel's warning. Despite Noel's words, he had never intentionally hurt a woman. He pursued only those who knew the rules of flirtation. Noel, on the other hand, had certainly hurt Katy more than once. "Look after yourself, Noel," he added.

"I want your word you will not—"

"Not what? Seduce her? You must think highly of my prowess, if not my character, if you think that I could perform in my current condition."

Noel sighed. "I don't think you would mean to take advantage, but women are . . . naturally drawn to you."

"You know nothing about me, Noel. You might have once, but not after years in the bloody British navy."

The tide of words rolled out of him. He had dreamed about returning home during those nightmare years, about seeing his family again and reveling in the warmth of their affectionate rivalry. He had finally found his way back, only to find his family divided, and his revered older brother giving aid and comfort to the enemy.

Noel's eyes pierced him. "I know you well enough, Jonny. I know you do not like being told what to do. But now you are going to do as I tell you." Noel's voice was flat, hard. "The British are combing the city for you. They are searching every inn as well as the homes of every rebel sympathizer, and even many who are not. They've searched the offices of every doctor in the city, including mine, despite my ties to . . . Howe. Only the fact that this house is a British hospital keeps them from searching here. The city itself is closed. I've never seen anything like it. Make no mistake, Jonny, they intend to capture the Star Rider. I'll not have you bring down the Careys, nor everything I've worked so damn hard to accomplish."

"What is so valuable that you turn your back on everything you used to believe?"

"You don't know what I believe."

"You can't possibly think we owe loyalty to England."

"That is exactly what I think. And you do, too, as long as you stay in this house."

"Then get me out."

"I will, the first moment I can," Noel replied. He looked at the closed door, then went over and locked it. "As long as you are here, you must have a believable background."

John Patrick wanted to continue the argument, but the conversation had drained what little strength he had. Every time he moved, new flashes of pain ran through him—and his conscience. He wouldn't admit it to Noel, but he hated taking hospitality under false pretenses.

And placing his brother in mortal danger. If Noel's role in hiding him was ever discovered, his brother could be hanged as a spy. John Patrick's anger came from worry, as much as his deep frustration at Noel's choices.

Yet even if he were physically able, he couldn't leave Philadelphia. He had to regain enough of his strength to rescue his men from the British jail. He couldn't leave them there to hang.

"Jonny?"

Each time Noel used his childhood name, new pangs of grief struck him. How far they had distanced themselves one from the other. Even though Noel was now protecting him, John Patrick could not expect him to do the same for his men. His brother remained the enemy.

He was reminded of Noel's question. A background. A British background. "I told Miss . . . Carey my name is John Gunn. A fine old Scottish name lurking in our history. Seemed fitting. Thousands of Scots have joined the British army in order to survive. Ironic, isn't it, Noel? The British destroyed the Highland clans, took away their land and livelihood, then turned around and employed them to destroy other lands. I just didn't think my brother would be among them."

"All right," Noel said, ignoring his last gibe. "You belong to the Fourth Fusiliers. The British are expecting a detachment from the South. If anyone asks, tell them you were sent ahead to check on quarters and were ambushed. I'll have some papers prepared."

"Papers?"

"I have a friend," Noel said. "He owes me a favor."

John Patrick mulled over that information. It was ominous. Why would his brother need false papers? Surely he wasn't more to the British than a sympathizer. "A Tory?"

"A businessman."

John Patrick studied his face. "Noel, you surprise me. More deviousness. I didn't think you had it in you."

"We have the same mother, remember," Noel said, a twinkle brightening his hazel eyes for a moment before disappearing. In fact, John Patrick wondered whether it had been there at all.

"Make me a captain then," John Patrick said, trying to push away the warmth he'd felt. "I've never cared for lieutenants."

"Greedy as always," Noel observed. "But no. A lowly lieutenant wouldn't be missed, nor would he be known," Noel said. "Someone would come looking for a captain."

John Patrick eyed his brother more carefully. Had he misjudged him? No one would ever mistake them for brothers—Noel had tawny hair and hazel eyes while he had inherited his father's dark hair and green eyes. Though Noel stood six feet, John Patrick was two inches taller. Noel's build, possibly because of his more sedentary lifestyle, was heavier.

Even their personalities were different. Noel had always been calm, deliberate, the peacemaker. John Patrick had a streak of recklessness, of defiance, that had often plunged him into trouble. The captain of the British ship on which he'd served had vowed to crush it. He had not, but John Patrick *had* learned to control his temper. Usually.

"Can you trust this man—this businessman?"

"As much as I can trust anyone," Noel responded.

The reply startled John Patrick. A cryptic answer for a man who was usually forthright. Had he needed forged papers before? For whom? And for what purpose? Again he studied his brother's face, noting for the first time the deep, furrowed lines that made him appear older than his thirty-eight years. He no longer smiled easily, though his eyes appeared as steady and honest as always.

Or were they a mask? For a fleeting moment, he wondered whether he'd ever really known Noel.

He wanted to ask more, but Noel was at the door, ready to leave. "I'll ask Annette to prepare the poultices. Remember what I said about her. Rein in that damnable charm of yours."

Noel's voice was hard again. John Patrick felt his own anger returning. Gratitude mixed with resentment was a bitter potion. He didn't want to be beholden to Noel, whose own choices went against everything he believed.

"Going to game with your British friends?"

Noel's lips tightened. "They are far more entertaining than you, brother." He left the room, shutting the door with more force than was necessary. He left John Patrick wondering why he continued goading his brother, especially after the risks Noel had taken for him. Yet the pain of his betrayal wouldn't go away.

Nor would the pain of depending on one's enemies while his own men suffered.

Annette accompanied Dr. Marsh as he checked the patients under her care. She took copious notes as he told her who needed dressings changed and how often, what kind of diet each patient required, the dosage of their medicines.

Most were on their way to recovery, though two of them had lost a leg after their wounds had festered. She had offered to assist during the amputations, but Dr. Marsh had said they would need her far more when they woke. And they had. She had spent hours reassuring them that their wives and sweethearts would still love them, that they had much to live for. She had felt their pain and their fear and heard their cries when they woke and found a part of themselves missing.

She'd prayed that would not happen to the young officer in Betsy's room. He had a devilish gleam in his eyes

that she didn't want to see dulled with pain and hopelessness. Even weak and ill, he had an energy she envied;
it was in his smile, in the fire in those remarkable green
eyes, in the teasing lilt of his voice.

She found herself worrying about him far more than
she should. Or maybe, she told herself, she was just
weary of hearing so much about the elusive Star Rider
and appreciated any diversion from the subject. Although she, along with nearly all of Philadelphia, was a
little in awe of his audacity in blowing up a British ship
so close to Philadelphia, she considered him no better
than a pirate who would soon be brought to account.

Printed stories from his captured men indicated the
privateer might well be at the bottom of the Delaware
River. If the captives were to be believed, the Star Rider
had remained on board the flaming ship.

Her aunt Maude joined them at the door. "Has there
been any more news of that . . . pirate?" she asked Dr.
Marsh.

He shook his head. "The entire city has been
searched, and searched again. Not a sign of him."

"Blackguard," Aunt Maude muttered. "Probably kill
us in our beds."

"I wouldn't worry about that, Mrs. Carey. I'm sure
he's much more interested in staying alive."

"Well, I am keeping my blunderbuss next to my bed,"
Aunt Maude said, her lips quivering with indignation.
More likely, Annette thought, her aunt would pull the
quilt over her head like an ostrich. She loved her aunt,
who had taken them in, but Maude Carey, a widow of
ten years, was a timid soul who fretted over the mildest
of misfortunes. It had been a miracle that she had succumbed to Annette's entreaties and agreed to house
British wounded. *Officers.* At least they were officers.
Gentlemen.

"I'm sure that the British can apprehend one man," Annette said, turning to Noel Marsh for confirmation.

"If he still lives," the doctor said. "I cannot see how he could survive. The river is icy, and there is no shelter along its banks."

"There're rebel sympathizers," she said.

Noel shrugged. "The British have checked them all. If he does live, I imagine he will soon be in British hands."

"They are saying they will hang him," she said.

"I think it would depend on whether he had a legal commission or not." He turned away. "It is time for me to leave. I have to go to the Quaker hospital, then I have some private patients." He hesitated, then added, "The lieutenant in Betsy's room needs as much rest as possible, after the fresh poultices."

Annette nodded. She watched him go, then went to the kitchen to prepare the dressings. The Scots lieutenant required lint dipped in oil to allow fluids to escape more easily. Others needed the milder—and more soothing—bread and milk poultices. Celia was already preparing the meals, a huge pot of soup for those who had not started eating solid foods, and a savory stew for those actively regaining their strength. Soon Betsy would be more than busy feeding their patients.

That left Annette to take care of Lieutenant John Gunn.

The prospect was devilishly tempting. She had not been able to get him out of her mind. Why this man and none other? She had always been drawn to thoughtful, solid men like her father, more like Noel Marsh than the rash lieutenant. Yet none of them had ever made her heart flutter as it did when she stood near Lieutenant Gunn.

Heart flutter, she thought in disgust. She was acting like a schoolgirl, not a responsible young woman who maintained a hospital and managed a houseful of dependents.

She straightened her back, went looking for Betsy to tell her that the poultices for the other patients were ready, then took the hot lint poultices to the lieutenant. For reasons she did not fully understand, she had to care for him herself, to see for herself that he was better. But it had nothing to do with heart flutters.

Just as she knocked on the door to the patient's room, she heard a crash upstairs. The door opened and Malcomb appeared, his usually dour face more morose than usual. "What was that noise?"

She shook her head. "I'm not sure. There are some other patients up there. Someone must have fallen. You're the only one with any strength in the house. Will you . . . ?"

He looked uncertain for a moment, then nodded and ran toward the steps. She took the steaming bowl into the room. The lieutenant was sleeping, but it was not an easy sleep. She touched his forehead, finding it warm. Annette swallowed hard. She hoped it wasn't gangrene. She debated over whether to leave the poultices and allow him to sleep, or take the chance of waking him. She thought of the two boys upstairs who had lost their legs.

"Please God," she prayed, not realizing she had said the words out loud.

His eyes opened. Slowly. Lazily. He moved slightly, a small groan escaping his lips as he did so. She wondered then whether it was the eyes that attracted her so. They were such a clear green, almost like emeralds, and they fastened on her with an intensity that spread through her body like warm syrup.

"This must be my lucky day," he said. "Two visits."

"Malcomb went upstairs to investigate a noise," she said, chiding herself for the defensive note she heard in her voice. She didn't know why he always managed to shatter her composure. She prided herself on that composure, and now it seemed like a willow branch in the storm of his gaze.

"I brought some poultices," she said.

He regarded her solemnly. "That is very kind," he said with his slight burr. She had the uneasy sensation that he found her sudden awkwardness amusing, just as he had earlier. She tried to become her usual efficient, practical self, taking her eyes from his face and turning down the bedcover.

That was a mistake.

He was wearing a linen nightshirt, though she was not sure how he had come by it. Dr. Marsh again? She inched it up to the exit and entry wounds on his thigh, careful not to reveal one inch more than necessary. Even then, she saw enough to bring a flush to her cheeks.

He was as fit a man as she had ever seen. His legs were muscled, and she could tell from the outline of his body under the nightshirt that it was lean but powerful. She tried to shake such unseemly observations from her mind and pulled the old poultices from his wounds. As gently as possible, she applied the fresh ones, watching him flinch slightly as the heat touched the jagged, raw wounds.

She finished tying the poultices so they wouldn't fall away. Then she quickly folded the sheet back up over his waist, and her gaze met his. She expected to find pain there, but instead she saw more amusement at her obvious discomfort. She bit her lip. She still had to do his shoulder, but at least that wouldn't be as intimate as his thigh.

She gently untied the sling that bound his arm to his chest. "Hold it still with your other arm," she commanded.

"Yes, lass," he said obediently.

She pushed his nightshirt down off his shoulder, then

pulled away the old poultice and replaced it with a fresh one.

"You are very good at this," the lieutenant said. "I would think a young lady would have better things to do than . . . change dressings."

"What is better than being useful?" she retorted as she awkwardly tried to tie the dressing to his shoulder. "Can you turn a little?"

He winced but did so, and as he did, the shirt fell open further and she saw ridges in his skin, deep scars etched in his side. He must have seen her eyes widen, because he immediately twisted back, away from her. "Malcomb will finish this," he said abruptly, and something like a curtain fell over those vivid eyes. "Thank you."

It was as curt a dismissal as she'd ever had, but the look on his face kept her from asking a question or even remaining another moment. "I'll send Malcomb back."

The amusement was gone from his face. So was that flash-fire charm.

All that was left was naked hostility.

Uncertain, she left, her heart aching for him, for the pain he'd once felt and obviously still lived within him.

Chapter 5

He didn't see her again until late the next day, and he worried every second of every hour he was awake. She'd seen the scars—the scars that revealed him for the liar he was, and the outlaw her precious British soldiers sought.

He had been a fool to let her close to him. He'd told himself that. Yet he'd found himself aching for a soft touch, for a woman's tenderness. Oh, he'd bedded a few women in the Caribbean, especially after the imposed celibacy of the British navy, but the occasions had been naught but mutual need and lust. He'd known most of the women would gut him for a ha'penny. In the last two years he'd been at sea most of the time, and the few times ashore had been hazardous at best. John Patrick Sutherland was a deserter, a pirate, then a gunrunner and privateer for the colonists. He was a wanted man.

He turned on his side and thought about the one trip he'd taken back to the Sutherland farm in Maryland. 'Twas then he'd learned a person could never recover innocence. He hadn't fit any longer. He was no longer the carefree young man who had said good-bye to them years earlier. He had killed and thieved and plundered, and he knew those chapters of his life were evident in his eyes. Though his mother and father had been overjoyed to see him, he saw grief in their faces when they looked at him—not unlike the grief that showed when they talked about Noel.

'Twas easy to claim that Noel had broken their hearts.

But he knew that what they saw in the younger son, in *him*, had hurt as badly.

The thought of Noel reminded him of his all-too-recent error in judgment. He never should have allowed Annette Carey to get close to him, and now he'd placed Noel—and himself—in great jeopardy. No British officer would carry stripes on his back. Would she realize the significance of what she'd seen?

Damn his own hide for letting a pretty face befuddle him. The fact that she was a Loyalist made his folly that much greater. He couldn't err again.

Still angry with himself, he sat up in the bed, putting his legs on the floor. Bloody hell, but his leg hurt. He put his good right hand on the end of the bed and tried to stand. The movement required every ounce of his strength. He fought the dizziness that made his body sway back and forth.

He grabbed the cane Noel had brought yesterday and leaning heavily on it, took a step, then another. Damn, but he was weak as a kitten, and warm, too warm. He took one more step, then returned to the bed and, breathing heavily, fell to it. His thigh felt as if he'd pushed a torch into it.

He continued to sit on the edge of the bed for several moments, trying to breathe easier, willing the pain to fade. He chafed at every moment he remained in this room, in this house. He kept waiting for the hammer to fall.

Noel had given him that piercing, disappointed look when John Patrick had told him what had happened.

"You just had to let her dress those wounds, didn't you?" Noel said. "You couldn't wait for Malcomb."

"Her hands are softer." But even as he uttered those light, defiant words, John Patrick felt a terrible guilt. He'd wanted her to touch him. Hell, who wouldn't prefer her nursing to Malcomb's? How could he tell Noel that at that moment he had been so utterly lonely?

John Patrick glowered. Annette Carey, Noel had said, had a lively, inquisitive nature, and he'd also claimed it wasn't like her to remain silent about things she did not understand.

But she had seen his back yesterday, and he had not seen her since, not since he'd levied that stare at her. Ivy had once told him that his icy expression was enough to send his sailors tumbling over the side to avoid his wrath. Over the years he'd partially tamed his temper, but his men—and his enemies—seemed to sense how fragile its cage was.

He hadn't been angry at her. He'd been angry at himself, angrier still when he'd seen the horror in her eyes. He was stung by it, humiliated that she had seen what he'd allowed others to do to him. Though he was loath to admit it, even to himself, his scars were another reason he hadn't sought out feminine company.

But what was done was done, and he could not change it.

He found himself breathing harder. Damn the pain. Damn the heat that seemed to be spreading over his body. He set his jaw and tried to stand again, cursing. At this rate, he'd be here forever. His men would be sent to the prison hulks, where two-thirds of the prisoners died of smallpox or fever or starvation. Or they would hang.

John Patrick hated this feeling of helplessness. He'd felt it much too often these past years.

He'd taken another step when a knock came at the door.

Expecting his brother or Malcomb, he bade, "Come in."

Instead, it was Annette Carey who stood in the doorway, and John Patrick became immediately aware of his nakedness under the linen nightshirt Noel had provided him.

Her gray eyes widened with surprise at seeing him standing. "You aren't ready for that yet," she scolded.

John Patrick's gaze lowered to the tray she carried. It held a pitcher, several glasses, and some small pastries.

"I . . . we . . . Betsy and I found some lemons at the market. We made some lemonade."

He took a step, then sat back down on the bed, heaving a sigh. "Thank you," he said, still painfully aware of his vulnerability in that damn nightshirt. He met her gaze and was pleased to see she returned it steadily. "I feared my scars offended you." He might as well face the problem head-on.

She set the tray down on the table next to the bed and poured him a glass of lemonade. "No," she said softly. "They didn't offend me. It's just . . . I couldn't bear to think how much . . . how painful—"

"There's only one good thing about pain, Miss Carey. Once it is gone, you forget it."

"Is that really possible?" she asked, as if she had thought about it and didn't believe him.

His voice gentled. "Yes, Miss Carey, it is."

"Do you think my father . . . could ever forget?"

He remembered Noel saying something about her father, that what happened to him had given her reason to support the Tories. "I don't know," he said honestly.

"He was tarred and feathered," she said. "He was burned badly."

His breath caught in his throat. Noel *had* mentioned it, but the impact did not hit him until now. He had never seen a tarring-and-feathering, but he'd heard about it, and doubted if there was a crueler punishment. "I'm sorry," he said.

"He almost died, first of the burns, then pneumonia.

They left him nearly unclothed on the road." Her chin trembled.

"You were *there*?"

She nodded. "They came to our home at night with their torches and their masks and the smell of whiskey on them. I wanted to fight them. Father had taught me how to shoot and I thought we could scare them away. But my father thought he could reason with them. He'd always been able to reason with people. No one listened. They just dragged him away. I—tried to stop them, but they held me." Her gray eyes misted over, and John Patrick suddenly yearned to take her hand, to comfort her. She had tended him with such gentleness, and now her pain radiated through the room. He could almost see, in his mind's eye, this slender reed of a girl trying to fight those who were torturing her father. "They made him watch as they burned down our home, the barn . . ."

Her hands were trembling. John Patrick felt his own horror at what had happened. "Dear God," he whispered.

"That's why I fled the other night," she said. "I thought about my father. I hate cruelty."

His eyes closed briefly as he heard the pain in her voice, the raw agony of memory. He'd lied about pain. He did remember. Just as she remembered. Only hers was worse, because she'd suffered for someone else.

"I'm sorry," he said in a low voice.

Her lips trembled. "I thought they were our friends, our neighbors. My father, he'd done so much for so many of them, and he'd committed no wrong. He just wouldn't sign their oath."

John Patrick's breathing became painful again, but not because of exertion. He fought down his revulsion. He'd never been under the illusion that the men who ruined his back were friends. They were officers who took pleasure in breaking spirits and men—not people who had grown up and raised families within acres of his own mother and father.

He wanted to move to her, he wanted to wipe away the horror in her eyes. But he could do none of those things.

"Your father? How is he now?"

She tried a weak smile. "He survived. But he hasn't talked since."

"Are there no other relatives?"

"Only one other aunt, Agnes. She's my father's only sister. But she lives in New York."

John Patrick suddenly understood Noel's interest in the Carey family. But he couldn't betray that. "I'm sure he will speak again," he offered, wanting to help in some way but having no idea how.

She stood straighter. "Of course he will. But I wanted you to understand."

She hadn't asked how or why his back had been shredded. He didn't want to lie to her. Not any more than he had to. But neither did he want her to mention those scars to anyone else.

He started to say something, then didn't. Instead he searched her face and saw only understanding. John Patrick had previously thought her attractive, if not exactly pretty. But now as he looked at her and recalled the gentleness of her hands, he thought her one of the most appealing women he'd ever known. Her gray eyes reflected compassion and intelligence. She asked for no sympathy for herself; instead, she'd told a painful tale to ease him. Instead of hating, she was helping men heal, even if they were Brits.

Her strength humbled him.

And he was using her, playing on her sympathies to survive.

He wished he could leave that very moment. But he

had no place to go, even if he could have taken more than a few steps. Nor could he leave Philadelphia without his crew.

"I hope you enjoy the lemonade," she said. "And Betsy's pastries."

"Thank you," he said again, even as the words threatened to stick in his throat.

Annette smiled, and it was like the sun emerging in a cloudy sky. It was just too bloody rare. He felt his heart constrict at exactly how beguiling it was.

He wished he wasn't beginning to care about her. Not only that, he was feeling the stirrings of desire. And those were two very deadly emotions for a man in his position.

Then their eyes caught, and he saw the same awareness flash in hers. The room was suddenly silent, leaden with the kind of expectation that precedes an electrical storm. It was as if the world was waiting.

Her eyes widened in acknowledgment, then confusion. The usual calm gray-blue turned to something more turbulent, the seas during a storm. There was a rebel beneath the calm facade she presented to the world. And, damn his soul, he wanted to tempt it out of its cage.

So did she. He saw it in her face, in the way her body seemed to sway toward him, in the way she suddenly licked her upper lip, then bit down on her lower one. He remembered Noel's warning, her obvious vulnerability after what she'd told him. He swallowed hard, trying to submerge the overwhelming need that had taken over his body.

He moved, a small groan escaping him as he did. "I think I need some rest."

Her face flushed a pretty rose. The storm had passed—for now. "Of course," she said. Then she slipped soundlessly out the door, leaving the room with only a faint flowery scent to mark her presence. It mixed with the fresh, sweet smell of the pastry. He took the glass of lemonade. He couldn't remember the last time he had one. Not since he was little more than a boy. Not since he'd left for London.

He sipped it, the sweetness almost choking him as he thought of her hands so trustfully preparing it.

He pulled on the nightrobe that Noel had given him. He wished he could dress more formally, but the uniform Noel had provided wouldn't go over the bulky bandages, nor was his shoulder strong enough to pass a shirt over his head. But, thank God, he had always healed quickly. Nothing had been able to keep him still for long, not even the fifty lashes he'd received from bloody Captain Wentworth. He grabbed the cane, and swearing, he took one step, then another. Pain cramped his leg. But he knew he couldn't stay here much longer. Not without doing something he'd regret.

So he walked until suddenly he couldn't stand any longer. His leg crumpled under him and he fell to the floor. He tried to get up, but his leg wouldn't cooperate. He crawled to the bed, but he was so dizzy. Hot.

He lost consciousness as a burning fever enveloped him.

Annette went to her room. She kept reliving that moment of magic, when the world had stopped turning for a fraction of an instant. Something in his green gaze reached out and embraced her as intimately as his touch ever could. Her body tingled, awakening a deep craving she never knew existed.

Attraction? She'd been drawn to him since the beginning, but these feelings . . . they were so much more powerful. She wished she could talk to her mother about them. Had she loved Annette's father with such passion?

She remembered only dignity in their relationship. Was it truly passion she felt now? Or something stronger?

But there was no one to ask. She could never talk to her aunt about this—it was so improper.

She wished she had more experience. But at home she'd been more interested in farming than in the few eligible young men she'd met. They'd all raised their eyebrows when she'd tried to discuss a book or, even worse, the benefits of rotating crops. And here—she'd never met anyone like the lieutenant, who listened to her thoughts, who praised what she was doing without that look of censure in his eyes. No one else had ever made her heart race merely on sight, nor given her such joy when that light appeared in his eyes.

The lemonade! In her flustered state, she'd left the pitcher on his table, and there were others who would truly enjoy the treat.

She turned back to his room, her stomach unsettled at the memory of the moment that had passed between them. She knocked briefly, but heard nothing inside. Opening the door, she found him crumpled on the floor. She knelt beside him and placed her hand on his forehead. He was hot, nearly burning up.

She couldn't possibly lift him herself. She had to get help. She was turning toward the door when she heard him muttering something, and suddenly her blood ran cold. It must be delirium. She hadn't heard right.

"Lower the lifeboats," he mumbled again, "the lifeboats . . ."

His voice was indistinct with fever but the Scots accent was most definitely gone.

"I will see to him, miss."

She whirled around. Malcomb stood in the doorway. Annette stared at him, the lieutenant's words echoing in her mind. He was a soldier, not a sailor, and yet even in his rambling the words carried a ring of command.

And the accent . . .

She stood slowly and stared at Malcomb. His face betrayed nothing. She didn't know whether he'd heard the words or not. Or whether he knew their meaning. She remembered the lieutenant's back again, the scars that ran like strips through his flesh. Not scars from a bayonet or bullet. Scars from a lashing.

But he was an officer. Officers were not punished in that fashion. At least, she did not think they were.

She looked back down at the lieutenant. Malcomb placed himself between them. "I will take care of him," he said again.

She found herself outside the door, leaning against the wall, her mind humming with so many different thoughts, all of them unsettling.

Noel treated a British officer's scratch from a carelessly handled saber with as much sympathy as if it were a major wound. Not once did he succumb to the temptation of telling the man he was a careless fool, and that he himself had far more important things to do.

In the midst of this benevolence the door opened, and Malcomb peered at him. His anxious expression and almost imperceptible nod told Noel he had trouble.

Noel finished hurriedly, giving the officer another glass of the fine brandy that drew patients to him.

After he ushered the man out, he gave his full attention to Malcomb.

"Jonny?"

"Aye. Found the bloody fool on the floor with the Carey lass beside him. He was mumbling about lowering boats. I don't know how much she heard, or understood."

"She said nothing to you?"

"No."

"We'll do a bit of praying then." Noel felt himself

going cold. "Dammit. I knew he was getting restless. Did he do any damage to himself?"

"Opened the shoulder wound. Might have some infection, but it's not gangrene."

Noel sighed. He wished he could have brought John Patrick to his home where he could keep a better eye on him. And he couldn't have Malcomb stand guard. It would arouse too many suspicions. He would have to trust Jonny.

"And now?"

"I gave him some opium. He should be unconscious—and quiet—for a while."

"Damn," Noel said. "I'll go over and see him. What about the Swede? He wasn't here when I returned."

Malcomb screwed up his face. "I think he's sneakin' around a bit. I donna' trust him."

"He's been prowling around the Walnut Street Prison," Noel said, nodding. "I saw him at a tavern near there last night as I was returning from Major Ames's residence."

"He's as much a fool as his master."

"Jonny won't leave his crew there," Noel said with a sigh. "He just won't do it. I know him."

"Even after all these years?"

"It could be fifty years and he wouldn't change that much. Loyalty's the most important thing to John Patrick."

"I don't see him being tha' loyal to you."

"Because he thinks I betrayed the family. Still, if I were in trouble, I think he would come running."

Malcomb snorted. "More likely, he would be the one getting you in trouble."

John Patrick saw the anger in Noel's eyes as his brother surveyed his wounds. God, but he felt terrible, and Noel's quiet rage did not help at all.

"What in the devil did you think you were doing?" Noel asked as he bent over the seeping shoulder wound.

"I cannot stay here," John Patrick said stubbornly. "I don't like lying to Miss Carey."

"And where do you propose to go?"

John Patrick knew, but he was not saying.

"Do you have any idea how tightly Howe has pulled his noose around this city?" Noel asked. "I had the devil's time getting you in. I'm not going to chance having you caught getting out. You know you're not strong enough to go on your own."

John Patrick closed his eyes. "How long?"

"Well, you just set yourself back at least two or three days, probably more." Noel continued to probe his shoulder. The stitches had parted. He swore aloud.

"You didn't tell me that her father didn't speak," John Patrick accused him.

Noel went perfectly still. "Who told you?"

"She did."

"Dammit. I told you to have nothing to do with her."

"She brought some lemonade and pastries. I couldn't very well stop her."

"What brought on these . . . confidences?"

John Patrick squirmed. "Nothing. She wanted to—reassure me about my back. She said she didn't run off because she saw something horrible or even because she thought there was anything odd about a British officer being whipped. She ran off because my scars brought back memories of her father being tarred and feathered."

"God's breath," Noel murmured.

"And so, brother, you don't have to worry."

"Do I not? Malcomb said you were mumbling something when he came in."

John Patrick stilled.

"She is a very intelligent young lady, Jonny. And she is vulnerable. She has lost everything of value to her. Everything but her father, and she feels she has lost much of him. Don't let her trust you, then betray her. It will likely destroy her. She must never know who you really are."

Another kind of pain, surprising in its intensity, ripped through John Patrick at that thought. For a moment, he wished she could know, could accept him. But that was folly. "She has steel in her," he said instead.

"And how would you know? You've spoken to her—how many times?"

"Three."

Noel swore audibly, a rare occurrence in John Patrick's experience. "Make them your last," he finally said. "Now be still while I stitch up the wound again."

John Patrick steeled himself even though he felt he deserved every ounce of pain. He was taking advantage of a heart far too soft for these times.

The sewing stopped and he opened his eyes. John Patrick's gaze met his brother's. "How much damage did I do?"

"Enough. From now on, tell her you need rest. No more heartfelt conversations."

John Patrick raised his eyebrows.

"And I want you to stay in this room."

Because he would promise no such thing, John Patrick changed the subject. "Have you heard anything about my crew?"

Noel hesitated long enough for John Patrick to be sure he had.

"Noel?"

"They're being sent to the prison hulks on the Hudson."

"When?"

"On arrival of a ship going that way," Noel said. "Two, three weeks."

"Few survive the prison hulks," John Patrick said softly.

Noel was silent.

"The papers you got for me—can you get more?"

"Why should I?"

"You took an oath to save lives. You know the death rate in those damnable ships."

"And you think one man can somehow rescue twenty prisoners from the king's finest troops?"

"If the Brits have twenty, that means thirty-five others must have made it to Washington's forces. Ivy can bring them back to the city. . . ."

Noel was staring at him. "You're mad. Even madder than I thought you were to sail this far down the Delaware."

"All I need is a paper giving me authority to take the prisoners. I can do the rest."

"No," Noel said. "I'll not help you kill yourself."

"With or without your help, I'll get them out."

Noel's expression was withering. "Not even a little gratitude, Jonny?"

John Patrick felt a bleakness flooding him. "I'm grateful, Noel, but not enough that I would leave twenty men in the hands of the British. They have been loyal to me these past four years, doing everything I asked of them, and more. If they go into the hulks, I go with them."

"No, Jonny, you're wrong. *You* would hang."

With that warning ringing in John Patrick's ears, his brother turned and left.

John Patrick sunk back into the bed. If only he weren't so damnably tired. He would have to regain his strength soon, for come what may, he planned to be the British officer collecting the crew of the *Star Rider* for transport.

* * *

For a large man, Ivy had an uncanny knack of blending into the woodwork. He had learned the art as an impressed sailor. His size alone had singled him out for attention by the officers, and he'd soon discovered he did not want that. So he'd learned to move in shadows, and to adopt a servile exterior, a fool's guise that produced laughter rather than blows.

Until Jonny had been brought aboard the ship, he'd succeeded. Ivy didn't know why he'd decided to risk everything to help the youngster. Perhaps it was John Patrick's courage. He did what no one else dared to do: He refused to give up. He fought Captain Wentworth with every ounce of his body and soul and heart.

He'd been lashed two days out when he refused to call the captain "sir," then two weeks later when he attacked one of the mates for striking a sick man. He'd taken on the duties of men too weak to work, sometimes working forty-eight hours at a time. He'd been a thorn in the side of the captain since the first day he was carried aboard.

Until John Patrick's arrival, Ivy had ignored the other sailors, intent only on survival. He'd watched when men were overworked, beaten, placed on reduced rations while the officers grew fat. But John Patrick had fought for each one of them, even the lowest among them, or perhaps especially for the lowest among them. And Ivy had watched, and envied his sense of honor, even as he saw John Patrick placed in irons, gagged, and lashed again. Then one day, Ivy stood beside him. And other members of the crew joined them. They saw real fear on the captain's face, because for the first time their crew had a leader.

Wentworth had pulled out his sword. He would have killed John Patrick, but Ivy had stepped between them. His arm caught Wentworth's, twisting it back until he dropped the weapon. Both he and Jonny were seized, given fifty lashes, and sentenced to hang two days hence. They were placed in irons and thrown into the hold.

Unwittingly, pirates prevented the sentence from being carried out. Even if they hadn't, Ivy wouldn't have regretted his reaction. John Patrick had given him back his manhood, his pride. Eric Iverssen would never cower before any man again.

But he still knew how to glide in the shadows. He knew how to avoid hunters, and over the years he'd been a pirate, he'd learned to hunt as well.

He owed the captain his soul. He would follow him to hell and back.

Ivy finished harnessing a horse to Marsh's phaeton. 'Twas near dark, and the doctor would be heading out to the general's ball, which was the talk of Philadelphia. Most of the British officers would be attending it as well. Tonight was the perfect time to try to slip through British lines and into Washington's camp at Valley Forge.

Last night, he'd slipped into the Carey house. The captain had told him to find any *Star Rider* crewmen who had escaped, and bring them back to Philadelphia. Then he should wait for word from the captain.

"Ivy." He heard the doctor's voice and turned quickly. He hadn't decided how he felt about the Tory doctor yet. Like his captain, Ivy hated the British with everything he had. They'd made him less than a man, until he'd met John Patrick. But Marsh had saved the captain's life, and Tory or not, that counted for a great deal.

Ivy met his gaze steadily. "The phaeton is ready."

"I'll be back no later than midnight."

The big Swede nodded. He would never use the word "sir" again with anyone except Jonny.

Dr. Marsh hesitated a moment, as if he somehow knew Ivy planned to disappear this night. His hazel eyes seemed to search Ivy's face. "My thanks for taking care of my brother. I don't think I've said that before."

"He would do the same for me."

Then the doctor said softly, "I saw you at the Walnut Street Prison. If I did, others might have. Be careful."

"*Ja.* You be careful, too, Dr. Marsh. 'Tis a dark night, and not everyone in Philadelphia likes Tories."

"I'll remember that," Marsh said dryly.

The doctor took the reins and stepped up to the seat, looked as if he wanted to say something else, but then he merely clicked the reins. The horse started forward.

Ivy watched as the carriage disappeared. Then he looked up at the sky. Clouds skittered across a small slice of moon. It was indeed a dark night.

A night for shadows.

Chapter 6

Annette tried desperately to be objective about each of the patients brought to her aunt's home. She'd learned right away how much it hurt if she wasn't. Her first patient had died, as had several following him.

Her heart broke each time. So many hopes ended.

It still hurt, but she'd learned to build a little fence around her heart.

In just a few days, the Scots lieutenant had torn it down. She'd been drawn to him even before she'd seen his back, but once she had, her heart had opened up and clasped him inside. His reaction to her seeing the scars had sent shivers of empathy through her.

It had been in such contrast with his usual easy manner, which already appealed to her. The teasing light in his eyes defied his grievous wounds, and his smile was pure rebellion against death. She liked that. And she liked the way his eyes seemed to see inside her, sense the part of her she'd had to keep hidden here in Philadelphia. It was disconcerting but compelling, as if he were asking her to go on an adventure with him.

And now she had something else to think about. The anomaly of his unconscious words. She'd tried to dismiss them. But they kept coming back.

At least that was the excuse she gave herself for approaching his room the afternoon after his fall. But in her heart, she knew it was something more. She felt like a lemming headed for the sea.

Dr. Marsh had tried to reassure her this morning.

The lieutenant just needed rest, he'd insisted after spending much of the night with the patient.

Today, though, she needed more than reassurance. She wanted to see for herself that he was improving. And she wanted to ask the questions that were pricking ever more insistently at the back of her mind. Celia had made meat pies and she'd put one, along with a glass of fresh cow's milk, on a tray. Annette had added a book from the library, a collection not nearly as grand as her father's, but still one containing some fine volumes.

Now she knocked on the door, and was heartened to hear his voice asking her to enter.

The lieutenant was sitting up in bed. His face had gained color, but he had bristles on his chin, making him look like a bandit. His dark hair was tousled, his lips smiling as he looked at her. Annette noticed the smile did not touch his eyes.

She set down the tray.

He sniffed appreciatively.

"Don't wait to eat," she cautioned him. "They are far better when hot."

"Did you make this?"

"No. Celia, our cook, did."

"Ah," he said. "The creator of soups and stews."

She looked at him searchingly. "No inflammation?"

Something odd passed over his face. "A little fever, nothing more," he said.

She found her eyes locked with a gaze greener than any she'd ever seen. His eyes had been slightly dulled before with pain, but now they looked clear. Very clear. And yet they revealed little.

"I . . . brought you a book. I didn't know if you . . ." She found herself stuttering. She never did that. Never.

"Thank you," he said. "I am grateful yet again. A good tale is welcome."

"You enjoy reading, then?"

"Aye. I grew up with it. I cannot imagine a world without books."

Her heart thumped hard. "I feel that way, too."

"And what else do you enjoy, Miss Carey?"

"Riding. I used to—" She stopped suddenly.

He waited for a moment, then pushed gently. "You used to . . . ?"

"I had a mare. Sasha. She was so very fast. I would race my father across the fields after the crops came in. Then we would wander over the acreage and talk about next year's planting, and . . ."

"No brothers?"

"No, just Papa and me. Mama died seven years ago. He taught me everything he knew about farming. He loved the land. I didn't realize how much I loved it, too." She paused. "Why do we never know how much we love something until we lose it?"

In answer he held out his hand. She took several steps toward him and laid her hand in his. She felt his warmth. It moved up her arm and flooded her body.

"And Sasha?"

She sat on his bed, careful not to jar him. "The night the raiders came, one of our people released the animals. I haven't seen her since." She felt his fingers curl tighter around hers, and she knew he understood. "I put an advertisement in the paper, but no one answered."

"What did she look like?

"She was a pretty bay with three white feet, and one black one. Her mane had a white streak. And she was among the fastest horses in the county. I helped foal and train her, and she followed me around like a pet."

He chuckled. "Is there nothing you can't do?"

"I couldn't protect my home," she answered, her voice more sad than bitter.

"No one could have protected your home against a number of armed, drunken renegades," he said gently.

"But I know how to shoot. I should have—"

"And they might have killed you, and I wouldn't have liked that at all," he said, bringing her hand to his mouth, touching it gently with his lips. "Never blame yourself."

"I will never be helpless again," she said, voicing something that had beat inside her for months. "I just wish I could help the British more. If only I were a man . . ."

"I am very glad you are not."

Annette felt the blood rush into her cheeks. For a moment she could not speak.

"I like your smile," he added. "You do not do it enough."

"There's little to smile about these days," she said wistfully.

He released her hand, and sat up a little straighter.

"Aye," he said. "That is so." Something dark had come into his eyes, as if he'd remembered something. His mouth thinned, and strangely she had the impression of a hawk. Powerful and predatory. The easy charm of a gentleman seemed to fade, and he looked every inch a soldier, a very dangerous man. She noticed the angles in his face, the recklessness that so oddly appealed to her.

The abrupt change made her remember the questions she wanted to ask. "Where is your family?"

He stilled. She'd often found that questions were a diversion for men in pain. And Lieutenant John Gunn *was* still in pain. She could see it every time he tried to move. But she was unprepared for the anguish that slipped across his face before it went blank. Had he suffered losses, too?

She rose. "I'm sorry. It is none of my affair. I just thought—"

"Yes?"

She tipped her head. "Your family might have something to do with the sea."

His eyes narrowed. "Why would you think that?"

A shiver ran through her. She hesitated, then, feeling like a moth flying too close to a flame, continued, "When you were unconscious, you muttered something about lowering boats."

His face cleared but his eyes remained cool, wary. "I did go to sea for a while in my youth, but I found I had no sea legs. Especially after my ship sank in a particularly bad storm. I spent several days in a longboat and nearly died of thirst. I decided if I was to fight, I would do it on land."

"Your scars?" She had not wanted to ask the question, but it nagged at her.

"A small disagreement between a mate and myself," he said. His tone was light, but she saw the chill in his eyes.

"And what happens if there is a large one?"

"I think that is no' for the ears of a bonny lass," he said. "Suffice it to say that when my time was up, I left."

His answers only created more questions in her mind. She knew about soldiering. She'd heard her patients talk. How did a common seaman become an officer? She was about to ask when he moved again, and she heard his swift intake of breath as pain struck him.

His gaze flickered to her, then away. "I'm more tired than I thought, Miss Carey."

It was as if she had suddenly ceased to exist for him. Was it the pain? The questions about his family? She felt responsible. Despite the brightness of his eyes, the crooked smile with so much charm, he was obviously still a very ill man. "I should go," she said. Yet her legs didn't want to move away from him. . . .

A muscle flickered in his cheek, but the corner of his mouth tipped in a piece of a smile. "Thank you again." It was a dismissal. Charmingly given, but a dismissal just the same.

She closed the door behind her before she realized she still did not know why his accent had disappeared the other night.

John Patrick tried a few prayers during the next few days, though he was quite admittedly out of practice. He'd stopped believing in prayer along with everything else in the British navy. But now he most assuredly needed the assistance of a deity. He prayed that Ivy had reached Washington's camp. He prayed that the men who hadn't been among the twenty in the Walnut Street Prison hadn't frozen to death or been killed. He prayed that Noel would obtain the papers he needed. He prayed that he would be well enough to masquerade as a confident British officer.

He prayed most of all that he could be cool and indifferent with Annette Carey.

But each time she fetched him clean dressings or food, she brought along a freshness and innocence that made her more alluring than any courtesan. She rarely stayed long and, as he'd promised Noel, he didn't encourage her visits. He usually answered in monosyllables, or feigned sleep.

Still, he found himself waiting impatiently for her to appear, and didn't quite understand his deep disappointment when she didn't. He'd never felt those emotions about a woman before. But he yearned for that rare smile that lit her face. He had to keep reminding himself it was a Tory smile for a British officer, and not for the man he was.

Noel appeared at the door of his room with a broad-side in hand.

5,000 Pounds Reward
For the capture of the pirate called the Star Rider
Believed to be in Philadelphia
Description: Black hair, green eyes, six feet tall

John Patrick winced. "I'd hoped they would believe me dead."

"I think they do. They're just not taking any chances."

"Where did they get the description?"

"Some British naval officer you apparently met while taking his ship."

"He's in Philadelphia?"

"Oh, yes. I met him last night at a soiree. He couldn't stop talking about the 'devil' responsible for the loss of half his crew, much less his ship. He was brought here from New York by the British to help identify you."

John Patrick couldn't quite control the anger flooding him at the image of Noel consorting with the enemy.

John Patrick crumpled the broadside.

"They are all over Philadelphia," Noel said wryly. "Malcomb's been taking them down as he sees them, but . . ."

"They have me two inches short," John Patrick replied.

"Aye, but close enough. Green eyes and black hair are none too common."

"Miss Carey?"

Noel winced. "I am hoping she's convinced you are who I say you are, who *you* say you are. But I want you to stay out of sight of the other officers, who might want some conversation."

John Patrick nodded. His stomach clenched. The

bloody broadside would make it that much harder to rescue his men.

"Give it up, Jonny. When you're strong enough, I can smuggle you out of Philadelphia." It was as if Noel knew exactly what he was thinking.

"I cannot do that. We've been together four years, some longer. I will not abandon them now."

A muscle throbbed in Noel's cheek. "Dammit, Jonny, you're not strong enough. You won't be."

"I'll be well enough in a few days."

"Ah, you're a doctor now, as well as a pirate."

"I've mended enough wounds."

"Did any of your patients survive?"

"One or two," John Patrick said with a wry smile.

Noel shook his head. "You've already planned this thing out, haven't you?"

John Patrick was silent.

"Nothing I say will make any difference?"

"No."

Noel's jaw set. John Patrick noticed gray strands in his tawny hair. Noel looked older than his years, the lines in his face more pronounced and his smile far less frequent than he remembered. He acknowledged the deep affection he felt for the man who stood beside him. Yet a war divided them. He knew he was placing Noel in an untenable position, asking him to support a cause of which he disapproved.

Yet the lives of his men were at risk.

He could not forget that. Even if his brother could. John Patrick sighed, easing back against the pillow.

"Noel, can you do something else for me?"

Noel's brows gathered together. "Rob the exchange? I don't think so."

" 'Tis much simpler and not as abhorrent to your sensibilities," John Patrick said with a grin.

Noel looked suspicious.

"Did Ann—Miss Carey ever tell you about her horse?"

Noel shook his head.

"She had a mare that disappeared when her home was burned. A bay. Three white feet, one black. A dark mane with a white streak. She worries about her. Can you make inquiries? I'll send you the money to purchase it back for her."

Noel stared at him for a moment. "Of course, I can look into it. But the money is not necessary."

"Yes, it is," John Patrick said. "For me."

Noel studied him for what seemed an eternity. "I will see to it."

Before he left, he threw the broadside into the fireplace. The gesture reminded John Patrick of how little time he had left.

He looked for suspicion in Annette's face when she brought him a glass of milk that evening, but found none. Instead, she gave him that special smile that made his heart warm, even though he warned himself that she would not give it if she knew his true identity, that he was the Star Rider all of Philadelphia searched for.

Five thousand pounds. It was a generous reward. Annette and her father had lost everything when their home had been burned, their land confiscated. If she knew . . .

But she didn't look at him as if he were the enemy. Part of him—the part that lodged his conscience—almost wished she did.

Instead, she regarded him solemnly. "You look much better."

"Dr. Marsh said I am healing quite well."

"I'm glad," she said.

"You look tired," he found himself saying, though he'd promised himself he wouldn't try to prolong any conversation with her. She filled a hole inside him, one that had eaten away at him for a very long time. The years of piracy had separated him from his family—in his own mind, if not in theirs. He felt alienated from them, from everything familiar.

He told himself he would soon be gone, and he would be no more than another former patient to her. He kept telling himself that, even though he knew it wasn't true. He'd tried to resist the raw, physical awareness that crackled between them every time she entered his room, but it was to no avail. His body glowed with a heat that had nothing to do with his wounds. But even more worrisome was the rare sense of belonging he felt with her. He didn't need that. He did not want it.

I wish I could help the British more. She would give him over to the gallows if she knew who he was. Did he really enjoy playing with fire that much?

But every time he looked into her blue-gray eyes, strange, unfamiliar feelings washed over him. Protective, possessive feelings.

"One of our . . . patients died." Her voice was almost a whisper. "We thought . . . he was getting better, but . . ."

A Brit. He'd killed his share of them. Yet, he felt a shadow of her grief flowing through him. He held out his hand again, and again she took it.

His fingers burned from the warmth of her hand, and a spark flared deep in his groin. A mistake. A terrible mistake. He knew it even as a moment of pure emotional intensity passed between them. He saw a tear hover at the corner of her eye, and he ached to touch it, to wipe it away from the delicate planes of her cheek—but that would not do. Not now.

She was so damnably pretty. Such an intriguing combination of strength and vulnerability, silk and steel. And dangerous as bloody hell.

He forced himself to release her hand.

Her eyes seemed to question him, but then she smiled, the rare sweet smile that he somehow knew was especially for him. No, he warned himself again. It was for the Scottish lieutenant named John Gunn. He swallowed at that knowledge.

"Sleep well," she said.

But he wondered whether he ever would again.

Annette closed the door quietly behind her, willing her heartbeat to slow.

She'd been so full of grief when she'd entered John Gunn's room. She didn't know why she'd permitted the young ensign's death to break through the wall she'd built around her emotions. Perhaps it had been the letter she'd written for him to his sweetheart, or perhaps because she'd believed him well on his way to recovery.

But two nights ago, she'd detected the telltale red lines jutting from the wound. No matter what Dr. Marsh did, the gangrene had proceeded lightning fast, and the soldier had died earlier in the evening. She'd washed well, then felt compelled to see the lieutenant, to assure herself that the same thing wasn't happening to him.

He'd always aroused something inside her, something stronger than the sympathy she felt for all the wounded young men she'd cared for. Was it the startling green eyes that always seemed to hold so many secrets, or the facial lines that didn't fit a man his age? It was a face that had suffered and conquered, but had never forgotten the suffering. Or was it the natural charisma of the man? Even when he had been so ill, his presence illuminated the room.

Whatever it was, he had worked his way into her heart in a way no other man had.

And he'd awakened a need in her she hadn't known

existed. She'd thought these past two years that she was destined to be a spinster. She hadn't minded, because she'd never met a man who'd warmed her, stirred her. But now, she knew she was not immune to feelings she'd only heard whispered about.

Whenever she neared him, a rush of heat drowned all sensibilities. As it did tonight when she'd let him take her hand. Grief shared by strangers, she told herself. It was natural enough. But she was honest enough to admit it was more on her part.

She knew nothing about him, about his home or family. He'd avoided her questions. Perhaps he was married, and that was why he was reluctant to talk about his life. She pushed her hair back. It didn't really matter. Once he was well, he would return to his regiment. General Washington's men were quartered not far from Philadelphia, and everyone said there would be a major battle after Christmas. She closed her eyes. The thought was devastating.

Walking on legs that were far too trembly, she made her way to her father's room.

She knocked lightly, then entered. He sat in a chair reading, and looked up when she came in.

He looked so thin, so slight, and his eyes had a lost, questioning look that made her want to cry. She went to him and bent over to kiss him on the forehead.

"Would you like a glass of brandy?"

He nodded, and she moved to a dresser where Franklin always kept a bottle of brandy and glasses. She filled a glass one-quarter of the way and handed it to him.

She looked at the book he was reading: *A History of the Crusades.*

"Is it good?"

A shadow of a smile passed his face, and he nodded. He laid the book in his lap and patted her hand. But the eager intelligence that had always livened his eyes was gone.

"There is a lieutenant here," she said suddenly. "He enjoys reading, too. I gave him one of your books. Perhaps you would like to meet him tomorrow?"

She watched his face anxiously. She always tried to stimulate him, to find some way to bring back the man she'd once known. Yet he only retreated farther into his world of silence and books. She saw it more and more each day and feared that he would disappear completely into it.

He didn't indicate that he even heard her. So she chattered on about the latest news. Mrs. Applegate was traveling to New York. Mr. Denning had joined the British army. Young Bruce Whitmore had joined the British navy. General Howe was said to be confident about defeating the ragtag American army. And oh, yes, there was a pirate said to be loose in Philadelphia. Most people, though, believed he had died when his ship went down on the Delaware.

"Dr. Samuel Johnson has published a new book, *A Journey to the Western Isles of Scotland*," she said. "Dr. Marsh said he has just finished it and will bring it over to you."

A slight glimmer of interest shone in his eyes and she rushed on, hopeful again. "The lieutenant I mentioned is from Scotland. Perhaps I will ask him to read it first, then he could talk to you about it."

The glimmer grew brighter as he took a sip of brandy. He had always been fascinated with Scotland. Although his father was English, his mother had come from the Scottish border country.

"Good," she said. "It is settled then. I'll ask Dr. Marsh to give the book to Lieutenant Gunn. Then the two of you can share a glass of brandy together. He should be well enough then."

She chattered on aimlessly until he finished his brandy. She leaned over and kissed him on the forehead again. "Sleep well, Father," she said.

Her heart hurting for his continual silence, she went to fetch Franklin to help her father to bed.

She would check on each of the patients, then head to bed herself. Optimism filled her. If anyone could pull her father from the silent world he now inhabited, she thought it could be the charismatic lieutenant.

Chapter 7

The sound of approaching thunder rolled through John Patrick's room. He put down the book Annette had brought him. Seized by a sudden restlessness, he walked around the room twice, then three times. He wanted to go out into the hall, but for once he heeded Noel's admonition. That bloody broadside *was* dangerous. As any questions about his fictional regiment would be if another patient tried to strike up a conversation.

But he felt like a prisoner. He knew only what Noel and Malcomb wanted him to know, or what Betsy or Annette innocently blurted out. He could hardly ask either of the women questions without creating suspicion—which left him completely at the mercy of a brother who had far different loyalties from his own.

'Twas a galling situation at best. Fatal to his crew at worst.

And he wished he had money in hand. He'd wanted to hand Noel a princely sum to find Annette's horse, but he would make sure he received it. Privateering was a lucrative business, and he had more money than he needed tucked away in Baltimore. Although he often donated British cargoes to the American forces, he had accumulated more than enough funds to purchase and outfit a new ship in the event he lost the *Star Rider*.

But he'd escaped his ship with a few coins in his pocket and nothing more.

He paused at the window. Eight days. He'd been here eight days. It seemed a lifetime. All his certainties—

about the war, about himself—were being tested in this house. The deep, bitter anger that had kept him alive so many years was fading. And that anger had been an essential part of the man he had become.

Because of a lass. A lass with eyes the color of the sky at dawn. A lass who had courage and determination and a heart so tender it was bringing life back to his. He looked out over the bleak and lifeless winter garden and forced himself to think of his crew. The sun was made all but invisible by the heavy clouds that raced across the sky. In the distance, he saw a streak of lightning. An ideal time for Ivy and whoever he'd found among the ship's crew to attempt entry into the city.

Time. He needed another week before he could rid himself of this limp. Even then, he knew it would take every ounce of strength he could muster to do what had to be done.

With the aid of the cane, he limped to the door and opened it. The room opened into a hallway that he surmised led to the front of the house, to the dining room and parlor where most of the British wounded were housed. To his left was a door that led outside. He longed to take the steps to that door. Yet what if a recuperating British soldier had the same thought?

Still, it was tempting. He wanted to feel fresh air. Wanted to feel the cool wind of the coming storm. He'd always liked storms, even at sea. He liked the challenge they presented, the skill they required. Of course, he felt fear. Only a fool wouldn't. But he also felt the exhilaration of sparring with nature, of guiding a dancing ship over heaving oceans. He wished now for a deck under his feet, dreamed of returning to a world where he had some control.

He heard a door open somewhere close by, and he stepped back into his room. He leaned against the wall and waited to hear whether footsteps would come toward him.

But another door opened and closed elsewhere.

He breathed easier. Every footfall brought the possibility of British soldiers. Of capture.

He started circling his room again. A step. Another. Keep going. One week, ten days, and he would be boarding a ship that would soon become his.

The storm released its fury at nightfall. Ivy and the thirty with him had waited patiently, then, as torrents of rain sent British sentries scurrying for shelter, they passed easily through British lines.

Ivy was anxious to return to the captain. He didn't trust the doctor and he trusted the irascible Scot who served him even less.

Ivy had found many of John Patrick's crew in General Washington's encampment. He'd decided to take all the men with him to Philadelphia. With scant food and scarcer blankets, the crew members were only too eager to follow orders, and grimly determined to rescue their companions.

Ivy was closer to the captain than any of the others, but John Patrick's fairness and personal concern for each member of his crew had produced a loyalty not often found on the seas. The fact that he had risked his life a week ago to give them a chance to escape had only served to deepen that allegiance. There was not one who wasn't eager to rejoin him and help free the others.

Thirty-two had escaped the fate of their fellow sailors when their lifeboats had been caught in the river's current and carried farther downstream than the other two boats. When they'd sought the other men, they found they had been captured by a large British patrol. Without weapons, the survivors had been unable to do anything but split up and try to bypass the Brits. Only two

of their number had not reached Valley Forge and were
presumed dead.

Now they were to filter into Philadelphia in twos and
threes. Each developed his own particular role. A patch
covering an eye lost in defense of the king. A farmer
driven out by the rebels. A simpleton begging for food.
A fisherman whose craft had been taken.

Such pretenses were not new to them. The captain
had often sent one or more to British-occupied areas to
obtain news of sailings. Subterfuge came as easily to
them as catching the wind in a sheet of canvas. To some
of them, even easier.

In Philadelphia, they would send representatives to
the tavern across from the Walnut Street jail every other
night until the captain decided it was time to act.

As they reached the outskirts of the city, Ivy whispered words of farewell to them and watched them fade
into the wet night.

Annette had gratefully accepted the Samuel Johnson
book from Dr. Marsh. She didn't tell him she planned to
give it to the lieutenant first; she'd noticed a certain
amount of tension between the two. It was, she'd specu-
lated several times, quite odd, since the doctor had an
easy manner with all his patients, even the most irritable
and difficult of them.

She'd tried to understand the cause of it, finally decid-
ing the problem arose from the kind of men they were.
Dr. Marsh was gentle, contemplative, slow to anger,
comfortable. Lieutenant Gunn, on the other hand, was
restless, brimming with energy even in his sickbed, and
not at all easy to be with. She sensed the impatience in
him, the anger. She knew it ran deep, and strong, and
probably came from those scars on his back.

And yet, the thought of his leaving created a great
emptiness inside her. He had made her hope and wish

and dream again. She couldn't bear to think how it would be to go into that room and find it empty. How it would be to wonder whether he lived . . . or was killed.

She shook the thought away. Nothing would happen to him. 'Twould be too much like quenching the sun.

"Annette?"

She pushed the unsettling thoughts from her mind and turned as Dr. Marsh came back into the kitchen.

"I do not believe Lieutenant Gunn needs more poultices," he said. "Just a great deal of rest. Can you see that he gets it?"

"I'm not sure that I can," she said honestly. "He keeps trying to walk."

"I know," the doctor said with a frown. "But keep visits to a minimum if you can. Tell Betsy just to leave the food."

She didn't explain that it was usually she who took the lieutenant his meals. She just nodded.

"Good," Dr. Marsh said. "He can move to a barracks in another five days or so."

Annette opened her mouth to protest, but didn't. A sudden bleakness stopped her. In truth, it frightened her.

But if he noticed anything, he didn't mention it. Instead, he began discussing the other patients, then spent several hours treating them before visiting her father.

As he emerged from the study in the late afternoon, his worried gaze met hers.

"He isn't getting better, is he?"

Dr. Marsh hesitated, then slowly shook his head. "No."

"Why?"

"I think he chooses to remain in a world where there is no . . . violence. But don't give up, Annette."

He stood there as if he wanted to say more, but after a moment, he merely nodded. "I'd best go. I have patients to see at the office."

"Have you heard any more of the pirate everyone is talking about?"

"No," he said. "I think even General Howe believes he went down with his ship."

"I saw the broadside. Are they really offering that much money?"

"Only because they don't expect to pay it," Dr. Marsh said. "I think it is more to reassure Philadelphians than any real effort to capture a ghost."

"It does seem an exorbitant sum. He must be a very dangerous man."

"Rest easy. If he's not dead, he's a long way from here."

Annette nodded and thanked him, following him to the door.

Still clutching the book in her hands, she dismissed the broadside and the pirate from her mind and walked toward the lieutenant's room. She knocked softly, then entered at his reply.

He was sitting in a chair that faced out the window, but started to rise as she came into the room. "Please don't," she said. "I just wanted to ask a favor of you."

Despite her admonition, the lieutenant stood, and she thought again how physically favored he was. He was wearing uniform trousers that stretched tight over muscled legs. The tails of a plain white shirt were tucked into the trousers. The laces at the neck were loose, and showed an expanse of sun-darkened skin. Without the nightshirt, he looked far less vulnerable than he had before. His face was still a bit pale from illness, but his green eyes glittered like brilliant stones.

He didn't seem to wonder at the way her voice faltered in midsentence. At least it sounded faltering to her.

"Anything, Miss Carey."

She hesitated, and he seemed to sense her discomfort.

He leaned against the window and looked outside. "I was just sitting here watching the storm."

"You like storms, too?"

"Aye, I do. But I'm surprised that you do. Most women do not."

Her stomach started churning at the intensity she heard in his voice. She felt his raking gaze studying her, and she knew a sudden uncertainty. "I don't believe . . . I am like most women."

"And why is that, Miss Carey?" His lips seemed to caress her name.

She wished she hadn't said anything. How could she explain that she'd always had such big dreams, along with what her father called a stubborn streak of independence? She'd wanted to use her mind, she'd wanted adventure, she could never be satisfied sitting in a parlor and agreeing with a husband. She'd thought she'd never find a husband who would want a *partner*, rather than a wife to stay at home and keep house.

His eyes bored into her, demanding an answer.

But she had none she could give.

After a moment, he gave her that crooked, charming smile that always made her heart rock back and forth. "I agree," he said. "You are not like most women. Not many young ladies would devote all their time to nursing the wounded, nor fight half of Philadelphia and risk the censure of the remainder to do so."

"How did you know that?"

"Dr. Marsh told me."

"You are fighting for something I believe in," she said. "I want to do what I can."

"Do you admire the king so much?"

Annette paused and considered the question. It was a strange one coming from a king's officer, and yet it was strange that some colonists were Tories and some rebels. She herself had questioned the king's actions and had

argued with her father about them, until the night that
forever drove away her doubts.

"He *is* the king," she said simply.

"Aye," the lieutenant said, and his eyes dropped to
the book in her arms. "Is this book for me?"

"It . . . it has to do with the favor I wish to ask."

"Aye?"

She hesitated.

"Come, lass," he said. "It cannot be that big."

"I told you my father does not—cannot—speak."
Suddenly, her words were flowing like a flooded creek.
"I'd hoped you could read this book and discuss it with
him. My father's mother was Scottish. He has always
been interested in that country, although he was born
here in Pennsylvania." She handed him the book. "I
thought . . . perhaps you might talk to my father about
Scotland. . . ." Her voice trailed off.

He took the book from her and looked at its title.
"I've already read it," he said. His eyes searched her face
for a moment and she feared he would refuse her request. Then, quite abruptly, he nodded his head. "I
think I would quite enjoy talking to your father."

She liked the way he didn't question, or become flustered, though she could not imagine this man ever being
flustered. He just accepted her father's condition matter-
of-factly. *Enjoy.* Quite different from a reluctant consent,
one given out of indebtedness.

"Thank you," she said.

His face went still. He merely bowed slightly.

A dismissal again. He was expert at it. She thought no
one could accomplish the task quite as gracefully, especially with no words. She looked up into his eyes, more
aware than ever of the magnetism between them, like a
piece of metal to lodestone. Or did *she* feel it—and he
felt nothing at all? She'd read romantic novels about love
at first sight, but she'd never quite believed them. Be-

sides, things like that didn't happen to her. And yet he'd already opened a new world to her, had made her heart sing and her soul warm.

"This evening?" She finally managed the question in what she hoped was a calm, tranquil tone.

"Yes."

"I'll come and fetch you."

"I will be waiting," he said solemnly, and the side of his mouth turned upward in that beguiling smile of his.

She forced her legs to move out the door, trying not to think about how much she wanted to stay.

Agreeing to meet with Annette's father was a damn fool thing to do. Noel would probably rant about it.

Yet he could not refuse the soft, desperate plea in her eyes, even knowing he was violating Noel's instructions. It didn't really matter, he told himself. He would be gone before long, and if everything went the way it should, she would never know she had harbored the enemy. Lieutenant John Gunn would just disappear into the maelstrom of war.

In the meantime, perhaps he could partially repay her for what she'd done for him.

His fingers opened the volume. He had found a copy of the book in Baltimore a month earlier when he was refitting the ship, but it had gone down with the *Star Rider*. He did not need the book, however, to remind him of the halcyon days in Scotland before his impressment, and he could talk knowledgeably about Scotland without ever turning a page. Prior to going to England, he had exacted every detail from his father, could remember each of his colorful descriptions and retell centuries of stories.

Oh, he could talk about Scotland, about its rich green borderlands and the stark beauty of the Highlands, where his family once lived. He could speak of them even to a Tory who defended the royalty that had stolen Sutherland land and nearly erased the proud Highland clans.

To a Tory like his brother.

And yet Hugh Carey had been wronged as much as John Patrick himself felt wronged. He had thought the issue was black-and-white, but he was beginning to wonder whether that presumption was entirely correct. What if one man's freedom meant another's loss?

He pushed the thought aside and opened the book.

The afternoon moved swiftly as he reread Dr. Johnson's book. Betsy brought his dinner: a large dish of stew with fresh bread and, for the first time, a glass of ale. His expectation started to rise in direct proportion to the sun's descent. He would be seeing Annette Carey soon.

He berated himself. He should be thinking about nothing but his crew. Still, his attention kept turning to Miss Carey.

When a knock finally came at the door, he pulled on the despised jacket of a British lieutenant and stood as he bade her to enter.

Annette stepped into the room. She wore a dark blue dress that was still far too somber for a woman of her age, its only decoration a necklace of pearl and sapphire he had seen her wear before. The deep blue of the dress emphasized the blue in her eyes and her shining, dark hair. For the first time since he'd seen her, her hair fell down in rich lustrous waves, held back by two braids fastened by a pretty comb. He caught his breath. Her face had strength and character and her eyes a lively intelligence. She was far more beguiling than a classic beauty. And every day he was misleading her, lying to her, deceiving her.

He felt sick at heart as he wondered whether she would ever discover to whom she'd been so kind.

"I'll take you upstairs," she said, then hesitated before adding, "Can you make it?"

"Aye," he said. "I've been practicing. But 'tis best if you take the book."

She saw it on the bed and walked over to pick it up. She moved gracefully. Very gracefully. Had he noticed that before?

She led the way, opening the door and moving down the hall, up the stairs to where the family lived. He used the banister as well as the cane. Each step was an obstacle, but also a triumph. When he reached the top, he had to rest a moment against a wall. He tried to even his breath as her anxious eyes watched him.

After a moment, he nodded and she moved ahead. An oil lamp lit the hallway, and she stopped outside a door, knocking first, then entering.

John Patrick hesitated for the merest moment, then followed her inside. An ancient in black stood protectively behind a man who was probably fifty, but looked seventy. John Patrick noted that the man's eyes were the same color as Annette's, but the similarity ended there. They had none of Annette's liveliness and curiosity.

Hugh Carey had a pleasant face, the kind that John Patrick felt would ordinarily draw people to him. He must have been a good man, since he'd incurred such strong devotion in his daughter. But now there was a vacuousness about him, a lack of focus in his gray eyes.

Empathy swelled in John Patrick, sweeping away some of the anger that had been festering inside him.

Annette introduced them, and only a flicker of the man's eyes gave any indication that Hugh Carey had heard.

"And this is Franklin," she said, nodding toward the cadaverous-looking man behind Hugh Carey. "He takes care of Father." If Hugh Carey looked seventy, Franklin looked one hundred. No wonder Noel often sent over

Malcomb. This was a household of women and elderly trying to nurse a goodly portion of the British army.

John Patrick nodded a greeting. "Franklin."

"Good of you to come, sir," the manservant said with great dignity.

John Patrick found a chair and pulled it up next to Hugh Carey. "Your daughter said your mother came from Scotland." He deepened his burr to sound more like his father, but not enough, he hoped, to make Annette suspicious of the inconsistency.

He didn't receive an answer, but he continued on. "My family comes from the Highlands. All crags and waterfalls. 'Tis nothing like this bonny land. But it is very dear to those who live there."

There was something in Hugh Carey's eyes. Somewhere, the man behind them was listening. "Miss Carey said your mother came from the borderlands. Could you be telling me her maiden name?"

Silence.

"Perhaps Miss Carey can." He turned toward her.

"Kerr," Annette said softly. "She was a Kerr. I remember her singing a Scottish lullaby."

" 'Tis a bonny part of Scotland," John Patrick said, "but I still prefer the Highlands. And the isles . . . they are truly magnificent. You will enjoy Dr. Johnson's book."

John Patrick chatted on, retelling old tales his father had told him, describing everything he himself had seen on his visit to Scotland: the fields of heather, the moors, the rugged coasts, the border swamps. He was inordinately pleased when Hugh Carey started leaning forward, his brandy ignored. Some of the vacancy seemed to leave his face, and John Patrick caught a glimpse of what he must have been.

For a moment, he was tempted to tell the family legend of the Starcatcher, who settled the feud between two families and won his Juliet, but that was sheer folly, leading straight to that damned broadside. He was astonished by his fierce desire to help this man.

This Tory.

He raised his eyes, and his gaze caught Annette's. Her eyes were soft, glowing, and they smiled at him in such a way that his heart jerked. Suddenly his throat felt dry, and he tried to remember what he had planned to say. Nearly every word seemed like a betrayal, and he longed to try to explain himself to her.

Instead, he turned his gaze back to Hugh.

His eyes lingered for a moment on a burn scar on the man's neck and he wondered how many other scars were covered by the clothing. For an instant, he remembered the pain of the lash, the feel of blood running down his back. The flash in his mind was so real, so vivid that his body trembled. He'd thought he had conquered those nightmares, but they kept returning. Hugh Carey probably suffered the same.

"You must go to Scotland—and England—some time," he said. "Have you ever been to England?"

Hugh Carey shook his head in the first active movement he'd made, and his eyes seemed to light. John Patrick wondered whether that trip wasn't exactly what the man needed, but travel was difficult, and dangerous, these days. And he himself was among the reasons why. Now that the French were discussing a treaty with the new American government, travel would grow even more hazardous.

Yet if the American forces outside Philadelphia won back the city, all Tories would be endangered, especially those who had actively assisted the British, such as the Careys. And his brother.

John Patrick dismissed the troubling thought and turned his conversation from Scotland to England, where he'd spent six months trying to petition the government. "London," he said, "is one of the most exciting cities on earth." He definitely had Carey's attention now, and he continued, pulling scenes from his memory. "The theaters and music are quite wonderful. I attended an opera by a musician named Mozart. It was truly magnificent."

Eventually Annette rose. "I think that is enough for tonight," she said, turning to her father. "Lieutenant Gunn is recuperating from very serious wounds. He needs rest even if you do not. But perhaps he will be back." Her father blinked several times, then he smiled. John Patrick knew a moment of victory, but felt the chill of deceiving yet another innocent person.

He stood awkwardly, favoring his bad leg, then gave a small nod, and followed Annette from the room. Descending the stairs was far more difficult than mounting them and it took every bit of concentration he had. He welcomed that need, however, for he did not want to think of the man upstairs or the fact that he was taking advantage of him, and his losses.

At the bottom he stumbled and nearly fell, but painstakingly regained his balance. Annette hovered next to him, ready to help if he faltered. He was determined to move under his own power, and he walked slowly to his room. Once inside his room, his leg gave way. Her hand reached out to catch him, but she managed only to fall with him, their bodies entwined, her face next to his.

Ignoring the pain in his leg, he found his arms around her. The light scent of roses clung to her, and her body was unexpectedly soft. He told himself to let go, to take a long breath and think things through. Yet the cold, ruthless part of him—honed by the years in the navy and with the pirates—wanted to take what had suddenly fallen into his arms, what he'd been desiring for so long now.

He had a man's yearning for a woman. A lovely

woman. A woman he wanted, and who, from the look in her eyes, wanted him. What prevented them from satisfying their needs?

His inner battle raged even as their lips came together, even as they sprawled together on the floor. He pressed his mouth tightly against hers, her hands curling around the back of his neck. He felt the warmth of her body, drank in the sweetness of it.

His body ached as hers instinctively stretched against him. Cautiously, his tongue licked at her lips, then found entrance into her mouth. Tension coiled in his body as he felt her respond. His lips instinctively softened as his mouth seduced hers. He savored the taste and feel of her as he probed inside her mouth and felt her shy reaction.

A groan reverberated deep in his throat. He was aware of a craving he'd never felt before. Lust was mixed with something deeper, richer, more enticing. And far more dangerous.

She was more intoxicating than anything he'd ever known before. Tentative yet eager, vulnerable yet ready to explore these raw feelings between them. There was an artless wantonness about her that made his blood warm and his heart hammer almost uncomfortably in his chest. He wanted her. He also wanted to protect her. And there was no one she needed protection from more than himself.

He drew away and looked at her. Her gray eyes smoldered. Her checks were flushed, her lips swollen from his kiss. "Annette," he said raggedly, as desire pulsed through his body.

His good hand stroked the side of her face then her neck in gentle movements, and he felt her pulse quicken and her body inch into his. His lips hungrily traced the lines of her cheek, then found her mouth again and deepened the kiss until he felt as if they were caught in a vortex, whirling around and around, oblivious of the danger at the core. Everything in him wanted her.

With another groan, this time born of frustration, he drew his lips away. In the light of the oil lamp he saw her face, saw the desire she couldn't hide, the wonder of an awakening body.

And he felt as low and treacherous as a man could possibly feel. He sat up, his hand catching hers until she, too, sat. He bent his leg, feeling streaks of pain as wounded muscles pulled. He welcomed that pain.

"I'm sorry," he said.

She fixed him with that level gaze of hers. No blame. No accusation. No regret. Instead, fingers wrapped in his trustingly.

He needed to pull away. He needed to stand and hobble over to the narrow bed. He needed to make her go. He couldn't do any of those things. Not as long as their hands were locked together, not when their breaths still mingled, not when their bodies still touched each other.

His desire coiled like a spring as he struggled to use some of that bloody discipline he'd once learned. Then he felt her fingers tremble in his much larger ones.

He'd been so righteous toward his brother, so condemning. And he was responsible for a betrayal far greater than his brother had ever imagined. Slowly, reluctantly, he released her fingers and reached for the cane he'd lost when he fell. He rose painfully, trying not to reach out to her again.

Annette got to her feet, too. Her gaze was wondering as she watched him.

John Patrick wasn't used to making apologies. Now they seemed to be tumbling out of him. And part of him didn't regret that moment when their lips had touched. He still tasted her, still smelled the scent that made his senses reel. He found himself reaching for her again, his fingers touching her cheek, tracing its hollow up to the corner of her left eye. He couldn't stop himself. Her face was still, but he saw her body tremble slightly. His fingers moved to her hair, feeling the silkiness of it, the fine texture.

"You are a very bonny lass," he said.

He'd heard his father say the same thing to his mother hundreds of times. He had always liked the sound of it, the musical quality of the words, but he'd never thought to use them himself. He wasn't saying them because he was pretending to be Scottish, but because he really meant them.

"Thank you for talking to my father."

"It was my pleasure."

She tipped her head. "You remind me a little of Dr. Marsh," she said. "He has also tried to talk to him, but my father has never responded to him as he did to you tonight."

John Patrick was silent. He could not believe that he had succeeded where his brother had not. Noel had always been the gentle one, the dependable brother. The healer. The conciliator.

"I am sure Dr. Marsh will help him."

"He has," she replied. "But neither of us has been able to interest him in anything." Her eyes misted, and he wanted to clasp her to him, soothe the furrows from her forehead.

He wanted, in fact, to give her everything he had, and he'd never felt that way about any woman before.

And the only thing he had to give her would destroy them all: the truth.

He limped over to the bed and sat down on it, keeping his eyes averted from her. He couldn't afford any more weakness.

"John?"

It was the first time she'd used the given name of the person he was pretending to be.

"Are you . . . is your leg all right? Should I call Dr. Marsh?"

Noel was the last person he wanted to see. John Patrick could already see the censure on his face, the disappointment if he learned about the kiss, about the intimacy that always seemed to wrap around Annette and himself when they were together.

"No, the leg is fine." It was another part of his anatomy that hurt. And she couldn't do anything about that. Not and leave with any self-respect at all.

She looked doubtful, but nodded. "I'll leave, then."

He wanted her to stay. Instead, he tried to control the need in his voice. "Good night."

Her eyes were puzzled, and again he longed to reach out and take her in his arms, to whisper endearments in her ear, to explore that hint of passion he'd awakened in her. But then he would be damned for all time.

"I'll see you in the morning." Her voice was low, and her cheeks were flushed again, but now with embarrassment. She'd taken his sudden coolness as rejection, and he saw the hurt in her eyes as she turned and went out the door.

If only she knew how much that coolness had cost him. If only she knew how much he wanted her.

He'd thought the first days on the British ship pure agony. But they were nothing like the hell he'd just made for himself.

Chapter 8

John Patrick worked at eliminating his limp. The pain was searing when he put all his weight on his leg, but he did it. One step, then another, until he could circle the room without a cane. Could he do it for as long as he would need to?

Thank God, he no longer needed the sling.

He was so bloody restless. He needed to leave this house, and yet he dared not step foot outside.

Or was the restlessness caused by the fact that he hadn't seen Annette today? It drove him to distraction how disappointed her absence made him. The last thing he needed now was to be unsettled by a woman, particularly a Tory.

Bloody hell, he'd never needed a woman before. Why, of all times, would he be plagued by such a need now?

God was not an accommodating deity.

He was even wondering whether He was on his side.

A step. Another. Each a punishment that drove deep into his soul. He wouldn't allow himself to think of Hugh Carey, much less his daughter. Where the devil was Ivy?

Thoughts and recriminations spun in his mind like whirling dervishes. He hoped they were products of his enforced isolation and inactivity and nothing more serious. Nothing he couldn't forget about when he left this place.

Only his brother's visit had broken the monotony of

the day, and he'd been curt as he studied the wounds. "You're a lucky man, Jonny."

John Patrick found himself at a loss. He owed his life to his brother. He knew he should thank him, but a firmly lodged lump in his throat stopped him. Noel had been forced into this, just as he was being forced into providing the papers John Patrick needed so badly. In the end, he stayed silent.

"Ivy returned this morning."

John Patrick sat up straighter.

"I imagine he will be over here tonight. I asked him to stay out of sight during the day. That British officer who described you is wandering the streets, and he might remember Ivy as well."

"I need information."

"Malcomb's getting it for you."

John Patrick stared at him.

"Not because he wants to," Noel explained. "But I brought you here, and my link to you is as strong as the chains we'll both wear if you're caught. I will help you, and so will Malcomb, because we must. You give me little choice, as long as you're determined to do this fool thing."

"I would never implicate you," John Patrick said.

"It wouldn't matter. I brought you here. I provided medical care. General Howe is not tolerant of those he considers traitors."

"Why?" John Patrick burst out. "Why did you join him?"

Noel's level gaze met his. "I haven't joined anyone. I'm just keeping out of it, and practicing my profession."

"You are serving Howe."

"My wife was a Quaker, and so is her family," Noel said quietly. "They support the British. And I support them." He paused for a moment, then continued, "I understand you've met Hugh Carey."

Pain rippled through John Patrick. He knew exactly where Noel was going. "Yes."

"Do you still feel that every Tory is your enemy?"

"Preach to someone else, Noel."

"I'd rather preach to you. I have a captive audience."

John Patrick's thoughts returned to his childhood. Although Noel was nearly ten years older than himself, he'd taught his younger brother to ride, fish, hunt. He'd been friend, mentor, guide, *God*. Noel had been God to a small boy.

"You do not have to," he said. "I understand your point."

"Humility, Jonny?"

"Perhaps a tiny bit," John Patrick said, unable to suppress a smile.

"Hell, that's worth all the trouble."

"Is it?" John Patrick said, suddenly serious. "Noel, I am sorry I dragged you into this. I'm sorry the Careys are involved. And I *am* grateful."

"I seem to remember I dragged you here, not the other way around. I should have expected you would then want to take on the entire British army and navy."

This time, John Patrick didn't smile.

Noel looked at him quizzically. "Why the long face? You're getting what you want."

"Perhaps I've had too much time to think."

Noel arched an eyebrow. "Ah, John Patrick admitting a weakness, along with humility. Miracles never cease."

John Patrick pretended to misunderstand. "Thinking is a weakness?"

"For some," Noel retorted, but his eyes smiled.

John Patrick sighed. "I admit that Hugh Carey has been treated unjustly. And yes, I agree that right is not always on one side." He paused. "Is there nothing you can do for him?"

"I've tried everything I know," Noel said. "Be careful, Jonny, or you will begin to care about Tories."

John Patrick glared at his brother.

Noel ignored him. "I know Annette cares about you. She'll be devastated if she finds out who you really are. I wish you would spend as little time as possible with her."

"She asked me to see her father. I could not say no without arousing suspicion."

"Is that why you did it?"

"Why else?"

Noel's steady gaze held a touch of sympathy. "Be careful, Jonny," he repeated. "For her sake as well as your own. I'll have the papers you want tomorrow. I will also see if I can't find a wig to cover that black hair of yours."

John Patrick nodded.

"And don't forget," Noel said as he opened the door to leave, "if you get caught, it's quite likely I'll hang beside you. Our mother would not be pleased."

Annette came later that day to take him to her father. Her eyes seem to twinkle as she saw him rise to his feet with more ease than on the day before.

"You look much better," she said.

"I am looking at one of the reasons why."

"I just think you are indestructible."

"Now that is a pleasant thought." Not as pleasant as taking her in his arms and kissing her, but he pushed the image out of his mind and followed her up the stairs to her father's room.

Hugh Carey was sitting in the same chair, his face still wearing a vacant look. Yet, John Patrick could swear he saw the man's body straighten as he entered the room. His head appeared more erect than it had before.

"I thought you might like to hear more about England." Even the word grated in his mind, his soul. England meant nothing to him but pain.

But to this man it was hope.

John Patrick didn't understand it. He didn't understand how England could mean so much to the subjects it had abused. But his feelings did not matter at the moment. Bringing life to Hugh Carey's eyes mattered. So did bringing pleasure to Annette Carey.

So he summoned up the images of London in his mind and related them.

The solemn Franklin stood behind his master, just as he had before, his stern mouth breaking into a smile only once, when John Patrick talked of the Thames and the hundreds of ships crowding the river.

"I remember that, sir," he said. "I sailed from London fifty years ago with my master. I thought never to go back, but I would like to see its shores again."

"I cannot imagine that many ships," Annette said.

"They are beautiful when sitting at anchor," John Patrick said, "but there is much poverty in London, and the docks are full of pickpockets and thieves."

"But no rebels," Annette said.

She said it lightly, but still John Patrick's heart skipped a beat.

"There are always rebels, Miss Annette."

Hugh Carey's gaze shifted from him to Annette and back again.

John Patrick turned back to Hugh Carey. "Have you started to read Dr. Johnson's book yet?"

Carey gave a barely discernible inclination of his head, and John Patrick felt a measure of satisfaction.

Satisfaction, and yet . . . his uneasiness deepened.

That uneasiness didn't fade as he pushed aside any offers of help when he pled exhaustion a half hour later and made his way back to his room. Franklin's frail form looked as if it would provide precious little assistance.

Annette, on the other hand, might raise other problems. He puzzled over the fact that he thought of her when he should be thinking of saving his men. He missed her when she was away, and wanted to hold her when she was in the same room as he was. In some odd way, she had become a part of him.

The lies were becoming unbearable. But her loyalties ran as deep as his own, and for equally good reasons. He could not trust her to protect his brother, nor could he ask her to choose between her own convictions and people she would consider traitors. He was discovering exactly how painful that was.

Perhaps someday, at the end of the war . . .

In the meantime, she must not know. Too many lives were at stake. Yet every day that passed meant more deceit and, he knew, more betrayal.

He made his way down the steps carefully, turning his face as several red-coated officers were admitted by Betsy to see wounded friends.

Once more, he was reminded of the danger here, of the danger he could be bringing on several heads, including a very pretty one. He made his halting way to his room, not looking forward to its loneliness, but aware that it represented a sanctuary of sorts.

Time to leave. In fact, long past time.

He found the big Swede sprawled on a chair in his room.

"Ivy," he said, closing the door behind him and tossing his cane on the bed. He made his way slowly toward his friend. Ivy stood, a smile spreading the usually cautious lips.

"How many men did you find?"

"Thirty made it to Washington's camp."

"Where are they now?"

"They are here, in Philadelphia, ready to do whatever you want them to."

"They know they can be hanged as spies?"

"*Ja.* They know."

"Have you heard any more about the imprisoned crew?"

"Your brother says a ship is en route for them. It should be here in three days, no more. It's the brig *Mary Ann*."

"Keep one of our men at the harbor. When the *Mary Ann* is sighted, we will act."

"They will be ready." Ivy eyed John Patrick's leg dubiously.

"I'll be ready, too," John Patrick said, following his friend's gaze.

"And the papers?"

"Noel will have them tomorrow."

Ivy eyed him carefully. "You trust him?"

"As I do you. He would not lie to me."

Ivy rose. "I'll go then and meet the others."

"Be careful. Apparently, there is a British officer in Philadelphia whose ship we liberated. He was sent here to look for me. If he knows me, he knows you. So keep to the shadows."

Ivy nodded. "The doctor already warned me."

"I should have known," John Patrick said wryly. "And, Ivy, I'm glad you are back."

Annette helped Franklin put her father to bed, then had a cup of tea with Aunt Maude, who had once again decided to ask the British patients to find another place to recuperate. This time, the search for the pirate had prompted her rebellion.

"All my friends are simply aghast, since we have no protection. Particularly with this pirate running around loose—"

"Just think, Aunt. We are safer than anyone in the city. We have all those young men here, and their friends visit frequently. Besides, the man is most likely dead."

Maude clucked nervously. "But it just isn't done, my dear. Not in Philadelphia. When there was an emergency, we could say we had no choice. But now I fear that it will ruin your chances for—"

"I'll risk that. Just think about the good you're doing, all these young men you've helped save. You have the undying gratitude of General Howe."

Her aunt preened slightly. "Yes, one of his aides did say as much to Clara Partridge. He said I was an angel of mercy."

Since Maude hardly ever had anything to do with the patients except writing an occasional letter, Annette smiled to herself. "And indeed you are. The British will never forget the assistance you've given them."

"Well, perhaps a few more weeks . . ." The older woman's voice trailed off.

The conversation had become a frequent one. Aunt Maude had to be convinced at least once a week. Annette changed the subject to local gossip, which Aunt Maude loved, then excused herself to check on her patients. There were only seven now, including the Scots lieutenant. And she suspected he would soon be gone.

She wrote a letter for a young ensign, telling him, "You will be writing her yourself before long."

He grinned up at her. "The captain says I'm going home soon."

He would be going home with a stiff leg, but at least he had kept his leg. So many others had not.

"That is wonderful," she said.

His face worked. "Thank you, miss, for all you've done for us."

Annette's eyes misted. She would miss these brave young men. Thank God there had been no more battles. Christmas was approaching, and there seemed to be an uneasy truce. Even the outcry over that pirate had dimmed, though she had heard there was an English ensign in Philadelphia searching for him.

After she finished with the last letter, she wondered whether she should say good night to the Scots lieutenant. *No.* He always confused her so.

Yes. She would take him a glass of port in exchange for his kindness to her father. She would deliver it, then leave. Surely there could be no harm in that.

She took a deep breath. She couldn't deny the quivering inside her when he looked at her, nor the wonder she felt at his patience with her father. There was something particularly appealing about a man whose profession was war being so sensitive—and gentle. She wondered whether he had ever had an occupation other than soldiering.

She still knew so little about him.

But he *was* honest and compassionate. For the first time, she was beginning to believe in people again.

She poured some of her father's port into a fine crystal goblet and took it down to Lieutenant Gunn's room. Outside the door, Annette paused to prepare herself. She was afraid she'd given far too much away last night when she'd melted in his arms. *What had he thought?*

Frissons of anxiety ran up and down her spine. Anxiety and something far more interesting. She hadn't realized a body could have so many varied reactions.

Still, she wished to see him. He would be leaving soon. She wanted memories of him, at least. More of them than she had.

She knocked lightly, and he bade her enter. He was still dressed in his uniform trousers and a white shirt, its sleeves rolled up. He was reading a book.

He looked up at her, but he didn't smile as he usually did. She suddenly wished she'd resisted this small indulgence.

"I didn't mean to disturb you," she said. "I thought you might like some port."

"And well I would," he said.

He was holding a book she had brought him, a history of Pennsylvania. "It is not very exciting," she noted.

"No," he agreed solemnly.

"I thought you might enjoy knowing more about where you are."

"I do," he said, still serious, but his eyes were beginning to crease with the wry humor that so charmed her. "Tell me where you lived."

She went to stand next to him, and turned the pages to a map. "It is not far from here, but now it is in rebel hands."

"Fifty miles?"

"More like sixty. It is a good two-day trip. But it is fine land, by a river. My grandfather sculpted it out of wilderness, even fought Indians for it. I think that haunts my father, that he lost something given to him in trust."

"You will get it back," he said with such confidence that for a moment she believed him.

A tiny ember of hope flared. Surely with men like him, the British would win. "Where will you go when you leave?"

"Back to my regiment, east of here."

"You will be careful?"

"I am always careful, Annette."

Her name sounded like honey on his lips. She looked down at his leg, then to his shoulder.

"Well, almost always," he amended.

"I'm surprised you haven't had any friends by," she probed carefully.

"I was sent ahead to find quarters for my unit. The doctor was supposed to send word as to where I am."

"You might find some friends among the other patients."

He was watching her intently with the emerald green eyes that so mesmerized her. He suddenly looked away and took a sip of the port she had brought.

"Your father has good taste."

"Dr. Marsh has good taste. He brings over bottles for my father."

"Ah, the good doctor. Do you know him well?"

She shook her head. "Only that he is a fine doctor and loyal to the king. He has paid a high price for it. It is said his family disowned him. But his wife was a Quaker, and most of the Quakers opposed the rebellion. Some were even hanged by the rebel government, and he was thrown in jail for protesting it."

Surprise flickered in his eyes, but he said nothing. Instead he stood, holding on to the chair with one hand for balance, and she moved quickly to take the goblet from his hand. Her skin brushed his, and somehow the goblet fell, the crystal splintering into glittering shards and the wine spreading over the floor like rich, red blood.

A small cry escaped her as she stared down at it. For an instant, she couldn't move. She'd seen more than her share of blood, but for an instant the wine . . . seemed to be *his* blood. A premonition? But she didn't believe in such things. Even so, her breath caught in her throat and her heart pounded uncontrollably. Suddenly she could only look at him, through eyes that were blurring with tears.

He moved to stand in front of her. "It is all right," he said in a low voice. "It is just wine." Using his cane, he lowered himself on his good knee, his hands gathering up the pieces of glass. One of them pricked his hand, and his blood mingled with the wine on the floor. He muttered something she took as a curse, and it broke the spell that had paralyzed her.

She took his hand and drew him back up. "We can

take care of that later," she said, as she investigated his cut and found it minor. The blood had already slowed. "I will get something to bandage this."

But instead he brushed it against his trousers. "No need," he said. "I am sorry for being so clumsy. You seem to have that effect on me."

She did? The idea was baffling, but intoxicating at the same time.

He lifted the hand. "See? It has already stopped." As if to prove its wholeness, he brushed away a lock of her hair with it, his fingers stroking the side of her face. Her pulse quickened, and her legs felt boneless as his touch ignited flames deep inside her. She lifted her face to him and she saw the glow in his eyes, like green fire.

"I will miss you, Miss Carey."

"When . . . ?"

"Soon. I must get back."

"Will you let me know you are well?"

"I will if I can." His voice was husky, his fingers still tracing the lines of her face as if trying to memorize them. She shivered.

He stepped back. "I'm sorry. I cannot seem to keep away from you."

Nor I you. But the words stayed in her heart.

"No matter what happens," he said, "I want you to know that I think you are quite unforgettable."

That was not exactly what she wanted to hear. She would rather hear words of love, or promises.

She thought she saw them in his eyes, and her soul started to sing.

She took a step toward him, and for a moment she thought he would turn away, or dismiss her yet again. But then he leaned down and kissed her. Hard. Passionately. She found herself kissing him back, her arms going around him, her hands entwining in his hair. He smelled of port and soap and some masculine scent that intoxicated her. A hot desire, so intense that she could hardly bear it, raced like a grass fire to the very core of her. She found her body pressing against him, felt a hardness against her that fueled the rampaging fire. It was as if her body had taken on a life of its own, instinctively reacting to his.

She heard him groan, then swear, and a second later he moved jerkily away. "Dammit," he swore. "I have no right."

She straightened. She had run the other night. She wouldn't do it again. "Yes, you do," she said, then stood up on tiptoe and kissed him lightly, little more than a breath. Then with all the dignity she possessed, she turned and walked out.

Hope had started to grow back inside her. Perhaps the war wouldn't last long. Perhaps Papa would get better. She knew he would if he regained the land he'd lost. And the only thing that would accomplish that was a British victory.

She would pray for one.

And for her British lieutenant to return.

Chapter 9

The next two days seemed to last forever to John Patrick. His leg was stronger, though it still took immense effort to walk without a cane. His shoulder ached when he moved, but it was certainly nothing he couldn't endure. He'd known far worse.

But the real pain came from thoughts of Annette and her father. Despite every effort to remain indifferent, he'd grown closer to both. He had not expected to feel the pleasure he did when Hugh Carey smiled, or the satisfaction when the man's eyes lit with interest at something he said.

The feelings were new, strong, and worthy. He had not felt worthy in a long time. He'd lost too much of his humanity in the Caribbean.

He didn't want to lose it again.

Nor did he want to lose Annette.

The two of them—father and daughter—had taught him to care again, even to love. He closed his eyes. *Love.* It was a frightening thought, far worse than facing a superior fleet of ships.

He wanted to stay. Instead, he would disappear from their lives. He'd already written a letter to her, telling her he'd been reassigned to another regiment and ordered to New York immediately. Of course, she would find no Lieutenant Gunn in that regiment—if she ever looked.

He limped over to the bureau and opened the drawer, adding the letter to the store of supplies Noel had brought earlier. His brother had produced a second, larger British uniform, this time that of a captain. John Patrick could wrap bandages around his chest and stomach, adding bulk to his body. A bewigged and bulkier British captain would bear little resemblance to the man described in the broadside.

Noel had left his offerings with a warning. The British officer who'd met the Star Rider was now visiting each Philadelphia residence, even Loyalist ones. Time was quickly running out.

He also brought news of John Patrick's crew. They were well enough, according to a surgeon with the British army, but they would be tried in New York as spies. Apparently, the Brits feared the repercussions of conducting a sham trial in Philadelphia; there were still too many neutral citizens. And it *would* be no more than a sham trial. Of that, John Patrick was quite sure.

After Noel had left, leaving John Patrick alone, the man sought by the entire British army wondered whether Noel was more adept at subterfuge than he.

He was still contemplating that question when the door to his room opened, and Ivy came in.

The Swede seldom showed emotion of any kind, but now his cool blue eyes couldn't hide a certain elation. "The British ship came in last night. According to a member of its crew, the ship will be resupplied, then take on the prisoners for departure day after tomorrow." He waited a moment, as if savoring his next piece of news. "Howe is having a ball tomorrow night. Most of the ship's officers, as well as half the officers in the city will attend."

John Patrick felt a surge of something like the old anticipation. He was damnably tired of being sedentary. And despite the pain that still accompanied his every movement, he was ready to get back into action, to leave the house where he felt like a liar and a fraud.

He would miss Annette Carey, far more than he'd

ever believed possible. She would believe he had left her easily, without even the courtesy of a spoken good-bye. She would never know that she'd carved a place in his heart. He swore under his breath, wishing that Noel had never thought of this particular haven. It was more like a hell, albeit one of his own making.

"Do we have enough uniforms?"

"We will. There's a detachment of marines that inhabits a particular tavern near the waterfront. We'll drug their wine." He looked at John Patrick. "Will you be fit enough?"

"Aye. I could go this night if need be. But tomorrow night is better. If the officers are busy, that means the enlisted men will be drinking as well. We'll meet at ten. The house should be quiet then."

Ivy's grin faded, his face hardening with seriousness. "What will happen to your bro—Dr. Marsh, if General Washington takes the city back?"

John Patrick had worried about that, too. And he wasn't worried about just Noel. Tories would not fare well in the city once it was retaken, and he knew Washington meant to take Philadelphia back. While Boston had been the fist of the revolution, Philadelphia was its heart—the place where independence was declared.

"I'm sure Noel is aware of the danger," he said after a long pause. In truth, Noel's role in his current predicament plagued him already. He'd never meant to put Noel in jeopardy, but there was no question he had. If anything happened to Noel because of him, he'd never forgive himself. And Annette . . .

He changed the subject. "The men?"

"Scattered throughout the city."

John Patrick moved about the room, stretching his muscles, testing his strength. He tried to move without a limp, although he could, if challenged, explain one well enough with a story about being anxious to return to service despite a rebel's bullet.

"Tomorrow night, then," he said.

Ivy nodded, his gaze going around the room, lingering on the vase of fresh flowers on the table, and the gay warmth of golden curtains. Then it returned to John Patrick. "What are you going to tell Miss Carey?"

"That I'm returning to my regiment."

"She is a kind person. Pretty, too," Ivy added cautiously.

"Aye," John Patrick said quietly. "Though I wonder if she would have been so kind if she knew . . ."

"Do you, Captain?"

"Perhaps not. But we will never know, will we?"

Once more around the room and back. He didn't want to think of Annette Carey. He couldn't afford to think of her. His men couldn't afford the distraction. Then he sat down with a sigh. It wasn't from weariness, though, or even the ache of healing wounds.

The physical pain was easier to endure than the thought of Annette Carey discovering who he really was. In his mind's eye, he could see the look of betrayal on her face. . . .

Hopefully she would never know. She might feel some sense of loss when he left, just as he would. Dammit, he had to stop thinking about her. Some British officer would court her, and she would forget all about him.

Why did the thought hurt so bloody much?

Ivy's brow furrowed. "I'll be meeting with the crew. He turned to go.

"Ivy?"

The Swede turned to look at him.

"Take care of yourself. I need you."

Ivy's large face turned red. He merely nodded once before he escaped out the door.

John Patrick continued around the room. Twenty-four hours. Twenty-four hours, and he would have a ship again.

He would be free, as free as he wanted to be. He waited for the familiar elation to fill him, waited for the sharp tingling of his senses to return.

But, instead, he felt something else altogether. Why did he feel so trapped? Why did his heart ache?

The next day went faster than John Patrick would have believed possible. He made one last visit to Hugh Carey, saying his own silent good-bye, wishing him well in his heart. He was stunned at how much the Tory had come to mean to him.

Leaving Hugh's room, he almost literally ran into Annette, his hands reaching out to steady her as she did the same. He knew immediately he should not have done it. Just the touch of her made him feel as if his flesh were suddenly burning, and when her eyes widened he knew she felt the same. Raw sexuality blazed between them, their eyes meeting, exchanging secrets—the kind lovers exchanged, not the deep, dangerous secrets he was trying so hard to protect. John Patrick forced himself to step back and let his hand fall. He grabbed the cane he had brought with him and held on to it for dear life. He allowed his body to slump slightly, even to sway.

The worry that filled her eyes was like a sword stroke to his gut. He had used that worry artfully these past few days, feigning sleep when she knocked, or pretending more pain than he felt. He was trying to keep his word to Noel. To himself.

"Let me help you," she said.

"No, Miss Carey," he said, softening the formality with a wry grin. "You've done enough. Stay with your father. Perhaps . . . tomorrow . . ."

Her eyes brightened, and she nodded.

But there would be no tomorrow. He would be gone, a note on a table saying only that he'd been fetched in the middle of the night and he had not wanted to disturb her sleep. His mind memorized the way she looked: the dark hair, the blue-gray eyes the color of dawn. The eyes that could become quicksilver with passion.

He knew she would haunt him for a very long time.

Noel knew John Patrick would do whatever it was he planned this night. The British ship was to leave tomorrow at late-evening tide. The fact that General Howe had planned a grand ball for this evening was an added incentive.

His gut tied in knots, Noel fed Aristotle, then went to the Careys'. He felt in his bones that his brother would be gone before the next morning. Hopefully, without a trace.

But first he wanted—nay, needed—to say good-bye. Jonny might think him a traitor, but he was still his brother.

At the Careys' home he knocked and Betsy answered, her face lighting with pleasure when she saw him. "Dr. Marsh."

"How are all my patients?"

"Well on their way, bless 'em," she said. "Not a new fever among them."

"It's Celia's chicken soup and your tender care, I think," Noel said.

Her smile deepened, dimpling her cheeks, and Noel understood why Malcomb was so besotted by her, and why he'd been even more cranky than usual since Ivy started spending so much time at the Carey home.

"How is our Scots lieutenant?" he asked after a pause.

She beamed. "The lieutenant is up and about. Even reading to Mr. Hugh."

Noel stifled his surprise. Jonny had said he'd met

Hugh Carey. But reading to him? After promising to keep his contact with the family to a minimum?

"Ah, that's fine. Is he in his room now?"

She nodded. "He's resting, just as you said he should. Miss Annette said to make sure he wasn't disturbed, but I know that doesn't mean you." She winked at him. "I think he has an eye for my miss."

Damn his brother's soul. He'd seen Annette's eyes light when John Gunn's name was mentioned but he'd hoped it was just a harmless flirtation. He knew his brother's attraction to—and for—the ladies. Few could resist him, and he'd moved from one to another as a young man. But he'd never been dishonorable about it. He'd never promised a young lady anything, at least as far as Noel knew, although he'd left a slew of broken hearts in his wake. The last thing Noel wanted was Annette Carey to be one of them.

But he followed Betsy inside silently, giving her his cloak.

"I'll see the lieutenant first," he said, and made his way to Jonny's room. He entered without waiting for an answer to his brief knock, closing the door firmly behind him.

Jonny was sitting on the bed. He started to rise, and relaxed only when he saw that the visitor was his brother. Noel looked down at Jonny's lap and saw the uniform jacket. And a needle in his brother's fingers.

Jonny grinned. "The uniform was a little large, even with the additional weight. But I am tailoring it to perfection."

"I didn't realize sewing was one of your talents."

"The British navy taught me a great deal. I rather enjoy using that knowledge against them now."

Noel noted the brightness in his brother's eyes. Anticipation. He'd seen it before when Jonny was far younger and about to ride a particularly dangerous horse.

"You are leaving tonight."

Jonny nodded. "Thanks to your papers. They really are quite good. I am in awe of your unexpected talents."

"You left me little choice, Jonny. I couldn't let you ruin what I've built here."

"It's that important to you?"

"Yes," Noel said simply.

"Then I'm sorry," John Patrick said, and meant it. He'd allowed his anger at Noel's own loyalties to destroy the closeness he'd always had with his half-brother. Because of Hugh Carey, he was beginning to understand that loyalties were a much grayer area than he'd wanted to believe. And he couldn't judge the actions of someone else, particularly when his own were so reprehensible.

Noel's face grew taut with restrained emotion. "I won't ask you when you're leaving. But . . . be careful. I don't want to lose my little brother."

Not so little any longer, John Patrick thought. He stood two inches taller than Noel. But he wondered whether Noel didn't stand taller in another way. John Patrick knew now—hell, he'd always known—that Noel was sacrificing his own principles to help him.

John Patrick held out his hand. "I know what you've risked for me. I won't forget it."

Noel took his hand, and for a moment, he couldn't say anything.

John Patrick released his grip. "What are you going to do when the British leave?"

"And why do you think they will leave?"

"They will have to consolidate their armies, and New York is more important to them than Philadelphia, despite this city's symbolism."

"Is it?"

"Aye. I've intercepted a few messages in the past few months," John Patrick said, his mouth twisting into a half-smile.

"Well, that's my worry and not yours," Noel said. "I understand you've continued to visit with Hugh Carey."

John Patrick's eyes hardened, all emotion leaving them. That was new. Noel remembered Jonny as open and easy to read. But that was ten years ago. He recognized other changes, the most striking being the aura of danger radiating from him. Noel knew his brother must be a very skilled captain; otherwise, he would not be so feared by the British. Yet he hadn't expected the ruthlessness he sometimes saw in John Patrick.

"Annette requested it," John Patrick finally said. "I could hardly say no."

"What do you think of him now?"

"I think he has been ill-used," John Patrick said wryly. "Is that what you wanted to hear?"

It was. Noel wanted to hear that his brother still had a conscience despite his years of pirating. "Someday you will have to tell me about the past ten years."

"I'm not sure you want to hear about them."

Their gazes met. Noel's was the first to drop. "Well, then . . . I'd best be going."

John Patrick stood there watching him, his eyes still shrouded. "If Washington retakes the city, get the hell out."

"I might. Or I might stay."

"Dammit, Noel. You will be a marked man. Don't be a fool."

"Look at who's giving advice. I can't imagine anything more foolish than sailing down the Delaware in the midst of the British navy."

Jonny suddenly looked like a boy whose hand is caught in the pie. The wry, startled expression softened the hardness in his face. Noel wanted to leave with that expression in his memory. "Good health and good fortune," he said, and closed the door behind him.

John Patrick was ready to leave at dusk.

Although he didn't think he would ever be ready to leave Annette. He felt a man's lust for her, but he also truly liked her. He liked her smile, her shining intelligence, even the anger that made her eyes flash and her lips set stubbornly. But his feelings went deeper. For the first time in ten years, he'd felt a kind of peace. And it was only in her presence.

Yet he was her enemy.

It was a damnably good thing that he was leaving tonight.

He took out the letter he'd so carefully written. He added a few lines. He wanted the Careys to know how very much he appreciated the care they had given him. He did not mention returning. He signed it, "Respectfully, John Gunn."

He placed the letter on the table.

Minutes seemed like hours.

Every squeak, every slight noise set him on edge. He'd never been good at waiting.

Especially now. So much hung in the balance. His men's lives. His brother's life. Perhaps even the Careys, if the British ever learned they'd been harboring a wanted fugitive, particularly one wanted as badly as he was.

He recalled Noel's comment about the wisdom of sailing down the Delaware in the midst of the British navy. He realized now how many lives he'd placed in jeopardy with that single act.

Then, finally, he heard the knock he was hoping for, a special prearranged signal. Ivy.

John Patrick opened the door to the big Swede, who stood there clad in his usual rough clothing.

Ivy's gaze met his. "We're ready, Cap'n. Samuels and two others are waiting outside with a horse."

John Patrick nodded. "Good. I have the papers we need."

Ivy gave him a rare grin.

John Patrick wished he could do the same. But the pleasure was gone from the game, and instead, he felt a deep foreboding. Still, he had no choice. He had to rescue the men who trusted him.

He started to pick up the captain's uniform that would disguise him when he heard footsteps in the hallway. He used his hand to signal Ivy to the side.

A knock. Light. Annette? He held his breath, hoping she would believe he was resting and go away. The gentle knock became pounding, and he realized that Annette wasn't alone.

Ivy reached behind the rough jacket he wore and pulled a pistol from the waist of his trousers. Then he stood behind the door.

John Patrick's heart hammered against his ribs. Too many lives depended on him.

The pounding grew louder, then he heard the doorknob turn. He moved to the bed and sat down. Anyone walking in would see him, not Ivy. He picked up the holster and belt that went with the captain's uniform and laid them next to him, covering them with a corner of the quilt.

The door opened. Two men, a British navy lieutenant in a blue uniform and a British army sergeant in red, waited at the door as Annette entered. John Patrick recognized one of them immediately. The recognition was mutual. Unaware, Annette started apologetically, "These men are searching every house—"

Her words froze as she heard the expletive from the officer behind her.

"Star Rider!" the man spat, his right hand going to the pistol at his side.

The door slammed behind him, startling the two Brits.

"Lower your pistols and stand very still, gentlemen," Ivy said.

Annette whirled around, momentarily placing herself between Ivy and the two soldiers. The British navy officer used that opportunity to draw his pistol and point it at John Patrick, who, at the same instant, pulled the pistol from under the quilt and aimed back.

"Bastard," the officer said as he pulled the trigger.

John Patrick's pistol went off a fraction of an instant sooner. The officer slumped to the floor, and John Patrick knelt next to him. Simultaneously, Ivy used the butt of his pistol to hit the other man's head. The Swede caught the sergeant as he started to fall and lowered him soundlessly to the floor.

John Patrick glanced up at Ivy, then stood. "He's dead. You had better see if there is anyone with him, or if anyone heard that shot. If they have, tell them I was cleaning my pistol." Then he turned to Annette.

Her face was white, her eyes disbelieving as she looked down at the spreading pool of blood beside the British lieutenant. Then her gaze lifted to meet his. She seemed to search his face for a denial of what she'd just seen.

He heard Ivy leave and close the door behind him, and then Annette dropped to the ground. For an instant, he thought she might be swooning. He started to reach for her, but the sudden movement sent pain rushing through his leg, and it gave way. He stumbled, but caught himself.

It was too late. She had the Brit's pistol in her hand, and she was pointing it at him.

Chapter 10

riends and neighbors!

For a moment, echoes of that night rampaged through her mind. The smell of gunpowder, blood, terror.

Annette willed her hand not to tremble. Her finger rested uneasily on the trigger mechanism. One bullet. She had one bullet to protect herself, her family.

She had sworn she would never be helpless again.

She kept her gaze on the man who'd called himself John Gunn, even as her mind's eye saw the spreading stain of blood just feet away. Blood pooling like the red wine he'd dropped the other evening. Her premonition had come true, though it hadn't been *his* blood.

Her throat constricted and her heart felt as if it had shattered just as the wineglass had. She'd thought she would never know a greater betrayal than that of her neighbors the night they destroyed her father and her home. She had thought she could never hurt so deeply again.

She had been wrong.

He took a step toward her.

"No!" Her finger tightened on the trigger and he stopped, his face grim, his green eyes enigmatic.

"Are you the man they're looking for? The man they call Star Rider?" Her voice was an agonized whisper.

A muscle worked along his cheek. She felt tension radiate from him.

"Are you?" Her voice was louder.

"Yes," he said simply, destroying her last small hope that this was some terrible mistake.

"You've lied to me all this time. Everything was a lie!" Her throat was so tight she could barely breathe. The kisses. The whispers.

She had almost believed . . .

The horror she had felt minutes earlier was nothing compared to the loathing and disbelief that rolled over her now. It was a terrible, stabbing agony that twisted her insides and made her want to double up in pain. But she couldn't. She couldn't let him see what he had done to her.

His gaze met hers, but he said nothing.

"You used me. You used my father." Emotions continued to crash over her, like hurricane-force waves. They battered her with ever-growing intensity until she felt herself drowning in them.

He took a step toward her again.

She took a step back. "Don't come any closer."

"Annette—I—"

She shook her head. "Don't. Don't say anything. No more lies."

His lips twisted into an odd expression. Not a smile. Not even a half-smile. "I can't stand any longer. I need the cane."

So cool. So indifferent to all the hurt he'd just inflicted. John with the soft words and gentle hands. *No, not John.* A pirate. A man as ruthless and dangerous as any alive . . .

John. Her John.

She shook her head. "You managed well enough to kill someone." She could hardly believe her own voice. Harsh. As cold as the bitterness flowing through her.

Cautiously eyeing the gun in her hand, he leaned painfully against the wall. "So you really think you can use that?" he asked softly.

She started to open her mouth, then clamped it shut. In truth she did not know. She didn't even know what to do next, but she had to do *something*. Ivy would be back soon. She had to force this man—this enemy—out the door, down the steps to where she could call for help.

Then what would happen to him? He'd shot a king's soldier while in a British uniform. He would most certainly hang. And sooner rather than later. Could she live with that on her conscience? The image of his gentleness with her father flashed into her mind. Could that have been faked?

The thought of him on the gallows was excruciating.

The memory of his hands on her, the soft words, lingered in her mind. She tried to equate that with the cool efficiency with which he'd killed a sailor of the realm.

She felt torn apart, her heart ripped away, her mind clouded with despair. "Why shouldn't I?" she asked after what seemed like an eternity had passed.

"Because if you shoot me, you can never go back," he said softly.

"I can never go back now. I trusted you, just as I trusted the people who nearly killed my father."

He closed his eyes for an instant, but not before she saw the raw pain there. The muscles at his throat worked convulsively. "I'm sorry," he said in a low, agonized voice. "I never wanted to hurt you." She almost believed him. But he was such a fine liar.

And even if she did believe him, it did not matter. He was the enemy.

She moved away from the door, taking small steps, staying away from him, all the while keeping the pistol leveled at him.

"Put the gun down." The words were cajoling. He took a step toward her, then another, even though his wounded leg was clearly shaky. The dead British officer lay between them. He separated them, an insurmountable barrier. But still John Gunn approached.

Another rebel intending harm, representing danger to her home, her father, all she loved.

They were coming for her father. She heard their taunts, their curses. She smelled the violence. . . .

She pulled the trigger.

John Patrick had been watching her eyes. He moved just as she fired—not quite soon enough. He felt an arrow of fire rip along his side, but his impetus carried him forward and he was able to take the pistol from her hand.

It was empty now, and she didn't fight him. Her face had paled to almost white, and her eyes were full of pain, an anguish so strong and deep that it nearly shattered him.

Twenty men depend on you. He was already behind schedule. But he couldn't leave her here. Not like this. Not with eyes that damned him. Not with what he had done to her heart.

And Noel? Christ, she could be his death.

He stood there, uncertain for one of the first times in his life. He would live with this moment forever, with the visible results of his own actions. He'd known almost from the first day he saw her what was happening. He had known it and allowed it to happen. Now she was the one who would pay the price. How much damage had he done?

He put a hand to her cheek and she flinched, jerking away. Then she stood straight, defying him with everything she had left. Except for one tear that wandered down the side of her face, one tear that belied the defiance. That tear hurt him far more than the whip had eight years ago.

Part of him turned cold and sour inside. "I'm sorry," he said softly.

"I wish I'd killed you." Her words were barely a whisper.

She looked down at where the bullet had passed through the uniform, where his fresh blood dripped to intermingle with the British officer's. She looked away. "What are you going to do now?"

His mouth quirked up at one side. "Stop the bleeding," he said, putting the empty gun down on the table and picking up the pistol dropped by the unconscious man. He tucked the weapon into his trousers as he pulled up his shirt. "I think you should sit on the bed."

Instead, she turned to the door. He moved even more quickly, placing his body between her and the way out. He bent his lips to cover her mouth as she started to open it, stifling a cry with a kiss. She fought him, trying to pull away, but he pulled her into him, trying to still the revolt inside her.

His lips pressed hard against hers, searching for the remembered response, but she remained cold, hostile. Where there had been only warmth, there was ice.

He felt her fury in the rigidity of her stance and reluctantly he let her go. "Do not scream."

"Or you will kill me?" she said bitingly.

"Remember, there is a household full of people," he said.

She stepped back. "You're threatening them?"

"I am saying your silence is best for everyone at the moment."

"Ivy belongs to you."

"He is my friend."

Her brows furrowed, but the door opened and Ivy appeared before she could ask her next question. "Captain?"

John Patrick stepped back, pulling her with him.

"Did anyone hear the gunshot?"

"Aye. Betsy. I said there were a couple of drunken

soldiers outside. She went to tell the remaining patients. Good thing I did, because I heard another one." It was a question as well as a statement.

"Miss Carey just put another hole in me," he explained. "It is naught but a scratch. Did our British friend have any company?"

Ivy shook his head. "Must have thought there was little chance of finding you here. Apparently they have orders to check every house not already searched. Others will come looking for them soon, I'd say."

"You'd better tie the sergeant here, then fetch two of the men outside and bring them here."

"You're bleeding."

"It's nothing."

"And Miss Carey?"

"I'll keep her here until you get back."

Ivy nodded and slipped through the door.

Annette was very still. Too still. He sensed she was only waiting for another chance at the door. He looked directly into her eyes. "Raise an alarm," he said, "and this British sergeant will die, and the rest of your household will be endangered."

She knew he meant what he said. He saw it in her face. Rage warred with fear. He knew she was remembering everything that had been said about him.

"Do you swear, Miss Carey? Do you swear on your father's life to do what I say?" He knew he couldn't show her a moment's weakness.

She resisted for a moment, unwilling to surrender, enmity and contempt swirling in her eyes, overtaking the pain he had seen earlier.

But he had no choice. He had to exploit a reputation he took no pride in. He had to make her afraid of him. Everything in him rebelled at the thought, but too much was at stake to do otherwise.

"Say it out loud, Miss Carey. You will follow my instructions. Completely."

"Or you will harm my father? *You* say it."

"*Everyone* in this house will be endangered," he said. "You've been harboring a fugitive. I don't think the British will quite understand."

Angry comprehension dawned in her eyes. "Dr. Marsh . . . ?"

"He is as unwitting as you," he said, "but I do not think that will matter to the Brits." He made his voice cold.

"You are contemptible."

He felt contemptible. But he couldn't show it. "No more sympathy for the newly wounded?"

"I wish I was a better shot."

"You were good enough. I simply moved in time."

"I'll remember that," she retorted bitterly.

He sighed. "Now we have that settled," he said, "I want your word. Now."

He watched her swallow before asking hesitantly, "And if I do as you demand?"

"No one will be hurt."

She looked down at the still body on the floor.

"*He* did not give me a choice," he said.

"And what do you plan to do to me?"

He hesitated. Again he had few options. He could not trust her silence, even if she gave him her word. One slip, and Noel might well pay for it. Unless he could find his brother tonight and warn him to leave.

But even then *she* would be in danger.

A plan started to form in his mind, but now was no time to tell her about it.

"You will be safe enough," he said. "You will stay here until I finish some business."

"And then?"

"I am not sure yet," he said. He disliked showing

uncertainty, but he wasn't ready to reveal his hand. "I did not expect this. I had hoped to simply slip out of here, but I can assure you that neither you nor your father will be hurt if you do as I say."

He saw her fingers balled into fists, her knuckles white. He'd felt helplessness like that during those years on the British ship. He knew exactly how she felt now.

"How can I believe you?"

"You have my word."

"I know how much your word is worth."

That one sentence was the worst injury he'd ever received, but he forced his voice to remain even. "You have ten seconds to decide."

"Damn you," she said, biting her lip so hard blood ran from it. His hand went up to wipe it away, and she flinched as if he were going to strike her. He dropped his arm to his side.

A sharp rap sounded at the door. Ivy and two of his men entered.

Ivy looked from Annette to him, his brows knitting together. The other two men were in British uniforms, and for a moment, he saw Annette revive, her face lighting.

John Patrick knew his next words would quench any hope she had. "Jeffrey, bind the sergeant. Tom, take these two to the docks and wait for us there. Spill some whiskey on both of them. If you're stopped, say you are taking them to their barracks. Ivy, you clean up these stains as best you can."

In minutes, both the Brits had been carried out, and the evidence of what had happened here was gone. If only it were as easy to repair a broken trust.

Still slightly dazed with shock, Annette marveled at the efficiency with which the dead and wounded were removed. She looked up at the man she had nursed, had shared hopes with, had dreamed about. But he was no longer John Gunn. He was a ruthless stranger who'd killed easily and without remorse, and who had threatened her and her family.

She felt removed, distant, but strangely enough she did not fear for her life.

She watched John Gunn, or whatever his name was, closely. Once, the control slipped from his face, and for a moment, she thought she saw anguish there. But then there was nothing again.

Annette turned away from him, pain glowing inside her like hot coals. He was keeping himself between her and the door. She would have to wait, bide her time until she had a chance to escape. Surely he would make a mistake.

So she tried to look broken while her mind conjured up ways to foil him. And wondered how she ever believed in him. She'd been inexplicably drawn to him from the moment she'd first seen him, and now she realized she'd allowed herself to care far more deeply than she'd realized. She feared she had even fallen in love with him. *What a fool she had been.*

He'd talked so easily about bringing harm to her family, to her father who had already suffered so much. Threats from a man who had taken their hospitality, who had taken her care. Who had taken her heart so easily.

There really was a fine line between love and hate.

She'd wanted to rail at him. She'd wanted to pummel him. Instead, she could only try to keep what pride she had remaining and find a way to outwit the man demanding that she betray everything she held dear.

Was he really as ruthless as his reputation? Had he really been the pirate and murderer he was rumored to be?

Her heart cracked as she thought of the wondrous

sense of safety she'd felt in his embrace. In the past few minutes, his eyes had been as icy as the Delaware River in January. How could she ever have thought they held compassion and warmth?

John Gunn pulled out a watch and looked at it. "It is well past ten. We are running late."

Then he nodded to Ivy. "Watch Miss Carey while I try to mend myself and change clothes." She watched as he unbuttoned his coat, then the shirt, which was covered with blood. He stood there looking—unbearably—splendid except for the ugly gash that ran alongside his waist. He tore a sleeve from his ruined shirt and wrapped it tightly around the wound, then picked up another shirt and slipped into it. Next, he started to unlace his trousers.

"You might wish to turn your head," he said, almost apologetically, the arrogance she had seen moments earlier gone.

She did. She had absolutely no desire to see him in a further state of undress. She would be happy never to rest her eyes on him again. She heard ruffling noises, then a moment later sensed that he had moved toward her. She turned. For a moment, she couldn't believe her eyes.

He was in a captain's uniform, and he looked far more sizeable than he had before. He wore a white wig that almost completely changed his appearance—or was it the supercilious smile on his lips? He bowed. "Captain Smythewick at your service," he said in a perfect upper-class English accent.

Ivy nodded. "You will pass, Cap'n."

She turned on him. "But you work for . . ." Her heart skipped as she suddenly realized what she was about to say. Ivy worked for Dr. Marsh. If Ivy was also working for John Gunn, then Dr. Marsh must be involved in all this somehow.

"The Tory?" Ivy asked with disdain. "It was as good as any place to seek employment. Better, in truth, than most. Where better to hide than in the midst of the enemy?"

Annette weighed the words, neither accepting nor rejecting them. She didn't think she would ever accept anyone completely again.

She looked back at the Star Rider. How could one man change so rapidly? From the kind and thoughtful John Gunn to the ruthless murderer and now to the pompous British officer. His expressions even changed to fit the different roles.

Then surprisingly, he leaned down and kissed her. His lips were tender, then hard, as if he were seeking something. She wrenched herself away. "Don't touch me ever again," she said in a low voice.

Emotion rippled across his face, but she couldn't identify it. Anger? Regret? But then his expression was blank again, and he merely bowed. "I will try to observe your wishes."

"What about my father? And my aunt and Betsy?"

"As I said, no harm will come to anyone in this house if you do exactly as I and my men say. Am I clear?"

A knock came at the door. He opened it to two men in British marine uniforms. Her heart sank when her captor greeted them. More impostors. Was no one what they appeared?

"This is Miss Carey," he said. "You will be staying in this room with her until I return. If anyone knocks and you feel you must open the door, she is not to be out of your hearing for even one second. You will simply be visiting me." He hesitated, then added, "She understands that the safety of this entire household is at stake."

The threat again. She understood. Completely. She tried to swallow, but her throat was dry, constricted. Her eyes met his, looking for something other than dispassion. But except for that one brief touch, he might have been a stranger. His face gave nothing away. Nothing but a hard determination.

She stood in stony silence.

He nodded to his men and without another word to her left the room.

"You might wish to sit, miss," one of the men said to her.

She glared at him.

He didn't seem to notice. He and the other man merely took up positions on either side of the door.

How long? How long before the—pirate returned? For a moment, she thought about the pistol in her father's study. She had acquired it after they had arrived in Philadelphia, a city torn by divided loyalties.

What she wouldn't give for one more shot at the man who had torn out her heart.

John Patrick muttered a colorful curse as he walked out the back of the house with Ivy. His leg hurt, and his side felt like fire. The chafing of the clothes did not help. How could everything have gone so wrong?

He had three fewer men than he needed, two of them with Annette, the other taking the dead officer and his friend to the docks. And he knew he would always see that look in Annette's eyes, the look of trust betrayed, of horror at the violent death of the British lieutenant. He'd hoped she would never know that her trust had been placed in a murderer.

It would only get worse when she discovered his plans for her and her father.

But first he had twenty men he needed to free.

Ivy glanced at him. "Are you all right, Cap'n?"

"Yes," he answered simply. "Are the others ready?"

"Aye, they are waiting down the road."

"Do I look like a proper British officer?"

"Much too fine for one."

John Patrick ordinarily would have grinned. But he had no humor in him at the moment. He wished he could wash Annette's face from his mind. But that was obviously not to be. He wondered whether he would ever smile again.

"Let's go," he said.

They avoided the carriages making their way through the streets to Howe's grand ball at the City Tavern. He and Ivy were soon joined by more men in red coats, by faces he knew. They joined him from taverns, from alleyways, until they numbered seventeen. No one spoke, but each acknowledged him with a nod.

Doors closed and windows lowered as they passed a street known to be sympathetic to the rebels. They became a cohesive unit then, marching together. A marine detachment off to do the king's bidding.

John Patrick patted his coat and felt the forged papers there.

He stopped a block from the Walnut Street Prison and turned toward the men behind him. "Careful now, lads. Look like the real thing. March in straight lines. Stick those legs out. Have your rifles ready." Ivy went among them, buttoning coats, telling them to pull in their stomachs and lift their chins, repositioning rifles.

Not bad for a band of pirates turned privateers, John Patrick thought, but then most of them had played similar roles before.

"At-ten-tion."

Each man jack clicked their heels. "You're from the *Mary Ann*," he said softly. "Don't any of you forget that. We take the prisoners directly to the ship. We'll release our men one at a time as we march, but they have to pretend they are bound. Pass the word to each one. Once we get aboard the *Mary Ann*, we'll take the ship and set sail. There's a ball tonight. Hopefully, most of the officers will be there and no one will know what has happened until we're well out in the Delaware."

There were no questions, only a straightening of ranks. John Patrick went to the head of the file, followed by Ivy, who'd found himself a sergeant's uniform.

He didn't look back as he marched to the Walnut Street Prison and presented his papers to the duty officer, who examined them carefully. The papers gave Marine Captain Jonathon Smythewick the authority to take charge of the rebel prisoners and transport them to New York.

"Thought you were taking them in the morning," the duty officer said.

John Patrick grinned conspiratorially. "The ship's captain decided to get an early start." He leaned over and whispered, "I heard him say he has a mistress in New York."

The officer, a young lieutenant, frowned. "I should have been notified of any changes."

"It's up to you," John Patrick said with a shrug. "We could wait until you check them. My men would just as soon have a tankard of ale across the street while we wait, but Captain Avery, he might be a wee bit upset."

The officer hesitated, then shrugged. "The papers look right. I'll have the prisoners brought to you."

"In irons," John Patrick said.

"Of course," the officer said. "Motley lot. No discipline. No breeding. I'll be glad to be rid of them."

"Do you require any assistance in getting them ready?"

The officer looked grateful. "I would be grateful. I'm shorthanded tonight."

"Sergeant. Take four men inside and help them secure the prisoners."

Ivy snapped to attention. "Yes, sir."

John Patrick leaned against the officer's desk and handed him a flask of drugged brandy. "The general himself gave me this," he confided as the man hesitated.

"You know General Howe?"

"A distant cousin," John Patrick said. He'd learned long ago the bigger the lie, the quicker the acceptance. "It is an apology of sorts because I've had to be on duty and could not attend the ball tonight. However, I still might make it because of your helpfulness. So you take the goods."

This time the lieutenant accepted gratefully. "My thanks."

"How long are you on tonight?"

The British lieutenant groaned. "All night."

John Patrick said a silent prayer of thanks. Because he was late, he'd arrived after the evening change of guards. "I'll put in a good word for you with the general," he said, peering at the man. "Your name, Lieutenant."

"Calverts, sir. David Calverts."

"Well, I think you will definitely come to his attention."

The lieutenant grinned. He rose from the desk and went to open the door. "I'll see if I can help them move these pirates along."

John Patrick followed him through the door and into the jail. He heard the clanging of chains, and he eyed the men being pushed into an unruly line as guards, including four of his own men, held rifles on them. Irons were attached to their wrists.

How long had he been here? Fifteen minutes? Twenty? Each moment increased the danger.

And Annette? Did each moment increase her fear? He cringed internally at the thought, even while he glared haughtily at the prisoners.

His stomach was clenched into a knot. He wished he

could get her out of his mind. He couldn't afford to think of her now. One mistake and—

Ivy stepped toward him and saluted. "Ready, sir."

John Patrick eyed the prisoners with contempt. Most looked away from him, glaring down at the floor or the prison guards. "Take this riffraff to the ship. Hurry now, the hangman's waiting in New York." He turned and led the way out the door, stopping at the duty officer's desk. "Again, my thanks," he said. "I'll certainly let my superiors know how helpful you've been."

The man preened as the prisoners shuffled out the door onto the street.

John Patrick gave the watch officer a neat salute, then followed them out, marching the prisoners down the middle of the street toward the docks.

Several carriages pulled over to allow them passage. British officers, attired grandly in their dress uniforms, jeered the American prisoners who, in mere weeks, had become gaunt, their clothes filthy and torn.

John Patrick permitted himself a small smile as he anticipated the consternation on the morrow when the British discovered that both the prisoners and one of His Majesty's ships had been liberated.

They continued on to the dock without being challenged. A cold mist had started to fall and that, together with the general's ball, emptied the streets. As the prisoners shuffled along, a key was being passed from prisoner to prisoner, the fetters unlocked and held together by hand. If they were challenged, John Patrick wanted more hands than his small band of armed men.

They reached the dock where the *Mary Ann* was tied. Its lanterns shone brightly, but John Patrick saw only a handful of men aboard. Most likely the officers were at the ball and as many of the crew as could be spared, in taverns. Philadelphia would be considered a safe harbor.

John Patrick located the man he'd sent ahead with the

dead body and the bound sergeant. They were both in a closed carriage his man had managed to liberate. He would have to take both Brits aboard the *Mary Ann*, and bury the dead man at sea. He did not want the man's body found; the Brits might discover that the last home he'd ever visited had been Hugh Carey's.

He chose five of the men dressed in British uniforms, leaving the rest in the shadows of the building. They approached the ship in formation, and John Patrick stood at the gangplank, waiting to be recognized by the watch officer.

"Permission to board," he said.

The petty officer looked down at the uniformed marines, then at John Patrick.

"We are to inspect the facilities for the prisoners," John Patrick said. "General Howe wants to ensure they are secure."

The officer looked indignant. "We've been transporting prisoners for two years."

"General Howe realizes that. Still, this bunch is considered extremely dangerous."

The petty officer hesitated. "The captain isn't here."

"We will be only a few minutes. I wish to attend the ball myself. I would hate to inform the general that I received no cooperation."

The officer relented, and John Patrick and his men boarded.

"We will try not to wake any of the crew. How many are still aboard?"

"Ten in all," the petty officer replied helpfully.

"Thank you," John Patrick said as one of his men sidled behind the officer and grabbed him while another stuffed a rag in his mouth. In seconds he was trussed and gagged.

Ten minutes later each of the sleepy crew was similarly trussed and locked in the hold, along with the sergeant who'd been taken at the Carey home.

John Patrick signaled the men on the docks, and they boarded, the prisoners grinning broadly at their escape.

Now he had to get the Careys and try to reach Noel. A throbbing pain ate at John Patrick's gut as he anticipated Annette's reaction.

God help them all.

Chapter 11

Annette hadn't thought her fury—as impotent as it was—could grow any stronger.

She'd been wrong.

Her home had been invaded for the second time, her father's fragile security smashed like a piece of glass struck by a hammer.

That the threat had been made by someone she trusted, and was beginning to care deeply about, devastated her. But even then she felt torn. As much as she despised him, despised what he was doing and who he was, she knew she couldn't go to the British authorities, couldn't be responsible for his death. She hadn't even meant to shoot him. Those images, the dreams, had clouded her senses, and his approach had triggered a compulsive reaction. Thank God she hadn't done more damage. She just wanted him to leave this house, leave her family alone. She wanted time for her heart to heal, for her mind to cease its pounding of contradictory emotions.

That he could invoke so many of them made her even angrier.

She forced herself to sit, to ignore the two men sitting in John Gunn's room, both looking intensely uncomfortable. When she explained that someone had to tend the British soldiers, one only raised his eyebrow in indifference. The health of an enemy, she gathered, carried little weight with these brigands.

They didn't look like brigands, though, with their clean-shaven faces and British uniforms.

They looked like ordinary men, except for the determined gleam in their eyes. No compliments or threats or bribes or cajoling had moved them. Their loyalty to their master, she discovered, was absolute and unbending.

She had thought the loyalty of pirates would be for sale. But neither showed even a flicker of interest when she offered what little she had. She'd tried pity for her sick father, and had even resorted to flirtation. Nothing.

John Gunn had made her feel pretty and desirable, but obviously that had been an act, a charade to keep his identity safe while he mended. The Star Rider. Even now, remembering the kisses she'd treasured, she found it hard to believe. Yet the coldness in his face, the hardness of his eyes kept returning to her mind, each time making another crack in her heart.

What would John Gunn—she couldn't think of him as someone else yet—do when he returned? She realized she represented a danger to him. Her whole household did. Would he kill them? If so, why wouldn't he have done so already?

And Noel Marsh—had he had anything to do with this? He had brought the man to this house. She remembered all his visits. The closed door. The special concern. But then he had paid similar attention to seriously wounded British patients.

An hour went by. Then another. It was midnight. She heard the chime of the large clock in the hall. Everyone in the house should be asleep. It seemed strange that they should be, when such violence was so close.

Just blocks away, the officers of the British army were gathered at General Howe's ball. She'd even been asked by one of her former patients, but she had no dress, nor had she wished to go. In truth, she'd known John Gunn would depart soon and she'd wanted to spend as much time as possible with him.

More fool her.

"I need to leave the room," she said as she stood, her face flushing red as her meaning became clear.

The two men looked at each other. One finally shook his head. "I'm sorry, miss, but the cap'n was very clear that you were not to be left alone."

"Surely, he did not mean . . . ?"

"I am afraid he meant exactly what he said," the speaker said firmly.

She sat back down. Her thoughts kept going to the pistol upstairs. But how . . .

If she screamed and woke the household, she didn't know what these men would do. Their "cap'n" had warned her it would put the household in danger. But there were a few British soldiers still in the house, and several of them were nearly well.

Nearly. She couldn't be responsible for them losing their lives.

Then she heard a noise outside the room, a soft knock. A name. The two men with her looked relieved, and one opened the door. John Gunn spared them only a quick glance. "The men are all safe, and we have the ship."

The two men grinned at each other like gleeful monkeys. She wanted to hit all three of them.

John Gunn looked at her for a second, then told the two men, "Wait outside for me."

She did not like the speculative gleam in his eyes. "What ship?" she asked, stalling for time.

"The *Mary Ann.* It was to take my crew to New York. We took it instead."

She bit her bottom lip. "With those few men?"

"And the others we just rescued from the Walnut Street Prison," he said with a jauntiness that turned her blood cold; it was obvious he was in the throes of success. Men and their games. They reveled in destruction while women and children and old men paid.

"You are mad," she whispered.

"It's been said," he agreed, then both his face and voice sobered. "But I do not have much time; we need to set sail before the general's ball ends." He hesitated, then said, "I want you to write a letter. Tell your aunt that you heard this evening that a relative is very sick and you had to leave to see to her. Your father is going with you. You did not want to disturb anyone."

"No one will believe it."

"Then you have to convince them. Either that, or I'll have to take everyone with me. Your aunt, Franklin, Betsy—"

"You wouldn't!"

"Yes, Annette, I would. I have more than fifty lives depending on me. I can't risk your alerting the British." He hesitated, then continued, "There is something else. None of your family knows about the British officer coming here. There will be no finger pointing at your household, but *you* know. And I cannot take the chance of something slipping out." His eyes were intense, emerald. "If anyone, anyone at all, suspected you had harbored the Star Rider, then all of you would be suspect."

She realized he was right. He had put her entire family in terrible danger. "Why my father? Leave him here."

"Would you go without him?"

He had trapped her. Very neatly. "Where?"

"Somewhere where he will be safe, where he can receive more help."

"Why should I believe you now?"

"Do you really think I would cause him harm?" His voice had gentled.

For a moment, she remembered his kindness with her father, the spark of interest only he had brought to her father's eyes. She believed him in this one thing. At least she believed that he *meant* no harm. Yet how could kidnapping him be considered "not harming"?

"You already have," she said. "As you said, the British may not forgive the household that gave comfort to a man they want above all others."

"We have no more time." His voice hardened again. "Write the letter."

"I have no paper."

He took some from the desk, paper he'd requested from her earlier to write a letter, paper on which he'd written his own note. "Now," he said.

She sat down and he stood above her, watching impatiently.

The pirate—the man she thought she'd loved—didn't feel she was working fast enough. "All right, then, I'll tell my men to round everyone up. The British wounded might be a problem."

She knew exactly what he was implying. "You wouldn't!"

"You think not?" he said. "I have men nearly dead from starvation in your British prison waiting for me."

His eyes were a cold glittering green. He looked nothing like the roguish young lieutenant now. She shivered. She believed him capable of anything. She couldn't take the chance that he might indeed use the wounded as pawns. She bent her head and wrote. She'd received word late tonight that her aunt Agnes was deathly ill with a fever, and had no one to help her. The lieutenant was leaving for New York. She had decided to go with him for protection. Her father would go with her; he and his sister were very close. But the journey would be too hard on Franklin, and Maude needed Betsy's help. She hoped to return shortly.

He took it and read it quickly. "Very good," he said

approvingly, and she wanted to slap him. He folded it. "I will leave it in the front hall."

He took her arm and guided her out of the room. Two men were standing there. "Take her to the carriage. I'll be there shortly." He looked at one of the men. "You stay with her in the carriage. Tom, go up the stairs to the second room on the left, and grab some clothes for Miss Carey, including a warm cloak."

"How kind," she said sarcastically.

"I try to please," he said.

Then he disappeared down the hall, leaving her in the hands of two rebels.

God's mercy, but how he wanted to reassure her. Despite her gallant attempts to hide her apprehension, he saw it in her eyes. Not for herself, but for her father. *I will never be helpless again.* He remembered her vow.

And it had taken every bit of will inside him to force the coldness into his voice, the threats to his lips. He had made her helpless again, and he knew she would never forgive him for it. She would never stop fighting him.

John Patrick hated everything about this. He'd sent a man to check on Noel, but his brother was gone, as was Malcomb. Noel was undoubtedly at the general's ball. He'd left a letter, quickly written in the captain's cabin of the *Mary Ann*, at Noel's house.

But his brother would never understand his actions, either, even though John Patrick did have good reasons for what he'd done. He was confident his family could help Hugh Carey. He was convinced of it, just as surely as he knew they would welcome the Careys. And he felt the Careys would be far safer in Maryland than in Philadelphia for the next few months. But he could tell her none of this. She simply wouldn't believe him.

He climbed the stairs, taking an oil lamp from a table in the hallway. God's mercy, but time was running out;

there was no telling when someone would discover the jailbreak. He didn't knock at Hugh's door but opened it gently. Franklin, he knew, slept in a small room next door.

John Patrick went to the bed and gently shook Hugh Carey. When the man's eyes opened, he put a hand to the man's mouth. "I don't want to wake everyone, but your daughter is going on a trip, and we thought you might like to go."

Hugh just looked at him. John Patrick was already gathering a pair of trousers and shirt from a dresser. He also found a heavy cloak and tossed it over his arms. "We have no time," he whispered. "It is going to be a grand adventure."

He flinched at the look of trust, even of interest, that flickered in the older man's eyes as he helped him dress.

Several minutes later, he was leading him out to the closed carriage. He helped him into a seat next to Annette, and took the one opposite her. The carriage moved forward with a lurch, and soon was careening through the streets toward the docks.

Annette was ominously quiet as she held her father's hand and pulled her cloak around her. John Patrick knew that only her father's presence kept her from lashing out at him. She obviously did not want to frighten him. But her knuckles were white, the fingers of her free hand balled into a fist.

The carriage came to a stop, and one of his men was there waiting, opening the door. Still no troops. Luck was staying with them.

As he hurried his passengers toward the gangplank, he held out his hand to Annette. She pushed past it, casting him a look of total contempt, only to have the hem of her skirt catch on the rough wood. He reached out quickly to steady her. But once more, she flinched at his touch, and he quickly released her.

He bowed slightly to Hugh Carey. "You will stay in the captain's cabin. Ivy will show you to your quarters."

John Patrick watched the two men go below, then glanced at Annette's white face. "You will have the first mate's cabin."

"And you, Captain?" she asked. "Where will you stay?"

"I think I've just been demoted to second mate." He hesitated, then looked up at the sky. "It's poor weather to be on deck. You should go inside."

"A pirate concerned about the health of his prisoners?" Her voice was stinging.

"Aye."

"Well, I do not want your concern, or your worry. I wish to stay out here." Her chin lifted in that singularly determined way.

He had no time to argue with her. "As you wish."

Then he turned and started issuing orders, watching her closely as the gangplank was pulled on board. Her last avenue of escape was gone, her last hope that somehow the British would stop them. He saw from her face that she knew it.

He stifled a curse, then turned his attention to the ship.

Despite herself, Annette's interest was piqued by all the activity around her. She had never been aboard a ship before, and it seemed like magic, the way the sails were so efficiently unfurled.

The sailors wearing British uniforms had already discarded their costumes, and worked companionably as they untied the thick ropes holding the ship to the dock. She heard their murmured comments as they unloosed additional sails. She watched the Star Rider move among them, observed their almost reverent glances as they looked at him. He seemed to have a word for each one, a warm clasp, a smile.

The smile he had once given her.

The lights on deck were quenched, then, but his tall form was unmistakable as he strode to the wheel of the ship, taking it from the man who had guided them from the dock. The ship shifted under her feet as the sails began to fill. The night was cold, and she felt the first drops of rain. She shivered, yet she couldn't force herself to go inside as the ship sliced quietly through the water. The lights on the shore faded as they moved into the channel, toward the Atlantic. Away from Philadelphia. Away from home. Away from safety.

The rain pasted her hair against her cheek. Her cloak was sodden. Yet she still didn't want to go inside. She was leaving everything familiar and safe. She was the captive of a ruthless man, and yet . . . yet she felt an odd excitement, an exhilaration she'd never known before. She didn't understand it.

She should feel fear and panic. Why didn't she?

She looked at the wheel, at the man standing there, and was caught by the power and confidence with which he steered the unwieldy vessel. She saw the white flash of teeth and knew he was grinning from the pure joy of the challenge.

The rain stung her face, but she leaned out over the railing. Even as his prisoner, she felt a curious sense of freedom. She had not realized how constricted she had felt in Philadelphia. She'd had to surrender freedom she'd never appreciated when her home was burned and she was forced into a society where her worth had diminished when her father's wealth had disappeared. How she'd longed to race across the fields, or dig her bare toes into fresh earth or sit in a barn watching new life being born.

She felt that same deep sense of elation now. It did not make sense, and she fought it, and yet . . .

She continued to stand in the rain, watching the shore rush by her. When would the British discover the disappearance of one of their ships? Would others come after them?

Annette was still looking toward the shore when she felt his presence. She didn't have to look to know who it was. Her nerve ends started to tingle, and heat rushed to her cheeks.

"It is cold out here, Miss Carey."

Why then did she suddenly feel hot?

"You said that before. I am no fragile flower."

"I've discovered that," he said softly. "My side keeps warning me to watch you carefully."

I did not intend that. She did not say the words, though. She had felt shock after the pistol had discharged, dismay at seeing the blood. She stared out at the water, not wanting him to see the regret in her eyes.

"Shouldn't you be steering the ship?"

"Ivy can handle it." His voice was seductive.

She shivered, but this time it wasn't from cold. Despite what she knew, he still had the ability to stir her, to awaken all her senses. She'd never been so aware of anyone before. She fought desperately against those wayward feelings. "Ah, Ivy. He is much more than a stable hand."

"He is my first mate."

"What ship is this?"

"His Majesty's ship, the *Mary Ann*, soon to be the new *Star Rider*."

"Where's the real crew?"

"I imagine the officers are at Howe's ball, most of the others in taverns, and the few who were on watch are now sleeping peacefully below deck."

"Where are you going to take us?"

"Somewhere safe," he said. "You and your father will be treated as guests."

"Where?" she insisted.

She could almost feel his indecision. It was rare for him, she'd discovered in the past few hours. "My home in Maryland."

She was surprised, but she hid it well. His home? "You cannot keep us there forever."

"Just until the British leave Philadelphia. I do not think that will be long."

She hadn't looked at him until then. "I *will* go inside now. I do not care for the company."

"You look as if you enjoy the rain and wind."

"I enjoyed the cleansing nature of it. I thought it might wash away the stench of betrayal, but I was wrong."

She turned away from him, but found his body blocking her passage.

"I never wanted to hurt you," he said.

She couldn't read his eyes. It was too dark, and the rain too heavy. "That's nice," she replied icily. "Good intentions often lead to—where?"

His hand wiped rain away from his face. "To hell? I might well find my way there, but for now I can only apologize."

"It means nothing, Mr. Gunn. Or shall I say Star Rider? That is what the broadside said."

"Gunn is an old family name."

"Really? I would have thought your family tree rather shorter than that."

The side of his mouth turned up. "A nicely turned insult."

"But true." Tired of sparring with him, she tried again to maneuver around him.

He stood aside. "I'll show you to your quarters."

"I would rather you didn't. If you can tell me where to go."

"Down the hatch, then turn left at the passageway. The first cabin is your father's. The next is yours."

"It has a lock?"

He chuckled. "Aye, Miss Carey, but a lock wouldn't keep me out if I wanted to enter."

"No, I don't suppose it would," she said, her voice dripping with contempt. "It is your ship, your crew."

Holding her head as high as she could, she made her way toward the hatch. He didn't try to follow her and she was grateful. Her hands clasped the wall to keep from falling; her legs seemed like tender young stalks, easily bent and folded. A chill caught her and she felt herself shake. The exhilaration of a few moments earlier was gone, lost in the weariness that suddenly overwhelmed her. Weariness and isolation.

She found the first cabin, knocked, then tried the door. It was unlocked. Her father was asleep, stretched out on a wide bed in a very large and elaborate cabin. A strange man was sitting in a chair when she opened the door, but he immediately stood. He was thin and haggard, his clothes in tatters, but his lean face was attractive.

He bowed. "You must be Miss Carey. The captain told me you would probably come by."

"Who are you?"

"I'm Quinn, the ship's surgeon."

"You are British?"

"No, ma'am. I was with the captain when our *Star Rider* sank. Then I was a guest of the British in the Walnut Street Prison," he said with some anger.

"You all escaped?"

"Thanks to the captain. We knew he wouldn't leave us."

"How—?"

"He is a man of many talents."

"Yes," she whispered.

"Your father is doing well," he assured her. "Ivy gave him a glass of brandy and he is sleeping peacefully now."

"You do not understand."

"Aye, but I do. The captain explained your circumstances in detail. You are welcome to come and go as you wish."

"We are prisoners," she said.

"Not according to the captain."

"You can call a pig a swan, but it is still a pig."

He smiled slowly.

"You can go," she said. "I will stay here for a while."

"As you will," he said. "Anyone can find me if you need help."

She didn't answer as the door closed behind him, and she sat close to the bed, beside her father.

Chapter 12

John Patrick watched Annette leave the deck. Her back was straight, her chin high, and that blaze of anger in her eyes remained with him.

She despised him, and rightly so.

Noel was going to be none too happy, either. How many times had he promised to do nothing to hurt the Careys?

He'd done damage to good people tonight, people who had helped him, befriended him. He wanted to go to her and take her in his arms, but she wouldn't welcome his comfort. And God knew he had caused her enough grief.

But neither could he leave her standing in the rain and possibly getting sick. If there was one thing he knew, it was that his presence outside would probably force her inside. And it had.

He stood in the rain himself after she left. He lifted his face to the sky, willing the elements to wash away the guilt he felt. He should feel elation as he watched his crew work together again, as he felt the ship race before the wind. He was free, his crew was free, and he had a ship once more.

Instead, he felt only defeat. Even at his worst moments in the British navy, he'd never experienced this kind of desolation. How do you reclaim your soul? Your honor?

How do you judge one set of loyalties against another?

He'd made his decision. He'd made it for his men, his

country. And in doing so, he'd betrayed a family that had taken him in, made him one of their own.

"Cap'n?"

He turned to see Seamus, an Irishman and his second mate. He had been one of the men taken by the British.

"Yes?"

"On behalf of all the men, we want to thank ye," Seamus said. "When we saw Ivy's ugly face, we knew you would get us out of tha' hellhole."

"You're welcome, Seamus," John Patrick said.

"Anyone else would ha' left us there. We all know tha'. We'll sail to hell with ye and back."

John Patrick tried to smile. "I hope it will not come to that."

Seamus grinned. "Not wi' ye as captain." He backed away before John Patrick could say anything else.

John Patrick knew he should feel better, but he didn't. He left the railing and went to the wheel. Wordlessly, Ivy moved over.

"It looks as if we've made it," Ivy said after a moment.

"Aye. For now at least. I suspect there will be British ships at the mouth of the Delaware."

"We're flying the British flag, and it's a British frigate."

"But we don't know their signals. The signal book was missing from the captain's cabin. He must have taken it with him."

"Or they are changing them."

John Patrick was silent.

"You didn't have a choice, Captain," Ivy said.

"Are you a mind reader now?"

"*Ja,*" Ivy replied. "Where are you taking them?"

"Home. To Maryland."

Ivy raised an eyebrow. "Your family? How are they going to feel about your delivering two Tories to their doorstep?"

"They are used to unexpected visitors, though probably not unwilling ones," John Patrick admitted. "But I believe my family will be very good for Hugh Carey. If anyone can help him, they can."

"And Miss Carey?"

He winced at that. "She will see how well her father does."

"You do not often delude yourself, Captain."

"Ivy," John Patrick said irritably, "I didn't have time to think it all through."

Ivy was silent.

"And what would you have done?"

"I'm not a captain," Ivy said with a hint of a grin. "Now I know why."

John Patrick grimaced. He doubted Annette Carey would ever forgive him. Even if, as he hoped, her father improved with his family, she would never forget his lies, his threats.

"Go down and see if they need anything," he said.

"Quinn is down there."

"Still, they may need food or linens or . . ."

"*Ja*, Captain, though I've never been a lady's maid before."

"You might assign one of the crew to them."

Ivy studied him through the rain falling between them. "You did what you had to do," he said again.

John Patrick didn't say anything. What was done was done, and now he would have to live with the consequences. He just wasn't sure he could.

Noel tried to pay attention to the cards in front of him, but it was well past midnight and he found his mind wandering, mainly in the direction of the Carey home. Most of the couples had already left the ball, but several of the bachelor officers had adjourned to a room for gaming. He had thought it wise to be among them.

Had his brother succeeded in doing what he planned?

Had he been caught? If so, he was sure he would have learned about it.

He yawned. He was ready to leave. He'd already lost enough money tonight, and he'd established his presence well enough. "It is time to go," he said, pushing back his chair.

One winning officer groaned. "You can't leave now, when we're finally recouping our losses."

"Another round, then, but just one," Noel said. "I have patients tomorrow."

But he couldn't keep his gaze from the door, and he was relieved when he lost, hoping they would be satisfied. They were not, but he gave his regrets and started for the door.

He didn't make it.

A marine corporal burst in the door, his eyes bulging with excitement. "General Howe?"

"He is having a late supper with his aides," one of Noel's companions said. "He won't want to be disturbed."

"The *Mary Ann* is gone. The captain returned to his ship, and she was gone from her moorings."

Noel stood absolutely still as his former gaming companions rose abruptly, overturning their chairs.

"A ship missing?"

"It cannot be."

"Who?"

"Mayhap it drifted from its mooring."

But the corporal had left the room, gone in search of General Howe.

Noel's companions looked at one another and followed the corporal, their winnings forgotten on the table. Noel looked at the money longingly, then followed the others into the room where General Howe was holding court.

The corporal almost collapsed under the glare of his commander as he told him of the missing ship. Howe's already ruddy face turned purple. "How could we lose a ship?"

The corporal cringed.

"The crew. I want every member of the crew found and questioned," Howe said. "I want every captain alerted." He stared ahead. "Wasn't the *Mary Ann* supposed to take the rebel prisoners to New York?"

One of Noel's recent gaming companions stepped forward. "Yes, sir."

Noel was well aware of the controversy surrounding the rebel prisoners. Some of Howe's command had wanted to hang them at once, but General Howe felt such an act would not be very wise in Philadelphia. He was attempting to keep the Quakers loyal, and a wholesale hanging might well offend them.

Howe swore. "You," he said, indicating a captain. "Find out which ship can take those pirates to New York."

Noel followed the captain out, looking for his phaeton. Malcomb had the night off, and Noel had told him to make himself very visible in one of his favorite taverns. Gathering his cloak around him, he located his phaeton and nodded to one of the privates who was looking after the carriages. He gave the man a coin, then hopped up to the seat before he was drenched.

He would go to the Carey home now. He had patients there, after all. But what excuse would he make for the hour of the morning? Calling himself every kind of a fool, he knew he could no longer wonder what was going on.

If all the lights were off, then he would drive past. Perhaps he would also drive by the Walnut Street Prison. It was not much farther.

But he already knew in his heart what had happened.

He knew John Patrick had succeeded. He knew that his brother had somehow stolen one of His Majesty's ships, and he wouldn't have done that without first freeing his crew. Then why had there been no outcry? He just hoped John Patrick had left no casualties behind him.

He drove past the Carey home. Lights were off, and he noticed no activity. He turned the phaeton toward the prison and was a block away when he heard shouts, then noticed several men, two on foot, one on horse-back, raising an alarm as they ran: "Prisoners escaped!"

Noel quickly turned the horse and headed home. Malcomb would know more. He might even send the man by the Carey home, once the alarm was citywide. He would have an excuse then to check on the safety of its occupants. He flicked the reins, urging the horse to a faster pace.

Escaped prisoners. A stolen ship.

His little brother?

A chuckle started deep in his throat, even as he couldn't quite still his worry over the Carey family.

The ship reached the mouth of the Delaware. John Patrick blessed the discomfort of the early-morning drizzle, and the fog that limited visibility. He'd rested only an hour in the tiny second mate's quarters, and he felt the weight of weariness on him.

In truth, he'd not gotten any rest. Quinn had poured alcohol on the raw wound and sewn it closed. It hurt like the very devil, though Quinn seemed to have little con-cern as he investigated the scars from his other recently incurred wounds. He'd just shaken his head. "You have more lives than a cat."

But it was the image of Annette's face as she'd dis-missed him earlier that kept him from sleep.

He tried to shake away the fatigue. Ivy stood beside him, as did the guide he'd found for his original ill-fated foray down the river. John Forth, who'd been one of those jailed by the British, had captained a small trading vessel that ferried people and goods from Philadelphia to Baltimore. He'd been neutral until his ship was confiscated by the British and he lost everything. Last night he'd navigated the *Mary Ann*'s voyage to the mouth of the Delaware, and as they reached the open sea, he had handed over the wheel to John Patrick.

The three of them, plus the lookouts in the crow's nest, kept their eyes peeled for British patrol boats. They spoke only in quiet whispers. Sound carried over water.

John Patrick felt the tension rising, in him and in the men around him. Surely the alarm had been raised by now and swift ships sent after them. The *Mary Ann* had good speed, but several of the corvettes in Philadelphia were faster. They would not have the cannon power he did, but he was desperately short-handed and the firing of even one cannon would bring ships of the line down on his head.

Great, dark gray clouds promised even worse weather than they were already experiencing. Lightning streaked through the sky, breaking through the shroud of grayness only briefly. He saw a shadow of a ship ahead and softly called out orders to pivot the square sails and add canvas. In minutes, the *Mary Ann* had changed direction, and John Patrick prayed that the lookouts on the ship ahead hadn't seen him.

The gray bleakness eclipsed the enemy ship again. He heard the sound of his ship slicing through water, the creaking of masts as wind blew against the great sails. Then he heard what he'd been dreading. The sound of cannon. A warning shot. A demand for recognition.

He raised the British flag, only too aware of his lack of proper signals. Dammit. He'd hoped to escape detection; now he felt as naked as a newborn babe. He would

have to run for it; he couldn't afford a fight with Hugh
and Annette Carey on board.

Another shot, this time closer. He knew its sound
would summon other ships. He would have to turn
closer to shore and hope not to run aground. He had to
lose them before the fog broke.

John Forth moved next to him, calling instructions as
the crew added sail, and the ship bucked and dipped in
rough waters. The cannon fire grew farther away as the
Mary Ann sped south, but John Patrick still expected
another hulk to rise in front of them. Surely they would
guess he was running to the south.

Forth ordered soundings to determine the depth of
water, and John Patrick heard the soft sound as men
relayed the information. They were running perilously
close to shore. But the sound of cannon faded to an
echo, and he ordered the sheets tacked to take the *Mary
Ann* farther into open sea.

The fog lifted thirty minutes later, although a light
rain continued with the occasional rumble of thunder
and bolt of lightning. Visibility was better, and he could
see the faraway shore. But he saw no British ships. He
called for full sail, and braced himself as the ship skipped
over the water toward Baltimore . . . and freedom.

Annette woke suddenly to the sound of thunder.

She was still fully dressed, and she realized she must
have fallen asleep sometime during the early hours of the
morning. It had been pitch-dark last night when she'd
entered the cabin, the doctor having warned her not to
use the lantern, and she'd lain on the narrow bed for
hours before going to sleep. Gray now filtered into the
room. It must be just after dawn.

The ship was bucking, and the sound of thunder—or
was it cannon?—resonated through the cabin. She'd
hurriedly, and blindly, braided her hair last night, and

now she tried to smooth it down. Her valise was on the floor by the bunk, but she didn't want to take time to see whether whoever packed it had included a brush. She had to see how her father fared.

She tried to walk, but the ship rolled and she was tossed from side to side, against walls and furniture that did not move when she did. It was all bolted down, whereas she, well, she went spinning around like a child's top.

Balancing herself against the sides of the rolling cabin, Annette headed out into the passageway, stopping only long enough to throw her damp cloak around herself. She knocked at the next door, and the ship's surgeon answered, looking as if he'd slept in a chair all night.

"My father?"

"He is awake and has already had tea," the doctor said.

"He's not ill?"

"Not at all. I gave him a bit of biscuit and apple. Apples are always good for seasickness. But he shows no sign of it." He looked curiously at her. "Neither do you."

In reality, she felt just a little queasy, but she was not about to admit to it. Instead, she took an apple he handed to her. He was a rebel and she didn't want to be grateful, yet it was difficult to be angry when he was so kind. He was also so terribly thin.

Her father was sitting up in a chair that was bolted down, and he looked confused but not displeased. She remembered he had always liked the sea and had talked longingly of a voyage to England.

Still, she sought to reassure him, even though she needed a great deal of reassurance herself. "Are you feeling all right?" she asked.

His eyes questioned her. "We are going on a trip," she said. "Do you have everything you need?"

He nodded.

"Would you like to go up on deck later? When the water is not so rough?"

He nodded, and his eyes lit.

She hoped it would be possible. She had to keep fear from her father's eyes. To bargain with a pirate, a man who obviously had no honor, was abhorrent. But the pirate owed her. And she would collect.

She leaned over and kissed her father's forehead, then drew the cloak around herself and left the cabin. She bounced back and forth along the walls until she reached the steps. At least, she no longer heard the thunder—or whatever it was.

She opened the door to the deck and the wind immediately threw her back against the cabin, whipping her hair around her face. She straightened. She was determined to see the Star Rider, and a little breeze was not going to stop her.

The sky was gray, and the rain had slackened. The wind was cold, but oddly refreshing. Invigorating.

The ship yawed and plunged and she caught the railing. She used that and the gun mountings to make her way forward toward the wheel. When she was within a few feet of the pirate's back, she stopped to watch him. The wind was whipping his hair, too, as well as nettling the oilcloth coat he wore. He seemed to control the wheel of the plunging ship easily, but then he appeared adept at everything, including lying.

Ivy, who stood with him, saw her and said something to the captain. The words were lost in the wind, and she ventured closer.

The captain turned toward her. "Are you and your father all right?"

"As right as captives can be," she said. "Was that thunder?"

"Cannon fire mixed with a little thunder. But we are safe now."

"*You* are safe," she corrected. "For the moment."

"I take it you would see me captured. And hung."

"With pleasure."

His lips twisted into a small smile. "You might still have your wish." He studied her, then gave her that crooked grin that too often made her heart beat faster. It still, she thought bitterly, had that power. "I was afraid you might be ill. I should have known better."

"You were afraid for me? What's a little seasickness compared to being kidnapped?"

"I didn't know you had such a tart tongue."

"I didn't know you were a thief and a traitor and a pirate who would take an ill man from the only safety he knows."

"I *am* truly sorry for that."

"And me? Are you *truly* sorry about me?"

He turned and gazed at her, his eyes unimaginably green, even in the gloom of the wet, soggy day. "No," he said. "I don't think I am."

He moved slightly, leaving space between his body and the wheel, although both hands stayed on it. "Would you like to feel the wheel?"

She didn't like the thrill of anticipation that suddenly jolted through her. She didn't want him to think she'd forgiven him, or that she didn't detest everything he was and everything he had done. Yet the wind, the spray, and the feel of the ship as it slipped through the waves aroused something deep inside her. She *did* long to reach out and touch the polished wood of the wheel, to feel the power in it.

She steeled herself against him, against the temptations that he offered like some dark prince. She stepped back, rejecting his offer, rejecting *him*.

She saw amusement in his face, and she realized he had read the longing in her eyes, had realized how close she had come to accepting his offer. Acceptance would make him a comrade, a companion, an accomplice in her own kidnapping. She felt that odd attraction again, the need to feel his arms around her. How could she? Her father was again in the hands of rogue Americans who cared little about life or justice.

She straightened her back and tried to glare at him. "Why are you taking us to Maryland?"

She didn't know what she expected, but certainly not his soft reply. "You and your father will be safe there. My father—he is a teacher as well as a farmer. And my aunt—when she was young, she had a problem similar to your father's. Perhaps they can help."

Annette was stunned into silence. She had expected the arrogance, even the ruthlessness, he'd displayed yesterday. She had not expected the compassion. Compassion she did not want. Not from a rebel who had lied to her.

But his comment also stirred something else. A memory. Dr. Marsh. Noel, too, had once said he had an aunt who had lost her speech. She looked up at her captor with dawning horror. They didn't look alike at all—Dr. Marsh and this man. Dr. Marsh had tawny hair and hazel eyes. This man had black hair and green eyes. But how could both have an aunt who once would not, could not, speak?

Dr. Marsh? A liar? A spy? A traitor?

Her heart sank. She recalled his gentleness, his care for her father, his genuine dedication to the British wounded—and his interest in this particular man.

She finally asked what she had to know. "Who are you?"

He stepped aside to let Ivy take the wheel, and moved toward the railing. He didn't touch her this time, as if he knew she would just jerk away. She followed, her cloak billowing around her, locks of hair escaping from the untidy braid.

At this moment she cared only about the answer to her question.

The man was staring out to sea, at the frothing waves that climbed against the side of the ship, spraying them with cold, salty water.

"Captain?" She tried to put as much contempt as possible into the word. "It is not John Gunn."

"Nay. It is John Patrick Sutherland. You will know soon enough, anyway."

Sutherland. Noel Marsh had Sutherland kin—the family that had disowned him.

"You are Dr. Marsh's . . . ?"

"Half-brother," he confirmed, his eyes intent on her.

"Then he is—"

"He is exactly what he says he is," her captor said evenly. "He is a Tory, like you. 'Tis his misfortune to have a rebel brother, and mine to have a Tory one."

"But he knew—"

"Aye, he knew, but what would you do if your father showed up unexpectedly on your doorstep when he was on the opposite side of a war? What if he was near death? Would you turn him in?"

"He used us, too. Lied to us," she said, ignoring his reasoning. She could barely breathe. She had liked Dr. Marsh, admired him. They had been partners against death. And he had introduced this pirate into her home, into her life, into her father's life, knowing how dangerous he really was.

"He did it to save my life. For no other reason. And if it helps you, he hated every moment of the deception. He warned me over and over again not to hurt you or your family." He winced. "I imagine he's already in a hell of his own after finding you gone."

How could she believe him now? How could she tell one lie from another? Dr. Marsh was probably a spy just like his brother, and his actions could cause incalculable damage. He had the ear of the British command.

Tears stung her eyes, mingling with raindrops. Waves of pain assaulted her heart. How could she have been so blind? So trusting?

"I do not want to go to your home. Leave us in Baltimore if you must. My father has friends . . ."

"I can't do that," he replied softly.

"Why?"

"Because you might go to the British about Noel."

"It will not matter, if he is as innocent as you say he is."

"Do you really think the Brits will believe that?"

"I know you and your brother don't care about truth or honor."

He stepped back as if taking a blow, and she knew she'd struck well and true.

His face seemed to shutter, the light of battle fading from his green eyes. "Honor is often a casualty of war."

"War?" she scoffed. "War against women and a sick old man? You're a pirate, growing rich, I assume, from the deaths of far better men than you."

His voice turned cool as he looked back at the churning water. "Do you and your father have everything you need?"

"Not our freedom."

"It is a precious commodity," he said. His gaze met hers.

"But you won't give it to us."

"I cannot."

"Do you have any idea how much I despise you?" she asked, frustrated at his calm denial of her desperation.

"I expect I do," he replied levelly.

She was unable to tolerate his presence any longer. What was so very painful was the fact that she was still attracted to him. She still felt a deep sense of connection. Her heart still beat a little faster, a little stronger, in his presence. Her blood still warmed too many degrees. She hated herself for that weakness even more than she hated him.

She took several steps away from him, then turned back. "Do you expect to meet any other British ships?"

"We might, but this is a swift vessel. We can outrun most others. I would not depend on being rescued. In the meantime, if you require anything, please see Quinn or Ivy. They will do everything they can to provide whatever you wish. Except my head, of course."

She refused to let his charm soften her retort.

"Freedom," she said, "is all I want. You've exchanged mine and my father's for your own. And I will never forgive you for that."

She whirled around and disappeared through the hatchway.

Chapter 13

reedom!

Annette's words echoed in his brain. She was right. He *had* exchanged her freedom for his.

But it hadn't been only his at stake, he argued with himself.

He returned to the wheel. He needed something to consume the guilt burning in his gut.

Ivy had been standing quietly beside him. "Get some sleep," John Patrick finally ordered. "If we see any sail, I'll call you."

Ivy hesitated.

"That's an order, Iverssen." John Patrick knew his voice was harsh. But it was far better harsh than uncertain.

Ivy looked him straight in the eye, then he turned and left.

The wheel took all his concentration. Once out of sight of land, the pilot, too, had retired to get some rest. A minimal crew was working the sails and keeping watch. He needed every man, but half were so starved they could barely handle the sheets.

And they would have died, either in the hulks or at the end of a noose, if he had not done what he had. But could he have found another way to save them without destroying the Careys? Not once the British soldiers had arrived at their door.

He'd never seen anyone quite as appealing as Annette Carey had been, standing at the railing, the wind whipping her hair, reddening her cheeks. Her chin had been so defiant, her gray eyes as turbulent as the sea around them. He'd not missed that momentary longing in her eyes when he'd offered her the wheel. She was born for the sea, whether she realized it or not.

John Patrick had expected to find her ill in the cabin as he would most inexperienced sailors, yet she'd not hesitated a moment to make her way on deck, disregarding both dark skies and cannon fire.

She certainly was not the reserved miss he'd first met. He sensed a reckless streak in her that needed merely a little cultivation. That she had defied the city to open a small hospital in her home was proof of it. He recognized a rebel, one who hungered, as he did, for adventure. She might not be aware of it herself yet, but he'd seen it in her eyes, in the way her body leaned into the wind.

He wanted her more than he'd ever thought possible.

And she hated him. With bloody damned good reason.

He hoped his family might temper that judgment. His mother, Fancy, was the most compassionate woman he knew and could tame the wildest of creatures. His father had a temper, true enough, but loved to teach, second only to his family. Derek, his brother, was kind and solid. His aunt Fortune was—like his mother—gentle with all creatures and could, he was sure, help Annette's father. The only problem could be Katy, who felt as passionately as he did about the rebel cause.

He didn't want to think how they would feel about their unexpected guests. There was room for them, plenty of room, with the house his father had built, along with the old Marsh manor he'd turned into a school. His father would like the studious Hugh Carey. And Annette? He suspected she, too, would fall in love with his family if only she would allow herself that pleasure.

But would she?

Katherine Sutherland Cantrell gave the coachman directions, then sat back in the seat as the coach headed for the home of Dr. Noel Marsh. She had not warned him of her arrival.

She'd always teased him about being his "aunt," though she was two months younger than he and they had grown up as brother and sister when her brother married Noel's mother. But there had always been an undercurrent of something deeper. She had adored him; he had watched over her. He had kissed her when she was seventeen and she had given him her heart. Neither of them said anything to Ian and Fancy Sutherland, though, afraid that they would frown upon the match because of their relationship, even if it were not by blood. The community, they sensed, would not look upon it that way.

At nineteen, Noel left for Scotland to study medicine at the University of Edinburgh. It had been his dream as long as she could remember, and yet the prospect of losing him had been devastating. He'd kissed her at the pier after the family had seen him off. The kiss had been hard and longing and promising. He'd asked her to wait for him.

But because she felt he *should* be more like a brother to her than a lover, she'd suffered a kind of guilt she'd never known before. She'd finally agreed to marry a man who had courted her for two years, the reckless and dashing young son of a neighbor. He had been everything Noel was not, and she'd honestly believed she would come to love him; he was, after all, much like her. It had not taken long to discover she'd made a mistake. She had not understood the life-sapping effect of living with someone she didn't love, the pain of deceiving someone who loved her.

And then Noel had returned, pain in his eyes when he'd seen her with her husband, and he'd left for Philadelphia. She'd known why. He hadn't been able to live near her. So he had left the place he loved, the people he loved. And he'd married another woman.

She had attended the wedding, painful as it was. She wished she hadn't. Her heart broke, and she realized her husband understood why she'd never been able to give herself to him. He said nothing, but she saw the hopelessness in his eyes, a grief that never went away. Two years ago, he joined the militia and was killed by the British. She'd never forgiven herself. She was, in fact, again plagued endlessly by guilt.

She'd hidden for the last eighteen months, teaching in her brother's school. Gradually she'd found a modicum of peace within herself. The school, once created for the slaves who had been freed by her brother and his wife, now served any child or adult who wanted to learn, regardless of whether they could afford schooling. There was always a mixture of children, some from poor farms, some from freemen. Prejudice was always a problem, even among these youngsters, but the school survived, supported by Sutherland lands and horses.

As the war deepened, she harnessed all her frustrated passion to the rebel cause. She heard that Noel had not joined the revolt, but then he'd always been deliberate, cautious. When his wife died, she thought he would return home to Maryland. But he didn't. She had not been surprised when she heard he refused to take the oath to the new country. She *was* surprised when she learned he was not only treating British soldiers but had become a confidant of the devil, General Howe.

She'd tried to forget him, forget the closeness they'd once shared, but she could not. Now, she had finally decided she would see him, to convince him to come home where he belonged.

But as she rode in the carriage, she wondered whether she was making a terrible mistake.

She had arrived by coach yesterday to stay with Ethan Taylor, a friend of her brother, Ian Sutherland. Ethan, a merchant, was a rebel by inclination but a neutral out of necessity. He and his wife had been pleased at her visit, but cautious when they spoke of Dr. Marsh.

The city of Philadelphia was in an uproar. British soldiers were everywhere, their tempers short. Her public coach had been stopped and searched three times before it reached the depot, and then again when she'd hired another to take her to the Taylor home. She'd heard, over and over again, the ravages caused by the man called the Star Rider.

John Patrick. Word had not reached Maryland that his ship had been sunk. Thank God, he'd survived. Her family would have been devastated if he had not.

She'd had to smile when she heard the stories being circulated, that the Star Rider had apparently absconded with twenty of his jailed men, then stolen one of the king's frigates from under British noses. She wondered what Noel had thought of such activities.

The coach stopped in front of a two-story brick home, and she waited until the coachman descended and helped her out.

"Do you wish me to wait, miss?"

Katy didn't feel much like a miss any longer. At thirty-nine, she felt long in the tooth. Still, she knew her dark hair showed little gray, and her love for riding kept her figure slim and supple. "No." She smiled at him and was rewarded with a true flash of admiration.

If Noel wasn't home, she would wait. If he was home, he could drive her back to the Taylors'. After she'd had her say.

She watched the coach disappear, wondering whether she had made a mistake. Her heart lost a beat or two. She remembered the last time she saw Noel. He was tall, almost as tall as John Patrick, but she thought him more handsome, with his calm hazel eyes and tawny hair and thoughtful expression.

She was probably a fool for coming here, but in truth, she *had* to see him again. The need had been growing in her.

Katy mounted the steps, then used the heavy brass knocker. She had visited the house once before. It had been at the time of Noel's marriage, and she had hurt every single moment she had been inside.

The door opened and she recognized Malcomb, who had been with Noel forever. A huge fierce-looking animal stood protectively at his side.

His eyes widened. "Miss . . . Mrs. Cantrell."

Startled that he remembered her, she hesitated for a moment, then leaned down and petted the huge beast, which looked as if he would like her for dinner. In seconds, the dog's tail was wagging frantically.

"Aristotle, Dr. Marsh's wolfhound," Malcomb explained, his eyes narrowing. "He terrorizes most people."

She couldn't help but smile. "He's just a big baby."

Malcomb winced at that. "He doesna' take to everyone."

"My whole family has a way with animals," she said.

"Aye, I fear so," Malcomb said, looking down balefully at the dog.

"Is Dr. Marsh in?"

"Nay, he is not, but he should be home soon. Will you wait for him?" He shifted on his feet. "I'm Malcomb."

"Yes," she said. "I remember."

His face seemed to brighten at her comment and he stood aside for her to enter.

She hesitated.

"He would wish to see you, Mrs. Cantrell," he said. "I can be making you some tea."

Tea had been in short supply in Maryland, in short supply everywhere, in fact, except in areas the British occupied. Though she would dearly enjoy a cup, she gave him a look of disdain.

"No," she said flatly.

His face fell, and she instantly felt regret. She had no quarrel with Malcomb.

"Cider, then?" he asked hopefully. "You can wait in the parlor."

She nodded and followed him inside, Aristotle plodding happily beside her. Malcomb left, and her gaze roamed about the room. She had liked this room since the moment she'd first seen it. The walls were lined with books; the furniture was comfortable, the colors muted and relaxing.

Katy looked at the journals sitting on a table. Medical journals mostly, but there were also Tory newspapers, including the *Pennsylvania Ledger*. She sat down in the most comfortable-looking chair and started reading the report about the escape of the "pirates."

She smiled as she read. She could well imagine the British army's consternation. And she could also see the devilish glint in her nephew's eyes. John Patrick had always been the rascal in the family, the bold and adventurous one.

Aristotle's nose nudged her for attention, and she rubbed him under the chin. A low moan of pure joy came rumbling out his throat.

"That beast is already hard enough to live with," grumbled Malcomb, who had appeared in the doorway with a tray containing a silver goblet and a plate of pastries. She looked up at him sharply. Noel never ate sweets; he'd never had a taste for them.

Malcomb seemed to ken her unspoken question. "A gift from a neighbor."

She narrowed her eyes. She wondered what neighbor. A Tory? A woman? She disliked the jealousy that surged through her.

Still, she took a sip of spiced cider and looked toward the window as she heard a noise outside, the grateful neigh of a horse returning home.

Malcomb went to the window. " 'Tis the doctor. I'll help him with the phaeton."

Before she could say anything, he was out the door. She stood and walked nervously around the room.

Then Noel came in and the air stilled.

He was wearing a cloak, and his tawny hair, accented with traces of gray, was windblown. His hazel eyes lit as they saw her, although she knew the manservant must have warned him about her presence. He studied her carefully, from the tip of her bonnet, lingering on her face. His gaze then moved over the green dress she wore, down to her boots. And finally to Aristotle, who had greeted him before returning to her side.

"So you've bewitched him already?" he said, amusement twinkling in his eyes.

Her heart pounded faster. She'd always loved that smile, the warmth that came so easily to his eyes. To hide her reaction, she stooped down and put her face near the dog's. His overlarge tongue took a giant swipe at her cheek, and she found herself laughing. "He's a great beast of a dog."

"He is that." His voice softened. "You look lovely, Katy."

"For an old lady?" she asked as she straightened her back.

"Ah, Katy, you will never be old."

His eyes caressed her, and achingly familiar warmth spread through her. He was still Noel. Friend and confidant. Almost lover.

"You look . . . prosperous." Her observation was not exactly a compliment, and he knew it. His eyes narrowed slightly.

"Appearances can often be deceiving," he said quietly.

"Yes. I see that a man called Star Rider cozened the British."

"Is that why you came to Philadelphia? You heard that he'd been taken?"

"No. I didn't hear until I arrived."

"Good. I would not like Mother and Ian to worry."

"They worry enough about you."

He looked uncomfortable. "There is naught to worry about."

"Except your politics," she said.

"And those, my dear, are my business."

She tried another track. "And did you see the Star Rider?"

"Yes," he said shortly.

She swallowed hard at the suddenly closed look in his face. After a moment, she asked, "He was well?"

"Aside from a few assorted wounds, I would say so."

"He really stole a British ship?"

"Yes, and stole two Tories along with it."

"Tories?"

"Hugh Carey and his daughter, Annette. She had been nursing him at the Carey home."

She questioned him with her eyes.

"Unfortunately, the daughter discovered his identity and he feared for me. He left me a letter. Dammit. I kept warning him not to . . ."

"Not to what?"

"I think he was falling in love with her. She certainly . . . had affection for him. I doubt if she does now."

"Jonny? Our Jonny? In love? With a Tory?"

"I am afraid so. And the father—he has lost his speech, just as Fortune did years ago. He was tarred and feathered, and nearly killed, by a band of renegades who called themselves rebels."

"Oh, dear." It was all she could manage. Jonny, who was even more rabid than she on the subject of Tories, was in love with one, and with one who had good cause to hate the rebel Americans. It bore far too close a resemblance to her and Noel.

"He's taking her home to Maryland. He hopes Ian and Fortune can help her father regain his speech. Thank God, he came up with an excuse for their disappearance, but I fear someone will start asking questions."

His lips thinned. That was unusual for Noel. Her heart gave a jerk. Something had happened between the brothers.

"Tell me about my mother and the rest of the family," he said, changing the subject.

But she would have none of it. "I want to hear more about Jonny. How did he happen to stay with that family?"

"One of his men came for me after his ship sank. The British were combing Philadelphia for him. I thought the safest place would be in a home caring for British wounded."

"Why didn't you keep him here?"

He gave her a chiding look. "Doctors' offices were among the first places searched."

She searched his face, then smiled. "Hide in plain sight?"

"I just didn't expect him to hurt people who helped him," Noel added.

"Do you know that he has?"

"The Careys would not have left willingly. Not with a rebel."

"A rebel? Not a patriot?"

Noel raised an eyebrow. "Did you come all this way to argue with me?"

"Not exactly."

"Then what exactly?" he said as he reached out and tucked a runaway lock of dark hair under her bonnet. His hand remained against her cheek for just a second longer than necessary.

Katy felt the gentleness of it. The tenderness. Her heart ached. She wanted to reach out to him. She wanted him to pull her into his arms. She wanted to step into them.

But her dead husband stood between them. He had died for the patriot cause. He had died knowing she loved another man.

She stepped back, swallowed hard.

"Why *did* you come, Katy?"

She loved the way he caressed her name. She tried not to imagine it drifting in the air. "I hoped to convince you to come home."

"Why should I do that?" He had gone very still.

"We need a doctor on the Eastern Shore."

"Is that the only reason?"

She knew where his questions were leading, but she wasn't going to throw herself at him. "Ian and your mother want you back. They miss you."

"Did they ask you to come and fetch me?"

It had been her idea, but she was not about to admit it. Too much time had passed between them, too many events, too much heartbreak. She just wasn't ready to lay bare her heart. "Yes," she lied.

His brows drew together and for the fleetest moment she thought he might be considering her proposal. "I cannot leave Philadelphia now," he said, dashing her hopes.

"Cannot or will not?"

"Both," he said, his tone cool. "Does it make any difference?"

"Yes. Is it because you want to stay with your British friends? Or . . ." Her voice faded away.

"My practice is here, Katy. My friends are here. My life is here."

Practice. Friends. Life. Each word was like a dagger to her heart. Her chin went up. "And a woman?"

His hazel eyes seemed to burn for a moment. "There's only been one woman for me," he said. "I think you know that."

"Felicity?" She hated herself for asking that question, but she wanted to know how he'd truly felt about his wife. Had he loved her?

"No, not Felicity." He did not elaborate. He did not have to.

"Then come home."

His hand went up and his fingers touched her cheek. "I wish I could, Katy, but I have things I have to do here."

She searched his eyes, not able to continue. Aristotle nosed his way between them and whined beseechingly.

"Go and lie down, Aristotle," Noel said.

The dog sat and his tail thumped once on the floor.

"No. Go to the fireplace and lie down."

The dog's ears drooped and he stood, then obediently went over to the fireplace and scooted all the way down, setting his head on his great paws as he looked pathetically toward Katy.

"You're cruel."

"Oh, he'll be rewarded later with a fine big bone. He's made an art out of looking doleful."

"How did you find him?"

"He was being mistreated. I don't think the man will ever make that mistake with an animal again." His voice was suddenly hard.

"My Don Quixote."

"Knight of the Sorrowful Countenance?"

They were sparring again, as they used to do, using literature as their weapons.

She looked at his face, which was anything but a sorrowful countenance. It was dear. Too dear. She had to force her hands to stay at her sides.

" 'The eyes those silent tongues of Love,' " she recited from *Don Quixote de la Mancha.*

" 'That's the nature of women . . . not to love when we love them, and to love when we love them not.' "

Their eyes met, and she couldn't counter the last verse. She had not waited for him twenty years ago. Was he now telling her it was too late?

And did she really want anything to do with a man who profited from the enemy?

"I had better go," she said after a moment.

"Where are you staying?"

"With Ethan Taylor."

He turned away to stare into the fireplace. His eyes seemed to catch the glow of the flames and turn golden.

"Tell him to be more careful. He is considered suspect by the British. After the past few days, they're ready to seize anyone they feel might hold sympathetic feelings for the . . . Americans."

His voice was cool, like a stranger's.

She didn't say anything for several seconds, then, softly, "Noel—"

He interrupted, unwilling to hear what he thought she was about to say. "When are you returning to Maryland?"

Wounded, she tried to hide her dismay. She shrugged. "I plan to stay for a while."

"I think you should return to Maryland. It may become dangerous here."

"It seems to be dangerous everywhere these days."

"Yes," he said. " '. . . Times that try men's souls.' "

"You quote Thomas Paine. I would think you might avoid him. 'A bad cause will ever be supported by bad means and bad men.' "

He raised an eyebrow. "He does have a way with turning a phrase. Ian would appreciate that."

"Yes, he does. He has a bound volume of Mr. Paine's writings."

Noel grinned. "I should have known."

"He really does want to see you."

"Despite my . . . unfortunate loyalties?"

"He's the one person in the world who doesn't judge."

"But you and Jonny do."

She bit her lip. "*Understand.* We do not understand."

He turned away from her. "I think it best if you leave Philadelphia."

"No," she said, suddenly making a decision. "I plan to stay as long as you do."

He whirled around, his brows knitting together. "I do not want you here."

The words hurt more than she'd ever thought possible. She didn't realize until this instant how much she'd hoped he would agree to return to Maryland.

Aristotle had risen at the heat in Noel's words, the pure desperation in his voice. He looked from one to the other with bewilderment in his big brown eyes. He whined.

"It's all right," Noel said softly, and the huge dog stood and came toward him. Noel held out his hand and scratched the dog's ears. The animal emitted a long moaning sound.

He was using the dog to end the subject. An old trick of his to avoid discord. Her anger started rising again.

"I don't really care what you want," she said. "The Taylors have asked me to visit, and I plan to do it." Her chin went up. "And I will enjoy myself in Philadelphia." She started for the door. "I can see myself out."

"Not now, you can't," he said. "The British are on a rampage. Malcomb will see you back."

Malcomb. Not himself.

She felt tears sting behind her eyes but she refused to shed them. Her fingers tightened into a ball, and she went over to say good-bye to Aristotle. He regarded her somberly as she scratched him under the chin. "Goodbye, Aristotle."

He panted with pleasure.

Because her pride wouldn't let Noel think he had hurt her, she straightened and turned to him, giving him a blinding smile. Then she swept royally from the room. She hoped.

He looked out the window. She waited on the front steps, apparently for Malcomb to bring the carriage around. She was wearing a green dress that made her eyes glow like emeralds.

She was so lovely it made him ache. When she had reached down to touch Aristotle, he thought his heart would explode into tiny pieces. He remembered her ferrets and how she adored them, and the way she'd always loved the most timid animals best. She always made them feel safe when no one else could.

And he had to get her back to Maryland where she would be safe. She wasn't safe here, not with her outspoken criticism of the British.

He felt as empty as one of those damnable brandy bottles his British friends had consumed last night. He'd never wanted anything as much as to take her hand and go back to Maryland with her.

But duty called here. He had too many patients, too many responsibilities, and most of all he had to clean up after Jonny. He had to make sure the Careys were all right, make sure Maude Carey could manage without Annette. He'd already found places for the remaining British wounded, and he tried his best to convince Maude that there was nothing at all unusual about Annette and Hugh leaving in the middle of the night to visit a sick relative. Betsy was also asking questions, and Franklin fretted.

He'd told Maude that yes, Annette had mentioned that another aunt was ill and that she was thinking about visiting her. She must have taken a turn for the worse. He sent Malcomb frequently to fetch them wood and do whatever needed to be done.

And now he had Katy to worry about, too. Noel knew how reckless she could be. He knew how she despised the British. A clash was destined, and that would endanger both of them. After Jonny's escape, the British were in no mood to tolerate dissension. In the past three days, they had confiscated property and driven suspected rebel sympathizers from the city. They threatened to hang others.

Noel looked down at Aristotle, who was pacing the floor restlessly. "So you need air, too, my friend."

Aristotle came over to him and sniffed his hand, then licked it, looking up at him sympathetically. He wanted her back, too.

Chapter 14

ohn Patrick anchored the *Mary Ann* in the Chesapeake and stood on the deck, looking out over the sandy beaches while Ivy supervised the lowering of a jiffy, the smaller of their boats.

He would have a long walk to his father's farm, but then he could arrange for transportation for Annette and her father. Looking out over the bay, he remembered the picnics on the shore, the days Noel spent teaching him to fish, the evenings his father spent giving them all the joy and blessing of books. He'd also taught tolerance and respect for the beliefs of others. But somewhere during his captivity on British ships, John Patrick had lost that tolerance. Until now.

He also understood why Annette now had little.

She had masterfully shown him her disdain during the past five days, and this time his smile and supposed charm had been fruitless.

They had met no more British ships after leaving the mouth of the Delaware, but the voyage had been rough. He'd sent a man ashore at Annapolis to report to the governor's office, and handed over the British crewmen, then continued on to Maryland's Eastern Shore. He'd seen Annette and her father often, but he made no attempt to force his company on them. He knew what kind of reception he would receive, and he had no desire to deepen her enmity. If that were possible.

He looked around the deck for her now, his heart bucking when he saw her emerge from the hatchway. Dressed in one of the subdued gray gowns he had seen so often when he'd first arrived in Philadelphia, she still looked prettier than any of the reputed beauties he'd seen either in England or in America.

He ignored caution and walked over to her.

"Maryland," he said, looking toward the shore. "My family's farm is not far from here."

Interest shone in her eyes, but only for a moment. It was quickly cloaked. "How far?"

"About ten miles."

Her brow furrowed. "Are we going to walk there?"

He turned and looked at her steadily. "I will. I'll be back in the morning with a carriage."

"What if your family doesn't want us?"

He smiled. "You've never met my father."

"And I do not wish to. I want to return to Philadelphia. My father wishes to return to Philadelphia. He feels safe there." Her defiant tone had turned pleading. That hurt him more than her anger. He knew how much it cost her.

John Patrick leaned against the railing. "If I thought you would be safe there, then I *would* send you back. But I don't want you to pay for something I did."

"I've already paid. It didn't seem to deter you."

John Patrick didn't have a reply to that. "You've enjoyed the voyage," he said instead.

She looked out over the sea. "I find I have a liking for the sea, if not for the company."

"Then it has not been too bad." He was trying to reassure himself.

She spun around to face him. "Yes, it has. Because I will never trust anyone again. You have taken that away from me, and I fear I will never find it again."

He saw the glimmer of tears in her eyes and he reached out to touch her, but she slipped from his grasp. And then she was gone, the soft whisper of her slippers

against the deck disappearing through the cabin door
and down the stairs.

Annette wished she hadn't wanted so badly to hold out
her hand to John Patrick Sutherland. She wished she had
not longed for his arms to sweep her against him and
make her forget the last week. She wished it were still
last week when she had her dreams and didn't feel the
weight of betrayal so strongly.

She went down to her father's cabin. There was only
one book there to entertain him, and she'd often taken
him up on deck. But now she would wait until the pirate
left. She kept thinking of him that way: the pirate. She
hoped it would take her mind away from other things,
like the green eyes that once touched her soul, or the tall
grace of his body, or the beguiling smile that often
lingered on his lips.

Quinn had just finished shaving her father, who
greeted her with that gentle smile she so loved. She took
his hand and held it in hers as Quinn wiped the last
traces of soap from his face.

He was already dressed in clothes her captor had hast-
ily packed several days earlier: pea green breeches, white
linen shirt, white vest, and a waistcoat that matched his
breeches. Except for the vacant look in his eyes, he
looked like any prosperous merchant with his neatly
combed white hair and spectacles.

Annette leaned down and hugged him. For a moment,
she wondered whether the pirate had been right. If he
spoke the truth this time, perhaps . . .

She had memorized every one of his words, trying to
pick them apart. His father was a teacher; his aunt had
had a problem similar to her father's. Perhaps they *could*
help her father speak again. But then Dr. Marsh had
been able to do little. At the very thought of the doctor,
misery balled in her stomach. He had been a friend for

years. How could he bring a man who was little more than a pirate into her home?

But she tried to let none of her despair show in her face as she told her father where they were and that they were to visit a teacher. She bit her lip, wondering whether it was possible to betray someone in order to help them.

Morality and ethics, which she once thought were a matter of right and wrong, no longer seemed that way.

It was a bloody damned long walk.

Even in the November chill, he felt sweat gathering underneath his cloak as he ignored the stiffness in his injured leg and made himself take long strides. He'd insisted on coming alone, leaving Ivy in command of the *Mary Ann*. He walked one mile, then a second and a third, passing acre upon acre of tobacco until he approached the Wallace farmhouse. He saw a tall, burly figure forking hay to several horses in a paddock, and he whistled.

The man looked up and John Patrick recognized Tim Wallace, who had married John Patrick's aunt, Fortune, thirty years earlier. Tim was quiet, almost shy, but he was also a man with a huge capacity for love. He would do anything for his family, for a friend. John Patrick liked him immensely.

Tim's face broke into a great smile when he saw John Patrick, and he came loping toward him, encasing him in a bear hug. "By God, we all have missed you." He looked at John Patrick critically. "You look like hell, boy. Too damned thin. And you're limping."

John Patrick winced at the word "boy," but he grinned. "The Brits sank my ship."

"The *Star Rider?*"

"Aye. Near Philadelphia. Grape from one of their guns caught my leg."

"Well, thank God you recovered."

"I probably wouldn't have, were it not for Noel," John Patrick said. "But that's a long story, too long to tell at the moment. Can I borrow one of your horses?"

"Aye, of course. I'll give you Little Ben. He's the swiftest. I'll be inviting myself over to hear the rest of your tale."

"Aunt Fortune?"

"She went riding. You know how she likes to be alone sometimes and go roaming in those woods of hers." He chuckled. "I think she wants to escape the lot of us."

John Patrick doubted the truth of that. Fortune dearly loved her big, burly husband and her two sons. "How are Michael and Samuel?"

Tim sobered. "Michael is with General Washington. Samuel's over at my brother's house, helping clear some fields." He turned toward the paddock. "Enough talking. Ian would bash me if he knew I was keeping you from him. I'll saddle up the horse for you."

In minutes, John Patrick was astride Little Ben, a misnomer if ever there was one. Little Ben was a large black stallion, who regarded him suspiciously when he approached. John Patrick whispered a few words to him, then ran his fingers along his neck. After making the horse's acquaintance, he stepped into the stirrups and swung easily into the saddle, controlling the stallion's uneasy steps.

He leaned over, uttered more nonsense into the horse's ear until it stopped fidgeting. Tim grinned at him. "You haven't lost your touch."

"Not much different from a bucking ship," John Patrick said, then he pressed his knees against the sides of the horse.

It was damn fine to have a horse under him again. He

walked the stallion through the gate and down to the road, then pressed him into a canter.

He was going home.

"You did what?"

Ian Sutherland glared at his son.

John Patrick felt like a boy again, wriggling under the disapproval of the man he admired most in the world. "I didn't have a choice. I was afraid they would implicate Noel."

"You should have kidnapped your brother, then."

John Patrick stiffened. He'd never even considered that possibility. He wondered for a moment if he hadn't considered it because he hadn't wanted to leave Annette.

"The British might still have taken it out on the Careys," he said. "If Annette or anyone in her household let anything slip—"

"You and Noel have certainly created one hell of a mess."

John Patrick sighed. He'd known his father, the most moral man he'd ever known, wouldn't be happy about what had happened. Yet he had not anticipated exactly how unhappy he would be.

His father continued to pace back and forth. "Now you want *us* to take responsibility for your actions."

"I would like you to *help* Hugh Carey," John Patrick said. "As they aided me. As you did Aunt Fortune."

"She finally spoke only because she thought I was going to be killed. I don't think I want to use that tactic with someone I don't know."

John Patrick didn't, either. He tried another tack. "You will like Hugh Carey. He loves books. He's quiet, gentle."

"He's a Tory, and we favor the American cause. That does not bother me, but from what you've told me, it does indeed bother the Careys. I do not intend to be a warden or make my home a jail."

"They will be endangered in Philadelphia," John Patrick said stubbornly. "They will come to understand that."

"Would you, if someone carried you away from your home in the middle of the night?"

The door opened and John Patrick's mother entered. "You are raising your voices," she said mildly.

John Patrick winced. He had already greeted her, and then had asked to speak with his father alone. He knew what was coming now.

"Do you know what your son has done?" His father's voice was indignant.

Fancy Sutherland raised an eyebrow. At fifty-three, she was an attractive woman. She was still slim, her light brown hair gently touched by gray. Her amber eyes had always been her best feature: soft and warm and compassionate. Now, they fairly sparkled with joy at his homecoming.

"I couldn't even hazard a guess," she said.

"He kidnapped a father and daughter and apparently expects us to keep them prisoner here."

She turned her gaze on him. "A father *and* daughter?"

"Aye."

"And why, may I ask, did you do this?"

Amusement flickered in her eyes, and John Patrick felt his confidence flooding back. She would understand. She always had. Perhaps because she'd always had a way with wild things. At least, that was what his father had told him, with no little disapproval.

"After the *Star Rider* sank, Noel took me to their house. They had a small hospital there for British soldiers. I thought I could leave without anyone knowing who I was, but a British officer recognized me in Miss Carey's presence and—"

"He broke his men out of jail and stole a British ship, my dear," his father broke in. "I imagine the British were rather irate, but that doesn't excuse—"

"He did *what*?"

John Patrick was beginning to feel there was an echo in the room. He decided to lean against a wall and allow his father to explain.

"Stole a ship, lass."

"You could not steal anything smaller?" his mother queried John Patrick.

"That is beside the point, lass," his father interrupted. "The point is—"

"By any chance, is this young lady pretty?" his mother interrupted.

Ian Sutherland glowered at her. "What difference—"

"Let John Patrick answer," his mother said.

John Patrick fidgeted. "Aye," he said. "But that has nothing to do—"

"Of course not," Fancy Sutherland said. "Now, how does she feel about this?"

"She is not happy, but I was afraid the British might retaliate against her. And," he added, "against Noel."

"And why take her father?"

"Her father has been ill. He has not spoken since he was attacked some months ago. I thought you might be able to help him."

His father frowned at him now, instead of his wife. Both John Patrick and Ian knew Fancy could never turn anyone away, particularly anyone with an illness or injury. In fact, his father was the same way, but he wouldn't admit it.

"Of course we will," his mother said. "And I would like to meet this young lady. Ian, send a carriage for them, and I'll get Jane and Pansy to freshen some rooms for them."

"Fancy!" Ian roared.

"What else would you do? Send them all away?" Fancy regarded him quizzically.

"They don't want to be here."

"I remember a time when you didn't want to be here, either," she replied mildly.

Ian mumbled to himself, and John Patrick dared to smile. His father had been sent to Maryland as a bond servant after the Battle of Culloden in Scotland. The last thing he had wanted was to stay. Until he fell in love with Fancy.

"I'll send the carriage," Ian Sutherland said, throwing his hands out in utter defeat.

John Patrick rode Little Ben. He had another horse on a lead for Quinn. Ivy would stay on board the *Mary Ann* in case of trouble. Ian had driven the carriage himself.

When they reached the shore of the Chesapeake, he signaled the ship. Immediately, a boat was lowered. Even from a distance, he knew Annette by the light way she stepped, the ease with which she moved despite the awkwardness of her skirts.

His father stood beside him. "How long do you expect this visit to last?" he growled.

"Until the Brits leave Philadelphia, or until I can ensure their safety."

"And Noel? You think he is safe?"

"Aye," John Patrick said, falling into his father's speech pattern. "No one but the Careys knew it was Noel who took me there. And Miss Carey's maid—but I don't think she'll say anything. She wouldn't realize the importance or even that I was the Star Rider." He looked at the approaching boat. "He is also a friend of General Howe's. I think he is safe enough."

"Katy went to visit him."

John Patrick spun around. "No."

"She left five days ago."

"You couldn't stop her?"

Ian shrugged. "You know my sister. She was determined to bring him back. I seem to have little influence on my sister—or my children." He hesitated, then added, "I hoped she might succeed."

"She'll fail. I tried to get him to leave."

"Katy might be a bit more persuasive."

John Patrick sighed. "I hope you're right."

The boat reached shore, and the rowers helped Annette and her father out.

John Patrick took a step toward Hugh Carey. "Sir, I would like to introduce my father, Ian Sutherland. He studied at the University of Edinburgh, and he has an extensive library of Scottish books. I hope you will enjoy it."

Ian Sutherland, who'd once been a marquis, stepped forward and bowed formally. "I welcome you all to Maryland, and to my home," he said.

Hugh smiled and nodded, taking his proffered hand to help him over the stones toward the carriage. His father, John Patrick knew, often had a soothing effect on people.

Annette looked discomfited. She apparently had trouble glaring at such an elegant welcome. Suddenly hopeful, he held out his hand to help her.

"I do not need help from my jailer," she said, glaring at John Patrick. She reached the carriage and helped herself up into it, gathering her skirts around her primly.

"I might enjoy this after all," Ian Sutherland said softly to John Patrick, before stepping up into the driver's seat.

John Patrick winced at the amusement in his father's voice. He certainly didn't see any humor in any of this. He turned to a waiting Ivy.

"I want you to stay with the ship. Send Quinn to me. He'll stay with us."

"Aye, sir."

He waited impatiently as Ivy climbed into the jiffy, and the rowers headed back toward the ship. It would take another twenty minutes to get Quinn back here, then he would have to catch up with the carriage.

He wanted to be there when Annette met the rest of his family. He wanted to see her relax. He wanted to see her smile. He wanted that smile back more than he'd ever wanted anything.

Annette could barely withhold her resentment. She wanted to lash out at the tall, handsome planter who was now participating in their abduction. But she didn't want to frighten her father.

She told herself instead to look at her surroundings, to memorize them, for she was going to escape this place. One way or another. She had been helpless aboard the ship, but not here.

So she rode in silence as Ian Sutherland attempted a conversation about the Eastern Shore, about Maryland, about horses.

Then he turned to her. "Do you ride, Miss Carey?"

She simply nodded her head. One owed no courtesies to one's captors. But an idea started to form in her mind. If she could get a horse, she could escape and reach some government authorities. Surely, even Maryland regarded kidnapping as a crime.

She stared out at the dry, gray fields, wanting to avoid any further conversation, but her father's face was alert, and he looked over the fields with interest. Annette realized his mind was forming questions even as his mouth seemed unable to utter them. Her father's silence—and hers—didn't seem to bother Ian Sutherland a whit.

They finally reached an impressive brick home. The carriage slowed and finally pulled up in front of a more comfortable-looking farmhouse behind the manor. A veranda stretched around the neatly painted edifice.

A woman stood on the porch, a warm smile on her face. She was dressed in a light brown gown that complimented her light brown hair and unusual amber-colored eyes. She hurried down the steps to meet the buggy.

Annette found it almost impossible not to smile back.

Ian Sutherland bounded from the buggy in one quick movement, and Annette was reminded of John Patrick. They moved with the same easy grace, despite their height. Instantly, she erased the thought and tried to make her face expressionless.

But after Ian Sutherland helped her down, the older woman clasped her hands in her own. "I'm Fancy Sutherland, John Patrick's mother. I know my son has treated you disgracefully," she said, "but we will try to make up for it."

"You can, by letting us all return to Philadelphia," Annette said.

"My son feels you would be in danger."

"That is his self-serving opinion."

"And you do not share it?"

"No," Annette said. "He wishes only to protect his brother."

"I'm afraid I share that sentiment," the woman said kindly.

"Then why not ask him to come to Maryland? Why should my family suffer?"

"I truly wish it were that easy, my dear."

The simmering frustration inside her exploded. "It *is* that easy, unless you approve of kidnapping. How would you feel if you were carted off in the middle of the night without knowing where you were going, or why?"

"I would be every bit as angry as you. But John Patrick feels we might be able to help your father, and he truly does believe you would be in danger in Philadelphia, whether Noel remains there or not."

Annette saw Ian's eyes meet his wife's. Some strong emotion flickered there, but she couldn't define it.

She wanted to retort, but her battle was with John Patrick. She unexpectedly found it difficult to be rude—or even angry—with his family. Still, that did not mean she would not escape at the first possible moment.

"I've had supper prepared," Mrs. Sutherland said. "You must be hungry. And tired. Let me see you to your rooms."

"Our prison, you mean," Annette said softly. Her father blinked suddenly, and she wondered how much he understood. She had told him it was an adventure, to keep from frightening him. Now she realized she had painted herself into a trap. She put an arm out for her father to take and tried to smile for him. "I think my father might indeed be hungry," she said.

Fancy Sutherland's eyes were full of understanding and compassion. "I have a story to tell you later," she said. "But in the meantime, we will do everything to make you comfortable. Jonny said your father enjoyed books. Ian has a very fine library, and your father is welcome to use it at any time and read any volume. Perhaps later he would like to go over to the school."

"The school?"

"The house you passed, the brick one, is Ian's school. He started it to teach the slaves we freed when we inherited Marsh's End. That was before Jonny was born."

Jonny? It seemed odd to hear him spoken of that way. And despite herself, Annette was intrigued with her hostess's last comment. She and her father believed in abolition, as did many Pennsylvanians. "Whom do you use as labor in the tobacco fields?"

"We employ freemen, my dear. Ian will have nothing to do with slavery."

Fancy Sutherland said nothing else, but Annette sensed it had something to do with that "story" she'd mentioned. Her own curiosity wanted to pursue the subject, but then she would be admitting to an interest she did not want to have. So she said nothing.

As she was moving toward the door, she saw two men on horseback arriving. She immediately recognized John Patrick Sutherland as one and Quinn as the other. To her chagrin, John Patrick looked as masterful—and as magnificent—on a horse as he did at the wheel of a ship.

His unruly black hair matched the black of his mount, and his green eyes glowed as he dismounted in one fluid movement. The ship's doctor, on the other hand, almost fell as he struggled to the ground.

Holding the reins of his mount, John Patrick approached Annette and his mother.

"You've met," he noted rather awkwardly, and only a flicker in his eyes betrayed any misgiving.

Annette turned away from him.

"Yes," she heard his mother say softly. "I am taking them to their rooms. You and your friend can stay at the school."

"You haven't met Quinn," he told his mother. "He's a doctor. You might well find much in common with him."

Fancy's voice quickened with interest. "We will have to have a long talk. I'm often called upon to help people on the farm. Perhaps you can give me some advice."

Annette felt bewildered. They sounded so *normal*. But what normal people condoned what their son was doing?

Fancy Sutherland put her hand on Annette's arm. "Come inside," she said. "Jane has prepared hot cider, and after seeing your rooms, perhaps you and your father would like some."

Annette was as attracted by Fancy's easy charm as she had been by her captor's several weeks ago. She warned herself against it and turned around, shooting the pirate a withering glance, letting him know that she had not succumbed to the Sutherland charm.

Chapter 15

Supper was a strained affair. John Patrick had
hoped for much better.

Despite Ian Sutherland's best attempts, conversation flagged when Annette refused to take any part.
Her father's silence didn't make things any easier.

Two large mismatched hounds of obviously undistin-
guished lineage sat on either side of Ian. A cat wandered
between them, occasionally batting one or the other, before settling down under Fancy's chair.

"This and That," she had explained when the dogs
had padded in, obviously confident of their welcome.

Annette looked perplexed.

"The dogs," his mother explained. "They are This
and That, for obvious reasons. The larger one is This.
The other is That."

"No one knows where they came from," John Patrick
added helpfully. "Mother found them as puppies on a
road one day, apparently abandoned. The cat is Queen
Mab, because she lords it over everyone and has no conscience."

A choking sound came from Annette, or maybe it was
a chuckle she was trying desperately to withhold.

Ian was watching her with amusement.

"Shakespeare," she finally said. Reluctant, obviously,
but compelled.

"Aye," Ian said delightedly. *"Romeo and Juliet."* He
beamed as if he'd found a pot of gold at the end of the
rainbow, then recited with great gusto, " 'O! Then I see
Queene Mab hath been with you! . . . She is the fairies'

midwife, and she comes in shape no bigger than an agate-stone . . .' "

Hugh Carey smiled.

Annette's eyes suddenly clouded, as if regretful at such a lapse in her studied animosity, and she turned her eyes back to the food that had been placed in great abundance on the table.

Throughout the meal, John Patrick watched for any signs that she might be succumbing to his parents' heroic efforts to make her and her father comfortable. The food—oysters, crab, and venison—was delicious, the result of special efforts by Jane.

His mother had never been comfortable with servants, and had always had only a minimum to keep the house presentable. For the last six years, she'd employed Jane, an Irish redemptioner, as housekeeper and cook; her husband, Terry, worked with the horses. Pansy, the daughter of one of their freemen, also helped with the housekeeping.

But John Patrick knew as often as not his mother would be working alongside both, helping with everything from cooking and polishing to mopping floors. Idle hands, she'd always said, led to idle minds.

Ian would just shrug helplessly, but he was often found pitching hay when he was not teaching. Both had earned the devotion of their workers, because they'd never felt above a bit of physical labor, and they provided a school for anyone who wished to learn. There was currently a full-time teacher, but John Patrick knew Ian frequently stopped in to teach a class or two. John Patrick had, in fact, met the latest teacher when he'd taken his very few belongings over to the old Marsh mansion which served as the school.

In the silence that had settled over the table, he asked about the man he'd met earlier. "I like your current schoolmaster," he said.

"Sweeney?" Ian said, a grin spreading over his face. "I was lucky with that one."

"Another redemptioner?"

"Nay, a convict. Wrongly accused."

John Patrick raised an eyebrow. His father was famous for attending auctions, finding promising redemptioners or convicts, buying their indentures, then setting them free. "Well, your Sweeney and my Quinn are getting along famously. They decided to find a tavern to exchange adventures."

"You are not to steal him," Ian said sternly.

John Patrick heard another choking sound from Annette, who was sitting wide-eyed, her food nearly untouched.

He realized the conversation had probably been disturbing. Talk of convicts and bonded servants and stealing. John Patrick winced at what she must be thinking.

His mother hurried to reassure her. "My husband wishes to save the world."

"Too bad his son does not follow suit," Annette retorted tartly.

"Ah, but he does," Ian said with a quick grin. "He just does it in his own perverse way." He turned fond eyes on John Patrick and quoted, " 'I love good creditable acquaintance; I love to be the worst of the company.' "

"Jonathan Swift," John Patrick said, playing the old game. " 'There is nothing in this world constant, but inconstancy.' "

" 'We are so fond of one another,' " his father said, " 'because our ailments are the same.' "

"Faults, he means," his mother interrupted, looking at her husband and son. "Rogues, both of them, but not a mean bone in their bodies."

Annette rose suddenly, pushing back her chair. "Is there not, Mrs. Sutherland? I cannot agree with your assessment of your son. You did not see him shoot a man in cold blood, nor threaten my father." Her voice cracked on the last words. Without waiting for an answer, she disappeared from the room, both This and That following her.

John Patrick started to rise, but his mother shook her head. "She has every right to feel that way. I think she's been admirably restrained."

Hugh Carey looked perplexed. As if nothing at all had happened, Fancy smiled sweetly at Hugh. "Why don't you have a brandy with my husband? Perhaps Annette needs some rest."

Hugh stood and followed Ian to his study. Fancy disappeared as well.

John Patrick was left alone except for Queen Mab. He looked at the unfinished meals, then the empty chairs around the table as the cat brushed against his leg.

"Ah, Queen Mab," he sighed. "I think I need a piece of your magic."

Annette made straight for her room. The infernal Sutherlands were seducing her father, and had well nigh seduced her.

For a moment, she'd been pulled into the warmth of the circle, into the game they fondly played with one another. She had basked in Ian Sutherland's approval when she'd recognized the quote from *Romeo and Juliet*. Too often, she'd been labeled a bluestocking, and scorned for being too intellectual for a woman. It had been amusing to listen to the conversation, to smile inwardly at the explanation about the dogs.

It *would* have been pure pleasure under different circumstances.

One of the dogs lifted a paw and touched her knee. They had scooted in before she'd closed the door, but now she welcomed their company. She couldn't blame them for their owners' failings. She could blame herself for falling into a silken trap.

It would have been her duty to her country and king to inform on Noel Marsh—had she had the chance. In the days since her abduction, she'd concluded that he must be a spy for the Americans; that must be why his brother would stop at nothing to protect him.

Of course, she didn't want him hanged, no matter what he'd done. But with her knowledge, she could force him to leave Philadelphia, where he had access to the highest levels of the British military.

This, or was it That, moaned aloud as she rubbed its ears, and his companion crowded in to receive his share. She bent her head against the short fur of his neck. She'd not had a dog since her childhood pet, King, died four years earlier. She'd thought none could take his place. Now, as she heard the contented rumblings of the two dogs, she wondered whether she'd been wrong.

She thought of Noel's wolfhound, Aristotle, and swallowed hard. His smile came to her mind. His intensity when it came to his patients. His grief when one died.

No, she told herself. She wouldn't think of those things. He was a spy, and she had to stop him, just as she had to escape this velvet prison. Remember that night the rebels came. Remember the cruelty, the hate, the devastation. John Patrick was little better. He had lied. He had taken what he wanted.

She felt a rough tongue swipe across her face, then knew the dog was tasting the salt of her tears.

John Patrick went out to the stables. He had to take Little Ben home to Tim and Fortune, and it would take several hours to make the round trip.

His mother was there, clucking over a new foal. She looked up as he came in.

"I have to return the horse," he said.

"I'm trying to think of a name for this little one."

He studied the colt. It was a gray, like many of the Sutherland horses. They were prized throughout Maryland. "She looks like a little duchess."

"Gray Duchess," Fancy said, rolling it around on her tongue. "I like it."

"I think Annette would, too. She lost a mare when her home was attacked. I asked Noel to try to find her, but I think it's unlikely now." He looked at the filly. "I wonder—could I buy Duchess from you? When she is weaned?"

"I don't think a horse will help at the moment."

"At the moment, no. But someday . . . perhaps it will compensate a little for what I've put her through."

"Then she is yours. But for a hefty price."

"I thought Papa was the horse trader."

"I let him think that," she said loftily.

He grinned, but then it faded. He had always marveled at the love between his mother and father. He had never thought to find such love. John Patrick wondered whether he'd destroyed any chance that he might.

"Give her time, John Patrick," his mother said, as if she'd read his mind. "She is going to have to learn to trust you again."

"I do not know if that's possible," he said.

"At one time, I didn't think Ian would ever trust me."

"You never lied to him."

"Now, that is not entirely true," she said.

He looked at his mother with interest. People often mistook her kindness and compassion for weakness. But he knew she had a core of pure steel when someone she loved was endangered.

She didn't give him a chance to ask any questions, though. "I have to go now. But your Annette has been wounded, not once but twice. You will have to be patient." She hesitated, then continued. "*If* you want her?"

"I do," he said softly. It was the first time he'd admitted to himself that he didn't just want her for a week, or a month, but forever. "You should have seen her on board the *Mary Ann*. She loved the sea as much as I do."

"You hated it for a long time," she reminded him.

"Aye, I did. I did not appreciate the way it was thrust upon—" He stopped, his eyes meeting hers. Understanding ran between them.

He appreciated then the enormity of his problem. It had taken him years to overcome his hatred of the sea, to see it as a source of freedom rather than captivity.

Years.

Flames climbed higher and higher as she heard her father's moans. Terror grabbed her. She felt the heat of flames, heard the hate-filled taunts of a drunken mob. She saw her father's pain-contorted face. The heat intensified. They were coming after her now.

She screamed.

A hand grabbed at her and she struggled to get loose. She struck out.

"Annette. Wake up. Annette. You are safe."

She continued to struggle, though, even as her mind slowly absorbed the sound, the quiet insistence. No anger. No hate. Slowly, she opened her eyes. Candlelight flickered in the room, sending eerie shadows cascading against the walls. She felt wet from the sweat created from fear and anguish.

"You had a nightmare," the quiet voice said, and she recognized it as belonging to the pirate's mother. "You're safe here."

Annette struggled to sit. "I'm sorry I disturbed you."

"You are not to worry about that," Fancy Sutherland said. "Can you tell me about it?"

The pain was so strong, so deep, Annette needed to share it. But not here. Not under these circumstances.

She felt she would be giving John Patrick Sutherland another weapon. He knew about the tarring-and-feathering. She'd told him. But she hadn't told him about the nightmares, about the fear that never quite left her, the endless sorrow she felt for her father.

"Would you like some warm milk?"

"No," Annette said. She wanted to be alone. Or did she? Her blood still ran fast. Her heart beat too quickly.

"May I stay with you a few moments, then?"

Annette smoothed the heavy comforter over her. "If you like."

She was suddenly aware of a big dog's head resting on the bed not far from her.

Fancy smiled. "This woke me up and led me here. He must have heard you."

Annette felt the terror seep away. "Are you sure it wasn't That?"

"Ah, now you understand the problem we all have. I'm not sure the names were very wise. But they do provide moments of amusement." She was quiet for a moment. "Noel particularly was good at names. He had a cat named Unsatisfactory that he loved more than life itself. At least he's graduated to 'Aristotle.' "

Gentle amusement. It was all around this house. She'd tried to resent it, but instead found herself drawn to it.

How could this family have produced a pirate and a spy?

How could she feel such warmth and such a chill at the same time?

She shifted her weight. "I think I can sleep now," she said.

Fancy Sutherland looked doubtful, then stood. "If you are sure . . . ?"

"I am."

"I wish you a good night then," the older woman

said. She leaned over and straightened out the bed-clothes as if Annette were only five years old. Then she quietly slipped out the door.

Annette waited a moment, then rose and went to the window, pushing aside the drapes to stare out. The moon was high, the sky clear, the stars so bright she felt she could reach out and touch them.

Star Rider. She thought she would never believe stars were quite as lovely and benevolent again.

Why was the one man who had come close to touching her heart so full of treachery?

She stared out for a long time, her gaze traveling from the oak trees that surrounded the house to the endless brown fields, then to the paddock next to the barn. A mare stood still, its head bowed. A colt lay next to her. Innocence. Peace. Two qualities she'd lost.

Despite what she'd told Mrs. Sutherland, she knew she would not sleep again tonight. She feared the return of the nightmares. She went to the trunk that had been packed for her and rummaged in it until she found a simple gown that laced in front. She slipped from her nightclothes and pulled a chemise over her head, then the dress.

Although the sky was fair, the temperatures were cold. Drawing her cloak around her, Annette opened the door. She might as well discover right now whether she and her father were being guarded in any way.

She slipped through a dark hallway, then down steps lit only by moonlight filtering through the windows. The house was quiet. She expected the two dogs to bark at any moment, but after one short growl, she heard nothing else.

The door was unlocked. She opened it and went out to the porch, expecting a hue and cry at any moment. She *was* a prisoner, after all. But there was silence, broken only by natural sounds: the hoot of an owl, the neigh of a horse.

Annette walked to the paddock. The resting mare snorted at being disturbed, then bowed her head, nuzzling her offspring. She was obviously ready to protect it if necessary. Puzzled at seeing no one, not even one of John Patrick's ruffians on guard, Annette made her way to the barn and entered, leaving the door ajar to allow some light in. She waited for her eyes to adjust to the dim interior.

The numerous stalls were nearly all filled. Like the mare outside, the horses lifted their heads, some snorting with disgust at being aroused. She found the tack room. *Easy.* It would be so easy to saddle a horse and escape.

She was a good rider. Not expert, but good. She'd ridden frequently on their farm. She wondered which of these horses would be easy to handle, which were the swiftest.

She could ride to a town and request the help of the authorities. But would she be back before the house awakened? Would she endanger her father?

In truth, she didn't know what John Patrick Sutherland might do.

Her hands curled into fists. She decided to wait a night or two. She would determine the best mount, discover the fastest route. If she left just after everyone retired, perhaps she could bring someone back before anyone realized she was gone.

She wouldn't let herself think what might happen to the Sutherlands. They were accomplices in a kidnapping. They were harboring a fugitive.

With a plan now firmly in mind, she returned to the house. She wasn't so cautious now about making a noise. If anyone questioned her, she'd say she'd just gone to get a breath of air after a bad dream. And why shouldn't she have a bad dream, after all that had happened?

But no one appeared as she made her way cautiously back up the stairs and into her room. She disrobed and snuggled back into bed, spinning a plan for a midnight ride.

John Patrick had watched her as she came into the barn. He had been sleeping in the small room in the back but had instantly wakened at the noise. He'd cracked open the door and saw her slender silhouette as she moved silently down the row of horses.

He'd brought back his father's horse and decided not to go to his room in the school. He'd never liked that house. None of the family did. Even the sound of children hadn't erased the ghosts that still seemed to haunt it—ghosts of people who had been mistreated by its previous owner.

The cot in the barn suited him just fine. He'd decided not to reveal his presence unless Annette made a move to saddle a horse. So he merely watched from the shadows and shivered in the cold. He always slept nigh on naked even on cold nights, trusting to blankets to keep him warm. He was very aware at the moment of his . . . vulnerability.

He found himself admiring her more than ever. He truly appreciated her spirit, even her misguided loyalties. 'Twas far better than not having any loyalties at all.

The unbidden thought stunned him. He'd been criticizing Noel, even shunning him, for holding loyalties different from his own. Noel, on the other hand, had not hesitated for an instant to help him. And in doing so had put himself in terrible danger.

Especially if Annette Carey escaped to carry the tale.

He'd watched Hugh Carey at supper. He appeared comfortable in the house, readily succumbing to its warmth. Annette obviously had not. He would ask for her promise that she would not try to leave the farm. And if she did not give it?

He knew his parents would not be her jailers. He had already asked enough of them, more than enough. He knew there was only one solution if she would not agree.

And he didn't like it one bit better than she would.

Annette did her best to avoid John Patrick the next day. She did ask his father to take her to visit the horses, neglecting to tell him she had already done so the previous night.

He had assented readily. His pride in the animals was obvious, as he told her some of their history, how a horse named Royalty had been the original sire of these horses, and his progeny had won many Maryland races. They were highly sought.

They obviously meant more to him than money, though. She noticed the way he spoke to each animal as he introduced them to her, and the affectionate way he pointed out their strengths and weaknesses, their odd little characteristics. Each received a piece of apple, and two of them nibbled his shoulder. He grinned as they passed a stall where a mare nuzzled a filly. "This is our newest addition. She's only ten days old."

Annette fell in love. The filly was all legs and eyes, and it regarded her curiously. "She's beautiful," she said wistfully. She remembered Sasha at that age, and she bit her lip to keep tears from filling her eyes.

"Let me introduce you to her papa," Ian Sutherland said as she looked up. Sympathy, or understanding, warmed his eyes. He led her down to the end of the barn, where a particularly large gray fellow stuck his head out and whinnied. "This is Shadow Prince," Sutherland said, taking a carrot from his pocket and giving it to the horse. "He's the fastest horse we have, but he's also the most difficult. Only a few riders can handle him, including John Patrick."

"I didn't think he was here often."

"He's not. But he enjoys working with the horses when he is. He raced them before he studied law."

"He studied law?" She couldn't keep the amazement from her voice. "But I thought he was—"

"A pirate?" Ian Sutherland asked. "That, too, but not from choice."

"I don't understand . . ."

"He's told you nothing about his years at sea?"

She shook her head. "What is there to tell?"

"Ask him," he said gently.

"I do not wish to ask him anything. I do not want to talk to him at all."

Ian Sutherland turned to her, his gaze meeting hers directly. "Do not judge until you hear him out," he said.

"He took us from our home. He lied to us. He used me. He used my family." She wished her voice didn't sound so choked. She wished the betrayal didn't still hurt so much. She wished she didn't feel such a fool for actually believing that John Patrick had truly admired her.

"I canna' say I approve of that," Ian Sutherland said. "I can say I understand how you feel."

"How can you?"

"I came to America as a bond servant, a slave," he said slowly. "Fancy's first husband bought me." He was silent for a moment, then added, "You canna' possibly imagine how that feels, to be auctioned like a horse or a cow. I do know the hopelessness in losing freedom, regardless of how small or how large it is."

She stared at him. She knew bondsmen. She knew many had been convicts.

"Yes, Miss Annette," he said, seeming to read her mind. "I was a convict. I was taken at Culloden Moor

when I fought for Prince Charlie, and convicted of treason. The sentence of hanging was commuted to fourteen
years' servitude. You canna' imagine how much I hated
the English, and how much I hated Fancy and her husband for buying the bond."

He had lapsed into a heavy burr as he talked. Annette
was stunned at the emotion in his voice, even the remembered anger. He had seemed so—so imperturbable.

"Is that why John . . . Patrick"—she found it hard
to say the name—"hates the English?"

"He has his own reasons, Miss Annette."

"And Dr. Marsh?"

He looked at her in surprise. "Surely you know he's a
Tory sympathizer. It has caused more than a few moments of disharmony."

"But he—" She stopped. John Patrick had said the
same, but she hadn't believed him. Yet Ian Sutherland
seemed perfectly convinced of his stepson's loyalties.

"My sons are extremely independent, lass. And Noel,
though he had another birth father, is as much my son as
John Patrick. But we do not always agree, nor, I suppose,
will we ever."

Thoughts were spinning around in Annette's head. A
family divided? It made no sense to her.

He seemed to understand and know the perfect rem-
edy. "Would you like to go for a ride?"

She nodded.

"A gentle mare or a spirited one?"

"Gentle," she replied. No sense in letting them know
the level of her skill.

He was saddling a pretty gray mare when the barn
door opened, and John Patrick entered along with a
black man. "We've been out looking at the new colts,"
he told his father. "Some more winners."

"Aye, they are braw lads. I'm taking Miss Carey for a
ride. Would you like to take Shadow Prince?'

The pirate looked at her. She felt like turning her back on him and returning to the house, but she wanted to know more about the horses, more about the land, more about the roads. She said nothing.

"Is it all right with Miss Carey?" he asked.

She shrugged with what she hoped looked like indifference.

He apparently took it as assent. "I'll saddle him." He looked at his father. "Is he still as stubborn as a mule?"

"It depends on who is riding him," Ian Sutherland said. "Now, he is rather fond of me, but you . . . ?"

Annette didn't want to acknowledge the warm competition between father and son, the comradeship they so clearly shared. She'd lost that kind of friendship with her father the night his dreams, his faith, his hopes, burned. Instead, she led the saddled mare outside to wait for them.

She stroked the mare's neck. "Pretty girl," she crooned. "You and I will suit each other well."

As if by prearrangement, Ian Sutherland came over to help her into the sidesaddle. She turned to see John Patrick swing easily onto the big gray, and watched as he quieted the horse's nervous steps with a whisper. Then Ian Sutherland mounted a bay gelding with the same natural mastery that his son displayed.

They rode down the lane for several miles, first in a walk, then a trot, and finally a canter. Annette appreciated the easy gait of the mare, but she admired the big gray, whose bunched muscles obviously longed to stretch out into a gallop. She also knew that John Patrick was restraining both himself and the stallion.

She was riding several lengths behind, and Ian gave her an apologetic look. "Would you mind if we rode on ahead?"

She could think of nothing she would like more. She was tense, and feeling any number of wayward emotions as she watched John Patrick. He was such a good horseman, and watching the power of man and horse together was nerve-jangling. She wanted to be alone. She wanted not to care. She wanted desperately to dismiss John Patrick Sutherland forever from her mind. And yet she knew she would always remember him like this.

She shook her head to let them know she didn't mind, and reined up her little mare as the two men raced down the path, the hooves thundering against the ground and throwing up tufts of grass. Both men leaned down on the neck of their horses; neither used a crop or quirt, but she recognized the communication between riders and horses as they disappeared into a stand of trees.

Annette thought about turning her horse for the nearest town. But she had no idea where it was, and she had neither money nor clothes with her. She also had no doubt that, tired as the Sutherlands' horses would be, they would still have enough stamina to catch her quiet mare.

She continued walking the horse, until she saw one solitary horseman returning. She knew immediately from the color of the horse that it was John Patrick. Where was his father?

As John Patrick approached her, tremors ran through her body. She didn't want to be alone with him. The presence of his father had diffused the confusion he always kindled in her.

She prepared to flee back to the house, but he was beside her and his hand reached out to take the reins.

"Where is your father?"

"He decided to go on to visit my aunt."

"I want to go back to the house," she said, trying to regain her reins.

"I had hoped you would like it here," he said softly.

"A gilded prison is still a prison," she retorted. "Your father knows that."

"He told you," John Patrick said in surprise.

"Yes." She wanted to ask him what his father had meant when he said John Patrick had his own reasons for hating the British. But that would mean sharing confidences. She was not going to do that. Not with a man she could not trust.

John Patrick gave her that crooked, charming smile. "He must like you. He never talks about those early days here."

She would not succumb to the sudden warmth she felt. Instead, she forced a coolness into her voice that was entirely at odds with the heat inside. "I want to go back."

"Annette?" His voice was suddenly low, serious.

"Miss Carey," she corrected him.

"Miss Carey, then," he said. "I want you to promise me you will stay here, that you will not try to return to Philadelphia."

"And why should I do that?"

"For your own protection. For your father's."

"For your brother's, you mean," she said.

"That, too," he admitted.

"I will give no promises to a liar and a brigand," she said, furious with herself for the tears gathering in back of her eyes. "I do not care how charming your family is. I cannot trust them, as I cannot trust you. Now please let me go."

She was surprised when he did so.

She clicked the mare into a walk, then a canter. She didn't look behind her, but the road ahead was blurred by the tears in her eyes.

Chapter 16

Two days passed. John Patrick continued to sleep in the barn. Annette's attitude was unchanged. He saw in her eyes that she would escape at any reasonable opportunity.

Reasonable was the word. He'd already discovered she would do nothing foolishly. She would bide her time. But she would strike.

She remained impervious to every attempt by his family to make her one of them. She was never rude after that first evening, yet any attempt to involve her in conversation was met with only the briefest of answers, and she disappeared as quickly as possible. She must have realized now that he was sleeping in the barn, because his father found him there one morning, and he'd seen the sudden alarm in her eyes when his father had mentioned the encounter at the morning meal.

He knew that look. She was not good at concealing emotions or intent. She was, in fact, a terrible liar. He then wondered how he'd become such a good one. It was a painful question.

He had hoped . . .

But now he had run out of time, and out of hope.

John Patrick had sent one of his men to Annapolis to inform the Maryland governor, who'd issued him his letters of marque, about the loss of his ship and his seizure of the British vessel. His man returned this morning with the governor's reply. He'd been ordered to sail to the French island of Martinique in the Caribbean to take aboard some cannon.

Legally, the governor had no authority over him, but since he had provided John Patrick with the protective cover of privateer, John Patrick knew he would do as asked. He would sail on the morning tide, but there was no way he could leave Annette here.

He wasn't sure how his family would feel about his plans. As much as they loved Noel, he knew they would argue that they had time to warn him now that John Patrick's brother Derek or Tim's son Samuel could race toward Philadelphia. They would not look approvingly on another kidnapping.

Perhaps the British wouldn't take vengeance on the Carey family for his misdeeds. He wished he could believe that. But he had scars on his back—scars that would never go away—because he had sat in a Scottish tavern minding his own business. And *he* had been innocent of any wrongdoing. He couldn't believe that they would not persecute a family that, knowing or unknowing, had sheltered a man they wanted so badly. He also realized that Annette would never believe that. She didn't want to believe it.

Or perhaps, God help him, he just didn't want to let her go. He knew that if she left him now, he would never have another chance to find that magic that had once flared between them. He was sure to the bottom of his soul it was the kind of enchantment that Ian Sutherland claimed happened only once in a lifetime to the men in their family.

He might never be able to reclaim it, but he wanted a chance to do so. Three weeks at sea. Long enough, he hoped, for her to realize he'd meant her and hers no harm, that he'd just wanted to protect them.

Bloody hell, he wanted her to look at him as she had that last day at her home, the day before she'd discovered who he was. Before he'd become the devil in her eyes.

Tonight, he would make it clear that he did not plan to stay in the barn. 'Twas a clear night, one she might well use to escape. And he would be waiting for her.

He knew what she intended. Annette was sure of it.

Why else would he choose to sleep in the cold barn at night, rather than in the mansion over the hill? Each night, after supper, she stood by her bedroom window and waited for him to go inside the barn.

It was the only time she allowed herself to watch him. She wished her heart didn't thump a little harder every time she saw him. He was limping far less now, and he had a grace of movement that fascinated her. She'd never known anyone who moved with such confidence, such intrinsic pride.

She wished she didn't see these things in him. She wanted to despise him. Yet . . . there was a part of her that reacted in rebellious ways to his presence. He did so many things well. He could tame a horse with his voice and a ship with his touch. He had a smile that could seduce angels. His laughter always seemed to surround her like a warm cloak, and press tight against her heart.

But she had only been a means to an end for him. She had to remember that.

That smile, the warm chuckle, the inherent charm that was so effortless . . . all of them made it imperative that she leave. There was only one place to go: the only home she had now, the only place of safety she'd known recently. Safety behind British lines—a sanctuary from him, and from her own wayward feelings.

Annette finally saw John Patrick stride across the yard to the barn and disappear inside. Minutes later, she was surprised to see him ride away.

Annette looked up at the sky. The moon was bright tonight, the weather cool.

She heard a whining noise and stooped down to pat

This. His canine companion nudged her. She found herself smiling. She would miss these two who had, apparently, adopted her. At night, one would first put one paw on the bed, then hearing no rebuke, would slink up next to her. The other dog would imitate the maneuver until both were happily ensconced deep in the feather mattress.

In truth, she would miss the whole family—except John Patrick—though she was loath to admit it. Warmth and love radiated in the house. She had done her very best to shield herself from it, but both crept into crevices of her heart.

She had to leave. Tonight.

When she reached a magistrate, she would demand the return of her father. She would lay all the blame on John Patrick and none on the other Sutherlands. She was sure now that they would not harm her father, even if she left. She tried not to think about the fact that her father might not want to be reclaimed. The Sutherland charm was insidious.

But Philadelphia was home. He would be pleased to be back there. Just as she would.

Wouldn't she?

Then why did she feel so empty?

She waited for silence, for the sign that the occupants of the house had gone to sleep.

Annette thought she should feel elation, not this terrible emptiness. She would be glad to get home. Back to the Tories she trusted.

These people were nothing like the drunken louts who'd tortured her father and burned their home. *But they sympathized with the American cause. If the colonials won, she and her father would never get their land back. Never.*

And though Ian Sutherland and his wife seemed warm

and welcoming, they were hospitable only to protect
their sons.

*John Patrick lied to you. He used you. He never cared at
all.* All the hurt she'd felt, all the misery and disbelief
welled up in her. She had been existing on anger, but
now she realized her heart had shattered that night, and
in the succeeding days when she'd realized how great a
fool she had been, to believe that a handsome rogue like
John Patrick Sutherland would, could, have any interest
in her.

She had to go home. She had true friends there.

And perhaps love wasn't so important, after all. She'd
always been realistic, but deep in her heart, she'd
yearned for a great love. She'd come to believe there was
no such thing—until the wounded "lieutenant" came to
her home.

She wiped a tear away from her eyes.

The house was quiet now. Annette pulled on her
cloak. She had to leave before John Patrick returned
from whatever errand he was on. She opened the door
quietly. The hall was dark. She went back into her room
and blew out the whale oil lamp next to her bed, then
allowed her eyes to adjust to the darkness. She returned
to the door and peered out again.

She wondered what time it was. Well after midnight,
she guessed. The occupants of the house retired early
and usually rose early.

Her slippers made little sound on the smooth floor.
She pulled the cloak tighter around her as she reached
the door, hesitating only a moment before pulling it
open.

The moon was bright enough to cast a glow over the
fields and pastures. They reminded her of her childhood
home. The sense of isolation deepened. Indecisive, she
stood there for a moment, then hurried to the barn, lift-

ing the heavy bar with some effort. Soft neighs greeted her.

Annette checked the barn thoroughly, just in case she had not seen John Patrick return. But it was empty.

She found a sidesaddle in the tack room, and hurriedly saddled the mare she'd ridden the other day. She was swift enough, and sturdy, as well as easy to control. Then she led the mare outside, found the mounting block, and climbed into the saddle.

Annette hugged the side of the barn, then tried to stay inside the shadows as she walked the mare out onto the road. The nearest city, she knew now, was Chestertown. John Patrick's ship was in the bay, in the opposite direction.

She urged the mare into a trot, and had gone approximately a quarter of a mile when a rider moved out in the middle of the road. John Patrick. Of course, he had read her mind even more clearly than she'd thought. There was no escaping him, not when he rode Shadow Prince.

Panic suddenly overtook her. Why had he allowed her to get this far? Why hadn't he just waited in the barn?

She turned the horse and started racing back the way she came.

She heard him behind her, even imagined she felt the heat of the horse as hoofs pounded against the road. Her mare stretched her legs as fast as she could under Annette's frantic urgings, but even without looking she knew he had reached her, was drawing even with her, and then she saw him lean over and grab the reins from her hands.

Annette tried to knock his hands away, but he was a better rider. She could only sit helplessly as he slowed both horses down to a walk.

"Should I bother to ask where you were going?"

"I would think you could guess," she said, forcing a

coolness she didn't feel. She didn't want him to see her tremble. "To the nearest sheriff. Even rebels have laws."

"I hoped you would enjoy your stay."

She looked at him with as much contempt as she could muster.

"I'm sorry, then," he said after a moment's silence.

Apprehension filled her then. "What do you intend?"

"I cannot let you go back. For your own sake, for your father's sake."

"You are truly mad. You attempt to justify acts that are completely unjustifiable."

In the bright moonlight, she saw a muscle work in his cheek. "Will you not even consider the fact you might endanger yourself?"

"It is *you* who endangered me, you and your brother."

His face was like granite. "I can do nothing to persuade you to stay?"

"I suppose you could threaten the life of my father again."

"I want to protect him, not hurt him."

"You are a liar. You only want to protect your brother."

Something in his eyes hardened. "You give me few choices."

"You give me none."

"I had hoped—"

"That I would enjoy being your prisoner? That I would believe your lies *now*?"

"Your father is content."

"My father is not aware of what is going on. He does not know you are a rebel pirate who used his home and hospitality for your own ends."

He said nothing for a moment, then he started down the road, her reins in hand, forcing her to follow. He drew the two horses to a trot, then a canter, and finally slowed to a walk.

Annette saw his face. It was set, just as it had been the night they left Philadelphia. Set and harsh. She tried to take back her reins, but he just turned and looked at her, and in the moonlight she saw the implacable grimness of his mouth. She gave up rather than seem any more a fool.

He was apparently taking her back to the house. But her heart thundered when he continued past the drive. She opened her mouth to protest, to scream if necessary.

"I wouldn't do that," he said.

"Why?"

"Because then I would have to gag you," he said in a conversational tone, as if it were an everyday chore he had to do.

"You are a bully and a coward."

His lips thinned. He sped the horses into a canter again, so talk was impossible. She could only fume as she held the pommel.

The ride seemed to last all night. Certainly hours. Her fury increased as they rode, as she realized where they were going: to the Chesapeake. To his ship.

The last place on God's earth that she wanted to be.

They finally stopped after hours of hard riding. Annette found herself on the beach. She could see the *Mary Ann* anchored offshore.

The pirate dismounted and, still holding her reins, approached her to help her dismount. She quickly slipped from the saddle by herself. She did not want him to touch her. As he took a step toward her, she backed away, and she saw contrition cross his face. Of course, she had seen it before, but it never seemed to stop him from more and more outrageous acts.

"I will not hurt you," he said. "You must know that."

"You already have," she retorted. And far more than he would ever know. She *wouldn't* let him know.

"You enjoy the sea."

"Not when you are on it."

His mouth turned up in that raffish expression that had once touched her heart. She despised the fact that it still made her pulse jump.

He didn't answer. He busied himself unfastening his saddlebags and removing a whale oil lantern and a tinderbox. After several tries, a spark turned into a tiny flame and he lit the lantern and turned toward the sea, swinging it several times. It annoyed her that he obviously felt no need to keep an eye on her, as if he took her helplessness for granted. She moved toward his stallion.

"I wouldn't do that," he said. "He's hard enough for me to ride."

He had not turned. How did he know that she had taken those few quiet steps? How did he know so much about her?

"What are you planning now?" she finally asked.

"A pleasant voyage to the Caribbean," he said lightly. Yet she felt the strain beneath the cool tone.

"My father . . ."

"He will be safe with my family. He will be told you decided to go with me to check on the house in Philadelphia."

She looked at him with stark horror.

"Does your family know . . . ?"

"Not yet," he said, his jaw setting. "This was my idea."

"You cannot take me away from my father. He needs me."

"He needs my father and my mother and Fortune," he said abruptly. "They can help him as you have not been able to."

She turned then, and hit him with everything she had in her. Her anger turned into a kind of fury she'd never felt before, not even when her father was being tarred and feathered. She heard the loud crack of her hand against his cheek, saw his face jerk with the impact. Then she turned and started running toward his horse. She was sure she could ride him . . .

But she felt John Patrick's hand on her shoulder and then she was falling, bringing him down with her in the sand.

She was totally aware of his body against hers, his face inches away. She felt his breath, heard the beat of his heart. She also felt his muscles tense, change, and her own grow hot and tingling. His gaze bored into her, and then his lips touched hers. They were incredibly tender, barely touching yet caressing. She tried to pull away from him, but there was no place to go.

He ran his hand along her cheek, his callused fingers rough yet somehow so very gentle. She swallowed, trying to catch the breath that was suddenly caught deep in her throat. Her body felt as if it had a will of its own, and she felt it moving just slightly, craving the feel of his. She forced herself to look into his eyes to see the lies there, but the darkness made it impossible to see anything. Yet his hands, his fingers, his lips . . .

No! With a great effort, she pushed against him, and he moved slowly away from her, his hand taking hers and bringing her up with him with such ease that she felt as light as a feather. He looked at her for a moment. "I'm sorry, Annette. I should not have done that."

Her body was so tense, so expectant, so—ready for something, that she was momentarily bewildered by it. She tried to summon back her anger, but somehow it had faded, replaced by a need and wanting so primitive and strong that she couldn't even speak. She looked at her hand still locked in his. His warmth burned her, then seemed to invade her body, moving like hot molasses through her blood.

She jerked away. Turned from him to stare into the scraggly trees that sat beyond the shoreline. How far to safety? How far to peace? But even as she wondered, she also questioned whether she could ever be happy again with what she had believed was, if not joyous, at least a contented way of life.

John Gunn, the pirate, had brought her to life, had turned her inside out, had given her a glimpse of real joy.

And she could trust neither it nor him.

"Come," he said softly, offering his hand.

She shook her head and knew she must look like a stubborn child.

"You will love the Caribbean. The emerald-and-turquoise seas, the warm sun, the feel of sand under your feet."

His voice was like music, like those sirens in the legend of Odysseus, as he held out a world to her, one that she had dreamt of before.

Still, she retreated to a coward's reasoning. "I would be ruined," she said.

He grinned suddenly. "Do you really care?"

When she looked at his reckless eyes, the defiant lift of his chin, she wondered. She wondered what it would be like to roam the oceans and visit exotic ports and feel the wind in her hair and run barefoot over sand.

Immediately, she stomped on the idea.

But she knew by the glint in his eyes, made silvery by the glow of the moon, that he had noted her moment's hesitation. Or maybe she had a gleam in her own eyes.

"Yes," she said, daring him to disagree. "I care. And I care about my father. I cannot leave him."

"Then," he said in a level voice, "give me your word you will not betray me."

"Betray you? There is nothing between us to betray."

His hand went to her face again, his fingers touching it, running up and down her cheekbones. "Is there not?"

The siren's song again. Smooth. Calculating. Manipulating.

"Never," she said as she turned around.

"You didn't answer me," he insisted, suddenly intense. The teasing note was gone. "If I allow you to go back, will you agree to stay with my family?"

"*Allow* me to go back?"

"Yes," he said, the silkiness gone from his voice. He was all seriousness now. "If you wish so badly to stay here, I need only your word."

"Someone without honor believes in the honor of others?"

His eyes narrowed. "Aye, Miss Carey. I do. And remember, I promised no harm would come to your father, and none has."

She bit her lip. "Damn you," she whispered.

"Your word," he pressed.

But she couldn't give it. And, God help her, she wondered whether it was principle that made her unable to utter the words, or . . .

No!

No, it *was* principle. She heard the sound of oars slapping at the water, the soft murmur of careful voices, and she looked back out toward the bay. A longboat was approaching.

"Miss Carey?"

A lump kept her from speaking as two men splashed in and pulled up the boat. One ran to the pirate.

"We are ready to sail."

John Patrick went over to his saddlebags and took out two letters. "Can you ride, Dan'l?"

"Aye."

"Well?"

The sailor looked at the mare and the stallion. The mare was standing calmly. The stallion was pawing the ground impatiently. "Her, yes."

"Then you can send someone back for the stallion," the pirate said. "Take the mare down the road about ten miles until you reach a two-story white frame house along the road. Give these letters to my father, Ian Sutherland, and tell him where to find the stallion. He will give you another horse, and directions to Chestertown. We will meet you there tomorrow afternoon while we take in supplies. Do you understand all that?"

The man nodded eagerly, basking in John Patrick's grin of approval, Annette noted with disgust.

John Patrick tied the reins of the stallion firmly to a tree, then his gaze returned to her.

"Willingly or unwillingly?" he asked.

"Never willingly," she said.

"Good," he retorted and picked her up as if she were a child. He carried her to the boat, and out onto the sea.

Chapter 17

Katy dressed carefully. She had met a British officer at Ethan Taylor's store, and had accepted his invitation to a soiree at the City Tavern.

Noel would be there. She knew he would. And she planned to tweak his nose. She had not missed the strain in him that day she had visited, and she felt sure she could persuade him—or drive him—to leave Philadelphia.

She had expected him to call on her before now. But he had not. So she decided to force matters when a Major Gambrell had asked to call on her, then to accompany her to General Howe's newest hospitality. The British leader was milking the city dry with his frivolities, even while Washington's army starved a few miles away. It was galling beyond acceptance—especially the fact that Noel was a part of it.

She had to get him back home to Maryland. When the Americans won this war, there would no longer be a place for Tory sympathizers. Why did he not understand that?

She had always thought Noel apolitical. He usually cared only for family, medicine, and animals, and she was never quite sure where the last two placed in importance. Family had always been everything. She simply couldn't understand why he had now placed politics above it.

Katy looked at her reflection. Her figure was fuller now than when she was a girl, but not much. She was almost forty now, and she felt the weight of those years.

She'd had no children with her husband, and she doubted whether she ever would. That, and Noel, were the sorrows of her life. She pinched her cheeks to bring some color to them, but her eyes needed no help. Just the thought of Noel made them glow.

She expected him to give her that solemn, measuring look when she appeared on the arm of one of Howe's officers, but she hoped she would startle him into a much greater response.

Ethan's wife, Sarah, had assisted her with her hair, pulling curls to the back, fastening them with combs in a sleek twist. Katy looked at herself critically. Her chin was too prominent, her mouth too wide, for beauty. But it was a face she'd learned to live with, and she seldom wasted time on things that could not be changed.

She would, however, spend a lifetime rectifying the one thing she thought she could—hoped she could—change. Noel had left Maryland because of her, and she would now do whatever was necessary to bring him back.

Sarah Taylor knew exactly what Katy intended. Katy had told her when she first arrived that she was in Philadelphia to lure Noel back home, and if she had to use the British to do it, then so be it. Sarah had not exactly been happy about the thought. Her sympathies were strongly pro-American, and she disliked having a British officer in her home socially. But hers was a love match, and she'd long known that Katy loved Noel Marsh.

For Katy, Sarah Taylor would hold her tongue.

"You look lovely," she said.

"Do you think Noel . . . ?"

"I think Dr. Marsh will be captivated."

"You haven't heard anything about him and—other ladies?"

Sarah shook her head. "No, but then we no longer move in the same circles."

Kate's cheeks flushed. She didn't mean to let anyone know her fears, her most secret feelings. She didn't want to admit that she'd expected him to sweep her into his arms. She'd never anticipated the cool greeting, the uncompromising refusal to return, the lack of explanation about his Tory sympathies. Even worse was the fact that he had not tried to see her again. That had hurt the most.

She'd sat in this house for a week, every day expecting a call that did not come. *"That's the nature of women . . . not to love when we love them, and to love when we love them not."* Well, he'd warned her. But then he'd touched her with such longing that she'd disregarded it.

Had she so mistaken him?

She heard the knock at the door, then Ethan's booming voice as he greeted the major. She looked at Sarah and swallowed hard. She had not been out with a man since her husband's death, and now she was being escorted by a soldier in the army that killed him. Was she a complete fool?

Major Gambrell had no knowledge of how her husband had died. He knew only that she was a widow. It had been easy enough to avoid questions. She simply allowed her eyes to fill with tears at the mention of him, and profuse apologies followed.

"Are you sure about this?" Sarah asked. "We can tell him you were taken ill."

Katy straightened her back. "I am very sure."

Sarah reluctantly handed her her green velvet cloak. "I expect Major Gambrell is a gentleman."

"If there is such a thing in the British army," Katy said softly.

Sarah looked at her worriedly. "You will not say anything unwise?"

"I will be the very soul of discretion," Katy promised, before heading for the stairs.

She saw the British officer, dressed splendidly with braid and decorations, look up, smiling with appreciation as she descended. He took several steps toward her, and held out his hand to take her arm. "You look lovely. I will be the envy of every man there tonight."

Hopefully one, anyway.

She gave him a smile that she hoped was only mildly encouraging. Surely, he must suspect that since she was staying with the Taylors she had some patriot sympathies. But he had not asked, and she had no intention of bringing it up.

A short time later, they entered the ballroom of the City Tavern, the same one where a similar event had been held some ten days earlier, while the Star Rider made off with the king's property. The thought made her smile, and her escort returned it. For a moment, she felt regret for deceiving him. She wondered whether Jonny had felt the same way when he'd stayed at the Careys' home. As children, each of them had been carefully instructed to respect individuals, regardless of their background, loyalties, or religion.

Did that include the plundering British?

Katy saw Noel the moment she entered. He was among the tallest men present, and his tawny hair immediately caught her gaze.

He saw her, too. His eyes narrowed slightly even as he continued to talk with a man who could be none other than General Howe himself, by the braid and decorations on his uniform. A handsome man, he was talking with animation, and his gaze followed Noel's, whose eyes widened when they saw her. He said something to Noel, who turned suddenly, and both men started toward her.

Katy's heart started to pound as they made their way through the crowd. She could tell nothing from Noel's eyes, not welcome or censure or the hoped-for jealousy.

Then they were in front of her, the general obviously waiting for an introduction.

Major Gambrell and Noel started at the same time. "General—"

Noel stepped back and allowed the major to do the honors.

"General, I have the pleasure to introduce Mrs. Katherine Cantrell. Mrs. Cantrell, General William Howe."

General Howe bowed. "Mrs. . . . ?"

"I am a widow, General Howe."

"And a relative, I understand, of our Dr. Marsh."

She met Noel's gaze for a moment. His hazel eyes were flat, impersonal.

"He is my nephew."

"Yes, he said that, but I would not believe it. *I* never had a such a lovely aunt."

She acknowledged the compliment with a sweep of her fan. "Thank you, General."

"You have just arrived in Philadelphia?"

She nodded.

"From Maryland, I understand."

"Yes, General."

He smiled. "I hope you will honor me with a dance later tonight."

"It would be my pleasure," she said, wondering how she could bear his touch. Perhaps she would have the vapors after all.

Her eyes met Noel's as the general left them to greet new arrivals. She saw a flicker of something there. "Would you mind if I had a word with my aunt?" he asked her escort. "Family business."

Major Gambrell agreed immediately. "Of course, Marsh. If that is agreeable with Mrs. Cantrell?"

She nodded, her speech suddenly buried in her throat. Noel took her by her elbow and steered her through the door, through the hall, and into an empty room. Then he turned on her. "What are you doing, Katy?"

His voice was low, angry. His eyes glittered in a way she'd never seen before.

She lifted her chin. "I am no longer in mourning. I have a right to enjoy an evening."

His fingers tightened around her arm. "With an officer in an army you hate?"

"Hate is a strong word."

"I want you to go home."

"Not without you."

"Is that what this is all about?" he asked. "Do you not know that Gambrell is a dangerous man?"

"He has been very courteous."

"He is married, Katy."

She felt herself pale. She had not known that. She suspected Sarah did not, either, or she would never have tacitly approved of Katy's accompanying him. "He is only an escort," she said defensively.

"He has a reputation as a womanizer."

"You seem to know him well," she said, a bite in her voice.

"I know him very well," Noel said mildly. "We frequently play cards."

Her gaze met his, and she saw his eyes soften, the corner of his lips turn up in a half-smile. "You do look lovely, Katy."

"I thought . . . you would visit me."

"I couldn't go to the Taylor home," he said abruptly. "They are known sympathizers to the American cause."

"Major Gambrell did not hesitate to call on me there."

"He can go where he wishes, and see who he wishes. His loyalty is not questioned."

"Yours is?"

"Since Jonny's escape, every citizen of Philadelphia

has been under a cloud. I just hope to God they do not learn who he really is—or you will be in as much danger as I am."

A chill suddenly ran through her, but she lifted her chin. "I will not leave until you do."

"Even if you condemn us both by doing so?"

"They are *your* friends."

"Aye, they are," he said. "But trust goes only so far, and if they suspect I might have helped Jonny, they will exact their justice."

Outraged, she stared at him. "Do you think I would say anything?"

"Not on purpose. Go home," he said wearily. "Go back to Maryland. What about your husband's estate?"

"I have a very fine manager."

He gave her a steady look. "Please, Katy."

"Not without you," she said stubbornly.

"I told you before, Katy, I cannot leave my practice. I am needed here."

She felt tears gather behind her eyes. "You will risk your life?"

"There would be far less risk if you leave."

His eyes were begging her. In all the years they had known each other, he had never done that before. They had teased and loved and argued. They had never begged.

A knock came at the door. "Mrs. Cantrell?"

"It's Major Gambrell," she said.

His gaze held her. "Will you go home?"

She was not going to surrender that easily. "I'll talk to you about it tomorrow."

"I'll fetch you at two."

"What about your reluctance to come to the Taylor home?"

He gave her a level stare. "The damage is done. Gambrell and Howe know about our relationship now. Let us hope they don't explore it any further."

Her heart sinking, Katy wished she had never accepted the major's invitation. She would never forgive herself if she put Noel in danger—all for a silly childhood dream.

Noel walked to the door. "Be careful with Gambrell," he said softly.

"I am very good at taking care of myself."

"Are you?"

She hated the doubt in his voice.

But he was already leaving her. "Thank you, Roger, for so generously sharing my aunt with me," he said.

Katy didn't miss the curious look Gambrell gave her. Perhaps he wondered if Noel had told her the detail Gambrell had so conveniently forgotten: his marriage.

"Good night, Noel," she said with as light a tone as she could manage.

"Good night, Aunt Katherine."

She flinched even as she accepted Major Gambrell's arm. "I believe you mentioned a dance," she said, sweeping by Noel and out into the room full of British soldiers.

Noel debated whether to fetch Katy on his own, or send Malcomb. He finally, reluctantly, decided to go alone, although he did not want to be alone with her. He'd used up all his willpower the day she'd appeared at his house. He'd wanted to take her in his arms. He'd wanted to kiss her and hold her. He'd wanted more.

Seeing her last night had been just as difficult, especially on Gambrell's arm. He'd never liked the major, and he knew the man's reputation with women.

She'd looked so pretty, so incredibly irresistible. He'd wanted to grab her and take her home. Which would have destroyed him.

He hesitated, then knocked on the Taylors' door, surprised when it opened quickly to reveal Katy.

He couldn't help smiling. Suddenly, he found himself weak in the knees. This wasn't going according to plan. "You arrived home safely."

"I think you know that," she said. "I saw a glimpse of Malcomb following us from the City Tavern."

"I'll have to speak to him about that."

"Roger Gambrell was a perfect gentleman."

"Did he ask to call on you again?"

"Yes, but I said I was uncertain about my plans."

He looked around. "Where are the Taylors?"

"They are both at the store."

He offered her his hand as they moved toward the phaeton and he helped her up into the seat. Her gloved hand was warm, and he smelled the rich, full scent of roses as he swung up beside her.

He remembered riding with her across the fields, her dark hair flowing like a mane behind her as she raced him. He usually slowed just a little, not because he wanted her to win, but because he loved watching her and enjoyed her intense competitive spirit.

Dear God, how he loved her. How he had always loved her.

His wife had been different, more of a temper like his, and theirs had been a pleasant if not passionate relationship. She'd been a Quaker, hesitant and reluctant about the intimate part of marriage. Like him, she'd loved books. She could sit for hours and work on a tapestry or on some other piece of needlework. Katy had always detested such sedentary activities.

Noel still saw his wife's family. Several of them had been exiled from Philadelphia by the American government, and just recently returned now that the British army occupied the city. The Philadelphia Quakers, particularly Noel's father-in-law, had been outspoken in their opposition to the separation of the colonies from Britain, and they had suffered for it.

Noel had hated that intolerance.

"Noel." Katy's soft voice stirred him to action, and he snapped the reins of the horse. Somehow he had to convince her to leave. He just wasn't quite sure how to do it.

In minutes, they'd arrived at his town house, and he helped Katy down while Malcomb saw to the horses.

He took her arm and led her inside the house, where they were immediately met by an ecstatic Aristotle.

Noel watched as she leaned down and rubbed the animal behind his left ear as Aristotle wriggled with pure happiness. "You've made yet another conquest."

"I take it you approve of this one slightly more than Major Gambrell."

"A little," he said equably. "Would you like a glass of claret?"

"Yes."

He went to the sideboard and returned with a goblet of claret for her and one of brandy for himself.

He purposely sat in a chair some distance from the one she'd taken. But she moved over and sat on the side of the chair. "You are too far away."

The air warmed, hummed. He felt his body tensing. He stood and strode to the other end of the room, leaning against the marble fireplace.

She didn't move this time, and he knew she would not. She had come to him and he had walked away. All he had to do was return to the chair and hold out his hand. He had only to smile.

And his shaky foundation would come crumbling down.

If he touched her, he knew he would never let her go again.

He took a sip of the brandy, letting it swish around in

his mouth. But when he looked at Katy, he almost choked on it.

Aristotle was trying to crawl up into her lap, all five stone of him, and she was made almost invisible by the half that had succeeded in his impossible mission. She was laughing, her eyes sparkling and warm with affection. She was simply the most beguiling sight he'd ever seen.

"Aristotle."

The dog looked around at him with huge soulful eyes.

"Aristotle," he said again in a little more authoritative tone, and the dog started slipping back to the floor, one reluctant leg after another.

"It's all right," she said.

"He'll suffocate you."

"I think not. And I appreciate the warmth of his greeting."

Her eyes were laughing at him and, heaven help him, he could do nothing else but take the several steps to her side.

He reached down to her. She took his hand, and he lifted her to face him. The laughter in her eyes died slowly.

The magic that had always been there between the two of them exploded with the longing both had held in check for nearly twenty years. He felt a muscle throbbing in his jaw as he fought against taking her into his arms.

But like two lodestones, they moved together anyway, and he surrendered to overwhelming need and opened his arms. She fell into them and lifted her head so his lips could meet hers. Their breath mingled, the sound of their heartbeats melding.

"Katy," he whispered roughly. Then his lips sought hers, first with infinite tenderness but then proceeding to something stronger, more demanding, his tongue urging her lips to open to him. As they did, his tongue explored her mouth, playing and teasing and arousing.

Katy's blood turned to warm honey, slow and languorous, and she responded to his every touch, his every caress. She had been waiting for this all her life, and now she felt, at last, she was coming home.

And what a home it was. The body she inhabited was no longer hers. New sensations were tumbling over each other: the overwhelming hunger, the excruciating tingling that ran from her neck to her toes. Their differences dissolved in their fierce need for each other, in her yearning to touch and be touched. He was her hero, her love. Her life.

She had wasted so much of her life because of one impulsive act. She intended to waste no more.

She wanted only to feel now, not to think, because she would go quite mad thinking about what might have been. His lips left her, and for a moment, their eyes met. Her hand reached up, tracing the weary lines in his face, touching the edges of those kind hazel eyes that were now roiling with emotion. His breath quickened and their bodies moved closer, hers pressing against his, feeling every change in his body. Her own responded to a deep hunger inside, an incessant craving that she'd never sated.

"Katy," he said again, his mouth caressing the word just as his lips had caressed her mouth a moment earlier. "This is not wise."

"I don't care about being wise," she said brokenly. "I've waited for you all my life."

His gaze seemed to sear through to her heart. "It does not matter that I am a Tory?"

"I don't care if you are the devil," she whispered. And she did not. He was Noel, and that was all she needed to know.

As his hands started to unlace the ribbons holding her

dress together, she thought it the most natural thing in the world. Then his hands stopped.

"I think we should go upstairs," he said.

"I think that is a fine idea," she replied, one hand holding her bodice together, the other locked tightly in his.

"I love you, Katy," he said, later. Wonder edged his voice, but something else, too. Something that sent a shiver through her.

She tried to smile, but she managed only a tremulous charade of one. She loved him so much, had for so long. Now she feared it, feared the next few moments.

Katy wanted to postpone them. She lifted her head to kiss him, her lips meeting his in her own proclamation of love. Their lips melded, some of the need gone, but none of the desperation that had colored and intensified their coupling.

Noel finally leaned back, sitting on the side of the bed, his hand clasping hers so tightly she felt he would never let her go. Yet the expression on his face, the worried, almost haggard look, frightened her.

"Oh, Katy. I did not want this to happen. Not now."

She sat up, indifferent to her nakedness. "But why? We can go home now and—"

"*You* will go home," he said. "If you truly care for me, you will go home."

She stared at the pain in his eyes, and she felt it streak through her, tearing the joy she'd just felt into small, ragged pieces. Yet somehow the last few moments had changed her. He would not have asked this of her, were it not vital to him. She had been a fool ever to think otherwise.

And what was important to him was important to her. She had made that commitment to him now.

"Yes," she said simply. "I'll wait for you there."

His smile was heartbreaking. Grateful, sad, regretful. He was so handsome, so true to those who loved him, to the principles in which he believed. If they were not hers, well, then she had to know that he had his own reasons, and they were noble ones.

He leaned over and kissed her. Passion edged it, but love, pure and sweet and tender, touched her and made her whole.

Not to disagree with poor Don Quixote, but the nature of this woman had changed. She was to love when she was loved.

Roger Gambrell sat in his carriage and stared at the two-story brick house.

He had gone to call on Mrs. Cantrell when he saw a phaeton stop before the Taylor home. Curious, he had waited and watched as Dr. Marsh descended, rang the bell, and returned to the carriage with the mysterious Katherine Cantrell.

As far as he knew, it was the first time he'd ever seen Dr. Marsh with a woman. He had often invited the doctor to events and extended the invitation to a woman of his guest's choice, but the doctor had always come alone.

Of course, Mrs. Cantrell was a relative. Still, Roger had felt the heat between the two. He'd felt as though he was standing amidst a storm when they stood together, although their expressions had both been reserved.

It had irritated him. He'd always had luck with women, and he knew he was considered handsome. Yet he saw nothing at all in Mrs. Cantrell's eyes when he tried gazing hopefully into them. He'd been stunned, then, to feel the sizzling heat between the doctor and his . . . aunt.

He'd started wondering then. The Taylors were known to have rebel sympathies, though they were tolerated as long as they made no overt comments. Then his mind took another leap. The jailer at the Walnut Street Prison had said the leader of the rebels who took his men from jail had a limp.

It was assumed now that the man was the Star Rider. If he had a limp, it meant he probably had been injured in the sinking of his ship. It also meant he must have had a doctor.

Dr. Marsh had said little about his family. Only that they lived in Maryland and that there had been a family split when he'd sided with the British. No one had suspected his loyalties, because he had been married to a Quaker, and most of the Quakers had been loyal to the Crown. His in-laws certainly had been, and he'd continued to call on many of the Quakers as well as on the British military. He had even been imprisoned by the rebels for his defense of royalists.

Still . . .

Roger decided that he might look a little further into the backgrounds of Mrs. Cantrell and Dr. Marsh.

He stayed in place for another hour, becoming more disgruntled by the moment. Then he snapped his reins.

He was damned if he would sit in front of some house like a lovesick schoolboy.

Chapter 18

Annette stood against the railing and watched the land disappear. The *Mary Ann* had anchored briefly in Chestertown to pick up a few members of the crew, add some new ones, and take on supplies.

She'd schemed to escape when they'd anchored, but she'd been locked helplessly in her cabin as she heard crew members load boxes and crates. Enough, she thought bitterly, to sail for a year rather than the three weeks she was told it would take to reach the French island of Martinique.

She'd thought about screaming, but the crew members obviously belonged to John Patrick heart and soul. Flirting had availed her little. Of course, she had never been adept at batting her eyelashes.

She didn't even have any clothes, other than the dress she'd worn when the pirate stole her away for the second time. It was already stiff with salt spray. Her hair was no better, and she felt the wind burn on her cheeks; she winced when she thought how red they must be. No wonder he scarcely seemed to notice her. In the three days aboard, he'd been polite and little more. He'd given her the captain's cabin, made sure she was fed on a regular basis, and otherwise ignored her.

That made her even angrier than her abduction had. Her *second* abduction. It was becoming a very disagreeable habit.

She tucked her cloak around her. The wind was cold,

freezing in truth, but she preferred it to the stuffiness of the cabin, spacious as it was.

The last of the land dissolved into the sea, and the sea seemed to merge with the sky. The ship, under full sail, appeared to rush across the waves, in a hurry for softer waters and warmer climates. At least, that was what the pirate had said this morning when he had knocked at her cabin and asked whether she wished to watch their departure from Maryland.

He'd been right. She had wanted to see everything. She knew she should feel regret and sadness, but instead she'd been seized by a very unfortunate exhilaration, and she suspected John Patrick Sutherland had sensed it. The Caribbean. The sound of the name alone sent thrills through her. Golden shores. Water the color of precious stones. A sun so brilliant it sprinkled the sea with diamonds. She'd read all those descriptions, and she'd often wished to see whether they could be true.

But not this way, not as a captive mouse being toyed with by a whimsical yet destructive cat.

At least she felt that her father was in good hands. It was her own self for whom she harbored fears.

She looked toward the wheel. Ivy was handling it with deft competence, though not the grace of his captain. She wondered if John Patrick was finally resting. He never seemed to need sleep. And, in any event, why should she care? He was a blackguard.

A chill crept into her cloak and she decided to head down to her cabin, though there was little to do there. The English captain had evidently had no use for books. She'd been reduced to studying charts she really didn't understand.

She opened the door to the cabin and went inside. A wrapped pile of packages lay on the bed. They had not been there when she left. She stared at them for a moment. They had undoubtedly come from the pirate, who had gone ashore yesterday morning. He must have put them in her room while she was on deck. He obviously hadn't wanted to give her a chance to refuse them.

Gifts. Remember the Trojan horse, she warned herself. Yet she found herself taking one step, then another in their direction. She should toss them out the door without giving him the satisfaction of her having opened them.

But she sat down on the bed and tentatively touched one. She knew immediately by the feel that it must be a dress. What was his taste?

No. She would wear this dress. Her own dress. Even if it fell apart.

Yet, her hand played with a string that held it together. Then she pushed the string to one side. Her father used to tell her that pride goeth before a fall. She did need some clothes, and it was the pirate's fault that she had none.

Her fingers slid the wrapping away and felt the soft cotton cloth, much more sensible than silk, but still, she knew, expensive. It was a soft blue-gray, trimmed with fine lace, and she thought it exquisite. She wondered how he had found it. Such dresses were usually made only by dressmakers, after extensive fittings. She would have to ask—

No, she wouldn't. She did not plan to ask him anything.

But still, her fingers untied the next package. This time, she found a wool dress the color of fine brandy. It had a high neck and long sleeves, and looked warm and comfortable.

A third package revealed a brush and combs, two pairs of worsted hose, two pairs of thread hose, two pairs of Spanish shoes, a pair of gloves, a petticoat and chemise. The latter made her blush but not as much as the white linen nightgown she discovered next. The bottom package included new books: *The Tempest* by William Shakespeare, and a book of poetry by Thomas Gray. Tucked among them was a very used copy of Daniel Defoe's *Robinson Crusoe*.

Her heart softened for a moment. He had thought of everything, and she saw him in her mind's eye going from dressmaker's shop to dressmaker's shop, probably paying a fortune for a dress meant for another woman.

She undid the ties on her own gown and tried on the wool dress. It was a little loose in the waist, a little tight in the bust. He had found garments that laced in front, which meant she needed no assistance.

He knew about clothes. He knew about women. He knew a great deal about sizing them both up. How many women had been in his past? She winced at the thought. She was probably plainer than any of them. More unworldly. His gifts spoke for themselves. He believed her a bluestocking.

Yet she couldn't stop touching the material. She'd never had a prettier day dress.

She tried on the other, and again it fit adequately, though not perfectly. She wondered whether there was a needle and thread aboard, and then realized they would of course be needed for the sails. Perhaps she could borrow . . .

Annette realized that, in her mind, she had already decided to keep the gifts. The pirate's scheme had worked. She would have thrown them back at him if he had given them to her in person, but now—

How did he know her so well?

John Patrick hesitated before the door of the captain's cabin. He had thought about sending someone to deliver his invitation to supper, but that was the coward's way out. He needed to know how difficult his courtship was going to be.

He rapped several times on the door.

After several moments, it opened.

Annette Carey was still wearing the dress she wore the night he kidnapped her. He had hoped against hope that she might be wearing one of the dresses he'd combed through Chestertown for.

He felt like a tongue-tied lad as he saw the frown on her pretty face. He looked down at her hands and saw she was holding the older book. He tried a grin. "That is our family's favorite book."

She looked down at it again. "Why would you give me a family treasure?"

"I thought . . . I was afraid you might find time on your hands, and I thought my family would approve."

"As they approved of your treatment of me."

"I do not believe they approve of that at all." He stood against the door. He was a supplicant now, and he realized it. He did not want to sail all the way to the Caribbean and back with a woman who, at best, detested him.

"But that did not stop you."

"There are reasons—"

"I know your reasons. I do not accept them."

"Will you let me convince you?"

"Why?" she said acidly.

He saw her swallow hard, and for a moment, he thought she might close the door on him.

"I hoped you would share supper with me," he said cautiously.

She opened the door a little wider, wide enough for him to see that she'd opened his array of carefully selected packages, as she seemed to consider his offer. Her hair was still windblown and she'd simply tied it back with a ribbon, but any number of curling tendrils had escaped to frame her face.

Bloody hell, but he wanted her in his arms. He

wanted to erase that doubt from her eyes, that suspi- cion—hell, the damnable accusation—that never went away when he was with her.

He had never been unsure with women before. He had been popular with women prior to his impressment, but since then he'd had little opportunity to be with "respectable ladies." He'd never had to pay for the women he met at seaports, but they had always been the "one-night" kind, women who made their way through the favors of men. He was bloody well used to taking and saying good-bye.

He didn't seem able to do either with the estimable Miss Carey.

Damn, but that long, searching look nearly undid him. "Where?" she finally asked.

Where? He hadn't even thought about where. In fact, he'd been certain she would turn down his offer.

"Your cabin?"

She gave him a cold look.

"Mine?"

A colder look.

The wardroom would usually serve, but extra stores had been piled high there, and the entire crew was using the reduced space already.

"I am running out of places."

"Where does your crew eat?"

"In their quarters, and believe me, you do not want to visit there."

"On the deck, then," she said.

He hesitated. All he needed was to be seen picnicking on the deck. He knew he would hear the tales of it for- ever. Her gaze held his.

He wondered whether she knew what she was asking of him. He saw the answer from the gleam in her eyes.

"A brilliant solution," he said.

"I think so," she replied.

"It might be a trifle cold."

"I've been cold before."

"At six, then?" he asked.

She nodded and closed the door.

Why did she do that?

She should have just said no.

Yet the word just wouldn't move from her mind to her mouth. It appeared to have detoured through her heart and crashed there.

John Patrick Sutherland had stood at the door with such humility that she'd almost broken into a smile. Humility did not fit him. She was used to the arrogant, confident, ruthless pirate.

Humility struck a chord in her that arrogance never could.

And, to tell the truth, she was tired of being alone. She wanted to be on deck. She wanted to enjoy the wind and the sea. She wanted to know more about the pirate.

He was not like the other members of his family. He could quote literary passages with them; he laughed with them; and she felt his affection for the others. But something had set him apart, and she wanted to know what it was.

Perhaps if she knew, she could better convince him to let her go home.

Of course, he affected her in such astoundingly physical ways that she prayed she would not be the one who was convinced of something.

She debated donning one of his gifts, but finally decided not to give him that satisfaction. Wrinkly, disheveled as she was, she preferred that to submitting to his whims.

Still, she would brush her hair and try to put it into some semblance of order, even though she knew the wind would soon change that. She could cover it with the hood of her cape, but she enjoyed the feel of wind blowing through it too much.

A picnic on a sailing ship headed for exotic ports. A year ago, she could never have imagined such a thing. Even a few months ago, she had been resigned to being a spinster. Now she had more adventure than she knew how to cope with. And she truly hated that small wriggle of excitement that wouldn't quite go away.

His crew was fascinated. John Patrick found them smirking already as he ordered a table and chairs on deck, then gave Ivy the wheel while he supervised the preparation of a feast. Tongues wagged, but quieted when he neared.

His reputation as a ruthless pirate was in dire jeopardy.

But he owed his captive what little pleasures he could offer.

He prayed that the rain would hold off. Clouds dotted the sky and were already changing in color, from billowy white to an ominous purple. The wind was growing stronger, the rhythm of the ship's path through the sea more erratic.

He hoped she would wear the wool gown, both because of its warmth and the indication that her reserve was melting. But he knew she needed time. She needed to learn to trust him.

Minutes before sunset, he was satisfied that everything was ready, and he went down to her cabin and knocked. He tried not to show his disappointment when he saw she still wore the same dress. She held her cloak in her hands.

He bowed in a courtly manner. "I thought you might enjoy the sunset."

A light jumped into her eyes, but was quickly quenched. "Yes, I would."

"You need not disappear every time I go on deck."

She did not say anything. He would rather have had accusations than the deadly silence.

But he took the cloak from her hands and assisted her in putting it on, then opened the door wider so she could precede him. He wanted to take her hand but resisted. He knew she would pull away.

He followed behind until they reached the hatchway, then he drew adjacent to her. He wanted to see her reaction. She stopped, and he saw her gaze move to a table and two chairs, neatly tied to the deck. The table wore a cover that looked like part of a sail, but it was festooned with fancy red napkins, also tied cunningly in place against an increasingly blustery wind.

Yet what was so completely incongruous was that the table was located between two very large cannon. John Patrick saw Annette's gaze move from the cannon to the table and back to the cannon. Then she looked at him, dismay in her eyes.

"It was the best place," he explained, even while he realized that any location would be near cannon except for the small area near the wheel, and the wind made that position impossible.

"Do you ever get used to war?" she asked.

He had no answer. He had known little else for a very long time. As an impressed sailor, he'd first fought the Barbary pirates, then the Caribbean pirates, and finally he had waged his private war against the British.

"Or destruction?" she added softly.

" 'Twas the British who taught me all about destruction," he said.

"How?"

"Do you really want to know, Miss Carey? It is not a pleasant story, and I wanted this to be a pleasant evening."

Annette turned her face toward the setting sun, and

he watched her reaction to it. The lower portion of the sky, the part below the clouds, was a vivid bloodred and colored the sea beneath it. Above, the clouds diffused the color, turning the horizon into gentler shades of coral and orange and pink. Violence and peace appeared to divide the sky.

He felt her shiver and her body angle toward his to escape the wind. He'd worn his own cloak and he drew it around her, drawing her into his arms, shielding her from the gusts of wind that filled the sails and blew up mists of sea.

"Would you rather we go back down?" he said.

Her eyes were still fixed on the sunset. "I have never seen one like it before," she said.

"You will see many of them at sea."

She stood motionless, partially in his arms. He summoned every ounce of self-control to keep from pulling her closer. Still, he felt her body against his, felt himself responding to it. She shivered, and he felt that, too.

"Perhaps we should go inside," he said again.

She turned and stared up at him. "And waste all the effort your men put forth?" she said, gesturing toward the sailors who had artfully tied everything down.

"They consider it a privilege."

He was surprised to see her eyes dance with merriment. "To serve you or me, Captain?"

He was immeasurably pleased at being upgraded from pirate to captain. "You, of course. They seldom have such a lovely lady on board."

"I do not need flattery."

His hand took her chin and forced it up until she looked straight at him. "I have never been good at flattery, Miss Annette."

"Nor the truth," she retorted.

He ignored the gibe, though it hurt. He wondered whether she would ever be able to relax with him again.

She was already moving away from him toward the table.

She was game. She always had been, ever since he had first met her.

His family had liked her tremendously, despite her often reserved—and sometimes hostile—attitude toward them. She had backbone, his father said. She had sense and courage, his mother said. High praise, indeed, from them both.

But even if they had not approved, he knew he would court her. Despite her British sympathies, he'd known, from the first moment she'd so gently tended his wounds, that she was the woman he wanted. Forever. The knowledge had danced around in his heart, though for a long time he'd refused to acknowledge it. Any doubts had been dispelled that day she had stood on the deck of his ship, trying desperately not to enjoy the rhythm of the sea, but betraying herself by the wonder in her eyes. There was so much she hadn't yet learned about herself, and he wanted to help her discover every facet.

He was learning there was much he didn't know about himself, either. He'd been startled by how much he wanted to share that marvelous sense of peace she carried within her. *Do you ever get used to war? To destruction?*

Perhaps he had. For the first time, he realized exactly how frightening that possibility was.

He helped her into a chair, then took the other. One of the sailors disappeared down the hatchway, only to reappear moments later with a tray of food. He set it down on the table with a triumphant flourish. "Beasley made this special for you, ma'am."

Annette's face creased into a spontaneous smile, and John Patrick felt his heart explode with longing. He wanted her to look at him that way. He wondered whether she ever would, whether he could ever overcome their ruinous beginning.

"Thank you," she said softly as he revealed a burnt chicken, overly crusty bread, and beans that had been cooked into mush. Then a platter of fruit—strawberries and sliced apples and oranges—was presented to her.

For the first time, he wished he'd taken more care with the food on the ship. He'd picked his crew for fighting ability—including the cook. After serving on His Majesty's ships and subsisting on a diet of beans and insect-laden bread with an occasional piece of rotten meat, he'd insisted on only one thing: a clean galley and as many fresh fruits and vegetables as possible, regardless of cost. He'd discovered long since that such a diet kept a crew healthy.

But now he looked at the ruinous chicken, and wished he'd bothered to find a true cook.

He looked up at her, expecting to find aversion. But instead, her mouth was twitching as if she were trying not to laugh. Her eyes fairly sparkled with merriment.

John Patrick felt a moment's indignation that all his efforts were resulting only in her amusement, but then he saw it through her eyes, and he couldn't quite contain a grin of his own as he thought of the absurdity of it all: sitting here at a table on a plunging deck with a tablecloth of sail and what must be the most pitiable of all chickens.

"Are you not going to cut it?" Annette queried.

"Do you really want me to?" he asked skeptically.

"We would wound their feelings if we did not," she replied, her gaze moving toward the sailors, who were pretending not to watch them.

John Patrick knew then and there that he would have her. One way or another, he would win her.

But he tried to hide that stubborn determination, and

instead started to hack at the chicken as she watched with intense interest.

In a pique of frustration, he stabbed at the chicken and it went flying off the table. The ship chose that moment to yaw, and he watched helplessly as the damned bird went skittering across the deck and tumbled into the ocean.

"Ah, so there is something you cannot master," she observed quietly.

"There are many things I cannot master," he replied, feeling like a lad who'd just failed his exams.

"Other than chickens, what are they?"

"To know is to conquer," he retorted wryly.

"I have no intentions of conquering. I just want to go home."

"Do you, Miss Annette? Do you really?"

He knew he'd made a mistake. Her eyes clouded, and the smile disappeared from her lips. She was discovering for herself the love of the sea, and in challenging her loyalties, he was forcing her back to the realties she had almost forgotten.

Pleasure faded from her eyes, and she looked away from him. The sun had set, leaving a grayness that suddenly seemed like a shroud. He saw her shiver, and he felt the increased chill in the air.

He wanted that one moment back, before he had forced her to remember everything he'd done. He wanted the delight reflected in her face, the amusement in her eyes.

Annette looked down at her plate. She took several pieces of fruit, but he noticed that now she was eating for appearance's sake; she didn't want to hurt the feelings of the sailors who had tried so hard. He admired her for that, but he also felt despair as he watched her.

He attacked a piece of the bread and the beans, but

the spontaneity of the supper was gone. She would tolerate him through the rest of the meal. Nothing more.

Patience, he told himself.

But as he watched her picking at the food, he wondered whether patience would be enough.

She finished just as the last daylight disappeared into night, and the wind began to pick at the flaps of the sailcloth covering the table.

Annette started to rise. "Thank you," she said solemnly.

He quickly moved to her side to help her stand on the unsteady deck. His offering, he feared, left a great deal to be desired. He had plucked a few moments of whimsy from the day, something he had not done in years, and he was a little unsettled by it. He thought he had lost whimsy long ago.

The ship plunged at that moment and she started to fall. Instinctively, he reached out to grab her as she slid along the deck toward the water. His hand caught hers and he pulled her into his arms, clasping her to him with sudden desperation. She clung to him, her breath rapid, her body trembling, her hands reaching around him for safety.

John Patrick tightened his arms around her. "It is all right," he whispered softly. "You are safe. You will always be safe with me."

She looked up at him then. He could still see panic in her face. He closed his eyes against it. What had he done to her? He'd had reason to kidnap her, but only because he and his brother had taken advantage of her selflessness and hospitality. He had placed her in great danger when he'd outrun the British ships at the mouth of the Delaware. He'd taken her from friends and home and all that she trusted.

If anything happened to her . . .

"I think we had better go below," he said softly. "The weather will get worse."

She did not move for a moment. Then she stepped back, and her hand clasped his as if she believed his promise. His long, callused fingers hurt from her grip but it was a hurt he welcomed. She was still trembling though not quite as much, and he watched as she slowly regained her composure.

After a moment, she spoke, her voice insistent. "You said the British taught you about destruction. How?"

Startled, his fingers tightened around hers.

"I was impressed when I was twenty-three," he said simply. "I was in Scotland, visiting my father's ancestral lands, which had been confiscated by the British government thirty years ago. I was a new lawyer, sure I could right all the wrongs in the world, and I wished to start with his. So I went to England to petition to have him pardoned and his lands returned." He stopped, remembering how naive he had been then, how young and idealistic.

"I was laughed out of the courts," he said. "I visited the Highlands where he'd once lived, then went to Glasgow to await a ship to take me home. Instead, I ended up with drugged ale, and a berth on a British man-of-war with the most sadistic captain who ever sailed the seas."

He was silent for a moment, but he felt her interest, perhaps even her empathy. "I was not very humble, I'm afraid, and I spouted a great deal of law. It was not appreciated. He was determined to break me."

"The scars," she whispered.

"Aye," he said. "Those and more. If it had not been for Ivy, I might never have survived."

"How long?"

"Three years," he said. "Most of them chasing pirates. But then Captain Wentworth ran into a trap, and the pirates took him. Ivy and I were in the brig, sentenced to hang for mutiny. We were given the choice of joining them or joining the others."

"The others?"

He didn't answer. He felt her shiver again.

"I would think you would hate the sea."

"I did, at first," he said. "But it wasn't the sea that took men from their homes and lives. It was the British. I soon learned I had an aptitude for the sea, for sailing. Like you, I never got sick as others did. I enjoyed the feel of a ship under full sail, and the sunrises at sea. There's a freedom like none other when you're running in a fair wind."

"But you hated to be captive on it, to have no choice."

"Aye," he said. His hand left hers and his arms went around her, but this time she was facing the sea and he stood at her back. "I know how you feel, Annette. Probably far more than you could ever believe. I know exactly how it feels to love and hate something at the same time."

He felt her shiver in his arms. He, too, was cold now, and he was used to gales and the chilled mist of seawater. He released her and took her hand. "We do need to go inside. I will not be responsible for you getting chilled."

Surprisingly, she made no protest, but allowed herself to be led to the hatchway. Then she pulled her hand from his.

"I can go alone now," she said. "I imagine Ivy needs you."

He was about to protest, but she shook her head. "I am quite capable of reaching the cabin on my own. But thank you for a—an interesting evening."

"More like disastrous," he said.

"No," she said with a smile that reached deep inside him. "Not quite that."

Then she ducked inside and disappeared down the stairs.

Chapter 19

John Patrick Sutherland was very adept at using people.

Annette kept telling herself that as one day faded into another. The *Mary Ann* had encountered one squall after another, and she saw little of its captain, even when she ventured up on deck. Though she enjoyed being outside during the storm, she was all too aware of how close she'd come to drowning on the evening of her dinner with the captain, and she did not linger on the heaving deck.

Only once did she see him. He was fighting the wheel, his form silhouetted against the dark sky and lit by an occasional flash of lightning. He did not see her, and she observed, fascinated by the strength in his arms, the skill he had in riding out the storm.

Beasley, the ship's cook, brought her food. It was all cold, and he apologized, explaining that they could use neither lanterns nor stoves in an ocean such as this. Fire was as great a danger as the wind and sea.

But he always saw to it she had fruit and hardtack and jellies with the hard bread. And during the daylight hours, she read in the swinging bed, which somehow was the only item that seemed stable.

And she thought about John Patrick and who and what he was.

A lawyer by education. A sailor by force. A pirate by choice. She didn't really know any of them. Yes, he had been kind to her father, but that had required little and gained him much. He had won the consent of those he'd used, betrayed, and wronged.

You cannot believe him.

Could she believe those scars on his back? She'd had only a fleeting glance of them that time she'd changed his dressings. But she still saw them in her mind's eye. But she could not imagine the proud captain of this ship being whipped. How much must it have cost him? Similar pain had taken her father's speech.

Part of the price for John Patrick, she thought, had been his humanity. She hurt for that young man whose youth had been stolen. But that should make him more aware of stealing freedom from others.

Yet she couldn't forget his wry expression as the dreadful chicken went spilling across the deck. Nothing he could have purposely done could have endeared him to her more.

All those thoughts nagged at her, making it nearly impossible to read, to concentrate on anything but John Patrick. Jonny, his family called him. But that seemed too innocent, too boyish for the hard, determined man she knew. If he'd once been full of idealism, it must have been taken from him, for she saw little of it in him now. He had been charming to her family, to her, yet underneath it all had been a man as strong and sharp as a blade of steel.

Remember that.

She tried. But despite nearly tumbling into the sea, the odd supper with him had been intriguing—exhilarating, even.

He was the most complicated man Annette had ever known. If he did not lie so easily, she knew she could well lose her heart to him. And she trusted neither his feelings nor his motives. He was the enemy. When the rebellion started, she had given her loyalty to the

Crown. She had not given it lightly. And how could her loyalty be any less important than his?

The sky cleared.

John Patrick could see for miles, but then so could the British. He clung to the shoreline as much as it was safe to do so, staying well away from the main shipping routes. He would follow the coast to Florida, then to the Caribbean—where the danger increased tenfold. He still flew the British flag, but that had limited value if they were boarded.

He'd already had his men check the cannon, clean them, and practice on them. They were more modern than the ones he'd had on the *Star Rider*. He didn't want to run into surprises. His men had seen sail—merchantmen most likely, since they had not been challenged—and he knew they chafed to go after them. But he had one goal now, to pick up the French cannon from Martinique and deliver them to General Washington. It meant another treacherous trip down the Delaware, but he knew no other way to get heavy armaments to Valley Forge.

In the meantime, he had to avoid battle. The cannon were more important than any merchantman. They could mean Washington's survival.

The sun was just peeking over the horizon, spreading a golden hue across the sky and spilling its dust across the waves. Porpoises trailed along the ship, leaping high into the air with an exuberance he remembered and wished he still had.

Ivy, who'd had the wheel last night, had finally gone to get some rest. He listened to the men singing some ditty as they struck the storm jib and raised full sail. At first light, one of his sharpest-eyed sailors, Taylor, had climbed up into the crow's nest with a glass John Patrick had found in the captain's cabin.

It was going to be a fine day after three stormy ones.

John Patrick looked around the deck, expecting to see Annette. She'd stayed in her cabin during most of the past several days, though he had seen her emerge from the hatchway now and then, breathing in the air, then turning back. He had been too busy fighting the storm to go to her, but he had set Beasley, who was obviously smitten by her, to seeing to her every need. He wished Quinn were on board, but he was still at Marsh's End, watching over Annette's father.

John Patrick missed Annette. He missed seeing her. He missed her tart tongue, her sharp intelligence, her eagerness to experience new things. He thought today he might ask whether she wanted to try steering the ship. In truth, he wanted to share something he loved with her. He'd never known until he'd met her how lonely he'd been, how he'd shoved every human part of himself aside these last years. He still had his family, but he'd never told them exactly what had happened on the British ship, even though he knew his father had experienced even worse when he'd been transported from Scotland.

He would do anything he could to see that the British never brutalized another member of his family, nor any American.

He turned toward the hatchway again, and this time Annette was there. Her cloak was caught by the wind and he saw the blue-gray of the dress he'd purchased. Pleasure filled him. She saw him, hesitated, then took the several steps up to the top deck and the wheel.

"You've survived the past few days well, it seems," he said. "No sickness?"

She looked out toward the gold-flecked sea. "Just a little."

"You are a born sailor."

Pride flickered across her face. "I always thought I would like the sea."

"Would you like to try the wheel?"

She nodded, and he stepped aside, keeping one hand on the giant wheel while she grasped it with both hands. It kicked suddenly, sensing perhaps that it had a sudden freedom.

"Steady," he said, watching as she strained with the effort. He took his hand from the wheel, giving her full control, and watched as she went from fighting with it to guiding it. She *was* a natural-born sailor.

Still, the wheel took all her strength, using muscles she'd probably never used before. He waited, expecting her to give it up, but she didn't. He stood behind her, his body just inches from hers. He wanted to move closer, to put his larger hands on hers and help her, but he restrained himself. He wondered whether she was as aware of the proximity of their bodies as he was.

After several minutes passed, he reached out and took the wheel again. She stood next to him, watching his every movement as if she were memorizing them. As if she knew this was all temporary. Then she turned her gaze toward the sun rising slowly over the ocean. "Where are we going?"

"A small island called Martinique."

"Are you going to be . . . attacking any ships?"

"No. I would not have brought you if I were planning that."

"Why are you going to Martinique?"

John Patrick knew the question had been coming. How could he explain? The French were supposedly neutral. For the moment, anyway. They could not ship cannon to the Americans without violating their treaty, and they were not quite ready to do that. Spies in France would know whether Americans had purchased cannon from the French, and the British would likely stop any

American ship in the vicinity of a French port. But a ship resupplying its stores in Martinique? He might well escape undue notice.

Especially when he changed the name of the *Mary Ann*.

Benjamin Franklin had worked it all out with the French in his usual wily way.

But John Patrick was not ready to explain any of this to Annette. The information could hurt France's position badly and thus delay further help to the colonies. And Annette was still a Tory with far too many British sympathies.

She was waiting for an answer, but he could give her none. He was not going to lie. He had done enough of that already. He retreated into silence.

She stood there several more minutes, then tried a different tack. "When will we return?"

"Four to five weeks, depending on the wind."

"And then will you . . . let us go home?"

He turned to face her. "If it is safe."

"And *you* decide whether it is safe?"

"Aye."

He saw her body tense. He knew, dammit, that he sounded arrogant, but he did not know how else to answer her question. He only knew he was not going to lie to her ever again.

She turned away from him, leaving the quarterdeck. She disappeared from sight, but he knew she would probably stay on deck. Frustration ate at him. For one fine moment, they had shared a common pleasure, but then it was spoiled by their differences. He wondered whether it would always be thus.

Annette went below to fetch her book. Perhaps this time she could stop thinking about John Patrick. About how angry he made her, and about how much he made her feel things she should never feel for an enemy.

The indisputable fact was that he performed some kind of magic on her whenever he was nearby. She had felt exhilarated when he'd turned the wheel over to her. She'd felt the heat of his body behind her, had felt every nerve ache with awareness. She'd even felt a . . . sharing with him—until that moment when he'd once more become a captor.

But she would not let herself feel imprisoned in the cabin. Despite the chill still in the air, she wanted to be out on deck, to smell fresh air and hear the wind snap against the sails. She took a pillow and made her way back up to the port side, finding a place between two coils of rope where she could see the pirate, but he wouldn't see her.

She only wished she could concentrate on the well-worn book. A treasure. Why then had he given it to her?

She soon became engrossed in the story of the man shipwrecked on an island all by himself. Having seen a storm at sea, the story became all too real to her. She was so engrossed that she was startled when a shadow fell over the page she was reading.

She didn't have to look up to know John Patrick stood over her. Her curiosity, unfortunately, made it difficult to ignore him. "You said this book was a family treasure?" she asked.

"My father used to read that to me," he said. "He taught my mother and Noel to read with it."

She was still trying to get used to all the family connections. "Dr. Marsh is your half-brother?"

"Aye. My mother was married to John Marsh before she married my father. They—she and John Marsh— bought my father at an auction." Without waiting for an invitation, he sat next to her.

She nodded, listening intently. "Yes, your father told

me something about his story. He was actually sold at auction?"

"Aye. He was at Culloden with Prince Charles. The British won, but winning was not enough for them. They slaughtered every man they could find, along with hundreds of women and children. They sentenced my father to hang along with his brother, Derek. After he watched Derek die, they told him he would be transported as a bond slave, instead.

"He was purchased by John Marsh. My mother had asked him to find an educated man, a schoolteacher who had been willing to indenture himself to pay for passage to America. Instead, he brought home a very bitter and angry convict."

"Your father?" Annette could barely believe what he was saying. Ian Sutherland was a gentle man, full of humor and compassion.

"Aye, my father. John Marsh died just days later, and his brother tried to take my mother's land—and her. But my father stayed, and taught her to read and write, and helped her build the farm, and . . . protected her from her brother-in-law. I think he always wanted to go back to Scotland, but if he returns, he would hang."

"So you went in his place."

"Little good I did except give the British another go at us."

"And so now you are trying to even the score?"

His gaze met hers. "It goes deeper than that, Annette."

"Does it?" she asked skeptically.

"It does, if you believe in freedom."

"That is incredibly arrogant," she replied frostily. "I believe in freedom. I believe in having the freedom to make choices without being tortured or having your home destroyed."

"That was a band of renegades."

"How do you know?" she asked. "Were you there?" After several seconds of silence, she added, "I do not see the Pennsylvania authorities returning our land; instead, it was confiscated, just as yours was. That land was just as important to us as your land in Scotland."

He dropped beside her, his green eyes almost opaque. "I will try to get it back for you."

"As a lawyer or a pirate? Or are the words interchangeable?"

"You have a quick tongue, as well as a sharp one," he said.

"I've learned not to trust your government."

He reached out to take her hand. She had not put on her gloves, and she felt a frisson of heat run through her. She tried to ignore it. But that was about as easy as trying to ignore a bull elephant charging down upon her.

"I am sorry," he said. "I'm sorry I took you from your home, from Philadelphia. I'm sorry for putting you in danger." His fingers caressed hers. She tried to gently withdraw them, but his grip tightened. "I owe you and your family," he said. "I owe you more than I can ever pay. I will get your land back, one way or another."

She melted under the sincerity and determination in his voice. She was sure, in fact, that he *would* try. She was not nearly as sure that he would be successful. Still, she was warmed by his vow.

Far more warmed than she should be.

The sun was shining down on them now, and despite the cool breeze she felt its glow. His fingers continued to run along the ridges on the back of her hand. The radiant heat she always felt with him intensified. She had never been so aware of her senses before. They all seemed to react at once. His barely discernible scent of soap and salt, the friction of his skin against hers, the almost caressing touch of a freshened wind, the lulling movement of the ship, the cries of the land birds that still followed them. It was the most intoxicating mixture she'd ever known, and when she looked at him, she knew he felt it, too.

He bent his head, and his lips touched hers as lightly as the breeze that brushed through her hair. His hand went to her hair, sifting it through his fingers, then traced her cheek, his fingers barely touching her. His hands were making love to her in the gentlest way a man could.

She had always had her doubts about his feelings toward her. She had been first useful, then a problem to be solved. But now . . .

He really seemed to care. She saw it in his eyes, in the odd tender twist of his lips. She felt it in his touch.

She knew they were hidden from most of the crew. She had selected this spot for just that reason. She'd wanted to avoid him, and in doing so she had avoided everyone else, too. She swallowed, but her throat was so tight she could barely breathe. Her blood turned thick and lazy, but his touch electrified her to her core.

His lips nuzzled hers, then moved to her neck, trailing kisses that ignited flames throughout her body, that turned her warm, lazy blood into lava. She sought her way back to sanity. But sanity was gone. His tongue teased her lips, and she opened them to him.

The taste of him was intoxicating, seducing, as his tongue explored her mouth, inviting her to join him. His hands moved inside her cloak, along her arms, and the cloth between them did nothing to shield her from the sparks that flared between them. Yet it was the gentleness, the restrained passion, that touched her. His eyes—those incredibly green eyes—seemed to love her even as they consumed her.

She trembled at the knowledge of how much she wanted him.

He must have felt her shaking and believed it to be

something else, for he drew away. His hand, though, caught hers and held it.

" 'Tis not a very private place," he said.

"No." Her word was a sigh.

"Will you have supper with me again?" he said. "And not in the blustering wind?"

No. "Yes."

Her mind said one word, her heart another.

But wrapped in the enchantment of him, for the moment, at least, she did not care. She only wanted more of the warmth and sensuality that had cloaked them.

He rose to his feet. "Would you like to stay here longer?"

"Yes." Perhaps the cold wind would quench all those blazes he'd ignited.

Perhaps.

She doubted it, because they did not fade as she watched him walk away. Why did even his walk make her heart jerk in peculiar ways? She tried to go back to her book, to concentrate on Robinson Crusoe, but Crusoe became John Patrick in her mind, competently building himself a shelter and making the best of a lone existence.

It fit him.

In many ways, he was a loner. She didn't know whether it had been those years aboard a British ship, or whether it was command, or whether it had always been John Patrick, but he was a man who didn't seem to need other people. That realization scared her as much as anything had.

After an hour of staring at the same page, she finally rose. The afternoon sun looked so big and close, she felt as if she could reach out and touch it. The sea did that. Everything was richer and grander and deeper. Even her perceptions, her emotions.

Annette really didn't want to return to the cabin. She

wanted to stay out here. But John Patrick haunted the decks of the *Mary Ann*—and her thoughts.

Reluctantly, she tucked the hood of her cloak over her hair, carefully picked up the book that was a family treasure, and walked to the hatchway. Such a beautiful day.

John Patrick was determined that this supper was not going to be like the earlier attempt. He hovered over the galley stove as a chicken roasted on a spit. Unfortunately, chickens, salt pork, bacon, beans, flour, and fruit were all that he'd been able to purchase on such short notice. But this meal, he determined, would not be overcooked. He'd also checked the former captain's wines and found one he deemed suitable.

After shaving, he'd dressed in his deerskin trousers and a white linen shirt. He felt almost boyish at the prospect of spending private hours with Miss Annette Carey.

When all was finally ready, he enlisted Beasley to help him carry everything to her cabin. The door opened almost immediately when he knocked, and he wondered how she grew prettier every time he saw her.

Her cheeks flushed as John Patrick entered and placed a bottle of wine and glasses on the table. Beasley, who'd once been a feared pirate in the Caribbean, turned bright red as he followed with the tray.

"You have my crew flustered," John Patrick said. "You've stolen them away from me."

"I would not like to test that. They think you are a god."

John Patrick did not feel particularly flattered at the description. He'd never had any ambitions to be a god. He'd never had any to be a martinet. He'd never even had any to be a captain. It had just happened. It had meant his survival. "They would do very well without me," he finally said.

"You bring them together. Because they trust you."

He didn't want to talk about the crew. He didn't want to talk about the war.

He only wanted to talk about her.

As if on cue, Beasley reddened. " 'Ope you enjoy the vittles, miss," he said, before disappearing through the door and closing it softly behind him.

"Where did you find him?" Annette asked.

"He was a pirate," John Patrick replied.

"An' he seems such a decent lad," she said, mimicking Ian Sutherland's accent perfectly.

He chuckled.

"I always thought pirates were dreadful people," she added.

"Pirates are fearfully misjudged."

"Are they now? They steal from the rich and give to the poor?"

"Not the pirates I knew," he retorted truthfully. "Most of them were the bloodthirsty villains you thought they were."

"But there were exceptions."

"Aye. Ivy and I were pirates only long enough to steal a ship from them."

"And Beasley?"

"I think he rather enjoyed the life."

"Then why did he leave them to go with you?"

"I do not know. You will have to ask him."

Her eyes were burning into him, seeking answers she could accept.

"Why did you leave pirating?"

John Patrick ignored the question. She most probably would not believe him in any event. She certainly had little reason to believe anything he said. Instead, he pulled out a chair for her and then sat down himself, taking several moments to open the bottle of wine and pour it.

But it did no good. The question remained in her eyes, and he knew from the jut of her chin she wasn't going to let it go.

"They operated off a small island in the Caribbean," he said. "Three ships, three captains. Once you signed on, you did not leave. It was similar to the British navy in that aspect. The difference was that you made money, a great deal of money if you didn't spend it on gambling and—" He stopped himself in midsentence.

"Painted women?" she concluded with an interest society would condemn as unladylike. But he had always liked that curiosity.

"Yes," he admitted.

"Of course, you saved your money?"

"Exactly," he said with a wry smile.

"And then?"

"I fought my way up to captain. It took two years. Even then, leaving was not an easy proposition. 'Twas a democratic society in some ways. The crew elected the captain, and they could unelect him in a very permanent way. Most of them liked the life, the money, even the destruction. I had to build a crew loyal to me before I could even think of leaving."

"And one day you just sailed off forever?"

"Aye," he said.

"And started raiding the British?"

"Not until the war started, and I received letters of marque from Maryland."

"Before that?"

She never gave up. He poured himself another glass of wine, aware that she had barely touched hers, or the food.

"I was a merchant sailor." True. He ran guns to the colonies. But he'd been paid for them. Sometimes.

Her gray eyes doubted him. He was sure his own betrayed him. But she didn't ask another question. She took a sip of wine instead, and he saw a drop hover on her lips. Bloody hell, but she was desirable.

He cut the chicken, and this time the bird looked edible. He was very aware of her gaze on him as he sliced the meat. He looked up and saw her smile as he finished with something of a triumphant flourish and placed the food on her plate.

"You've restored my faith," she said.

"Your faith?"

"It was considerably weakened when a chicken defeated you."

"It was a very gallant chicken."

She giggled, locking her laugh in her throat. It wasn't a silly giggle, but true merriment she obviously wanted to contain. After several seconds, though, she surrendered and burst into full laughter. He had never seen her laugh before, and he delighted in the sound of it. It made him start laughing, too, and before long they were both nearly doubled over with mirth.

When he regained his composure, his eyes met hers, and through the amusement, he saw the same need that was suddenly filling him. He was aware, barely, that their shared laughter had broken through the barrier she'd tried so hard to erect against him. Heat radiated between them.

The smile faded from her lips. But the gentle softness he loved replaced it, even as he realized the gentleness was laced with a strength as tempered as steel. 'Twas what he admired most about her.

Admired?

Loved.

The sudden realization stunned him. He had wanted her from the beginning. He had grown to like her immensely. But love?

He reached over with his right hand, surprised when she took it. He rose, and she rose with him, both of them ignoring the food on the table. John Patrick guided her from the table and she was in his arms, clinging to his neck as their lips met in explosive desire.

Annette was unprepared for the driving need inside her, for the ache, for the yearning that had made her body into something unfamiliar. The explosion, so close to erupting during the past few days, had finally come. Her world seemed to rock with it as his kiss deepened, his lips plundering hers until she thought she would drown in the sensation.

She opened her lips to his as his arm tightened around her, drawing her hard against him. Her hand circled his neck, touching the thick dark hair that curled ever so slightly around her fingers, her other hand caressing his nape in a round motion that grew increasingly smaller as her body reacted to his. Instinctively she drew into him, her curves fitting so neatly into his, as though they were made to do exactly that.

Her body shuddered as his lips moved away from hers, his tongue feathering her cheek, his lips caressing skin now burning with his touch. Desire ripped through her, overtaking her distrust, her reservations. His lips traveled down her cheek, to her ear, then her throat, creating a tense expectation deep inside her.

"Pretty Annette," he whispered into her ear, making her name into a song. He pressed his lips against her cheek for the barest of moments, and felt his straining need.

She drew a shaky breath, trying to restore some calm in a body shaken by a tempest, trying to tame the feelings betraying her, but his every touch seemed to spark even more fevered responses. She touched his face, ran her fingers along the crevices that had been carved there by hardships she could only imagine from the few words he had spoken. Fierce tenderness made her hands tremble as they traced the lines, then fell to his mouth. She knew then she was lost. She could control passion; she could not control the love she felt.

His lips caught her fingers, nibbled on them for a moment, before he crushed her to him, then she felt his hands on the ribbons that held the bodice of her dress together. As they came undone, his fingers caught the brooch she wore on a chain.

He looked up at her. "You always wear this."

"It was my mother's, the only possession of hers that I have. I almost lost it years ago when the clasp broke, and my father asked a jewel maker to put a chain on it. That is why . . . it survived the fire."

"It is beautiful," he said. "Like you."

She looked up at him. She knew her heart was in her eyes. Her hand touched his, even as she realized it was an invitation.

She saw him hesitate, uncertainty cross his face. "Are you sure, lovely lady?" he asked.

His hesitation was her downfall. If he had just tried to take, she probably could have rebuffed him. But the tender concern in his eyes made her very, very sure.

"Aye," she said.

His hands were gentle as he finished untying the bodice. His fingers fumbled for a moment, and she suddenly knew he was not as sure as she had thought him to be. But then he pulled the dress down, then her chemise, and he bent his head, his lips touching her right nipple. Despite the gentleness of his touch, the caress sent waves of sensation flowing through her, and she felt a wonderment that her body had these feelings, amazement that one built upon another.

His hands moved over her body, somehow dispensing with each and every piece of clothing. His hands then took the combs from her hair, letting it fall around her face. She knew she should feel embarrassment, but she couldn't take her gaze from the possessive gleam in his eyes, the tender crook of his mouth.

"You really are beautiful," he said. "So beautiful."

She felt beautiful. Beautiful and cherished. Tremors ran through her as his hands moved up and down her body, the pressure building inside her. His hand slid down to the triangle of hair, his fingers soothing, even as they created ripples of raw need.

He picked her up, and set her gently on the bed. He sat, pulled off his boots, then untied the laces to his trousers. She watched as intently as he had looked when he undressed her.

He left his shirt on, though, when he bent back over her, his mouth raining kisses over her body until she was almost crying with a need she still didn't quite understand.

Her eyes met his, and her face must have given him the answer he needed. Her pirate moved slightly, positioning his hard body above hers. "This will hurt at first," he whispered.

She didn't care. She didn't care about anything but feeling his closeness, his warmth, anything but finishing whatever it was he had started with her body.

She strained against him, and she felt his body lower, his swollen manhood probing, teasing, seducing. But she needed no more seduction. "John Patrick," she said, hearing the ache in her own voice.

He entered her then, slowly, and she felt an odd sensation, then sudden pain. She couldn't help but cry out, and he stilled. The pain faded, and her arms went around him, urging him down, cherishing the warmth and feel of his body while seeking something more.

He moved slowly inside her, and she felt an increasing fullness, then, astonishingly, ripples of pleasure. She felt her body arching up suddenly, then, as he moved slowly inside her, waves of delicious sensation.

Vestiges of that first pain vanished, swallowed by streaks of exquisite pleasure as her body responded, clenching around him, quivering in response to his quickening rhythm. She heard his groan, then a final thrust, and she felt as if her body had become a comet racing through the skies, only to explode in one brilliant ball of fire.

John Patrick held Annette in his arms for a long time. Neither said anything. He just relished having her in his arms, feeling her cheek against his chest, hearing her soft breath.

For the first time since Glasgow, he felt a measure of peace. The hate that had haunted him these past years faded away.

His arms tightened around her, and he heard what sounded like a small purr.

His fingers ran through her hair. How had he been so lucky as to find his little Tory? The word no longer raised anger. He knew now he would never again judge anyone by labels.

The fingers of his other hand ran up and down her arm. "Are you . . . all right?"

She looked up, her eyes glowing. "Oh, yes."

"No regrets?" He didn't want her to have any, but he had to know.

"I should have some," she said, her gray eyes fairly dancing. "Any properly raised young lady would." She paused for a moment. "But I'm discovering I am not so proper after all. I should not enjoy being kidnapped, or being the lone woman among a ship of pirates, or—"

"I thought we had settled the question of pirates."

"No. You never did tell me why we are going to Martinique."

"I thought you might like it. 'Tis a lovely island."

His light answer was a mistake. He knew it the moment he saw her eyes cloud. He should have learned by now not to underestimate her intelligence.

She drew away from him, her gray eyes intent on him.

He didn't want to tell her that he was picking up cannon for Washington's army. He was only too aware they would be used against men she had nursed, had sheltered, had befriended. But he wasn't going to lie, either. He would lose her forever if he did. It had been his lies, not his politics, that had turned her against him.

"Supplies," he said, choosing a partial truth.

"Guns?"

"Aye." Very large guns.

She did not say anything for several moments. "I will stop you if I can," she finally said.

"I know," he said softly.

She put her fingers to his cheek. "Beloved enemy," she said.

It was the "beloved" that lingered in his mind.

She settled back down in his arms. But the words remained between them, intruding on the magic that had so securely, and briefly, wrapped around them.

Chapter 20

Martinique *was* truly beautiful. It rose out of the sea like some ancient empire, its range of blue mountains crowned by misty clouds.

The afternoon was bright and clear, the sea a deep indigo blue. The sun's rays made the sea sparkle as if diamonds had been sprinkled across its surface. The town across from the ship seemed to shimmer, the red tiles on the roofs of the buildings reflecting light.

Annette watched the shore as the *Mary Ann* sailed into the harbor. Now it was the *Star Rider*. John Patrick had purchased paint in Chestertown, and while still at sea, his crew had painted over the old name and painted on the new.

She wondered whether it was bad luck to name a ship after a deceased one.

She had asked John Patrick that, but he had merely said a man made his own luck. His ship, he added, would always be named *Star Rider*. He would, he'd added, find an American flag to fly.

Annette knew John Patrick far better now than she had the day he had taken her from Philadelphia, but there were still parts of him she thought she would never know. Despite their lovemaking, she knew he still withheld parts of his story. He never allowed her to see him without a shirt, and he'd never spoken again of those years that apparently shaped him into what he was.

They had not made love again, though he had spent as much time with her as he could. He had not wanted

the crew to see him spending the night in her cabin.
Supper, yes. All night, no.

She knew he wanted to preserve as much of her reputation as possible, but she was aware, if he was not, that
once this voyage was known, she would be ruined forever. Respectable young women did not sail without fe-
male companionship on a ship with what most of her
acquaintances would consider a pirate crew. Kidnapped
or not, she would be quite ostracized.

As far as she was concerned, in for a penny, in for a
pound.

But John Patrick obviously felt differently, and he'd
been careful since that first time not to let their caresses
go farther than a kiss. He'd asked her if she had regrets;
but it appeared that it was John Patrick himself who had
regrets.

Because he did not love her? She didn't know. He was
too adept at keeping his own counsel, at masking his
emotions.

She often just watched him, hoping he did not know
she was doing so, trying to equate the man with such
gentle hands with the one who had apparently sent many
men to their deaths, who would send even more unless
she could convince him otherwise.

And that, she suspected, would be as likely as asking
the stars to tarry after sunrise.

Star Rider. A whimsical name for a serious man.

Had it always been thus?

The harbor was filled with ships—tall-masted ships
flying the French flag, and numerous fishing boats of all
sizes and conditions. A wall of gaily painted storefronts
faced them, and they appeared backed up to the mountains behind.

She knew the French were close to signing a treaty
with the American colonies. She would receive little help
here, even if she knew what to do to keep John Patrick

from taking guns aboard. And how to do it without hurting the man she loved.

It sickened her, however, to know that this ship would be used to convey weapons that would kill the very men she'd nursed back to health. Perhaps men could look at concepts, at strategy, at winning and losing, but she saw only individuals. She *knew* what cannon and musket balls could do to a human being.

Of course, he did, too, being the recent recipient of a musket ball, but the experience did not seem to have changed his dedication to the cause.

As she stared at the buildings, she became aware of John Patrick's presence. Even though his steps were almost soundless on the deck of the ship, she knew by the electricity that touched her.

"Fort Royal," he said. "Capital of Martinique. It is a lovely island. I will take you riding, if you wish."

"How long will we be here?"

"I hope no more than two or three days."

"Then where?"

His mouth tightened slightly.

"John Patrick?"

"I don't know yet," he said. He placed a hand on her shoulder, and she felt it burn straight through the cotton dress she wore.

"We will have to get you more dresses here," he said. "There is a fine shop with all the latest French fashions. They call this Little Paris."

"You are changing the subject."

"Only because I truly do not know," he said. "I haven't yet decided."

"And when you do, you will be kind enough to let me know?" She couldn't stop the asperity in her voice. He always did that to her: disarm, then demonstrate his power. "It is not long until Christmas. I want to be with my father."

"I will try to get you there before Christmas."

"Where is 'there'? My home or yours?"

"I'd hoped my home was becoming yours," he said softly.

His words were as close to a declaration as he'd made. Yet he had never said he loved her, had never mentioned a future.

She did not know how to answer him, so she remained silent.

After several seconds, he took his arm from her. "I have to go into the town and conduct business. I'll leave you at the dressmaker if you like. Then we can take a ride through the hills."

"Are you not afraid I might try to flee?"

"On Martinique? There is no place to go, love."

Love. He made it sound such an easy endearment, one he might give any woman. Her heart splintered. He had been so careful since that night, careful with his words, careful with his touches. Had he merely taken what he'd wanted, then considered her only a nuisance?

She looked over at the French ships. Perhaps . . .

But she had no money. And what would she do in France?

Yet she felt she must get away from John Patrick, whose presence sent her usually sensible heart into a muddled mess, and made her conscience into something unrecognizable. He affected her in ways no man ever had.

He was waiting for her to answer.

"I don't have any money for a dressmaker," she said.

"I took you without any more clothes than you were wearing. 'Tis my responsibility to see to your wardrobe," he offered gently.

Responsibility. She hated that word.

But as she looked out over the town, she found she desperately wanted to see it. Despite her anger, she wanted to walk the streets, to feel the soul of the place. She had never been anywhere exotic and different. Her curiosity, spurred by her days on shipboard, by the senses the sea had teased and beguiled, hungered for more new experiences.

She nodded. "I do not have a bonnet."

"You need no bonnet here," he said, and one of his fingers wound itself in the curls that fell around her face. "The climate forces its residents into much less rigorous convention. And it would be a pity to cover such lovely hair."

Another compliment, this time in a warm voice. She yearned to touch his hand, his mouth, watch that quirk of a smile appear.

But before she could do anything, he turned and ordered the gig to be lowered.

She watched as his command was obeyed and a rope ladder was flung over the sides. Several sailors scampered down the ladder and took their places in the jiffy.

"I'll go before you," he said.

"So you can catch me if I fall?"

"Aye," he said.

"You have no faith in my prowess."

"I have every faith in your competence," he said. "But a moving ship is something else altogether."

"I have gotten my sea legs," she replied indignantly.

"But maybe not your ladder legs," he said as he effortlessly dropped over the side of the ship, then climbed down several feet. He waited for her.

She tried to put her legs over gracefully, but she couldn't quite do it in her skirts. It had been far easier going up than going down. Her legs got tangled in the cloth. She held on for dear life as she lost her footing and started slipping. She grabbed for the rope again, her breath caught in her throat as she lost purchase. She knew the jiffy was swinging against the ship, and how easily she could be crushed.

John Patrick's arms clasped around her and the ladder swung outward, then back again, smashing her hand against the side of the ship, but she hung on for dear life, afraid she would throw both herself and John Patrick to the boat below.

"It's all right," he whispered into her ear. "I have you."

Pain pounded in her hand, but his soft words took away the fear. Gradually her body eased into his.

"Slowly," he said. "One step at a time."

She took one step, making sure her slipper was free from her skirts, then moved her hand. Pain intensified as she unclenched her fingers. She forced them to move again, to tighten again into a fist around the rope.

Another step. A third. Her hand ached more with each movement. Then finally, she knew John Patrick had reached the bottom of the boat and he lifted her down, settling her on the board next to him. She held her aching hand in her other fist, willing the pain to leave.

John Patrick took her hand, his fingers gently probing her fingers. She stifled a cry, but he must have seen her face because his somber one suddenly reflected pain of his own.

She saw a muscle move in his throat as he examined the rip in her skin, the dark purpling around it. He tore off a piece of his shirt and bound it tenderly, careful not to tighten the cloth more than necessary to staunch the flow of blood. "We might have to postpone your visit to the dressmaker. A physician will be our first call."

"What about your business?"

"That can wait."

Her gaze met his. His eyes were tender, worried. He was not hiding behind a mask now.

She found her body leaning into him, even as he put her injured hand on his. Waves of pain flowed through it, one after another, and she wondered whether it was broken. She tried her fingers, and each worked, if painfully. She felt a fraud, though, when she recalled the extent of his injuries.

"I always seem to be falling into you," she said.

"That's because I keep putting you in dangerous places." His lashes shaded his eyes as he spoke. They reached the wharf and one of the sailors jumped out to fasten the rope. She started to rise but John Patrick was on his feet a second before her and held her back for a moment, both of his arms around her protectively. Then, unexpectedly, he picked her up and lifted her to one of the waiting sailors. When she was safe, he leaped up himself.

"I'm not taking any chances with you again," he said, as the sailor handed her back to him.

Held close to his chest, Annette felt safe. The pain seemed to fade from her hand.

After a time longer than necessary, he set her down. "I'm sorry," he said. "I'm so sorry for everything."

But in that moment, there was absolutely nothing for him to be sorry for.

John Patrick wanted to protect her forever. Instead, he seemed destined only to hurt her.

He had tried to keep away from her. He had tried so bloody damn hard. It had been sheer hell after the night when they'd made love, but he would have to take the cannon down the Delaware, and he wasn't quite sure he would live through that experience a second time. How could he, then, leave her with a child? And he couldn't tell her why he might have to leave her. He loved her. He thought she loved him. But what of her sense of loyalty to the British, if she knew he was taking cannon to General Washington?

Somehow, once-clear lines were becoming blurred.

When Annette had started to fall, his life seemed to stop.

If he had not caught her, she might well have been caught between the ship and the jiffy.

He had felt her heart beating against his. No tears, but then he'd never seen her shed tears. "We have to find a surgeon to look at that hand," he said now.

She didn't argue as he took her arm. He walked slowly, apparently aware that the land felt like it was rocking as much as the ship. She had to clasp his hand to keep steady. He smiled down at her. "The land will feel like the sea for a day or so."

He guided her down the street past several noisy grogshops, then past shop windows with any number of exotic goods—silks and lace and carved ivory combs, all, he knew, imports from faraway countries.

He knew these streets intimately. He knew every grogshop and pleasure house on the island, having both visited them and pulled members of his crew from them when he was pirating. Flying at various times under Dutch, French, and American flags, John Patrick had often refitted his ship here. The government, he knew, was not overly particular about the law as long as sufficient coin changed hands.

He'd always loved the raucous island and felt well at home on its waterfront.

Despite her recent mishap, he saw the same excitement in Annette's face as she studied the goods in the windows. She slowed, forcing him to do the same, when she saw a brightly colored parrot.

"It probably came from Curaçao," he said, watching as a look of wonder flitted across her face. He waited several seconds, thinking she looked like a child staring into a toy store, then he steered her away. He wanted to have her hand attended to immediately.

"I have never seen a parrot before," she said. "Do they really talk?"

"Yes," he replied. "I had a mate once who had one."

She turned around and looked wistfully at the bird again. "It is beautiful."

"Their feathers are."

"Are you trying to tell me that they are . . . undesirable?"

"Stubborn," he corrected. "And their vocabularies are not always for gentle ears. Sailors seem to take delight in teaching them . . . questionable phrases."

"I know about stubbornness," she said, looking him straight in the eye. The accusation was unmistakable.

"Ah, know thyself," he said with a grin.

He steered her back to the road, to some stairs that led to a door above a shop. A small sign claimed the occupant to be Louis Fortier, Physician.

She turned and looked at him. "My hand is fine now."

"All the same, I want him to look at it."

"You know this man?"

"Aye, Louis is a friend."

She looked at him from under her dark lashes. "You know a lot of physicians."

"Unfortunately," he said with that crooked smile of his.

She moved her hand suddenly, and she swayed for a moment. He knew she was feeling far more pain than she wanted to admit. His hand tightened on her arm as they went up the steps.

The physician was in, thank the saints, because if he had not been, John Patrick was prepared to hunt him down and do him physical harm. It had been a year since John Patrick had brought several British prizes into port, and had summoned Louis to care for the British wounded. The man had not changed at all since then. He was still a large man with a large belly, and an even larger smile.

"More customers for me, Captain Smith?" he asked in heavily accented English. "I always like to see your ship come in. My purse fills twice as fast as when you're gone."

John Patrick could have strangled him. Especially when he saw Annette's eyes widen at the reference to the increase in business when he was in town.

"Only this young lady," he said. "She fell coming down a ship's ladder and injured her left hand."

The physician's eyes immediately went to her, taking her hand in his with a gentleness that belied his size. "Come in, Miss . . ."

"Smith," John Patrick said.

"Ah, I see. Mr. Smith and Miss Smith. A sister, I gather?" The twinkle in his eyes told John Patrick he did not believe that assumption for a minute.

John Patrick saw her bite her lip as she hesitated. He suddenly wondered whether he had been a fool to bring her to Fort Royal, wondered whether she would blurt out that she'd been taken against her will and ask for help from the French government. The governor, though he often turned a blind eye toward a ship's origin, considered himself a gentleman and would most likely arrest him and claim the cannon as his own. *That* would certainly defeat his mission.

He hadn't really considered that before, but he should have. Hadn't she said she would do anything she could to stop him?

But he'd so wanted her to see the island, with its profusion of orchids and the other richly blossomed tropical flowers. He wanted her to see the magnificent waterfalls, and the fine white beaches, and the pineapple bushes. He'd always loved it here, even the first time he'd come, when he was little more than a prisoner aboard the British man-of-war, sailing these seas to capture pirates. He had never been allowed to go to shore, but he would gaze out at the neat buildings with their iron balconies and the lush green hills behind him. It had always represented freedom to him. Was it the same for her?

She said nothing, though he was aware that she had considered her alternatives. He had seen them in her eyes.

Instead, she followed Louis to a chair and waited while he drew another close and sat down to unwrap the bloody piece of John Patrick's shirt. He winced as she sat motionless, her face set against the pain he knew she must feel.

Louis washed the blood from the wound and probed each finger, then looked up at her. "The gash needs stitching," he said, "and it will leave a scar. There doesn't seem to be a break, though your hand is badly bruised and will ache for a while." He retrieved a needle and thread, hesitating when he returned. "This will hurt, Miss Smith."

She nodded.

"Miss Smith has done some nursing," John Patrick said. "She is aware of what must be done." He put a hand on her shoulder.

Annette didn't move or cry out as the physician punctured her skin. It was all John Patrick could do to keep still, to keep a comforting hand on her. Every puncture hurt him far more than any musket ball, or even lash of the whip, had.

When Louis was finished, he wrapped the wound in clean cloth, then gave her an approving glance. "Most young ladies would have fainted."

"Annette is not most young ladies," he said.

Louis smiled as he looked from John Patrick to Annette. "I can see that." He paused. "You might wish to have some sherry or brandy tonight. It will help the pain."

John Patrick took a coin from his pocket and tossed it to Louis. "Thank you."

"Will you be here long?"

"I fear not."

"I regret that. I do not suppose you have time for a supper together?"

John Patrick shook his head. "Not this time."

Dr. Louis Fortier picked up a small bottle from a case, then handed it to John Patrick. "Herbs for a poultice to prevent infection. Use it on the wound for the next few days."

Once outside, John Patrick turned to her. "Why didn't you say anything to him?"

"About abduction? He is *your* friend."

"He is a gentleman who would be appalled at my conduct and offer you help."

She looked at him with her great gray eyes, but she said nothing, and he wondered exactly what was transpiring in that quick mind of hers. For once, he did not know. He had not known since he'd made love to her. She had never said she loved him, just as he had not said the words, but he'd hoped . . .

Yet she'd also made it clear she had not changed her loyalties.

"Would he?" The doubt in her voice made him wonder whether she was just waiting for the right opportunity, as she had waited in Maryland until she knew something about the area.

Trust. Dear God, how much he wanted it from her. But he'd given her precious little reason to have any.

He changed the subject. "Do you feel well enough to go to the dressmaker?"

Her eyes lit slightly, and he saw her glance around at the town and the park in its center, then at the sea.

Despite her injury, she was savoring the island, just as he always had. "I would rather walk around the town."

He glanced down at her hand. "I think a carriage would be better," he said. "I'll rent one, but first the dressmaker."

"What about your business?"

"That can wait," he said, surprising himself. Right now, all he wanted was a smile on her face, in her eyes.

One day would make no difference.

You can stop him from carrying arms back.

Annette kept telling herself that. Over and over again. She could go to the authorities and accuse him of kidnapping. What penalty was there for such an offense? Prison? Worse?

Could she do that to him?

No.

But the thought lay in the back of her mind, even as she sniffed the flower-scented air of the island, felt the warm breezes off the sea, watched with astonishment the varying hues of emerald and green and dark blue that colored the water, listened to the musical cadence of the language. All of her senses were vibrantly alive, and despite the throb of her hand she wanted to run down the street, visit every store, go up into the hills that looked so incredibly green.

Her feet fairly danced along the cobblestones as John Patrick guided her to the dressmaking shop. He was at his most charming as he soothed an indignant Madame into selling him two dresses meant for someone else, and fitting them immediately. He tried to buy a third, but no amount of bribe could change the woman's mind about a dress destined for a girl named Josephine, the young daughter of one of the island's most prominent families.

Then John Patrick hired a carriage and drove Annette over dirt roads, past a magnificent waterfall. He pointed

out a mountain with a smokelike cloud hovering over-
head. "That is a volcano. Mont Pelée."

Everything was so strange and exotic and incredibly
beautiful. Her good hand slipped into his, and she felt
burned by his touch. They stopped at a broad, empty
expanse of beach, and he swung her down from the seat,
stopping long enough to take off his boots and her slippers and stockings. He then took her hand again, leading
her down to the water.

The sun-warmed sand trickled through her toes. The
tang of the sea mixed with the thick sweet smell of flowers. The cry of seabirds and the soft sound of water lapping against the sand provided a seductive music. She
was so incredibly aware of the man next to her, of his
fingers against her skin.

She looked at him. His green eyes were even more
vivid than the sea as he looked down at her. He touched
her face, then fingered her hair.

And there was suddenly no one else in the world.

Chapter 21

John Patrick had vowed it would never happen again. God help him, he had meant it.

But never had he been so tempted.

Her close call this morning had made him realize again how terrified he was of losing her. Now, with delight dancing in her eyes, she was more appealing than ever. And, although she was obviously unaware of it, more seductive.

Her hand was warm in his. Trusting as it had never been before.

She used her injured hand to pull her skirts up to her knees, and her toes wriggled in the clear, sun-warmed water. She looked up at him with that wonder that never failed to touch him. "I never knew the sea could be so warm."

She closed her eyes, and he recognized the sensations washing over her. He knew them well, but they were never so vivid as now, when he shared them with someone else, someone who brought even more light to an already glittering day.

He reached out and drew her to him. Her skirts dropped, and he felt a gentle wave wash over the bottom of his trousers as well as the hem of her dress. She appeared as indifferent as he to being drenched. His body no longer obeyed his brain. He had already tasted the forbidden fruit, and now it was irresistible.

He ached from wanting her, from needing her, from that roaring passion that blazed between them. How could he need her so badly? He who had always believed he didn't really need anyone, who had sought out the most disreputable taverns, who had looked for women who would never claim his freedom?

His hands moved along the sides of her dress, and then he leaned down, his lips barely touching her sun-kissed cheek. He meant then to let her go, to retreat and watch her, but her hand wouldn't release his, and she turned her face slightly so her mouth touched his. Her other hand touched the darkened skin of his arm where he'd rolled up the sleeves of his shirt.

Raw, physical need struck like a hammer in his groin as she leaned against him. He savored the sound of her heartbeat, the taste of her, the feel of their bodies together, the gentle friction of skin against skin. He had never felt at one with another person before, and he relished the exquisite pain of feelings too deep to express.

When he looked up, the sun was setting. Together they watched splashes of crimson spread across the sky, then blend into soft shades of coral and gold. The sea glazed with the last glittering rays of a lazily descending sun. The first star was barely visible, and the warm breeze cooled and played with the loose edges of their clothes.

He had never seen a more beautiful sunset. He looked down at Annette's rapt face.

"Why did you ever leave here?" Annette's voice was tinged with awe.

He shrugged. "I love Maryland, too."

"Do you?"

"Oh, I never want to be a farmer. Neither do I want to be a lawyer." He held her close, and told her his dream, the one he had told no other. "I would like to build ships, fine ones that could sail from the Continent to America in far less time than it takes now. There is talk of a steam-driven ship that sailed on the Seine. I would like to build one like that some day."

"And continue to sail around the world?"

"Aye," he said. *With you.*

She leaned back in his arms, and her fingers touched his mouth. Her body ached with tension, with savage wanting. The intensity of his words, the sharing of his dream, made her best intentions slide away like the particles of sand swept back into the sea. She didn't understand the depth of her feelings; she only knew she loved him, and that she loved with a fierceness that frightened her.

His eyes blazed with passion as his hand stroked her neck. He bent his head. His lips met hers with such restrained yearning that she felt her heart crack. He nuzzled her cheek, then the lobe of her ears and finally her neck, until her legs were useless and her body meshed into his.

He turned her, guiding her behind an old washed-out log. He took her good hand and gently pulled her to the sand, sitting down next to her. The sand was still warm from the sun and fine, like sugar. Together, they watched the very end of the sunset, then the beginning of twilight, and the coming out of stars.

"Why do you always call your ships *Star Rider*?" she asked.

"Stars have meant good luck to my family," he said. "They called one of my ancestors the Starcatcher. My father refers to himself as the Starfinder, for finding my mother."

"They truly love each other, do they not?" she asked wistfully.

"Aye," John Patrick said. "I once thought it very rare."

But not now. Could it be? She tried to make her voice steady. "I would think you would want to stay near them." She would. Family had always meant everything to her.

He was silent for a long time, but he held her good hand tight in his. He wanted her to understand who and what he was. "I always lusted for adventure. I did not realize the price adventure often exacts. I was . . . uncomfortable when I returned home. I was no longer the Jonny they loved and respected. I think my father understood; he fought at Culloden, and watched his brother hang. He knew about killing, and"—he hesitated—"vengeance."

"Do you still want vengeance?" she said, staring up at him.

"No," he said softly.

She seemed to hold her breath for a moment. "Then why don't you start your shipbuilding? Now?"

"I still have a duty, love."

"To whom? You are not in the army or navy."

"To my country, Annette."

"Vengeance," she insisted.

"No. The anger is gone. But I believe in the American cause. We are a different people from those in England, with their classes and strictures."

"Your family held titles."

"Ah, the Scots were different. They followed a leader because they respected him, not because of how he was born."

"There would be no colonies without England."

"The English did not settle the colonies out of the goodness of their hearts," he growled. "They saw riches, and they saw markets for their goods. They wanted a vast empire to lord over."

"No vengeance?" she asked with a raised eyebrow.

"Perhaps still a little," he admitted. "I do not want anyone else forced to serve England's navy." He put a finger to her mouth. "No more politics, little Tory. 'Tis much too fine an evening."

"Will your crew not miss you?"

"I think not. They are used to my . . . absences."

His fingers were stroking her shoulders, and he felt her tremble under his touch. They were alone, far away and out of sight from a road seldom used. It was as if they were on a deserted island of their own.

A full moon climbed into the sky, its initial transparency taking on substance and brightness. One star after another filled the heavens, joining the early ones that had sparked her question.

But her gaze was on him, now. Her gray eyes smoldered. Her body was taut and her hand played a sensuous rhythm on his arm.

He had vowed . . .

She *would* be his wife. He bargained with himself, with the devil, as his hands untied the laces of her dress, pulling it away from her, then her chemise. His mouth trailed kisses down her silken curves.

Annette heard a sigh, like the rustle of a gentle wind against sails, and he pulled her close.

She looked up at the startling green eyes that always seemed to hide so much. The shadows made them more enigmatic than ever. The only hint of what he felt was the slight movement of muscles in his jaw.

But his hands reflected what his face did not. They caressed, seduced, loved until her body felt like a jewel, as bright and glowing as the moon above.

So many sensations flowed through her. The tropical night—the sea, the sky, the warm fragrant breeze—gave her feelings she'd never known before. She'd accused him of taking her freedom. Now she realized he had given her the first true freedom she'd ever known.

The hesitation, even the fear, she'd had when he'd first made love to her was gone. Her body remembered every ripple of pleasure after that first pain, and now she felt it reacting to the memory.

Annette had always believed love would come slowly, that it formed quietly and naturally between people with the same likes, the same values, the same loyalties; that it required trust and commitment; that it should involve friendship.

John Patrick offered none of that. He was lightning to her quiet dusk, a tempest to her April shower, a rogue to her dutiful spinster. She had spent her life trying to please people and do the right thing; he had spent his rebelling against them.

Star Rider. It fit him, fit his restlessness and his curiosity and his hopes. No woman could tame him, especially not her.

That knowledge was anguish. Because she loved him to the depth of her soul. She didn't know why or when or how it happened. She only knew it was the painful truth.

She also knew she was going to seize every glorious second, memorize the sounds and scents and touches of this night, keep them locked in her mind and heart forever.

Her body was tingling, aching, arching. They were both unclothed now, except for his shirt. The shirt he always wore.

When he kissed her this time, her lips responded with reckless abandon, with that freedom that was still so astonishing to her. His kiss deepened, and the heat between them became blue hot, like the core of a flame. Shudders ran through her as his hand went to the most sensitive part of her, caressing and teasing until her body convulsed with a series of exquisite explosions.

"Jonny," she heard herself cry, only partially aware of adopting the name used by those who loved him.

"Lovely lady," he whispered as his body came down

over hers, moving slowly down on her, entering with a deliberate slowness that created an agonizing need inside her. She found herself moving against him in instinctive, circular movements, drawing him deeper and deeper inside her.

Waves of intoxicating pleasure flowed through her, filled her. Even a kind of bliss numbed her mind with the plain joy of being with him, of having him become a part of her, of feeling his hands touching her with something like worship. She wanted to capture that feeling forever.

But then his movements increased in tempo, in rhythm, and she wanted even more. Her body responded wantonly to his, moving as frantically as his as they rode an incredible wave, a great force that rushed them along. Then he plunged one last time, filling her, a satisfaction that defied any definition. He stilled, then pulled away, turning away from her.

She heard his groan, his deep breathing, and she knew that he was sacrificing for her, that he didn't want to risk giving her a child. The thought saddened her, drained away some of the euphoria she'd felt, even though she knew it the wise thing. He did not want to be trapped, and she did not want to trap him. No matter how deeply she felt about him, how much she wanted him, she could never do that.

He took her hand and she clutched his tightly, though she said nothing. Instead, she listened to the primitive sound of sea and birds and wind, and allowed her body to savor the still exquisite aftershocks of their lovemaking. She leaned against him, feeling his heartbeat, listening to his labored breathing.

Her hand ventured gently beneath his shirt, and she felt the scarring on his back. He tensed, but then slowly, very slowly began to relax. Then her fingers climbed, caressing the scars. The shirt inched up, and she couldn't quite stifle a gasp.

She had seen just a fraction of his scars during that day in her home, but she had never seen the mass of them. Deep ugly ridges and jagged white scars criss-crossed the whole of his back. It was obvious they had not been treated, nor sewn, and had healed slowly and unevenly. She couldn't bear to think of the pain he'd endured.

He started to move away, as if fearing she'd been re-pulsed, but her hand restrained him. She pulled the shirt all the way up, to his shoulder blades, and she leaned over, her lips touching the scars with all the tenderness she had. She wanted to go back to those years and take away the pain, pain she now knew lingered to this day. John Patrick Sutherland was the proudest man she'd ever met; she couldn't even imagine what it had done to him to endure such barbarity.

So her lips and her fingers tried to tell him that those scars didn't matter, not to her, not to anyone. She wanted to tell him she loved him, but she feared he would feel trapped by her feelings as surely as he would with a child. Bittersweet regret filled her, but still she sat beside him, touching him, unable to move away.

He turned slightly and his gaze met hers, then his hand caught her fingers. She wondered whether his heart pounded as strongly as hers. She wondered whether he thought the moon brighter, the stars closer, the air more scented.

Then he stood and pulled her up with him. He took off his shirt, then led her into the sea. The water was cool but not cold, and marvelously sensuous on skin still heated by making love. The coolness felt like moving silk; the warm, fragrant breeze brushed Annette with in-toxicating softness and his fingers, intermingled with hers, played against hers with a rhythm that revived the sensations still humming in her body.

She looked at him, at his lean and powerful body, and she thought how astonishingly beautiful he was. Her heart hammered inside her chest as she suddenly saw herself: she, Annette Carey, standing naked, unashamed, in the moonlight. She could barely believe herself, and yet . . . the wicked sorcery was irresistible.

They stood in water that advanced, then retreated, leaving sands trickling through her toes, and then he went to his knees, bringing her with him, and his lips met hers with a fierce hunger. Her senses spun and whirled as the kiss deepened into something frenzied, and then she was lying down, the water washing over her as he entered once again, his movements in rhythm with the pull of the sea. An elemental, primitive need, raw and savage, seized her body, and she wrapped her legs around his, her hands clasping his back. She heard him whisper to her, but the words were lost in the soft lapping of the water. His lips were suddenly gentle, his breath on her cheek mingling with the drops of cool water that washed over them, and his movements inside her slow and languorous, until her body was so wondrously aching, so needy for more, that she cried out.

His lips moved, and his mouth nibbled her throat, even as her hands caressed his back, his neck, moving back and forth with love she still feared to whisper but conveyed in so many other ways. His body stilled for a moment, and she felt her own body love his, wrap around and cosset him, and then he moved again, deeper and deeper until he reached the essence of her, and this time his slow measured strokes, his soft whispering kisses, brought a tender sweetness to their bonding, a giving so complete that her heart nearly burst with it. Together, their souls joined as their bodies merged and

danced in a soft sea with millions of stars as their wit-
nesses.

Later, they lay together, their bodies still clasped together, the water cooling the fever of their bodies.

He brought her hand to his mouth and kissed it, the
edge of his thumb teasing hers.

Annette held tight to his hand, wondering how a body
could absorb so many feelings, how it could melt into
another and now feel all the echoes of their mating, still
so warm, so rapturous, so magical. How could she love
so totally, so poignantly?

She kissed his shoulder, then nibbled on his neck, unable *not* to touch him, to feel and share every single
instant of the extraordinary magic.

"I love you," he whispered then, his words mixing
with the sounds of sea.

Her finger touched his lips. She had just given him
her heart. But she couldn't, for some reason, say the
words. As miraculous as she felt, as her body felt, a voice
deep inside her warned her that this was an isolated
piece of enchanted time. He would return to his world,
and she to hers.

But he didn't seem to require an answer. He rolled
away from her, looking down at her. "You were meant to
be a sea sprite," he said softly, and she knew for sure
then that they saw two different people.

She tried to smile, tried to believe him, even as she
saw that fine glimpse of splendor drift away.

John Patrick swore to himself as Annette's face paled
when she watched the cannon loaded on the ship.

The day of reckoning.

He'd had three days of heaven, of introducing her to
the place he loved best after Maryland. He had watched
her eyes light with pleasure as she tipped her feet in
springs warmed by the island's volcanos, and taught her

to swim in a cold pool underneath a hundred-foot water-fall. He'd rejoiced in the delight in her eyes at the dresses he'd purchased for her. They had shared suppers of fresh fish at the city's most respectable tavern, and she browsed through every shop in Fort Royal, her gaze devouring everything new and different.

On the second day at anchorage, he had gone alone into Fort Royal and made the final arrangement for delivery of the cannon, which had arrived two weeks earlier from France. Officially, they'd been purchased on the credit of the new young nation, and he was only the delivery agent, but in actuality, he knew, they were a gift from France. On his way back from the meeting, he'd stopped at the shop with the parrot and emerged with the bird in tow.

He had his doubts about the bird. The shopkeeper had sworn he spoke only the cleanest of language, and John Patrick was only slightly mollified when the bird kept insisting hopefully, "Billy's a good bird." John Patrick's experience told him that those who most often spoke of their virtues were more frequently apt to have none. Was that also true of birds?

But any reservations he'd had were quickly quenched when he saw the pleasure in Annette's eyes as he handed her the cage with the bird in it. The bird had promptly informed her that she was now the owner of a very good bird.

Something in its beady eyes, though, told John Patrick that Billy might be exaggerating things a bit.

Still, she had regarded the parrot with absolute delight, and that disquieting reserve in her eyes faded. He'd had trouble leaving her then, but if he had broken some of his rules, he was not going to break the one about spending the night in her cabin. What his crew suspected, and what they knew, were two different things.

Then this morning—their fourth in Martinique—he had moved the *Star Rider* to the wharf. He had been issuing orders when she appeared on deck, and he'd watched the horror wash over her face as she saw massive guns rolled to where the ship was tied. And looked at him accusingly as a gang of dockworkers rolled eight large pieces of artillery on board, all of them far uglier looking than the guns on his ship. He watched, occasionally issuing instructions, as they were dismantled and stored in the hold.

When he looked back to where Annette was standing, she had disappeared.

His stomach clenched. He was now used to her confronting him. The fact that she had not stormed over to him left him with questions and uncharacteristic worry.

He called to Beasley, who had been looking after her. As large as Ivy, and as rough-looking as any brigand, he had taken to his duties as maid and butler with startling alacrity. Beasley had been watching the loading with the other crew members, and now ambled over.

"Keep an eye on Miss Carey while we're docked here," he said. "And you might see whether she needs anything."

"Aye, sir."

John Patrick turned his attention back to the cannon. He'd had the hold cleared yesterday, the remaining stores distributed throughout the ship. He'd used his own funds to purchase large amounts of fresh fruits, which he knew would be welcomed by Washington's hungry troops. They would be delivered after the cannon, his first priority.

He was supervising tying down the various parts of cannon in the hold when Beasley came to him.

"I can't find her," he said worriedly.

John Patrick swore under his breath. He couldn't leave now. The weight of each twelve-pounder exceeded

3,200 pounds, and if it weren't distributed and secured properly, the first storm could well sink the *Star Rider*.

Where had she gone? And how? He hadn't been able to keep his gaze on the gangplank, but he thought he would have noticed if she left the ship. *Someone* would have noticed.

Beasley was still standing in front of him.

"Take a couple of men and look for her in town."

The crewman hesitated. "Ah . . . sir . . . then what do I do? If she don't want to come back?"

"Bring her anyway."

Beasley's eyes widened, then he nodded reluctantly.

Ivy approached then, perhaps aware of the tension in his captain. "Sir?" he said, as he always did on board.

"Miss Carey is missing."

"She cannot have gone far. And she can't do any harm."

She could if she reported being kidnapped. The governor might well hold the ship. Or confiscate it. But even that consequence paled as John Patrick realized how *she* must feel at this moment. He had broken through that reserve she'd clung to so tightly. She'd trusted him with her body, even, he thought, with her heart.

He closed his eyes. He should have told her days ago. He'd known it would matter to her, but he hadn't been able to force himself to shatter the magic they had created together.

"Dammit," he whispered, his voice rough with frustration.

"I can see to securing the cargo," Ivy said. "You go look for her."

"No," he said. He trusted Ivy, but this was too important. "Beasley will find her."

He worked through the afternoon, until the last barrel had been securely tied with hemp and cable.

Then he went up on deck. Beasley had not yet appeared.

John Patrick gave orders to Ivy about storing the fruit, then combed the ship. No Annette, though Billy was still in her room, as were most of her clothes. "Bad boy," the parrot scolded, then clucked as if he knew exactly what he was talking about. John Patrick knew he was going to regret purchasing the bird, but that was the least of his concerns now.

Where had she gone?

Where?

Annette stood for a long time in front of the building that housed the government offices.

She could stop the cannon from reaching America. Neutrality laws were openly being broken. And then there was the matter of kidnapping.

From the moment she saw the cannon being loaded, her blood froze. So did her heart. Though John Patrick had not lied to her, she suspected he knew exactly how she would feel about being a party to wholesale slaughter of the men for whom she had cared. His silence was nothing less than a betrayal. He had made love to her, had made her fall in love with him, knowing all the time he was doing something utterly repellent to her. Small arms were bad enough. But cannon! Even she knew that the cannon were larger than those needed to protect a ship. Even she knew they were meant to tear soldiers on the field to pieces.

She *could* stop it. She could be loyal to all she believed, to the men who had believed in her, who trusted her.

And in doing so, she would be sentencing John Patrick to death. Kidnapping was not something taken lightly. The French authorities would be forced to hold him, to try him for piracy.

She felt a tear trickling down her cheek. She couldn't

forgive him. But neither could she be responsible for his death. The lump in her throat constricted her breathing. Her heart felt as if it were breaking. All that joy, all that wonder had been naught but a mirage.

Deep in her heart, she knew she couldn't betray him as she felt he had betrayed her. But neither would she sail with him again. She would not allow his sorcery to subjugate her again.

Where would she go? She knew he would come after her. He could not afford to allow her to wander about. But she had no funds, no clothes other than those she was wearing. How would she get back to Philadelphia? How could she reclaim her family?

Her fingers went to the antique sapphire-and-pearl brooch she always wore around her neck. As the only remaining piece of her mother's life that had survived the fire, she treasured it as she treasured no other possession.

If she could make her way to St. Pierre on the other side of the island, perhaps he would not be able to find her. Perhaps there she could find a ship headed toward some port, where she could then find a British ship. She would need a horse, and she had no idea how much the brooch would bring.

Fighting back the tears behind her eyes, she entered the first store that looked promising. The shopkeeper smiled, having seen her the day before.

"I am interested in selling a piece of jewelry," she said in the halting French she had learned as a girl. She took the brooch from around her neck and handed it to him, watching as his fingers gently touched the intricate design.

"Mademoiselle," he sighed. "It is truly beautiful, but I cannot give you its worth."

"How much?" she asked.

He named a sum in francs that she tried to translate, and her heart plummeted.

"*Merci,*" she said, shaking her head and taking back the brooch.

Three more stores yielded similar results. The fourth shopkeeper, however, studied it longer. And finally made an offer higher than the others. It was not all she hoped for, but she knew now she would receive little more.

She nodded, and watched as he counted out gold coins.

How much more time did she have?

She looked out the door and saw Beasley far down the street, pausing at the entrance of each establishment. He would catch up with her soon.

She put a hand to her head and swayed.

"Monsieur. I feel . . . faint. Do you have somewhere I can sit down for a moment?"

He rushed to the other side of the counter and took her arm. "*Oui,* in the back."

He took her through a curtain to a room in the back of the store. It was piled high with boxes, but several chairs were scattered around a table and he helped her to one. She sat and lowered her head into her hands. "The . . . heat," she said. "I will be fine in a few moments." She gave him a weak smile. "Please, I do not wish to worry anyone."

He frowned. "The physician?" He asked in French. "Should I not find him?"

She shook her head. "It will go away."

He stood undecided a moment, then nodded and headed back toward the front of the store.

She waited for an agonizing five, then ten minutes. The storekeeper came in twice to check on her, and the third time, she rose. "I feel much better," she said. "*Merci.*"

Moments later, she had purchased a horse and

sidesaddle she intended to sell again in St. Pierre. Beasley was nowhere to be seen. He was probably, she thought bitterly, reporting back to Captain Sutherland. She bought a map of the island, so she would not need to ask any more questions.

She mounted the horse with the help of the hostler. Then, praying she would not be seen, she avoided the main road that ran along the waterfront in preference to a smaller road running behind the buildings. Soon it met the main road, twisted around the bay, and she was out of sight of the anchorage. And the *Star Rider*. The road, she thought with no little dismay, led to the beach where he had taken her three nights ago. The memories caused her throat to constrict. She tightened her knees, and the mare quickened into a canter.

She was free.

But there was no elation in the knowledge. Only a terrible loneliness. She wasn't running to anything. She was running away.

And her heart felt as if it were crumbling into a thousand pieces.

Chapter 22

WOULD Annette go to the government house?
If so, John Patrick's crew and General
Washington would pay the price.

He should have told her at the beginning of the voyage exactly what he was doing. He kept seeing her face as the cannon was loaded: the bleak despair, the look of betrayal as she looked up at him.

John Patrick swallowed through the thickness in his throat. He felt sick inside, sick at what he had done to her, done to himself. Would she ever look at him again the way she'd looked at him yesterday, and the day before? And this morning? Had he completely destroyed any future he might ever have with her?

But through all the soul-searching, which yielded little, he could not avoid the possibilities her disappearance presented.

She had been gone hours. Surely, if she'd gone to the authorities, his ship would be thick with police and constables.

He knew her. At least, he thought he did. So he started his search among the shops and soon discovered that a woman had visited them hours ago, seeking to sell a piece of jewelry. The brooch. It was the only thing of value she had. His heart sank lower. She must have felt even more desperate than he believed if she'd been willing to sell the cameo.

He continued along the line of shops until he saw it in a window. He went inside. "I am interested in the brooch in the window," he told the shopkeeper in French.

The man beamed. "I just purchased it, not more than two hours ago. A treasure, is it not?"

"*Oui*," John Patrick said. "How much?"

The shopkeeper mentioned an amount that made his brows rise in surprise. But he had no time to bargain. He quickly paid for the brooch and hurried out. His next stop was the livery where he'd rented horses for their outings. As he thought, Annette had been there. And buying, not renting.

"Do you know where she went?"

"*Non*, monsieur."

But he thought he did. She had few alternatives. She had little money, no clothes, no resources. Just her courage. And her outrage.

He knew how great that was. How far would it take her?

He could think of only one place she might go, only one place she *could* go.

John Patrick knew he should return to his ship. She could do nothing to stop him now, and his duty was to get the cannon back to America. To the war.

He couldn't do it. He couldn't leave her here. Not without money, or friends, or any way to get home. He could only guess what she planned: She would try to find passage from St. Pierre. But he was only too aware of the ships that called into St. Pierre, and he trusted none of them.

John Patrick rented a horse, and at a gallop headed toward St. Pierre, praying every mile he was right.

Annette stopped and dismounted at the beach where she'd made love with John Patrick. She justified the short detour as necessary to rest the horse. In reality, she could not force herself to pass it by without one final look.

So much had happened there. She'd given her heart, and now she had to take it back. She just didn't know how. How do you stop loving someone? Yet how can you continue to love someone you cannot trust? How can you love someone whose loyalties and values are so different from your own?

She'd thought love would mean safety, protection, friendship, trust.

She'd never thought it meant lightning bolts, suspicion, doubt, betrayal.

John Patrick was like a meteor flashing through her universe, bright and full of splendor, but destined to burn itself out.

Then why did he still fill her mind and soul? Why couldn't she let him go?

The beach still looked beautiful, but now it also looked lonely. Seabirds hopped across the sand before taking to the sky and starting their graceful dives into the green-blue sea for their supper. The sand glistened with the rays from the sun, as did turquoise-colored waters. She saw the log they had used for privacy. She saw in her mind's eye the two of them—herself and John Patrick—together. Loss flooded her, and she fought back tears.

Her hand ran over the mare's neck and she leaned against the animal for support. All the underpinnings of her life had been swept away. She had never done anything so rash, but she knew she could not face him again, could not look into John Patrick's face without feeling explosive emotions that threatened everything she was and wanted to be.

Time to go. Time to set out on her own. The thought gave her courage. She'd defied so many when she'd convinced her aunt to take in wounded. She had risked her reputation, yet she had been safe. Safe! She was sick of the word. She wanted to control her own destiny.

Annette led the horse over to the rotted log and climbed up on the mare, then had the strangest urge to ride the horse along the beach. She turned the horse toward the surf, then urged the mare into a trot, splashing through the clear water, feeling the wetness against her legs. The sun shone down on her, warmed her. The wind made her hair fly free.

She wondered whether she would ever know these feelings again. If nothing else, John Patrick had given her this awareness of being alive, given her the confidence to determine her own fate. She had lost. But she had also won.

She turned the horse, and then she saw him. John Patrick, astride a bay, rode toward her. She thought about racing away, but she knew now she must confront him, confront her own demons.

Annette slowed and met him. Her gaze caught his and refused to falter under its intensity.

"I am going to St. Pierre," she said.

"I'm sorry," he said. "I should have told you."

"Yes," she said simply.

She saw his uncertainty, and it unexpectedly touched her. He was never uncertain.

"I have a proposition to make."

"That would be unique. Usually, you just take what you want." She heard the chill in her voice.

"Aye," he said, surprising her again. "I'm afraid I have grown used to that. I truly didn't mean to do it with you."

"You *truly* didn't," she mocked.

"No. I never wanted to hurt you."

"You think you hurt me?"

His gaze seemed to bore directly into her heart.

"Well, you are wrong. You've given me strength, and I thank you for it."

"You've always been strong, Annette. You just did not recognize it."

Why did he always have the ability to disconcert her, to disarm her? But it would not happen this time.

"Believe it," he said softly.

She turned her horse, trying to pass him. He didn't try to stop her, but turned and walked his horse next to hers. "You haven't heard my proposition," he said.

"I am not interested. You lie as easily as you smile, and that's far too facile for me."

She saw pain flicker through his eyes. She hardened herself against it.

"Come back with me," he said. "I swear I will not come near you. I will take you to Baltimore and then, if you still wish, to Philadelphia."

"I can get there on my own."

"You might," he allowed. "Then what of your father?"

She turned. "Is that a threat?"

"Nay. You should know by now I would never hurt any of you. But I know the captains of the ships that ply these waters. You would not be safe with them. Then what would happen to your father?"

"And I am safe with you?"

He was silent.

The only sound for several moments was the cry of the seabirds, the gentle pounding of the sea, the dull thud of hoofs on the sand. She turned her horse away from the sea, toward the road.

"Annette."

She didn't turn. Her hands twisted around her purse of coins, her only defense against him.

"If you will not go on the *Star Rider*, stay with

Louis—Dr. Fortier, until he can find a reliable ship, and a chaperon."

"It is a little late for that," she said. She kept her eyes straight ahead, trying to hide her surprise that he hadn't merely attempted to take her reins and force her back. "You can always kidnap me again. You are very good at that."

"I will never again force you into anything you do not want," he said.

She looked then. "Sugar instead of pepper?"

"I've always preferred pepper," he replied with a wry smile.

She had, too, but that was not what she meant. And she knew he realized it.

"I should have said poison."

A muscle moved in his jaw. His voice was barely audible. "I had hoped . . ."

"That your charm would substitute for honesty?"

"No."

The horses reached the road. She started to turn toward St. Pierre.

"I meant what I said," John Patrick said, stopping her. "I *will* take you home."

"To Philadelphia?"

"If that is what you want, yes."

She eyed him skeptically. "You will no longer make decisions for me?"

"No."

"Why should I believe you?"

His gaze met hers. "You have no reason, I know." His eyes were brilliant. "If you can't . . . trust me, then stay here in Fort Royal until Louis can find you safe passage."

Annette studied his face. He would let her go. How long would it take her to find a ship? How long to return to her family? But could she really trust him to fulfill his part of the bargain? Could she trust herself?

"I have tried not to lie to you, Annette," he said. "I have not told you things, but I have tried not to lie."

"You said you were John Gunn," she challenged.

He had the decency—or the wit—to look embarrassed. But he didn't defend himself.

Annette felt herself weakening. She knew her plan would be difficult to carry out.

And she wanted to go home. The lure of the island had turned sour.

She looked ahead, her hands tightening on the reins. Could she really stay away from him in the close confines of the ship? Even now, she wanted to touch him, to run her fingers along the ridges of his face. Her body was already tingling in reaction to his closeness. She was beginning to understand what he meant by choices. How difficult they were.

She could spend months trying to get home, leaving her father alone in Maryland, Aunt Maude and Betsy alone in Philadelphia—or she could trust him. And herself.

"I will sail with you. On my terms."

"On your terms," he agreed.

Then he took a small package from his trousers and handed it to her.

"You forgot this," he said.

She took it, holding it for a moment. Then she slowly opened it. She already knew what was inside. Her throat constricted. She looked up at him, but she didn't know what to say.

"We had best go," he said softly, and turned away before she could say anything else.

Her terms were pure hell.

The only thing that saved John Patrick's honor—and

sanity—was the weather. Storms buffeted the *Star Rider*, one after another. He stayed awake twenty hours a day, napping only briefly while Ivy took command. Day after day, they encountered one squall after another until he thought surely the ship would become as exhausted as the crew.

He saw her infrequently. She ventured on deck during the few calm hours, then once just as a storm was brewing. He felt as if she were a thousand miles away, rather than a hundred feet. She had built a wall around herself again, and it was one he couldn't breach. She would have to open the gates herself.

As one day disappeared into another, he doubted that would happen.

On the thirteenth day, the sun appeared. The twentieth of December, according to his calendar. He remembered what Annette had said about wanting to be with her father for Christmas.

And again he weighed his loyalties. He should head directly for the Delaware River, and the treacherous trek to Washington's winter headquarters. But he could take a few more days and run down the Chesapeake.

Several days would not a battle win. Washington would not move until after Christmas.

John Patrick chose the Chesapeake.

Noel started packing the few necessities he needed, and made arrangements for someone to care for the house and horses.

It was time, past time, to leave Philadelphia. There was no question that he was under suspicion by British authorities. No officers came to his home for afternoon brandy and games of whist. He received no more calls to attend Howe's officers, and he was certain he was being watched.

At least he'd managed to get the last of the Carey

household out of town four days ago. As suspicion started to fall on him, he feared it might also touch Maude Carey, since he visited there so often. He was not unaware that the British suspected the Star Rider had received medical attention from someone.

He'd also finally found Annette's missing mare, Sasha, and it was the least he could do to get her back to her owner.

Telling Maude that her brother-in-law needed her, Noel had arranged for a private coach to take her out of the city, and then for one of his couriers to see her safely to his family's farm. Sasha was to go with them, along with Betsy and Franklin.

No one, he thought, would stop an old woman, a maid, and an ancient manservant who thought they were going to New York. Hell, he was as Machiavellian as John Patrick, but he'd not had time to explain that Hugh Carey was not in New York but in an American home in Maryland.

Malcomb had informed him just this morning that they had passed through British lines and were safely on their way.

Now all he had to do was get himself and Malcomb out. They planned to leave tonight after dark.

Noel had told Malcomb to avoid his house and office. If he were taken, he did not want Malcomb arrested as well. Yet the Scotsman continued to report to him, moving through the dark streets and entering through the back door.

Katy had been right. He should have left weeks earlier, right after Jonny's theft of the British ship. But he had been one of General Washington's most effective spies, and he'd kept putting off his departure. After Howe ordered a lunge at Washington's forces in early December, Noel had been asked to stay and report any talk of another attack on Valley Forge. In the last few days, though, he realized that his time as a rebel agent had run its course.

He'd never fancied swinging at the end of a rope.

John Patrick's unexpected—and unintentional—visit had started a leak that now threatened to tear down the dam. Katy had not helped. Roger Gambrell had become decidedly less affable after her visit, and he suspected that Gambrell's sudden interest in Noel's background had much to do with Katy's spurning of him. She had provided an opening to Noel's complicated history.

After an officer turned his back on Noel at the City Tavern last night, he knew it was time to leave. A Christmas visit home was his excuse, if anyone bothered to ask. He had sent his final message to general Washington this morning, praying that the courier would get through.

Noel finished packing several changes of clothing in his saddlebags. He added a pistol and cartridges. That and his medical bag were all he would be taking.

He looked around the house he loved. Well, he would be back when Washington retook the city. Noel did not think it would be long. Howe was already talking about returning to New York. The proposed French alliance with the rebels, and the consequent threat of French naval activity, would force Howe to consolidate his forces with Clinton's.

And then . . . then he would probably return, though many of his Quaker friends might well consider him a traitor. Most of them had stayed true to the king, had cheered when Howe had entered the city. Just as the rebels had shunned him when they believed him a collaborator, his Tory friends, he knew, would turn on him.

But now he had to worry about leaving the city in one piece.

He would go to Washington first and hope that the general had received the messages Noel had sent by courier. If not, he would give him all he had. Then Noel would turn toward the Chesapeake—and Katy.

Darkness shrouded the city. Time to leave. He would take his fastest horse, a dark bay, which would easily fit into the shadows. He had left the horse at the blacksmith shop and told the smith he would pick him up tonight. Malcomb would steal a horse for himself. Neither of them wanted to be seen leaving the house on horseback.

Noel took the saddlebags and the medical bag and slipped out the back door, taking Aristotle with him. He trusted no one with the dog, and he knew the animal would stay with him. He moved silently behind the houses of his neighbors and through narrow streets, feeling unseen eyes on him.

Thank God, clouds drifted heavily across the sky, eclipsing even the smallest light from a waning moon. He heard the sound of wheels on the road. He knew Malcomb would be waiting near the tavern across from the blacksmith's to make sure he made his escape. Then Malcomb would follow.

Noel reached the blacksmith's shop with its attached stable. He tried the door, found it unlocked and slipped inside.

Suddenly he was surrounded by redcoats. Major Roger Gambrell stepped in front of him.

"Going someplace, Doctor?"

Noel lifted his bag. "A call."

"Strange. No one appeared at your home."

Noel gave the major a look of outrage. "You've been watching my house?"

"Oh, for some time now. I suspect you know that," Gambrell added, "since you felt it necessary to sneak out the back door."

"I often go out the back," Noel said. "By what authority do you question me?"

"General Howe's," Gambrell said. "Now if you

would be so kind as to accompany me." He took a step closer, and Aristotle growled.

"If you don't want me to kill that beast, tie him up, now," Gambrell said.

Noel did what was asked as the huge dog looked at him with betrayed eyes. Noel had never tied him before. "Stay," Noel said softly.

"Now it is your turn, Doctor," Gambrell said, then turned to one of his men. "Put irons on him."

Noel's heart sank. There was nothing Malcomb could do now but retrieve Aristotle and report to Washington. Thank God, they had not been together.

"Your hands, Doctor," Gambrell insisted.

Noel looked around. Ten men filled the stable. He had no chance other than to protest his innocence, and innocent men did not run. He did as he was told, and felt the hard, cold bite of iron around his wrists.

The game *was* over. And it looked as if he had lost.

Ah, Katy. Now there would never be time for them.

Malcomb watched the detachment of soldiers march Noel from the building. Dressed in beggar's rags with a patch over one of his eyes, Malcomb looked nothing like the doctor's assistant.

He, too, had felt the noose tightening, and he had taken every precaution not to be caught.

He saw the major send several men back to the Marsh house, probably to watch for him. The dog must be inside the stable, either dead or secured in some way. Otherwise, he never would have let Noel out of his sight.

Malcomb debated with himself several moments. Was the animal worth being caught? He knew Noel would never ask it of him. Hell, Malcomb didn't even like the bloody beast. Aristotle had no use for anyone but his master.

Malcomb swallowed hard, then edged forward. The

stable was unlocked, and he wondered briefly whether the smith had betrayed them, or whether he was under arrest, too. Had the major left anyone inside? If so, then he was probably a dead man along with Noel. The door opened at his touch. No one was there. Probably the bloody British didn't think anyone would be insane enough to risk their life over a dog. Calling himself every kind of a fool, Malcomb went over to the beast, who was whining and straining at the rope that held him.

"Want to go after him, donna' you?" he said.

The dog whined again.

"Well, you canna'. But I will get you back to him if you help me."

The dog stopped whining and stared at him, as if trying to understand. It was, Malcomb thought, almost uncanny. The dog had always ignored him, but now seemed to be trying to decide whether or not to trust him. The animal's tongue suddenly darted out and licked his hand.

"All right, then," Malcomb said. He untied the rope from the post, and led the dog out, still keeping to the shadows. What in the hell was he going to do with the beast? If the animal would follow him quietly, then all would be well.

He had no more time to waste. He had to leave the city and notify Washington, then Noel's family. He had to mount some kind of rescue. That damn fool brother of Noel's escaped and took half the prison with him. Certainly Malcomb could do as well. But he needed help, and he had no one in the city he could trust. Not now. They—Noel and he—had played their roles too well. No rebel would trust them, and now no Tory.

"Stay with me, Aristotle," he said, and the dog obediently moved closer to him, hopeful he would be taken to his owner. Malcomb moved silently through the streets he knew so well, until he reached a disreputable tavern where he knew certain officers went to game. He looked over their mounts carefully and chose what looked to be the swiftest. Arrogant bastards, leaving their horses unattended.

He put a hand to the chosen mount's neck and ran his hand up and down, talking to it softly as he had seen Noel do. He was nowhere the horseman that his friend was, but he had picked up the custom of making friends with an animal before mounting it. The horse shied as Aristotle neared, but Malcomb's hands gentled him. Then Malcomb took the reins and led him quietly down the street, moving aside as a noisy band of redcoats drunkenly stumbled down the street. Malcomb leaned over and stopped Aristotle's soft growl, then once the soldiers had passed, he mounted the horse and whistled to the dog as he'd heard Noel do.

His prayers were answered when the dog followed obediently, trotting just behind the horse. Perhaps the beast wasn't as bloody stupid as he'd thought. The next problem was filtering through British lines with the animal.

Malcomb did something he had never done before. He prayed.

Chapter 23

Annette stood at the railing of the *Star Rider* as the ship rounded a bend and its crew prepared to anchor off the Maryland coast.

She was going home. Why, then, was she so miserable?

John Patrick had kept his word. For nearly three weeks, they had scarcely exchanged a word. When she saw him, she left the deck and retreated to the cabin. Her willpower was sorely tried in his presence, and she did not want to test it again.

How could someone love so much, so painfully? How could someone tolerate the feeling that she was betraying everything she believed in?

They had sighted three British ships during the voyage. John Patrick had either outrun or outwitted each one. Her mind told her she should want the *Star Rider* taken, the cannon destroyed. Her heart wanted something else altogether. She could not bear harm coming to its captain—or his crew, who had tried so hard to make her comfortable.

In any event, she could only stand and watch, or retreat like a child to the luxurious cabin that was a mockery. Only Billy Boy was available for companionship, and the parrot's vocabulary was definitely limited. Despite the alert interest in his beady eyes, she found little stimulation in reciting her woes and hearing a sympathetic "bad boy" in reply. He was, in all truth, a hurtful and constant reminder of John Patrick and Martinique.

She felt her heart being torn in two.

Be true to herself, or true to him. Could she do both?
She no longer knew.

She didn't even know whether he really wanted her.
He had never mentioned marriage or a future together.

Annette tried to unravel all the warring emotions as
the anchor was dropped, and the jiffy lowered. She was
anxious to see her father and, hopefully, to hear of Aunt
Maude and Betsy. She wanted to know that they were all
well. And yes, she wanted to go home.

Or did she?

Be careful what you wish for.

All her adventures gone. The freedom. The pure joy
of sailing on a fine day, of walking into a jeweled sea, of
exploring new lands.

Even worse was the knowledge that all those other
wondrous, enchanted emotions and sensations would
disappear into practical, work-filled days. She would re-
open the hospital and care for her father. She would try
to do good works. The magic would fade into shadows
that would probably haunt her until the day she died.

She felt a tear trickle down her cheek.

Then she sensed John Patrick behind her. She did not
turn. She did not want him to see her despair, when she
should feel elation. He had finally agreed to give her
what she told him she wanted.

"You will be back in your home in another week," he
said in a low soft voice.

This was her home. This ship. Maryland. Wherever
he was. Why had it taken so long to realize it?

She didn't answer.

"Will you change your mind?" he said. "Will you stay
in Maryland?"

She turned and looked up at him. His eyes were intent, searching. She knew his gaze would probably seduce her into jumping into a school of sharks if he asked.

He put a hand on her shoulder. It was so natural a

movement, yet so powerfully explosive to her heart that
shudders ran through her. "Will *you* be here?" she asked,
wishing she hadn't as his eyes clouded.

"Not as long as the war continues," he said.

"Ah, war," she said bitterly. "The call of the sirens."

"No, love," he said. "I admit it was that once, but no
longer. Too many people have been killed, too many
lives ruined. But neither can I turn my back on something I believe."

She leaned against him, feeling his warmth. Yet still
she shivered. She wanted to stay with him. Dear God,
how she wanted that. Could she watch him sail away
over and over again, knowing he would be attacking
British ships, killing British soldiers? Could she wait,
never knowing if he would return?

"Then I cannot stay," she said, her heart breaking
into shards of glass, each piece slicing through her.

His fingers touched her hair. He leaned over and
kissed her lips ever so lightly.

Then he turned and became the captain again, his
voice barking out orders.

Annette's heart lurched as she walked through the door
of the Sutherland home. She had not wanted to wait, and
so she and John Patrick had walked to Tim Wallace's
farm. Then John Patrick had borrowed a buggy to bring
them here.

The sound of the approaching carriage must have
aroused the house, because John Patrick's mother
stepped out just as they pulled up. Fancy Sutherland met
Annette as she jumped down, not waiting for any help.

Mrs. Sutherland embraced her, then stepped back,
looking at her. "Are you all right, Annette?"

She nodded, moved by the warmth in Fancy Sutherland's eyes.

"I am going to have to take my son to task," the older

woman said, "even as big as he is. But that can wait. I have a Christmas gift for you."

After giving John Patrick a baleful glare, she took Annette's hand and led her inside to the parlor, gaily decorated for Christmas. This and That barked loudly, clamoring for attention, but all Annette saw was her father as he stood, a smile lighting his face. "Annie," he said as he held out his arms to her.

Annette stood still for a moment. He had not called her Annie since she was a child. She remembered that, even as her heart thudded at the sound of his voice. She ran into his arms and felt them close around her just as they had years ago. She buried her head against his heart. He was back! Her father was back with them. The Sutherlands had somehow accomplished a miracle.

Just as Jonny had said they would. She had not believed him. Just as she had not believed so many things.

She swallowed hard, then leaned back to look at his face. Life glittered in his eyes, even as a long-awaited smile played over his lips. "You look wonderful," she said.

"So do you, daughter," he said slowly, his eyes studying her face. "I missed you, but you look well and— healthy."

"Is that sun in your complexion?" Aunt Maude said worriedly as she appeared on the stairs and hurried to embrace her niece. "And I certainly hope you had a chaperon . . ."

Annette looked at her aunt in amazement. "How . . . ?" Her voice trailed off.

"That nice Dr. Marsh sent us here. Betsy and Franklin and I." She looked puzzled for a moment. "I am not quite sure how we got here. I thought we were going to New York. But we ended up here, and dear Hugh is so much better."

Betsy flew into the room, hugging Annette. "I am so

glad to see you. Isn't it wonderful about your papa?"
Then she added in a whisper, "There is another Christmas surprise for you."

But Annette had every surprise she needed; her father
was back again from wherever his mind had retreated.
She went back to him and touched his cheek. "But how?
When?"

Hugh spoke slowly and deliberately. "Ian took me
over to the school each day, and I watched over the
children when they played. Then one of the children fell
from a swing, and I . . . had to call Ian for help."

Fancy added, with a little catch in her voice, "Now he
teaches at the school."

"And the child?"

"She's fine. She just lost consciousness for a few moments, but Hugh clucked over her like a mother hen. He
still does. I think," Fancy Sutherland said, "he needed a
purpose."

Gratitude swelled inside her, as Annette looked back
at her father. Why had she not guessed that? Why had
she not involved him more in the hospital, instead of
sheltering him? Had she, by wanting to protect him
from further hurt, actually crippled him?

With sudden insight, she wondered whether she had
tried to do the same with John Patrick. By wanting to
keep him from danger, would she actually destroy all
that she loved in him?

She looked toward the door. He was standing there,
tall and commanding, as the two dogs sniffed and madly
wagged their tails. He'd apparently listened to at least
the last part of her conversation with her father, and his
lips had twisted into a smile. But she saw no pride, only a
certain wistfulness.

Fancy Sutherland went over to her son and looked up,
then put her hand to his cheek. Annette watched him put
his arms around her and give her a bear hug.

"Welcome home," she said.

"I am afraid it is not for long. I have to leave tonight."

Dismay clouded Fancy Sutherland's face.

"But I'll be back soon. I promised Annette I would take her to Philadelphia, her and her family."

Silence suddenly filled the room.

"Annie—" her father started to say.

"But—" her aunt chimed in.

Her family had been entirely seduced by the Sutherlands—as she had been. Could she now force them back to Philadelphia, where, if John Patrick was right, they could be in danger? She didn't think so, but . . .

"You are all welcome to stay," Fancy said hurriedly.

"We have to—" Annette broke off the words as she saw her father's eyes lose some of their glow. He had apparently found some kind of peace here. Could she really take him back to war-torn Philadelphia?

Fancy looked worried. "It will be dangerous. Noel sent a note saying he'd sent your family here for that reason."

John Patrick's brows furrowed together. "Did he say the Careys were under suspicion?"

"No. He just said Philadelphia was becoming dangerous and that there might be another battle soon."

Annette knew now she couldn't take them back. But *she* could go back and make sure Maude's house remained safe. It would be the least she could do for the aunt who had taken her in. She would be safe if the city remained in British hands, and if not . . . well, surely even the rebels wouldn't hurt a woman, especially if she held a note from their hero, the Star Rider.

"No." John Patrick's denial was low. So he suspected again what she was thinking. "If Noel thought it dangerous for your father . . ."

"You promised," she said flatly.

A muscle throbbed in his cheek.

"Daughter?" her father said.

"You can stay here," Annette said. "You and Aunt Maude. I will look after the house in Philadelphia." She knew she had to get away from him, from the feelings he aroused in her.

Both of them looked at her with amazement.

Fancy broke in. "Why don't we wait until Ian returns home? Tomorrow is Christmas Eve. He will surely be back then. He might have a letter from Noel or some news."

Annette looked toward John Patrick. She had sensed his urgency on the voyage back.

He hesitated, then nodded his head curtly. She knew he meant to change her mind, but she had no intention of allowing him to do so.

"Where is my father?"

"Chestertown," Fancy said wryly. "Delivering a horse someone wanted as a Christmas gift."

John Patrick grimaced. "He actually *sold* one?"

Annette must have looked curious, because Fancy turned to her. "Ian does not like selling his horses. Buyers have to meet certain criteria. If he had his way, he would never sell one, but our stable is quite full at the moment, and the Hayeses are friends. It's a mare for his oldest daughter." Then she turned her attention back to John Patrick. "Will you stay? At least through Christmas. And I am sure Annette wants to spend it with her family."

Annette did. She turned pleading eyes on him, and she saw surrender.

"Until Christmas Day," he conceded.

"You can leave me in Chestertown," she said. "I can take a coach from there to Philadelphia."

His face was a mask.

"You did promise," she reminded him again.

"So I did." Then he turned back to Fancy. "I'll stay through Christmas."

She'd won.

So why did she feel that she had lost?

After supper, John Patrick asked Annette to go out to the barn with him. She didn't want to be alone with him or leave her father, but the plea in his eyes made it impossible to refuse him.

She remembered the last time she was here, when she had so desperately refused to accept the Sutherland hospitality. So much had happened since then.

John Patrick opened the barn door and led her to a stall. A bay mare stuck her head out of the stall, whinnying a welcome. Annette stood stunned for a moment, then buried her head in the soft neck of the horse. "Sasha," she murmured.

The horse whinnied again, a soft equine expression of delight. Annette closed her eyes and heard her heart beat faster just as her throat seemed to close. Finally, she turned her head.

John Patrick was leaning against a post, watching, a smile on his lips. "Merry Christmas," he said softly. "It's a little early, but I couldn't wait."

"How—?"

"Before I left Philadelphia, I asked Noel to try to find the horse. He hired someone to search the county where you lived."

She could barely comprehend his words. She had mentioned the horse to him only once, and yet he had remembered.

The man she had thought unfeeling.

"Thank you," she whispered, her heart constricting.

He fished a carrot out of his pocket and handed it to the mare. Sasha nibbled daintily at it, her eyes watching her mistress as if afraid she might disappear again. Annette stroked the soft neck. "You look thin," she whispered. "We have to fatten you up."

But where? She had no place in Philadelphia to keep the mare. She swallowed. "Will you . . . keep her here?"

"Then you insist on going to Philadelphia?"

She turned to him, afraid her heart was in her eyes. "We cannot expect you to keep all of us here forever. I must see if I can bring them back to Philadelphia."

"You can all stay as long as you like."

"No. I don't think I can stand to watch you sail off to war, not knowing whether you will come back, not knowing if . . . you are responsible for killing a friend."

His hand touched her cheek, and he leaned down and kissed her gently, tenderly, before backing away. "I said I would never force you into anything again," he said with a voice that broke in midsentence. "And I won't. I will leave you to a proper reunion with Sasha."

The next day passed swiftly. *Christmas Eve.* Annette tried to smile for the others. She tried to be happy even while she knew her heart was breaking.

She saw very little of John Patrick. She suspected that he was staying aboard the ship.

Ian returned, and she was surprised at how pleased she was to see him. Her family had always been small, and she reveled in the warmth and numbers of this one. Relatives seemed to be all over the place, including Aunt Fortune and the famous Katy. The latter was staying at the house over the holiday.

Annette found she liked them all enormously.

Still . . .

She tried to warn herself not to care so much, and she prepared to return to Philadelphia.

"Are you sure?" her father asked anxiously.

She wasn't. But she also knew she could not stay here and spend her life waiting for John Patrick, to wonder whether he was coming back, or whether he lay somewhere in the sea's depths.

If nothing else, she could start the hospital again. She could try to help preserve lives, even though everyone else seemed bent on destroying them.

So she replied, "Yes," even when doubts racked her.

That evening, she rose from her bed and went to the window. The night was dark, the moon invisible above a layer of dark clouds. A wicked night, she thought, wondering why that image flitted through her mind.

Annette sat on the window seat for a long time. She would miss this house, and everyone within it. Then, as her eyes grew accustomed to the dark, she saw a horseman approach, riding as if the devil himself were chasing him. Another silhouette followed behind him.

She knew instantly it wasn't John Patrick.

The burly form seemed to fall rather than dismount, and then she heard a heavy pounding on the door. She put on a nightrobe Fancy had loaned her and hurried downstairs, other family members joining her in the hall. She was momentarily reminded of another such pounding, another rush downstairs, and her heart jerked frantically.

Fancy was the first at the door, and she threw it open. Katy, who was staying for the holiday, followed.

Annette immediately recognized Malcomb. Beside him was Aristotle, Noel Marsh's dog.

Fancy seemed to recognize him, too. "Malcomb?" Annette heard the fear in her voice.

"Dr. Marsh has been taken by the British. He's been charged with treason," Malcomb said, collapsing against the wall in exhaustion..

Behind her, Annette heard Katy's anguished cry.

* * *

Summoned from his ship, John Patrick strode up and down the room, questioning Malcomb sharply. His face had grown harder as the Scotsman repeated his tale. He had gone to General Washington, but the general had reluctantly decided that he could do nothing. Ironically, after John Patrick's rescue of his men, security at the Walnut Street Prison had become unassailable.

Noel's trial was set for next week.

He had not been hanged immediately, Malcomb had learned, because the evidence was still being compiled. The Quakers still considered Noel one of their own, and the Quakers were the bedrock of British support in Philadelphia. They would require hard evidence. But the Brits, according to the information Washington had received, were determined to make an object lesson of the doctor.

Annette had listened carefully, her mind muddled. After her kidnapping from Philadelphia, she had partially blamed Noel. But now she saw him in her mind's eye. She saw the generosity, the compassion, the utter decency of him.

He was a spy. A spy for the rebels.

And she didn't care. She felt only a deep sickness that a man like him might die in an ugly public way. She rubbed Aristotle's ears, felt his head bury itself in her lap in a forlorn gesture. Noel had brought the dog to her aunt's house several times, and she'd always thought him rather unfriendly. But now the great beast needed comfort.

"Dammit," she heard John Patrick say brokenly. "Why did he not say anything to me? I—"

Malcomb frowned. "No one knew. No one but Washington. It was safer that way."

"We have to free him," John Patrick said.

Malcomb's face brightened for a moment, then folded in on itself in weariness and despair. "I donna' know how you can do that. For some reason, Major Gambrell, the general's adjutant, started investigating Noel's background. Howe now knows Noel's connection with the Star Rider, that you are brothers. I think they will be expecting you."

"It's my fault," Katy said in a broken voice. "I went out with Major Gambrell to make Noel jealous. The major was very angry that I wouldn't agree to go out with him again."

John Patrick walked over to her and put a hand on her shoulder. "We all made mistakes, Katy. We have to decide how to correct them."

Hugh Carey, who had joined them, coughed. Everyone looked at him.

"They will set a trap for you," he said in slow, measured terms. "They know you rescued your men. Of course, they will believe you will try to do the same with your brother."

Annette couldn't remember when she'd been so startled, not only that he was speaking, but by the authority with which he spoke.

"Do not look so surprised, daughter," he added. "I was not completely unaware of what was going on. I just could not find it in myself to care. I am sorry about that. I'm sorry I caused you so much pain."

Annette looked at him, puzzled. Her father was a Tory. Why was he warning John Patrick?

Hugh was sitting next to her, and he reached out and took her hand, squeezing it. "The British broke laws and violated decency, just as some of the Americans did. I despaired for both sides. It took the innocence of children to show me that there are still things to live for, and fight for." He gave Annette a small smile. "Among them, friends."

John Patrick was staring at him, too.

Malcomb stood. "Tha' is all well and fine. But what about Noel?"

"We will get him," John Patrick said.

"How?" Katy asked, biting her lip.

It is people who matter, not blind loyalties. "I have an idea," Annette said.

The cold wind whipped at Annette's cloak, the rain drenching her through the sturdy cloth. She shivered, and reached out to touch her father. He must be even more miserable.

But they had to be wet, and cold and miserable. They *had* to be escaping from their captors.

John Patrick reached out and took her hand, squeezing it hard. Then he lowered his head and kissed her hard.

He had already tried everything he could to dissuade her, even though his eyes told her that she offered the only real hope for his brother. Katy had also wanted to come. Only John Patrick's warning that she would put them all at risk quieted her pleas.

"Go now!" The harsh whisper came from the man who had guided them to the British lines.

John Patrick broke off the kiss. "I love you," he whispered, and though she was chilled as much by fear as by the freezing rain, she felt warmed to the bottom of her soul.

She knew he and the others were retreating, disappearing through the rain to their own lines. So much was up to her now. Up to her and her father. Their clothes were already in disarray, their faces and bodies smudged with dirt.

She took one look at her father, the gentle man who'd always avoided conflict. He was determined. Dr. Marsh was his friend, regardless of the side he had chosen, or the way he'd chosen to fight. Annette had never intended for her father to be a part of this, but when he'd heard her plan, he'd insisted on accompanying her. Everyone knew he was disabled. He would be far more believable than a young woman; the two of them together would not be doubted.

She reached out and touched his gloved hand, and he smiled. Waves of love rolled through her. Fancy Sutherland had guessed out loud that he'd needed a purpose, a challenge. He certainly had one now. They had one together. The life of a friend hung in the balance.

They stumbled along in the underbrush. They had to be careful not to get shot by British patrols, yet they had to make it seem as if they were frantic to reach help. They could not use the road; that would be too simple, too suspicious.

"Help," she cried out, hoping her voice carried in the wind and rain.

Finally they heard a sharp challenge. "Approach and be recognized."

Her father's hand clasped hers as they slowly approached the sentry.

Her father fell to the ground on his knees and clasped the soldier's hand.

Annette could barely believe the man in front of her was her father. The Sutherlands had apparently awakened a passion and strength in him she never even knew existed. Just as John Patrick had in her. Her fingers tightened into a fist.

"It's a woman and an old man," she heard one sentry exclaim.

"Get the sergeant," said another.

Another swore volubly. "They look ill-used."

Ten minutes later, Annette was explaining to a sergeant that she and her father had been kidnapped by the pirate, the Star Rider. They had finally escaped from a small hut where they had been held captive these past two months.

Tearfully, she said, "I want to go home."

The sergeant had looked at her helplessly, then ordered two of his men to find horses and take the Careys into Philadelphia. "I'll send a messenger to headquarters," he added.

"General Howe," she managed between sniffles. "I can't talk to anyone but General Howe. It was just . . . it's just too terrible . . ." Her voice trailed off.

The sergeant looked even more helpless, his face turning red with outrage. "We will catch the wretch," he said. "We already have his brother—"

"I hope you hang both of them," she said.

The sergeant turned to her father, "Sir?"

"He does not speak," she said. "Not since rebels burned our farm and tarred and feathered him."

The sergeant cursed, then apologized to her. "You are in safe hands now, miss."

Two men holding four horses materialized in the rain. "I fear we do not have a sidesaddle," the sergeant said.

"I just want to get home," she said through sobs. Then she allowed her legs to go weak and she would have tottered over if one of the sentries had not caught her.

"Faint," she said. "I feel faint." Then she closed her eyes and swooned.

They were surrounded by sentries, all of whose attention was on the father and daughter. Annette kept it there while John Patrick's men filtered through the depleted lines. She waited to hear another challenge, but there was none.

Annette made a show of struggling to mount, requiring the assistance of several men. Her father fell once, then stumbled to the horse, also requiring help.

Annette quashed the guilt she felt at deceiving men who were most certainly sympathetic. If all went well, no one would be hurt, and one man would be saved. She kept telling herself that, as she and her small escort headed toward Philadelphia.

John Patrick and Malcomb reached Walnut Street. John Patrick had aged forty years. A gray wig, obtained during a short stop in Chestertown, covered his black hair; stage makeup made his face look lined. He leaned on a cane as Malcomb, his sandy hair dyed black and cotton balls making his cheeks puffy, helped him along.

His other men had taken on various disguises: farmers, peddlers, Dutch sailors. No soldiers this time. After the last escape, one unconscious soldier might alarm the entire city.

The Carey home, according to Malcomb, was currently empty, all the wounded having been transferred after Annette and her father disappeared. Their home was no longer needed as a hospital, in any event, since both armies had settled in for the winter. There were small skirmishes but no great battles, and the sick and wounded were easily served by the Quaker hospital.

John Patrick and Malcomb tried the back entrance. It was locked. Malcomb pulled out a piece of metal and in moments had it open.

They slipped inside. John Patrick waited several moments, allowing his eyes to adjust to the darkness. They could use no candles.

Annette and her father should be here soon. John Patrick knew he couldn't risk being discovered by their escort.

He and Malcomb found the stairway. They made

their way up to the second floor before locating, with some difficulty, a trapdoor in the hall ceiling.

The two men worked swiftly and silently. Malcomb fetched a chair from the hallway. John Patrick mounted the chair, opened the door, then pulled himself up. Malcomb set the chair back in place, then returned, stretching his arms upward until John Patrick could reach them. Slowly John Patrick pulled him up. They closed the trapdoor just as they heard the front door open.

Annette and Hugh had done their job, delaying their arrival at the house. He marveled at their courage, at their determination to help Noel and himself after all they had put the Careys through. Dear God, he loved her.

The two men lay stretched out on the floor of the attic as they heard noises beneath them. Men's boots tramping upstairs. Voices. Doors being opened and closed. The rooms were being searched by the British soldiers who had accompanied the Careys.

One hour went by, then another. Finally they heard a tapping on the door, and John Patrick cautiously opened it. Annette and Hugh Carey stood underneath them. Hugh gestured for them to come down.

"They have gone," Annette said. "But they said they would send several soldiers to guard the house, since we have information about Dr. Marsh and the Star Rider. Some officers will be over in the morning to take our evidence. I said I would talk only to either General Howe or Major Gambrell, and that I could not leave my father."

John Patrick's gaze went to Annette. Her dress was still dripping wet, and her hair lay in limp ringlets, but he thought he'd never seen anyone quite as beautiful.

Her eyes met his. He saw regret in them. She had

never been made for deceit. But her gaze was steady. She would go through with the plan.

The trap was set.

Annette fidgeted as she met John Patrick's eyes. 'Twas her plan, but so many things could go wrong, and she would never forgive herself if someone were hurt—or killed.

She knew Major Gambrell, knew his ambition, knew his weakness for women. Even though it was known he had a wife in England, he had repeatedly tried to call on her, and she'd often been the unwilling recipient of an "accidental" touch. She had asked for General Howe. Gambrell would come instead. And he would come alone.

John Patrick and his men probably could have taken Gambrell on the street. But the major was seldom without his men, and John Patrick did not have time to wait for the perfect opportunity

Annette had understood that, when they had sat talking in the Sutherlands' home.

She had never liked Gambrell, and given the choice between him and Noel, she would take Noel any day. She'd known exactly what to do, once Malcomb had said the British needed evidence against Noel. What better to rile Philadelphia Quakers than a kidnapped woman?

She would never be able to return here again. Nor would her family.

Annette knew they were happy enough, ensconced in the bosom of the Sutherland family. But they couldn't stay there forever.

She knew all her doubts were reflected in her eyes as John Patrick took her in his arms. Malcomb turned away and quietly disappeared down the stairs to join her father.

"You need to get dry," he said in a voice oddly unsteady.

"So do you," she said, "and all we have for you is Father's clothes." She eyed him critically. "I do not think they will fit."

"No," he said with amusement. Her father was four inches shorter, and thin. "I've been wet before."

An unwanted image jumped to her mind. The sea washing over them. But that had been warm sea, and this was freezing rain.

"Perhaps you can start a fire," she said.

"Aye, I can do that for you. But I'm not sure it is wise for me to stay down here."

"I don't think they will come in again," she said. "They believe I am hysterical and prone to fainting after my terrible experience with pirates. I said I wanted to see no more uniforms except for General Howe's."

He grinned, and for the first time she felt totally at ease with him. Despite the tiny interior voice that still asked questions, they were comrades, together in something important. She was a partner, not a victim. She enjoyed the feeling. Indeed, she enjoyed it very much. She even relished the feel of danger, the surge of blood rushing through her when she played her part. Was that how *he* felt when he engaged in a ship in battle? She understood now how it would become addictive.

She tried not to let him see that in her. She didn't think it a becoming quality in a woman.

But he had a gleam in his eyes that seemed very appreciative. And very dangerous. They should not be thinking of *that* at the moment.

He appeared to come to the same conclusion. He leaned over and very gently kissed her, then reluctantly straightened. "I will start a fire in your room."

He put his arm around her and led her to her bedroom. Briefly she wondered how he knew where it was, then remembered the night they had all left the house. She'd been so angry, so wounded, so betrayed. Now . . .

Now she felt like a different person. She still didn't like his lies, but she admired so many other things about him, and *she* had changed. She hardly recognized herself, yet the seeds of rebellion, of adventure, must have always been deep inside her. She wasn't sure she was comfortable with this new Annette, who could deceive as well as he had.

She watched as he placed wood in the fireplace, found the tinderbox, then quite efficiently struck the flint with the steel until he raised a spark. The tinder, a piece of linen, suddenly flamed and he added it to a pile of chips underneath the logs.

"Put on some dry clothes while I fix something hot," he said. Then he grinned again. "Please."

She wondered whether that was the first time he'd said that word in a long time. It sounded rusty. And pleasant. Very, very pleasant. "There is some cider in the cupboard," she said, "and brandy in my father's room."

He nodded. He and Malcomb would have to be careful, though, to keep out of sight of the windows. He disappeared down the steps.

Annette looked around the room. She found a warm if not particularly attractive dress, right for what she had planned. Yet she remembered the dress he had bought her, full of color and lace. She thought of the warm breeze and hot sun. She thought of being in his arms.

What would happen after they rescued Noel? John Patrick had said he loved her, yet could she really believe that? He still wanted something from her, and he had used her before.

She shook the thought from her mind and started to dress.

* * *

How long before their quarry arrived?

John Patrick did not think it would be long. Not if they were as hell-bent on hanging Noel as Malcomb had indicated; and they believed Annette could give them the evidence they needed.

Who would come? She had specified General Howe, but he doubted the great man would come on his own. According to Annette, the most likely candidate was Major Gambrell, the man who had arrested Noel. He would do, especially if Annette was right about his character.

John Patrick wished Ivy were here. But he had left him with the ship. Ivy's large size was even more distinctive than his own, and more difficult to disguise. His other nine men—selected for their unimposing looks as well as their skills—should be somewhere around the streets by now. He had learned in the past days that Malcomb was far more than the physician's assistant he had appeared to be.

He closed his eyes at the thought of Noel, at the charges he'd hurled at his brother. Noel had been far braver than he, had risked far more than he had. Knowing Noel as he did, or thought he had, John Patrick could only imagine the price he had paid for his role in this madness.

And the thought of his brother in the Walnut Street Prison was devastating. He knew from his own men how horrific the conditions were.

He shivered even as he started a fire in the stove, located the cider, and poured a large portion into a pan. They were all cold. Then he looked for food in the cellar. Peas, which could be boiled. Perserves. Flour. Applesauce. Pickled cabbage. Pickled asparagus. He took several jars up the narrow stairs.

Hugh was in his room, changing, and Malcomb was watching the street from behind a curtain. Since it was still dark and they had lit no lamps in the parlor, he should be invisible from the street.

It was nearly dawn now, and none of them had had any rest. After a glass of cider, he would urge Hugh and Annette to get at least a few hours of sleep.

Just thinking about her aroused an undeniable warmth inside. A strange feeling. After their days in Martinique, he hadn't thought he could love her more, but when she'd volunteered to help Noel, when she'd risked all she cared about for his family, he'd felt an explosion of love he'd never thought possible. The light of battle in her eyes made him think of her as an ancient warrior princess. Their peaceful gray color turned as turbulent as the sea during a storm. He wanted both: the peace, and the vitality and courage that were so rare.

If anything happened to her . . .

He couldn't even think about it. Why in God's name had he allowed her to do this?

It was too late now.

He had set things in motion, and there was no going back.

Chapter 24

A peddler appeared at the back door just after daybreak. He was hawking freshly made bread, and Annette, who had been unable to sleep even a little, welcomed him and his wares. She smiled as the older, slightly bent man entered, carrying a full sack over his shoulder. His load smelled wonderful, and she wondered where he'd found such riches early in the morning. John Patrick and his crew, though, had ceased to surprise her. They apparently were capable of any number of miracles.

"Quinn," she acknowledged.

He gave her a broad grin as John Patrick emerged from the basement.

"Captain?"

"See any patrols?"

"Aye, sir, but nothing unusual, I think. There are two men watching the front, but no one in back."

"Good. All our men here?"

"Aye, not one was taken."

"I want three men in the house. Several others to buy horses—four of them. Two sturdy and fast; two decrepit-looking." He hesitated, then added, "Don't steal them. Tell the others to stay within sight of the house."

He didn't explain further. Annette didn't ask questions. She now knew how they could blend into the street, into shadows, into the night.

Quinn nodded. He took several loaves of bread and placed them on the table, along with some pastries. Then, still carrying his sack, he disappeared out the back door. Thirty minutes later, he had returned to the rear entrance, the sack gone. In short order, a fruit peddler had arrived. A chimney sweep presented himself at the front door, and an hour later a large black woman dressed in voluminous skirts appeared at the rear entrance.

"Mr. Beasley," Annette said delightedly, as the woman stomped loudly through the room.

He looked chastened that she had recognized him.

"How can I not recognize a friend?" she asked, and was rewarded with a big grin.

"Best be going about me duties," Beasley said under John Patrick's steady gaze.

She could only shake her head. "Where . . . ?"

"I bought stage makeup," he said. "Before we went to Martinique. You never know . . ."

But her amusement faded quickly when Malcomb whistled from the other room. He held up two fingers, then one.

"Gambrell," John Patrick said with satisfaction. "He has one man with him." They had already gone over every possible scenario, she hoped. No, prayed.

She nodded, and he and Malcomb disappeared into the basement.

The chimney sweep was upstairs, Beasley was polishing furniture. Quinn and the fruit peddler had disappeared. Her father was sitting at the table with her, and he put his fingers over hers.

Seconds later, a knock came at the door, and her father went to open it. She followed him.

She'd met Major Gambrell many times. Too many. She had seen him at homes of other Tories. He had asked to call on her, but she knew he was married, and she had refused him.

He smiled, though, when he saw her now. She shrank back.

"Mr. Carey, Miss Carey," he said. "I understand you have had a very harrowing experience. May I come in and talk to you about it?" He looked expectant.

Her father stepped back.

"Mr. Carey?" the major said.

"My father cannot talk," she said. "He hasn't talked since the rebels burned our house. And after . . ." Her voice trailed off.

"May I speak to you, then? You must know that Dr. Marsh—"

Her eyes went to the sergeant who stood just behind him. "I . . . I think I can talk about it. But not . . . in front of . . ."

Major Gambrell's eyes took on a gleam, even as he obviously tried hard to look sympathetic. She had never liked him. Now she despised him. He really didn't care what misfortunes had befallen her and her father, as long as he got evidence against Dr. Marsh.

But he understood what she was trying to say. "Wait for me outside," he told the sergeant.

She grabbed for the door as if she were about to swoon. He caught her, his hands going around her waist in a too-familiar manner. She allowed him, though, to help her to a table. He sat across from her. "Are you all right, Miss Carey? Did that brigand—?"

The question hung in the air. Her face reddened.

Her father hovered nearby, but the major ignored him.

"Dr. Marsh was working with him, wasn't he?" he finally asked. "He was the one who brought the man to your home, was he not?"

A tear started to roll down her cheek as Beasley entered the room, still dressed in his women's clothes. Major Gambrell didn't even spare a glance for him, not even when the figure moved behind him, extracted a large pistol from under the skirts, and pointed it at him.

"Gambrell." The voice was little more than a growl.

The major turned in his seat, his eyes widening as he saw the large woman hold a gun on him. He started to move.

"I wouldn't do that," came a voice from the other side of the room.

Gambrell half stood, whirling around.

John Patrick stood in the doorway, his pistol also pointing at the hapless major. Standing next to him was Malcomb.

"Sit back down, Major," John Patrick said.

John Patrick had removed his wig, though remnants of the facial makeup made him look older than he was. Major Gambrell looked frantically around the room, then back to John Patrick, who was obviously in control. Bewildered, he demanded, "What in the hell—?"

"I believe you were looking for me," John Patrick said in the lazy voice Annette loved. But now it was underlaid with menace.

Gambrell turned his attention to Annette, then to her father, comprehension spreading over his face. "You can't be—"

"They are not," John Patrick said firmly. "Unfortunately, I hold Mr. Carey's sister. Believe me, they are here under duress."

That had not been in the plans. He was trying to keep her and her father from being considered spies. She didn't think it would work.

John Patrick lowered his gun, but the other two armed men who had entered behind him kept their pistols leveled at Gambrell. He strode over and sat nonchalantly on the edge of the table, lazily folding his legs as if he had all the time in the world.

"What do you want?" Gambrell said harshly.

"Your life for my brother's."

"He's alive!"

"That is very fortunate for you, but I understand you are doing everything you can to change that."

"He's a spy."

"No, he just has the misfortune to be my half-brother."

"I don't believe you."

"You don't have to. You just have to have him brought here."

Gambrell looked at him as if he were mad. "I cannot do it. He will not be released under any orders."

"Oh, I think General Howe's might do it, along with your signature, of course. You were the one who charged him."

Understanding glimmered in the man's eyes. "I won't do it."

"Of course you will. Unless you want to die today."

He said it in such a matter-of-fact way that chills ran down Annette's back. She suddenly realized that he was very, very capable of doing exactly what he said.

So, apparently, did the major. His hands trembled slightly on the table, and she saw him swallow hard.

"You will never get out of Philadelphia alive."

"Then I have nothing to lose, do I?"

"You will all be hanged."

"You will not be there to see it. I am going to give you several choices, Major."

Gambrell looked at him suspiciously.

"You can tell that sergeant out there to send for the general, that you have news of great importance for him."

Gambrell's face paled.

"Of course, then your career would be ruined. You would be known as the man who led your general into a trap."

John Patrick continued conversationally, "Or you can try to get away. However, there are four guns on you.

There are several others in this house. As I said, we don't feel we have a lot to lose if you try to escape. I really don't know how brave you are feeling at the moment, but I assure you one wrong word will send you to hell.

"Or . . ." He left the word hanging in the air. Gambrell leaned forward in his chair, fascinated despite himself, like a moth circling too close to a flame.

"Or"—his voice was low and deadly—"you can salvage your career by saying you made a mistake, that the Careys completely cleared the good doctor, and in good faith you released him. Since you were the one who made the accusation, I think you would be believed. The Quakers here will be happy. Since the general's control of the city depends on their goodwill, *he* will be happy. Your career will survive."

Annette couldn't take her eyes off him. If Gambrell was like a moth to his flame, then she was a snake to his charmer.

He had found the one way to protect her father and herself, if they wanted to stay here. Once committed, Gambrell could not backtrack.

"Marsh cannot stay in the city," Gambrell said.

John Patrick nodded.

Gambrell looked toward Annette and her father. She made every effort to look pitiful. So, she noticed, did her father.

"Did you harm them?" The major's color was returning, and his voice tried to reflect outrage. It didn't quite make it. He was still trying to determine how best to save himself.

"They were . . . uncomfortable," John Patrick said. "Very uncomfortable. And very frightened. Nothing more. Believe me, she fought me every inch of the journey. If I didn't hold Maude Carey and Mr. Carey's manservant, they would never have agreed to—"

"I don't want them in the city, either." *Someone to tell the tale of a devil's bargain.*

John Patrick waited. Annette sensed he did not want to appear eager. He looked toward Annette. "Will you agree to leave?"

"This is my home," she said with indignation, tears welling up.

Gambrell closed his eyes for a moment, then opened them. "I will not agree unless they leave the city."

"You will not accuse them?"

"Why do you care?"

"*I* do not. My brother might. They are all innocents in your nasty little game."

"Damn you," Gambrell said.

Annette sniffed. "We will go if it helps Dr. Marsh. I know he is no spy. Just as we are not. We only tried to help your wounded. General Howe . . ."

Gambrell had the look of a trapped rat. "If I agree—?"

"We will leave you someplace you cannot extract yourself from. I'll give someone a key to release you several hours after we leave. Just to make sure you keep your end of the bargain."

Gambrell looked furious. His darting eyes told her he was looking for a way out. Finally he gave a curt nod.

"One last word, Major. You know how easily I can slip in and out of this city. If you violate any part of this bargain, I'll kill you. If you try to return to England, I'll send evidence to Howe proving you a traitor. If I do not return back to my own lines, that evidence will also go to him."

"You can't. I haven't—"

"Who will believe you, when your gambling debts have just been paid?"

Gambrell's brows furrowed in confusion. "How?"

"They are no secret. As we speak, a solicitor is paying them off. A stain will forever be on your name."

Annette saw Gambrell's face go from pale to red in a matter of seconds. He started up from the chair. "You blackguard."

John Patrick's face didn't change, nor did the ice in his eyes or the ruthless bend of his lips. He frightened her now, and yet she realized he was accomplishing his aim without gunfire, and making it possible that no one learn of her family's role in all this.

"Your answer?"

"I'll still see you hang someday," Gambrell blustered.

"And well you might," John Patrick conceded.

Gambrell's face returned to its natural color. Annette realized John Patrick had just given him a straw of pride to preserve. She had never seen someone twisted in so many knots before by so skilled a sailor.

"You swear your brother was not involved," Gambrell said. "You swear on your mother's life."

"He was never involved with me," John Patrick said. "Never. He's been an embarrassment to us all."

Annette wasn't sure whether Gambrell heard exactly what John Patrick said, or only what he wanted to hear.

"Give me some paper," Gambrell said.

Noel's stomach ached from hunger. His wrists chafed from the irons he wore. He sat in his corner of a crowded cell, shunned by the other prisoners, who believed him a Tory, even if he was suffering the same deprivations as they. The fact that he continued to claim his innocence had not improved matters with either the king's soldiers or the embittered rebels held here.

The only damning thing they had, he knew, was his relationship to John Patrick. The fact that no one had seen him care for his brother or take him to the Carey house had hampered the king's case. Supposition and coincidence were not good enough, not in a city where he knew every single Quaker elder. No one had ever actually seen him with the Star Rider. No one except the Careys, and thank God they were already safe.

He tried to turn, but the prison was so crowded, he bumped into the man next to him and received a rough curse.

Katy. He couldn't stop thinking about Katy. And his family. He longed to see them all again. He yearned to take Katy back in his arms and compensate for all those years they had wasted. Unlikely now.

He tried to move again. His clothes were stiff with dirt, and their odor nearly more than he could bear. It was no worse, though, than that rising from the other men crammed into the small area, with only several buckets for their waste. He now understood Jonny's determination to release his men. Too bad his tactics wouldn't work twice.

He wondered where his brother was now. Probably somewhere on the seven seas. But alive. He fought despair. He was not yet ready to give up. Katy was waiting for him.

He heard the rasp of doors opening, the sound of boots. None of his fellows looked up. Most of them had been here longer than the three weeks he'd inhabited their little corner of hell, and hope had drained from them.

Several, though, stirred when the iron door to their particular cage opened. A lantern shone in their faces.

"Marsh." The name was little more than a growl from a large sergeant who had taken a dislike to Noel.

Noel slowly stood, his weakened body reluctant to move. Another beating?

He stepped over bodies, trying to keep his back straight, not bent as it was wont to be after sitting, and lying, for days on a stone floor. The manacles on his wrists clanked a most uncharming melody.

He reached the door and one of the guards pushed him out, then locked the door again. He was led down a corridor to the guardroom, then brought to a stop in the blacksmith area where his irons had been attached earlier. Now he was astonished when a burly soldier unlocked them.

No one had said a word yet.

The sergeant led him through a door to the front area where another sergeant stood, waiting impatiently. This one, unlike the prison guard, was immaculately uniformed.

"Here 'e is," the prison guard said with disapproval.

The other man nodded, then turned to Noel, sniffing disdainfully, as if a particularly foul piece of rotten fish had been offered him. "You've been ordered released. Major Gambrell wants to see you first, though. If you will accompany me . . ."

It was not a request. What was Roger's game now?

He followed the sergeant at a distance. He was tempted to run, but his freedom was too precious to risk. God's breath, but the air felt clean and fine. He hoped the rain was washing some of the filth from him; he didn't even mind the cold.

He was more than a little surprised when the sergeant led him to the Carey home. The first floor was lit throughout. Why? When had the Careys returned? How?

John Patrick, he realized instantly. The Careys had been with John Patrick. His heart started to pound. No. His brother would never return to Philadelphia. It was far too dangerous. . . .

Yet already he was seeing the fine hand of his Machiavellian brother in this. Roger would never have released him, even if he couldn't prove Noel was a spy. His step grew a little lighter.

The sergeant reached the bottom of the steps leading up to the house. "The major is waiting inside," he said, knocking at the door, then stepping aside.

The door opened, and he saw Hugh Carey first, a huge grin on the man's face as he led him into the kitchen.

Roger was sitting at a table, scowling. John Patrick was sitting on the edge of it, holding a pistol but looking as relaxed as if he were attending a soiree.

John Patrick's gaze met his. "You look like hell, brother."

"I smell worse," Noel said. "What are you doing here?"

"Convincing the major here that he has made a terrible mistake in arresting an innocent man. He finally saw reason."

Noel's gaze went to Roger. The scowl on the major's face deepened.

John Patrick's nose crinkled as the full impact of Noel's odor reached him. "Hugh will get you some clothes. They may not fit well, but—"

"And then?"

"Major Gambrell has made your departure from Philadelphia a condition of his most generous release of you. We will be leaving in thirty minutes."

Noel's gaze flickered from John Patrick to Annette, who was standing beside her father, then to the burly woman who also held a pistol. It finally rested on Malcomb, who had just slipped into the room. Noel grinned. "Dammit, but I am glad to see you."

"Aristotle is safe," Malcomb said.

Relief washed over him. He had worried endlessly about both Malcomb and the dog.

"You had better hurry," his brother said.

Noel just nodded, his heart too full for more words. He followed Hugh up to his room. The older man closed the door, then turned to him. "They will be small, but—"

Noel just stared at him. "When . . . ?"

"A few weeks ago, at your father's home," Hugh said. "But I will explain all that later. I think—"

"We'd better get the hell out of here," Noel finished, as he quickly scrubbed himself at the washbasin.

"Exactly," Hugh Carey said as he tossed Noel some clothes, watched as he struggled to get into them, then offered a heavy cloak. "Annette has some food downstairs. We will be riding all night."

"We?"

"Major Gambrell does not want us in Philadelphia, either, though John Patrick tried valiantly to make him believe we are only innocents in all this."

"How did he—"

"Some information from your man, apparently. He knew exactly how to get the major to agree."

Noel shook his head. "And Annette?"

"I believe she loves your brother."

"I've been worrying about your family. When you disappeared—"

"John Patrick took excellent care of us. We've been staying at Marsh's End. I've been helping at the school," he added proudly.

How many more miracles had Jonny wrought in the past few weeks?

But now was not the time to explore them all. He followed Hugh back down the steps. Roger was nowhere to be seen now. A huge pastry sat on the table, and Noel grabbed that and a glass of ale, downing the welcome liquid in three swallows, clearing the last lingering feel of prison from his head.

In another minute, Annette appeared. She was wearing trousers and a shirt, her hair invisible under a seaman's cap. Gone was the prim miss. Her eyes sparkled, and her steps seemed far lighter than they had before.

How many miracles?

"Where is the major?"

"John Patrick took him down to the cellar to make sure he does not change his mind for the next few hours. He has paid someone to come in tomorrow morning and open the cellar, then lock up the house."

A chimney sweep and another man Noel didn't recognize appeared in the room, then the burly cook, who calmly took off layers of skirts to reveal seaman's trousers. The wig came off next.

John Patrick returned from somewhere in the back of the house. He'd aged considerably, with a gray wig and an old hat pulled over his head. "The horses are ready. We'll go in twos. I'll ride with Annette. Noel, you and Hugh take the other two horses. You're not strong enough to get through without them. We had better take different routes out of the city. I assume you know how to get out of Philadelphia."

Noel nodded. There was no sense in both of them being caught. "What about the others?"

"They will filter through on foot. Or steal horses. It will be safe enough now."

"Shouldn't we wait until dark?"

"It will be by the time we reach British lines," John Patrick said. " 'Tis better to move honestly during daylight in the city."

"Honestly?" Noel lifted an eyebrow.

John Patrick chuckled. "Still a stickler with words?"

Noel found himself grinning back. "Thank you," he said.

"A debt only partially repaid," John Patrick said, "but we will talk about that later."

Minutes later they were mounted, John Patrick and

Annette on a pair of nags that looked as ancient as he did, Hugh and Noel dressed as prosperous merchants. The others had already slipped, one by one, from the house.

"I'll see you at Valley Forge," John Patrick said.

Noel nodded, and they turned in different directions.

"Come in out the rain, missus."

But Katy wouldn't, couldn't.

She paced outside one of the makeshift huts of Washington's army headquarters. She had come with the others, survived the treacherous trip down the Delaware in a moonless night to avoid British guns. The cannon and food were unloaded. Then the *Star Rider* left under the command of Ivy, while John Patrick and a small party of his men stayed, along with the Careys.

Katy had wanted to go on to Philadelphia with them, but John Patrick had threatened to bind her if necessary. "You will only endanger Noel," he said, finally convincing her. But they had been gone three full days now.

One of Washington's colonels came out the door. "We have men waiting outside the British lines with horses," he said. "It shouldn't be long now." His hands fumbled with a pipe. "General Washington wants to congratulate Dr. Marsh personally. He has been our most effective agent in Philadelphia. We hate to lose him."

Because of her. Guilt had filled her ever since she heard of Noel's imprisonment. She had directed unwelcome attention toward him. She remembered all the barbs she had thrown at Noel, all the accusations, and she wanted to die inside. She should have known. But even if she hadn't, why hadn't she just supported him, been there for him?

Please God, bring him back to me. She had not stopped praying since she had heard the news. Neither hell nor

John Patrick had been able to keep her from boarding the *Star Rider*. It had only been the knowledge that she might indeed hurt their chances of freeing Noel that she'd agreed to stay here. And wait. And wait. She determined, then and there, that she would never let Noel out of her sight again.

Rain pummeled her. It had rained steadily for the past three days, turning roads into mud, quenching fires, making everyone miserable, particularly all the young soldiers in inadequate clothing.

She drew her cloak around her as the colonel continued to try to engage her in conversation. She didn't want conversation. She wanted Noel.

She finally turned to the colonel. "Can we not ride to where they will cross the lines?"

The colonel nodded reluctantly, perhaps knowing it was pointless to try to dissuade her. "I'll saddle two horses. But we don't have any sidesaddles."

"I don't need one," she said.

They started down the muddy road toward Philadelphia, toward the woods that separated the two armies. More and more of it was disappearing with the need for firewood.

They passed straggling groups of soldiers returning from patrol. Then, finally, in the distance she saw two riders coming toward them. Her heels touched the side of her horse, spurring her mount into a trot, then a canter. As she approached, she saw what appeared to be an old man and a younger, wiry rider. She recognized John Patrick and immediately rode to him. "Noel?" she asked.

"He shouldn't be far behind us," he said. He grinned. "Damned if I want to go after him again. I think I've worn out my welcome in Philadelphia."

"You got him out of prison?"

"Aye, but it was up to him to get out of the city. He said he knew a way. We thought it best to separate."

Katy looked over at Annette. "Thank you."

Rain dripping down from her knit seaman's cap, Annette smiled almost shyly as she looked at John Patrick. Katy suspected they would be sisters-in-law before long. She was delighted. In the short voyage from Maryland to the Delaware, she had come to like Annette. And it was ever so obvious that her nephew and Annette were very much in love.

John Patrick stretched in his saddle. "He might be coming out along the river," he said.

He turned south, off the road, and the four of them rode for an hour before encountering several sentries. "Have you seen anyone go through here?"

"Yes, sir. Two men. They've been taken to headquarters."

"Both in civilian clothes? One older?"

The sentry nodded.

The four riders grinned at each other and rode hell-for-leather toward camp.

Noel had finally convinced General Washington's officers he was who he said he was. He was elated, but exhausted, as he waited for an audience with the general. Suddenly, the door to the general's quarters burst open, and Katy flew into his arms.

He held her tight. She was sodden, just as he was, and they dripped on the floor, but neither cared as their lips met in front of half of Washington's staff. He hadn't thought he would ever hold her again, hadn't thought to see those magnificent green eyes stare up at him as if he were all she ever wanted.

"Ahhh-hum . . . hum . . ."

The clearing of a throat finally gained his attention and he turned, still holding Katy. General Washington stood there, a smile on his face. He held out a hand. "So that rogue brother of yours succeeded."

"Yes, sir."

"He has more lives than a cat. So, apparently, do you."

Katy's hand squeezed tight in his. "Yes, sir."

"Where will you go now?"

"Home, I think. For a while."

"You've earned it, Dr. Marsh. Then come back to us. We need good doctors." He held out his hand. "We owe you a great deal." He then turned to John Patrick, who had followed Katy in and stood near the door with Annette and her father. "Captain Sutherland, my thanks," he said simply.

John Patrick nodded, and Noel saw him catch Annette's hand in his. "I do have something to ask of you."

General Washington nodded. "Anything within my power."

"These people's land was confiscated because he would not take the loyalty oath. He acted out of principle—"

"I understand," General Washington said, the smile gone from his face. "I promise you I will remember their services, and do what I can."

He turned then. They were dismissed.

The five of them walked out, Noel and Katy, John Patrick and Annette, Hugh.

"Where are you going now?" Noel asked his brother.

"I thought I might go home with you. The *Star Rider* needs some repairs in Baltimore. If Ivy got her out of the Delaware."

"Then you can come to our wedding. Katy's and mine."

They must have made a strange procession, Annette thought, as they crossed the Delaware in two small boats and finally arrived at Wilmington, then traveled south to the Chesapeake. John Patrick, who seemed to have an inexhaustible purse, bought sturdy, if not beautiful, horses for all of them. The sailors grumbled; few of them were good riders, and several fell more than once. At the Maryland border, Quinn split off from them and took the crew members toward Baltimore, where John Patrick had told Ivy to take the *Star Rider*.

Katy, Noel, John Patrick, Annette, and Hugh headed toward the Sutherland home. They rode hard and stayed in wayside inns at night, Katy and Annette sharing a room if one was available. If not, they shared with other women. There was little time for intimacies.

Yet there was a comfort now between John Patrick and Annette, something that had never been there before. Love, yes. Comfort, no. But now, Annette realized, they had finally forged a trust, one as strong and inflexible as steel.

On the fourth night, the rain stopped, and the weather moderated. They stopped at an inn for food but, after seeing the accommodations, decided not to sleep there. They made camp beside a stream instead and built a fire, sharing the bread, cheese, beef, and ale they'd purchased from the inn.

John Patrick took Annette's hand, and they wandered down the stream. Noel and Katy went in the opposite direction, leaving Hugh to tend the fire.

John Patrick finally found a log and they sat down together. He touched a lock of her hair. "You've never been more beautiful," he said.

She knew how she must look. His comment did not reassure her.

But still, the touch of his hand warmed her. So did his mouth as he started nibbling at her ear, then her lips. It had been so long since they'd had any privacy. Despite the chill of the evening, she felt a familiar heat.

"I haven't thanked you properly for saving Noel," he said against her skin.

Gratitude. The last thing she wanted.

She looked away from him. Up into the sky. She'd heard his stories about the Starcatcher, the Starfinder. It was just her luck to find the one family member who was not content just to catch and find. She had to fall in love with someone who wanted to ride the infernal things.

The problem was she wanted to ride with him.

Suddenly he left his seat on the wet log and kneeled on the ground. "Will you marry me?"

She narrowed her eyes.

"Out of gratitude?"

"No, love. I would never marry out of gratitude," he said. "I love you."

She stared at him. He had said it before, but she hadn't let herself believe him. "Your knees are getting wet," she observed stupidly. Then she felt her face flame red.

He chuckled. "Very wet, and I feel like a fool, but I thought I should do at least this right. We did not start out very well, you and I."

She felt herself breaking into a smile. "No," she said as her fingers touched his lips, tracing the cherished curves. Dear God in heaven, but she loved him. She had always been afraid to say it.

"I'm sorry. . . ."

"No," she said, hushing him with a finger. "Do not ever be sorry. You and your family healed my father. You made me understand and believe in myself."

"I love that self."

But she still wasn't sure. "You are the Star Rider, the adventurer, the explorer, the seeker," she said.

"No," he said slowly. "That is who I *was*. Now I want to be the Star Keeper in the family. And you, love, are my star." A slow smile came to his lips. "*Now* will you marry me?"

It was what she needed to hear. "Yes," she replied. "Oh, yes." Then she looked at him suspiciously. "Or do you just want to get off your knees?"

"That, too, love." His eyes glittered as he stood, his mouth quirked in that wonderful half-smile of his. He pulled her to him. "But know this. You will always glow for me. Bright and shining and indispensable to my world."

She held his hand tight, as her body melded to his, and his other arm encircled her. He kissed her long and hard, almost taking her breath away, then he just held her as if he would never let her go.

She turned in his arms, her fingers touching his face, and finally she said the words she'd held in her heart. "I love you."

Annette stood at the top of the steps waiting for her cue, holding a bouquet of flowers.

The banister was laced with evergreen. The Sutherland home smelled of freshly cut greenery.

It was her wedding day.

Along with Katy's.

There had been no time to plan a grand ceremony. They had obtained a minister with only two days' notice. But neither had wanted to wait. Love was too precious to waste.

Politics didn't matter any longer. Annette's loyalty— and John Patrick's—now was to the people they knew, respected, loved.

Katy had already descended the steps, and now Annette followed. The house was filled with Sutherland relatives and friends. She'd always wanted a large family. Now she had it.

She walked slowly among them to the front of the

room, where she took her place next to John Patrick as Katy stood next to Noel. Katy winked at her, then gazed lovingly at Noel.

Annette turned her gaze to John Patrick. His green eyes smiled at her as he reached for her hand.

She thought her heart would burst with love for him.

Her pirate. Her rogue.

Her husband.

Her Star Keeper.

Epilogue

November 5, 1781

Annette had been riding out each day to the bay where John Patrick usually anchored on his visits. In front of her, on the saddle, perched two-year-old Katherine.

Annette had been riding to this spot every morning since she'd learned of the surrender of Cornwallis at Yorktown.

Noel, who had been with Washington, had sent a letter with a dispatch rider. He would be tending the wounded for several more weeks, then he would be coming home. Katy had left four days earlier to be with him and render whatever assistance she could. Annette had no idea where John Patrick was. But surely he must have heard the news. Surely he must be on his way home. Betsy was also on tenterhooks, waiting for her two suitors to come home. She still hadn't decided between Ivy and Malcomb, and very definitely enjoyed being courted by both. Annette secretly thought she favored the Scotsman.

Aristotle, who had stayed at the Sutherland home while Noel was a surgeon with Washington's forces, whined. Annette was acceptable to him, but she was not his master, and his discontent was becoming more obvious day by day.

At least she and Billy Boy, the parrot, communicated. The parrot's vocabulary had expanded to include something like a whine. It also included "pretty baby" and "come home," the latter obviously aimed at her errant husband. She had constantly demanded of the bird, "Why doesn't he come home?"

But he *did* come home, between raiding British shipping and taking supplies to Washington; the news she had of him verified that. She smiled as she thought of the new baby growing inside her.

She was just about to give up when she took a last look, shading her eyes with her hand. A sail. A lovely beautiful sail.

As if sensing her excitement, Aristotle barked. "No," she said softly. "It is not your person. It is mine."

Still, Aristotle ran back and forth in frenzied welcome.

She thought for a moment. She could ride over to Tim's farm and get another horse for Jonny. She would have time. Yet she liked the idea of riding double. Triple?

Quadruple?

With that possibility in mind, she had chosen one of the large, broad-backed geldings.

She grew warm inside just thinking about sitting behind Jonny and clasping his body tightly. She had missed it so very much.

The sails on the ship were lowered, and the anchor dipped into the sea. Then she saw the longboat being lowered. Katherine—little Katy—squirmed in her arms, and Annette slid from the saddle, then lowered her daughter to the ground. She had chosen a regular saddle, not a sidesaddle. Just in case . . .

"Your daddy is coming," she whispered to her daughter.

"Daddy?"

Her daughter's face lit with a blinding smile. John Patrick had been careful to make enough trips home to be sure that Katy recognized him. He was the man who lifted her up and whirled her around and gave her great big hugs.

"And he will stay awhile this time." She hoped. She prayed. He had said that, once the war ended, they would move to Baltimore, where he planned to start his shipbuilding company. They would test their own ships, he said with laughing eyes, on trips to Martinique.

A home of her own. She loved the Sutherlands, but she yearned for her own household. Her father, however, planned to stay here, despite the fact that Washington had kept his promise and pressured the Pennsylvania government to return their land. The house was gone, though, and the fields overgrown. He had no wish to start over. He'd sold the land, and accepted Ian's offer to take over the school when the schoolmaster left to join the army.

Annette had never seen him so happy. Maude lived with him now, on the second floor of the grand house. Franklin still tottered along, fussing over them. Any suggestion of retirement and a cottage was met with outrage and wounded feelings.

And now the country would be whole again. At peace. Both she and her father had come to see that independence was bound to happen. The Americans' spirit could never be ruled from a distant place. She had learned a great deal about independence since she met John Patrick.

She only wished that so many lives had not been lost.

The longboat was approaching. She leaned down to lift Katy and ran down to the beach, uncaring when a wave caught her skirt. She watched as John Patrick stood and waved, a broad grin on his face. He didn't wait for his men to pull the boat up out of the water, but jumped into the shallows and ran to her.

Her heart swelled as she reached out a hand to touch him.

"Annie," he said lovingly, leaning over Katy to kiss his wife hard as Katy wailed for attention. He reluctantly stepped back and took Katy in his arms, kissed her on the cheek, and tossed her in the air, chuckling at her screams of delight.

Then he tucked her in the crook of his arm and pulled Annette close to him with the other.

"Let's go home."

"All of us?" Annette asked him mischievously, her hand resting lightly on her stomach.

John Patrick's eyes widened and a grin lit his face. "Yes, my star, all of us. Together."

About the Author

PATRICIA POTTER has become one of the most highly praised writers of historical romance since her impressive debut in 1988, when she won the Maggie Award and a Reviewer's Choice Award from *Romantic Times* for her first novel. She has received the *Romantic Times* Career Achievement Award for Storyteller of the Year for 1992 and its Career Achievement Award for Western Historical Romance in 1995. She was recently nominated for a Reviewer's Choice Award for Best British Isles Romance in 1996. She has been a RITA finalist three times and has received a total of three Maggie Awards. Prior to writing full-time, she worked as a newspaper reporter in Atlanta. She has served as president of Georgia Romance Writers and currently is a member of the board of Romance Writers of America.

Bestselling Historical Women's Fiction

⚡AMANDA QUICK⚡

____28354-5 SEDUCTION ...$6.99/$9.99 Canada

____28932-2 SCANDAL ....$6.99/$9.99

____28594-7 SURRENDER ....$6.99/$9.99

____29325-7 RENDEZVOUS ....$6.99/$9.99

____29315-X RECKLESS ....$6.99/$9.99

____29316-8 RAVISHED ....$6.99/$9.99

____29317-6 DANGEROUS ....$6.99/$9.99

____56506-0 DECEPTION ....$6.99/$9.99

____56153-7 DESIRE ....$6.99/$9.99

____56940-6 MISTRESS ....$6.99/$9.99

____57159-1 MYSTIQUE ....$6.99/$9.99

____57190-7 MISCHIEF ....$6.50/$8.99

____57407-8 AFFAIR ....$6.99/$8.99

____57409-4 WITH THIS RING ......$6.99/$9.99

⚡IRIS JOHANSEN⚡

____29871-2 LAST BRIDGE HOME ...$5.99/$8.99

____29604-3 THE GOLDEN

                BARBARIAN ....$6.99/$8.99

____29244-7 REAP THE WIND ......$6.99/$9.99

____29032-0 STORM WINDS ....$6.99/$8.99

Ask for these books at your local bookstore or use this page to order.

Please send me the books I have checked above. I am enclosing $____ (add $2.50 to cover postage and handling). Send check or money order, no cash or C.O.D.'s, please.

Name _____

Address _____

City/State/Zip _____

Send order to: Bantam Books, Dept. FN 16, 2451 S. Wolf Rd., Des Plaines, IL 60018
Allow four to six weeks for delivery.
Prices and availability subject to change without notice.

Bestselling Historical Women's Fiction

⋇ IRIS JOHANSEN ⋇

____28855-5 THE WIND DANCER . . . $6.99/$9.99
____29968-9 THE TIGER PRINCE . . . $6.99/$8.99
____29944-1 THE MAGNIFICENT
                          ROGUE . . . . $6.99/$8.99
____29945-X BELOVED SCOUNDREL .$6.99/$8.99
____29946-8 MIDNIGHT WARRIOR . . $6.99/$8.99
____29947-6 DARK RIDER . . . . $6.99/$8.99
____56990-2 LION'S BRIDE . . . . $6.99/$8.99
____56991-0 THE UGLY DUCKLING. . . $6.99/$8.99
____57181-8 LONG AFTER MIDNIGHT.$6.99/$8.99
____57998-3 AND THEN YOU DIE. . . . $6.99/$8.99
____10623-6 THE FACE OF DECEPTION. $23.95/$29.95

⋇ TERESA MEDEIROS ⋇

____29407-5 HEATHER AND VELVET .$5.99/$7.50
____29409-1 ONCE AN ANGEL . . . . . . $5.99/$7.99
____29408-3 A WHISPER OF ROSES .$5.99/$7.99
____56332-7 THIEF OF HEARTS . . . . . $5.99/$7.99
____56333-5 FAIREST OF THEM ALL .$5.99/$7.50
____56334-3 BREATH OF MAGIC . . . .$5.99/$7.99
____57623-2 SHADOWS AND LACE . . . $5.99/$7.99
____57500-7 TOUCH OF ENCHANTMENT.$5.99/$7.99
____57501-5 NOBODY'S DARLING . . . $5.99/$7.99
____57502-3 CHARMING THE PRINCE . . $5.99/$8.99

Ask for these books at your local bookstore or use this page to order.

Please send me the books I have checked above. I am enclosing $_____ (add $2.50 to cover postage and handling). Send check or money order, no cash or C.O.D.'s, please.

Name _____

Address _____

City/State/Zip _____

Send order to: Bantam Books, Dept. FN 16, 2451 S. Wolf Rd., Des Plaines, IL 60018
Allow four to six weeks for delivery.
Prices and availability subject to change without notice.   FN 16 2/99